FULL THROTTLE

BLACK KNIGHTS INC.

JULIE ANN WALKER

sourcebooks casablanca

Published by Sourcebooks Casablanca, an imprint of Sourcebooks, Inc.
P.O. Box 4410, Naperville, Illinois 60567-4410
(630) 961-3900
Fax: (630) 961-2168
www.sourcebooks.com

Printed and bound in Canada.
MBP 10 9 8 7 6 5 4 3 2 1

To my big sister, Dana.

When I was younger, I thought being known as "Little Dana" was a curse. I wanted people to see me not as your mini-me, but as myself. Now I realize being "Little Dana" was a blessing. It gave me big shoes to fill and made me always strive to be better, do better, and reach higher. That drive has served me well in life. Thank you for that!

All great things are simple, and can be expressed in a single word: freedom, justice, honor, duty, mercy, hope.

—Winston Churchill

Prologue

Georgetown Campus
Washington, DC
Eight years ago…

"HEY, LITTLE *NEÑA*. WHERE ARE YOU GOING IN SUCH A hurry, eh?"

Abigail Thompson's heart took flight at the sound of Carlos's smooth baritone calling from directly behind her. She spun around, bracing herself for the impact of his laser-black eyes and that oh-so-tempting dimple in his left cheek. But the stupid sidewalk chose that moment to go all wonky, like the floor of a fun house. And instead of the graceful pirouette she'd planned, she ended up tripping over her own two feet. Down fell her books, her purse, and her enrollment papers as she lurched sideways toward the curb.

"Son of a biscuit!" she yelled as her ankle rolled over the lip of the sucker. But no matter how she pinwheeled her arms like a cartoon character, there was no stopping her momentum.

Honk! A car horn blared. *Errrrrttt!* A set of brakes squealed. Her entire body flashed hot and cold in the early autumn air, the hair on her head standing stick-straight as she squeezed her eyes shut, preparing for the bone-breaking blow. But she was saved from becoming a hood ornament by the grace of God—*Hallelujah!*

Amen!—and Carlos's quick reflexes. He snagged her wrist in a firm grip, deftly yanking her out of oncoming traffic and into his arms.

And speaking of the grace of God…

Heaven, that's what she was now in. With her face pressed against his solid chest and the heady smell of soap and…*man* filling her nose, that was the only way to describe it.

Well, if she was splitting hairs, nirvana, paradise, or wonderland probably worked, too.

Your body is a wonderland… When John Mayer penned those words, he had to be talking about Carlos, right? Because the dude was flat-out *ssssmokin'*! Adonis come to life. Er…Carlos, that is. Not John Mayer. Though, in all fairness, Johnny Boy was sort of cute, too. But she digressed. Because it didn't really matter which term she used—heaven, nirvana, paradise, or wonderland—since it all came down to the simple fact that from one second to the next, her distress was replaced with desire, her terror with tension. *Sexual* tension.

And it was delicious!

Unfortunately, it lasted for all of about two seconds. *Gah!* Because Carlos gripped her shoulders to hold her at arm's length—much to the lament of her rapacious nineteen-year-old libido.

And, yes, she fully realized how irrational it was to be cursing the fact that she'd only been given two seconds to revel in his arms when she should be thanking her lucky stars she hadn't ended up as roadkill. But there you go. Because the man had been making her think and act irrationally since the first moment she laid eyes on him, standing there on the sidewalk by the South Gatehouse. He'd had his arm looped through Rosa's, his twin sister and Abby's new—at the time—premed academic advisor, and *pow*! His swarthy, exotic beauty had hit her like…well, like that sedan had nearly hit her.

That had been a year ago. And since then, she'd come to love Rosa like family. As for Carlos? Well, she wouldn't say she loved him like family, but she certainly felt *something* for him. Something her Bio 101 textbook had called a biological imperative, i.e., the overwhelming and intrinsic compulsion to mate. Or, in layman's terms, the need to Get. It. On.

"*Jesús Cristo!*" he cursed now, dragging her away from her heated thoughts. "Are you okay, *chamaca*?"

Okay? Well, a few seconds ago, snuggled against him, she'd been *better* than okay. She'd been great! But now he'd gone and called her *chamaca*—which Rosa said was slang for "little girl"—driving home for the bazillionth time that he viewed her less in terms of a willing bed partner and more in terms of a pesky kid sister. So now it was safe to say she was pretty far from okay.

"I'm fine," she lied, bending to grab her dropped belongings, slapping her hand down on the sheaf of enrollment papers when they caught the wind and threatened to blow into the street. "Thanks for that save, by the way. A bad case of road rash would have seriously put a damper on my day."

"Not a problem." He squatted next to her, helping her stack her books. She couldn't help but notice how tan his hands were compared to hers. *Just imagine how we might look together naked, his warm brown skin contrasting against my paleness?* Her knees weakened at the thought. And *gah* again! "Especially considering I was the one who startled you into tripping."

"No. That wasn't your fault. I'm just clumsy," she assured him, leaving off *whenever you're around* from the end of the sentence.

"Hmm. Are you sure it's not all that sangria you guzzled last night at the drama club's little fiesta? Hangovers can be a bitch."

"You were there?" She found that hard to believe. Not only had it been mostly underclassmen at the party, but it also seemed impossible she could have missed him. When Carlos Soto entered a room—or, in the case of last night's party, an abandoned warehouse—everyone *knew*. He just had a way, a...*presence* about him that seemed to command attention.

Case in point: When she glanced up to discover that damned irresistible dimple of his winking at her, every cell in her body came to a hard stop like her father's old English setter did when he spotted a squirrel. And like that dog, she was pretty sure her whole body was now quivering.

Does he even know he's doing it?

Probably not, she decided, which made it worse.

"I just stopped by for a second to pick up a friend who found himself in need of a designated driver," he explained. "And who was also in need of a voice of sanity to keep him from going home with a philosophy major who was *far* too young for him."

"Too young for him? Let me guess," she groused, standing and slinging her purse strap over her shoulder. "This philosophy major was what? Eighteen? Nineteen? Last I heard, that's past the age of consent."

Carlos mirrored her movement, rising in one graceful motion that was the polar opposite of her near face-plant into the grille of the Buick. He held on to her books, tucking them under his arm, causing his brown suede jacket to bunch up and reveal his trim waist. What she wouldn't give to turn back the clock a couple of minutes so she could take the opportunity to wrap her arms around that waist. "She was twenty, and… Don't you roll your eyes at me," he grumped when she did exactly that. "That's too young to be carousing around with a guy who's my age."

"Yes, because twenty-five is positively *ancient*." She wrinkled her nose. "I see daily doses of prune juice and Bengay in your immediate future, you poor thing."

He made a face at her.

She made one right back.

"And to get back to the point," she said, "I don't have a hangover."

"You don't?"

"No. I prefer to think of it as wine flu."

He barked out a laugh, and she would swear she felt the sound low in her belly. When the cool breeze tousled the hair near his temple, she hastily reached out to take her books from him. Not only was she already running late for her meeting, but she also needed something to fill her hands lest she find them burrowing themselves through his sleek, black locks.

"Which reminds me." He glanced toward one of the three Secret Service agents who had melded back into the landscape the instant it became clear she wasn't in danger of falling into the street. "What's the matter with your security detail? Don't they know better than to let you drink? You're underage. Do I need to have a talk with them?"

Oh, geez. It was bad enough she hadn't had a single moment of privacy since her father made public his bid for his party's nomination to be the next president of the United States. But it was worse still that everyone was highly aware of the presence of the requisite Secret Service agents who came part and parcel with her being the next prospective first daughter—the next *likely* first daughter if all the political pundits and talking heads were to be believed. It made most people act funny around her, like they were afraid they were ten seconds away from taking a bullet to the brain or something. Or in the case of Carlos—the big, beautiful buttmunch—it made him constantly try to enlist the agents into curtailing what she considered perfectly *normal* college-girl activities.

"You'll be glad to know"—she grudgingly informed him as they turned to continue up the sidewalk. From the corner of her eye, she saw her security detail fall into step with them—"that Agent Mitchell already gave me some donkey barbecue over the two measly glasses of sangria I drank. He informed me, in that gruff tone of his that's far too much like my father's, that I need to be more careful than the average university student. That I have to consider how my actions could impact the upcoming election. Which means, no. There's absolutely no need for you to have a talk with them. But thanks for offering all the same."

"You're welcome."

She shot him an exasperated glance. "I take it you missed the sarcasm in my tone."

"Oh, I caught it. I just chose to ignore it," he admitted as a young woman, one Abby was almost certain had been in her calculus class last spring, brushed by them. The brown-haired Barbie eyed Carlos with what Abby suspected was supposed to be a *covert* look of longing. But the blushing and giggling Barbie did when he glanced her way completely ruined her ruse. Abby rolled her eyes and made a gagging sound.

Carlos nudged her with his elbow.

She rammed her shoulder into his arm in retaliation.

"Stop it," he said.

"*You* stop it," she countered.

With a wide grin making his already handsome face just that much more…well, *handsome*…he tucked his hands into the pockets of his jacket. "So, uh, what exactly *is* donkey barbecue anyway?"

"It means ass chewing. Duh." She would have teased him about being an old coot who no longer kept up with youthful slang, but that would do nothing to forward her campaign of making him realize their six-year age difference was really nothing in the grand scheme of things.

Again he barked out a laugh, one that reverberated somewhere in the vicinity of her womb. "The things that come out of your mouth…"

Yep, that's me. Silly little Abby. Always good for a chuckle.

"So where are we headed?" he asked, shortening his steps to match hers. A breeze blew the smell of the changing seasons at them, and there was the promise of turning leaves and long rainy days in the air.

"Well, I don't know about *you*," she said, "but I'm meeting Rosa at the coffee shop around the corner."

Motioning with her chin to the batch of papers now sandwiched between two textbooks, she continued. "She's going to help me with enrollment for next spring. Tell me which courses to take, which professors to avoid, yada, yada. I need to pick her brain now, before you two begin your next round of clinical rotations and I don't see you for weeks on end. And speaking of rotations, Rosa said she's looking forward to spending some time in pediatrics. Are you still leaning toward general surgery?"

"*Sí.*" He nodded. "It's the most fun."

"Fun?"

"Sure." He nodded again.

She sighed. Sometimes getting the man to expound on a subject was like pulling teeth. "Fun it what *way*?" she prodded.

"Fun in that I like the challenge of never knowing what's coming through the doors of the emergency room or what operation I'll be required to perform next. Every day is an adventure in GS."

"Ah." She nodded. "I guess that makes sense. You know, given that you're *you*."

He turned to look at her, one dark brow quirked. "Now what is *that* supposed to mean?"

"Just that between you and Rosa, you're definitely the thrill-seeker and she's definitely the staid, responsible one."

And if he handled a scalpel the way he handled that motorcycle he roared around campus on—with deft precision and quick, confident assurance—it was a safe bet he'd quickly make a name for himself as one of the country's most sought-after surgeons. "I'm going to choose to take that as a compliment," he said. "And speaking of my staid and responsible twin sister, I wonder why she didn't tell me she was meeting you?" Another young woman came toward them then. But unlike the previous girl, this one made no bones about the fact that she was extremely interested in fixing herself a big, heaping helping of Puerto Rican man-meat. The only way the blue-eyed tart could have been more obvious was if she unbuttoned her blouse and flashed Carlos her tatas. And when the big idiot had the audacity to hit the woman with the full force of his dimple, resulting in said tart sending him a saucy wink as she brushed by them, Abby decided *this* was what it was like to want to murder someone.

But the question was, did she want to execute Carlos or Miss Obvious?

"I suspect she didn't tell you because you're not her keeper," she informed him haughtily while shuffling her books to one arm so she could wave her hand in front of her face. She coughed dramatically.

"What's that? What are you doing?" he demanded.

"Sorry," she said. "It's hard to breathe, what with all the hussy and nitwit floating around in the air."

He jerked his chin from side to side, cracking the vertebrae in his neck while his black eyes glittered with amused affront. "And I'm assuming *I'm* the nitwit here?"

"It's dealer's choice," she told him as they rounded the corner and the neon sign hanging above the coffee shop came into view.

"For such a little thing, you sure know how to bust a guy's b—"

BOOOMMM!

The whole world exploded...

Or at least that's what it felt like, the thundering roar so immense that total global destruction seemed the only natural result. But it was obvious the planet remained intact when Abby found herself kissing concrete. She'd gone from standing on the sidewalk to pancaked flat on the ground with her books smashed beneath her arms in a nanosecond.

"Wha—?" she managed, her ears ringing. The frightened screams and blaring car alarms all around her seemed muffled and distant by comparison.

She turned her head to lay her cheek against the rough coolness of the walkway, trying to determine if anything was broken. Fortunately, nothing hurt save for a small sting on the inside of her bottom lip where she'd apparently taken a chunk out of the thing on her way to the ground. But she'd just go ahead and file that under The Least of My Worries, because in the next instant, she saw Agent Mitchell barreling toward her, yelling something into the tiny radio transmitter he kept attached to his cuff. And the stark terror on his face said it all…

Whatever had happened, it was bad. *Really* bad. Her heart took off like it was running a race and someone fired the starting pistol. Her lungs expelled the last bit of air inside them until she was woozy from lack of oxygen.

"Stay down! Stay down!" Agent Mitchell commanded as he knelt beside her head. His voice came to her as if from a great distance. "Don't move, Soto. Stay right where you are," he continued as the black sneakers of the remaining two agents came into view, their voices weirdly echoey as they barked orders to the other people on the sidewalk.

Stay where? Where are you, Carlos? And then she answered her own question. He was sprawled atop her, covering her body with his own. Later she would think about how quickly he had reacted—how selflessly—because right now she needed to find out what was going on.

"What's happening?" she demanded, not surprised when her voice came out raspy and thin, barely above a whisper. No one heard her above the racket of a world in chaos. The blare of sirens screamed from up the street. The pounding of running feet was a stampede. And the fearful cries of a dozen people reverberated through the air, each one an acoustic assault. She swallowed, the metallic taste of blood slipping from her bitten lip down her throat, and tried again. "Somebody tell me what's happening!"

This time her voice actually had some volume behind it. Still, no one answered her. And her fear quickly turned into panic. She began to struggle.

"Shh, Abby," Carlos's low baritone sounded in her ear, his hot breath fanning her cheek. "Stay still until the agents tell us it's okay to move."

"What is it?" she begged him, a strange sense of foreboding tickling the back of her brain. There was something… "What's going on?"

"I can't tell," he said. "There was some sort of blast and—"

The squeal of tires on asphalt echoed a second before the big knobby wheels of a black, government-issue SUV bounced over the curb not five feet from her head.

"Okay, let's go!" Agent Mitchell shouted as two of

her bodyguards grabbed Carlos's arms to haul him off her. The next instant she was plucked from the pavement as easily as she and her mother plucked the bad buds from the rose bushes planted around the beech tree back home.

And it was strange she should make that comparison. Because as the agents wrestled her toward the open door of the waiting SUV, she was finally able to take in the scene around her. Glass and debris littered the sidewalk and street. Smoke and flames billowed from somewhere up the way. People were darting wildly this way and that or else huddled together in tight packs on the ground. And speckling everything, the road, the people, the wreckage, was a slick crimson substance the exact color of the roses on those bushes.

Blood. That was *blood. Jesus...*

She struggled against the agents, that sense of foreboding having morphed into a terrible, sickening dread. "Stop it!" she shouted at them, needing to get to Carlos. He was standing on the sidewalk, staring straight ahead. And the look on his face was indescribable, some sort of horrible mix of terror, disbelief, and denial. "Let me go! I need to—"

"Abby?" He turned to her, his voice raspy and barely audible above the turmoil around them. "Was Rosa in the coffee shop?"

The coffee shop? Had the blast come from there? No. *No!* It couldn't have. But she couldn't *see* to assure herself of that, not with agents and the SUV's door blocking her view. Her heart was poised to explode inside her chest. "P-probably. I was running l-late," she told him.

She barely finished the sentence before he took off

up the sidewalk, screaming Rosa's name over and over again in a voice she was sure to hear in her nightmares. The very next instant she was shoved inside the SUV, agents piling in all around her and pinning her arms and legs when she fought them with everything she had, biting, hissing, scratching.

Rosa! Oh God, no! The phrase blasted over and over again inside the confines of her skull, and with each repetition the very fabric of her soul ripped anew. "Let me go!" she yelled at her security detail. "I have to see! I have to find Rosa! I have to help Carlos! I have to—"

"Abby!" Agent Mitchell bellowed from beside her, slapping his wide palm over her mouth. "There's nothing you can do! We're getting you out of here!"

On that cue, the driver threw the vehicle into gear. She could feel the big tires spin violently before their tread gripped the pavement, shooting the SUV forward. Thrown back into the bucket seat with head-whipping force, she wailed, "No, no, *no*!" when Agent Mitchell's hand fell away. Panic and shock had turned her into a wild animal that bucked and heaved and desperately fought for freedom. That is, until the gaping, charred hole that used to be the coffee shop buzzed by outside the window. She stilled as the full measure of what had happened dawned on her. And an awful, *horrifying* thought slipped through her mind.

This is my fault...

With that, she began to scream in earnest. Scream until her vocal cords shredded. Scream until a blood vessel in her right eye burst...

Chapter One

Hotel Novotel
Kuala Lumpur, Malaysia
Present day...

Carlos Soto, known to everyone in the spec-ops community as "Steady," lounged at the end of the ritzy hotel bar, casually watching his best friend, Ethan "Ozzie" Sykes, work his masculine wiles on the cute off-duty Secret Service agent seated at a nearby table.

"Ozzie is a serial seducer," Dan Currington observed from the barstool beside him. Dan was the third and final member of Black Knights Inc. to accompany him on this mission. BKI being the covert government defense firm that operated under the guise of a custom motorcycle shop—okay, and sometimes Steady still had trouble believing such an entity actually existed; it was like something out of a bad spy novel.

"*Sí*," he admitted with an affectionate chuckle, smiling as Ozzie leaned over to whisper something into the shell of the agent's ear. The woman blushed and giggled, and Steady could only shake his head. "But the ladies never seem to mind. I don't know how he pulls it off time after time."

"You don't?" Dan turned to lift a dubious brow as he took a leisurely sip of seltzer water. "I thought you two were neck and neck in that whole notches-on-the-bedpost race."

Steady frowned at the bottle of Tiger beer in his hand. It was true. For a couple of years there, he'd given Ozzie a run for the money in the bedding of bar bunnies. But recently the…er…*hunt* had lost its allure.

"I think I'm about done with all that, *hermano*. It just seems so…" He twisted his lips, searching for the word. "Superficial, I guess. Unfulfilling? I don't know." He shrugged. "And besides, I was never as good at it as Ozzie." He tipped his beer toward the table where the unrefuted king of casual relationships was now fiddling with the agent's fingers. Julia Ledbetter. That was her name. And she resembled a Secret Service agent about as much as a Chihuahua resembled a Doberman. But Steady supposed that was part of it. Protection through subterfuge and meek-but-mighty camouflage. Although, if you asked him, there was something to be said for the fierce, bulldog demeanor that good ol' Agent Mitchell had sported.

He wondered what had happened to the guy. Come to think of it, he wondered what had happened to *all* the agents who'd been assigned to Abby's protection detail back in the day. There wasn't a familiar face among the seven in her current bunch.

Then again, a lot could change in eight years. Just look at him. He'd gone from medical student to soldier to clandestine government operator in the space of that time. Hell, even his *name* was different…

"Never as good as Ozzie?" Dan's second eyebrow joined his first somewhere near his hairline. "Well, I, uh…" He cleared his throat. "I hafta say, that's the first time I've ever heard a man admit his sexual prowess lacked in comparison to—"

"That's *not* what I meant, *pendejo*. And you know it."

Dan tucked his tongue in his cheek, nodding. "The beer bottle incident?"

Steady fingered the small scar cutting through his scalp above his right ear. He'd received it courtesy of a one-night stand whom he'd *thought* understood the nature of their relationship. But when she caught him locking lips with a curvy little *mamacita* outside the back door of Red Delilah's Biker Bar—his local watering hole in Chicago where Black Knights Inc. was based—she'd shouted obscenities that questioned his mother's morals before hauling off and smashing a bottle of Bud over his head.

"I *told* her I wasn't interested in anything serious," he said in his own defense. "I don't know how much more specific I could've been."

"Mmm," Dan answered noncommittally, causing Steady's scowl to deepen. His entire life he'd been accused by family, friends, and teammates of being oblivious when it came to dishing out details, but he disagreed. He said what needed to be said *when* it needed to be said. He just wasn't all that elaborative, that's all.

"Look," he continued, choosing to ignore Dan's nonanswer and getting back to the point. "I'm only saying I might be ready for something...*more*." He blinked. A little astonished he'd climbed out on this conversational limb. After all, the Knights were a far cry from the touchy-feely sort. In fact, their discussions tended to center more on the latest weapons, motorcycle exhausts, and Chicago Cubs scores than anything that came close to resembling, you know, actual *feelings*.

He waited for Dan to say something along the lines

of *whoa there, compadre, what are we? Girlfriends?* So he was shocked when instead Dan went with, "Are you telling me you've sowed your last wild oat?"

"I don't know about *last*." His frown kicked into a grin. "I'm not sure that's even possible. I'm Puerto Rican, man. My oats are endless."

Dan rolled his eyes. "I can't believe that Latin lover shtick actually works."

"What can I say? Chicks dig my Rico Suave."

"Rico Suave?" Dan turned, cocking his head to study him. "Nah. I'd say you're more of a low-budget Enrique Iglesias."

Steady punched him in the arm before quickly reining the conversation back in. Experience had taught him it was either that or devolve into a good, solid hour of swapping insults. Fun? Sure. But not at all productive. "The deal is, I'm thirty-three years old. And I can't help but wonder if it's time to start thinking about"—he made a rolling motion with his hand—"commitment."

And would you look at that? He said the word without choking on it.

Dan turned to face him, the picture of shock and awe. Seriously, George W. Bush would've been proud. "Well, well, well." He shook his sandy blond head. "Will wonders never cease?"

"I know." Steady shrugged. "I'm a bit surprised myself. Or maybe I've been drinking too much of the Kool-Aid being served back home. I mean, you *have* noticed the rate at which our teammates are taking the plunge into happily-ever-after, haven't you?"

"Staggering, isn't it?"

In the last couple of years, six, count them, *six* of the

BKI boys had strapped on the ol' ball and chain. And talk about wonders never ceasing? They actually made the condition look…well…*good*. Preferable even. *God help me.*

"Or maybe this sudden attack of fidelity has something to do with the way you've been staring at"—Dan glanced around to make sure they were out of earshot of anyone who might be listening—"*you know who* for the last three days."

The blood drained from Steady's head, leaving his face cold and his forehead clammy. "What do you mean?" he asked, shooting his cuffs and tilting his head from side to side in an attempt to loosen the tension that gripped his neck. Suddenly his clothes were too tight. He wanted to chalk it up to the fact that he was accustomed to wearing combat gear or jeans and a biker jacket. But deep down he knew the real reason his suit coat was now a straightjacket, his necktie a silk anaconda, was because Dan's assessment hit far too close to home. "How have I been staring at her?"

"Like Winnie-the-Pooh stares at a pot of honey."

"Pssht. You're imagining things. If I've been watching her, it's only because that's what we're being"—he lowered his voice to a whisper—"*paid* to do."

"Yeah, but there's watching and then there's *watching*," Dan insisted.

Steady squeezed the beer bottle so hard it was a wonder the thing didn't shatter. Dan was right. Since President Thompson had tasked him with flying to the other side of the globe to help protect Abby while she attended the New Frontiers in Horticulture Convention—*sí*, it was a thing. Who knew?—he hadn't been able to take his eyes off her. And although he hadn't seen or heard from her in eight years, she was just as he remembered…

Slim, blond, pretty in an all-American kind of way, which seemed appropriate given she was the youngest daughter of the president of the United States. She still had those arresting green eyes that'd stopped him in his tracks when he met her on the Georgetown campus all those years ago. She still had that same sweet, luminous smile that'd fueled his fantasies back then and most of his daydreams since.

She's too young for you, he remembered the scolding tone in Rosa's voice. *And even if she isn't, she's too far out of your league. You think her father wants her dating a* maldito bori *when he's got a national election to win?*

He'd winced at the slur while at the same time knowing his sister was right. The difference between Abby's age and his had seemed insurmountable at the time. A gulf in life experience as wide and impassible as the vastness of space. But she was all grown up now, wasn't she? A woman, as in *whoa-man.* Everything guaranteed to rev his engine in one fair-haired little package.

Unfortunately, that whole *maldito bori* thing hadn't changed. Even with his multiple degrees and that Army Ranger pin stuck to the lapel of the uniform hanging in his closet back home, he was still just the son of uneducated immigrants who'd spent their lives slinging *cervezas* and serving rice in a greasy corner café in Miami. And any illusions he'd had that *Abby* didn't care about such things was stripped from him the day of Rosa's funeral.

He'd gone to her thinking maybe she would be his hand to hold, his shoulder to cry on. He'd gone to her thinking they were friends…maybe *more* than friends, though she had still been far too young for him. He'd needed her so badly that day he'd been willing to ignore the gap in their ages, the impropriety of his making a move, because his remorse, his grief, his need to comfort and be comforted had outweighed anything else. But he'd been wrong to think she might consider him worthy of her affection. She'd made it obvious that Rosa, and Rosa's position as her academic mentor, had been the only glue holding the three of them together.

Abby may have exchanged her premed degree for one in botany, she may have traded in her scalpel for a garden spade, but like her appearance, nothing else about her was any different. She was still Abigail Thompson, the first daughter. America's princess. And he was still…well…*him.*

"So, are you gonna let me in on the history between you two?" Dan asked when Steady had been quiet for too long.

"No history," he quickly replied. *At least none worth speaking of.*

"Yeah, I call bullshit."

And now it was his turn to pull out the ol' Black Knights' tried-and-truism. "So, what if it *is*? You think I want to *talk* about it? What are we? Girlfriends?"

Dan rolled his eyes. "Then you're happy we're headed out tomorrow? Happy to wave your good-byes to her?"

And *that* thought made Steady's scalp itch. "I know I've said it a hundred times since we took this gig"—he kept his voice barely above a whisper—"but I don't buy that nonsense about Abby's big sister being the likely target of this prospective kidnapping just because she followed in her father's political footsteps to become a congresswoman." He used his thumb to pick at the beer's label, succeeding in peeling the corner away. He attacked the glue left behind with the blunt edge of his nail. "Being a government bigwig doesn't make Caroline any more attractive than Abby to those factions looking for leverage to use against the president."

"Look, man, you read the NSA Intel the president gave us as closely as I did. All signs point to Caroline." Dan loosened his tie. They were here at the hotel under the guise of businessmen. Only the president, his JCs, and the Secret Service knew their real assignment—to provide auxiliary security for Abby when she wasn't safely ensconced in her room for the night. Like she was right now.

And Dan was right, of course. All signs *did* point to Caroline. And since that was the case, President Thompson, who secretly ran Black Knights Inc. along with the Joint Chiefs, was only requiring Abby be given BKI protection when she was OCONUS—outside the contiguous U.S. Whereas Caroline had had a supplementary BKI force assigned to her every day of the last six weeks. Ever since the first peep of a possible kidnapping came over the wires.

"Chin up." Dan elbowed him. "By oh-seven-hundred tomorrow morning we'll be hopping on a plane. And then none of this will be your problem. It'll be bye-bye bullet-catcher duty and bye-bye you know who."

Bye-bye you know who? After eight long years apart, was he really ready to bid farewell to her again so soon? The answer to that question shouldn't make his heart ache. *Mierda.*

He took a sip of beer, hoping the pain in his chest was simply indigestion brought on by the *nasi kerabu* he'd eaten for lunch—*I mean, the blue rice should've been your first clue,* pendejo. But the minute the suds touched his tongue, he grimaced. Plunking the beer on the bar, he scrubbed the back of his hand over his lips. "*Madre de Dios,*" he grumbled. "Why can't they brew a decent beer on this side of the planet?" Dan's expression hardened when his eyes landed on the abandoned bottle. "Sorry." Steady winced. "I, uh, I guess *any* beer sounds good right about now, huh?"

Dan "The Man" Currington had crawled into the bottle and stayed there for a full year after his wife was brutally gunned down inside the gates of the Black Knights' compound. It'd taken ninety days of rehab and a dogged mental fortitude Steady couldn't help but admire in order for Dan to pull himself back out.

"It's not the taste that tempts me," Dan admitted, his tone stiff. "It's the oblivion it offers."

Steady motioned for the bartender to come take the beer away. "And speaking of finding oblivion and sowing wild oats"—he tipped his chin toward the tall, lanky woman ordering a drink at the opposite end of the bar, happy to change the subject—"I can't help but notice how you and Agent DePaul have been making googly eyes at each other for the last seventy-two hours. Why don't you take a page from Ozzie's book and use the fact that you're both off the clock tonight to sow *your* wild oats. Seek oblivion in bed instead of the bottle. You know, get your freaky-deaky on."

"Freaky-deaky?" Dan grunted. "Wow, Steady. Spoken like a true prodigy." But when he glanced toward

Penni DePaul, the look he gave her exactly matched the one he'd given the beer only seconds ago. Two words: abject longing.

In true BKI form, Steady called Dan on his bullshit. "It's obvious the woman puts you in a state of forlorn yearning, *hermano*. Like, seriously, I'm afraid if you don't do something about it soon, I'll find you locked in your room upstairs listening to Air Supply's greatest hits." Dan sent him a look meant to curdle his balls, and Steady shook his head, clapping a hand on the guy's shoulder. "Besides, Patti wouldn't want you to spend the rest of your life as a eunuch. She'd want you to be happy. She'd want—"

"No." Dan shook his head. "It's too soon."

"That's a pile of *caca* and you know it. It's been almost two years since Patti's accident." Dan opened his mouth, but Steady preempted him. "And don't give me that same old self-recriminating song and dance about it being your fault she's gone. You know as well as I do the only person to blame for what happened to Patti was the guy who pulled the trigger on that sawgun. It's time for you to move on. To start living again." He let his gaze drift over to Agent DePaul. She was staring at Dan, her big brown eyes soft, concerned. *Sí*, she was exactly what Dan Man needed right now. Something comfortable and caring. Something sweet and willing. Something that *wasn't* a memory. "And I think you should begin with pretty Agent Penni over there."

Dan shrugged, a muscle in his jaw flexing. "I don't care what you say. Two years is too damn soon. Besides, the similarity of their names is just…it's weird, man. Patti spelled with an 'I' and Penni spelled with an 'I.'

I'd probably end up calling her by the wrong name in the heat of things, and how awful would *that* be? For *both* of us." He feigned a shudder.

There were times, like now, when Dan Man's Michigan accent really showed, adding an "L" to the word *both* until it sounded more like *bolth.* Steady sat back, crossing his arms over his chest, sucking in the bar air, which was a combination of Red Bull, whiskey, and high-priced perfume. He tried to decide what to say next. But before he opened his mouth to recite another platitude about it being time to *carpe diem* and whatnot, Ozzie arrived on the scene.

Throwing an arm around each of their shoulders and flashing that white-toothed grin guaranteed to make panties drop in two seconds flat, Ozzie leaned in and whispered conspiratorially, "Guess what's in my pocket, boys?" He wiggled his eyebrows. "Why, it's the room key of a certain delectable little government agent who'll wake up tomorrow morning completely ruined for all other men!"

"For Chrissakes, Ozzie," Dan grumbled, staring at the ice in his glass like he was attempting to melt it with his gaze. "You're an ass. Like, seriously, one or two chromosomes away from a farmhouse donkey."

"Aw, listen to you sweet-talking me," Ozzie quipped right back. "But don't roofie me and call it romance. Besides, it takes one to know one."

Dan turned to glare. "How do you figure?"

"Only an ass would pass on the invitation in the eyes of that tall drink of Secret Service agent over there." Ozzie hooked a thumb toward the table where Penni had joined Julia.

"Dan says it's too soon," Steady informed him.

"Hmm," Ozzie hummed. "Well, one of the things I've learned in life is that bullshit stinks. And, dude, what just came out of your mouth reeks like week-old sushi wrapped in unwashed gym socks."

"That's what I've been saying," Steady agreed.

"Oh, fuck off, you two," Dan harrumphed. "Stop talking about me like I'm not here. And besides, I'm not interested in Penni DePaul."

Steady and Ozzie exchanged a look that called Dan a raging *mentiroso*—a liar. Dan caught them. "I'm *not*," he insisted a little too forcefully. And then the truth of the matter came out. "Anyway, I wouldn't have the first clue what to do. I haven't tried to seduce a woman in more than a decade."

"Well, you're lucky the role of wingman is right in my wheelhouse," Ozzie boasted, slapping him on the back before turning toward the women. "Come dance with us, ladies!" he crowed, grabbing Dan's arm and hauling him off the barstool. "We have grind on the mind! And we plan to make good on the impulse until you're forced to head upstairs in an hour to make your curfew."

"It's not a *curfew*, Ozzie!" Julia Ledbetter called back, laughing and rising from the table. "It's protocol. And that's *vastly* different!" She rolled her eyes to signify how much she was irked by the new Secret Service code of conduct enacted in response to the group of agents who'd found themselves front-page news after they were caught boozing and carousing with some… erm…*questionable* female companions down in South America. Uncle Sam, never one to take kindly to that kind of international embarrassment, had tossed off the role of *uncle* and donned the garb of *dad* by implementing a new set of guidelines by which off-duty agents had to adhere. And one of them was…wait for it…a frackin' midnight curfew.

Not for the first time, Steady was glad that after his stint with the Army he'd chosen door number two when President Thompson—who for some odd reason had taken an interest in his career—offered him a position either within the Secret Service or as an operator for Black Knights Inc. Of course, at the time his decision had less to do with a lack of regard for the already stringent rules of the Secret Service and more to do with not wanting to run into Thompson's youngest daughter at every turn. Or worse…get himself assigned to her security detail.

Damn, but look at me now! Assigned to her security detail!

And, *sí*, he totally appreciated the irony.

"Steady? You coming?" Dan asked, dragging him from his thoughts. When he glanced at the guy, it was to find Dan's expression just this side of panic.

Ozzie slung an arm over his shoulder and murmured, "Dude, if you'll just stop dragging your feet and cock-blocking yourself, I might be able to get you some squish tonight."

Dan's expression morphed from panic to consternation. "Squish?"

Steady shook his head. "Don't get him started," he advised, well-versed in where this was headed next. Unfortunately, he was too late. Ozzie was already expounding.

"You know," Ozzie said. "Get you back in the V-saddle. Have you re-conquer the V-dragon. Put you back on top of the V-mountain. *Now* you understand what I'm saying to you?"

"No." Dan shook his head, his expression repulsed. "You were so very subtle. Maybe use sound effects next time."

Ozzie opened his mouth and Dan rolled his eyes, lifting a hand. "That was joke. I get it."

"You do?" Ozzie grinned, wiggling his eyebrows.

"Yeah." Dan nodded. "I totally get that you lower the bar of evolution by at least three rungs."

Impervious to insults, Ozzie grinned and hauled Dan toward the cleared floor space in front of a raised dais where a five-piece band and an exotic singer in a red sequined dress were doing some pretty strange renditions of the current Top 40. When Dan glanced back in his direction, he implored, "Come on, man. Come with us."

"Not me, *hermano*." Steady threw some colorful Malaysian ringgits atop the bar. "I'm headed up to bed." *Where I* won't *lay tossing and turning, hard and aching because little Abby Thompson is just four doors down.*

Sí. Sure. Right. And if anyone believed that, he had a bridge he could sell them…

Chapter Two

ABBY READ THE FINAL WORDS OF HER SPEECH ON THE need to protect Malaysia's jungles from deforestation, assuring herself she'd hit all the major points—even if she'd flubbed a line here or there when she'd given the damn thing a few hours ago. But the horticultural convention attendees hadn't seemed to notice when she'd tripped up—a public speaker she was not—so all in all, she was chalking this one up as a success.

And maybe it will make a difference in the way they're managing their land here. Though she wasn't holding her breath. Southeast Asia's vast wildernesses, though rich in the biological treasures of plant life, were not nearly as profitable as the rubber tree plantations that were edging them out more and more each day.

But at least I gave it a shot. Said my piece. And, really, that's all she could hope to do. Folding away the speech and tucking it into the back pocket of her slacks, she leaned against the molded concrete ledge of the narrow hotel balcony, watching the golden lights of Kuala Lumpur twinkle all around her. A thunderstorm had blown through the city a couple of hours ago, cleaning most of the smog from the air and upping the humidity a few more degrees. *Like it needed it.* But despite the film of sweat that threatened to slick her skin if she remained outside too much longer, she couldn't force herself to return to the air-conditioned sanctuary of her room. Because she knew the moment she did, there'd be nothing to distract her from thoughts of Carlos.

These last three days had been some of the longest of her life. Seeing him again. Being near him again. Noticing that in most ways he was still the same man she'd known back in DC. Smart. Handsome. Quick with a smile. But in others ways, he was entirely different. Harder. Edgier. *Sexier...*which she wouldn't have thought possible had she not witnessed it with her own two eyes.

Oh, Dad, why did you agree to his coming along on this assignment? Why couldn't you have sent him to guard Caroline and given me another one of your super secret operators?

And, yes, she knew all about Black Knights Inc., the clandestine group of men and women her father had formed a couple of years after becoming president and learning there were some things that could only be done outside regular government channels. She knew all about them because making sure Carlos was always taken care of had been part of their deal.

Their deal... That mothersucking, whackass, craptastic deal...

Which brought her back to the question of *why* her father had sent Carlos here. She'd been shocked as shit to see him that first day. Hadn't her father thought about how difficult it would be for her? Hadn't he given one second's contemplation to how hard it would be for her to have to smile and flirt and tease like she'd done back in the good ol' days? To have to act as if nothing had—

She sensed a dark presence move up behind her a split second before the dainty, almost delicate bite of—was that a needle?—pierced her neck. Her heart slammed against her sternum with enough force to snap a rib. She opened her mouth to scream, but a loud, gurgling groan like that of a dying animal was the only sound to escape.

It *was* a needle. And the substance shooting through her veins was powerful and fast-acting. It locked her vocal cords in place and caused her muscles to go limp. Instantly, she lost the ability to grip the hotel balcony's rough ledge. And although she could feel the sticky sweat on the forearms of the mysterious man straightjacketing her arms to her sides while pushing the syringe's plunger home, she could not for the life of her do one thing to fight him.

Oh God, no! Her horrified mind screamed the words her mouth couldn't form. And as the stuff shot through her veins like the drug it obviously was, burning, festering, polluting, it ignited her blood and sent a thousand stinging ants skittering across her nerve endings. Then, like a light switching from *on* to *off*, all her senses dulled. She knew the breeze drifting up from the dark street below was hot and moist, redolent with the burning scent of car exhaust and the more pungent odors of dried fish, cardamom, and freshly cut chili peppers. But she could no longer feel its sultry kiss on her skin or smell its uniquely Southeast Asian flare.

She was trapped. Trapped inside a useless body. And not to go all *Apocalypse Now* or anything, but the horror of it! The absolute horror!

Struggling to hang on to some semblance of coherence, she fixed her watering eyes on the Petronas Towers, off to the north. The massive skyscrapers pierced the blackened sky with their bright, silvery glow…twin beacons of hope showing the world just how far the country had come in the last twenty years.

And where is my hope? My salvation? Where the frickin' sticks is my security detail?

She let her gaze slide to the balcony on her left, looking for Marcy Tucker, the Secret Service agent who'd been assigned the room next to hers for the night. But, to her utter dismay, her eyes landed not on Agent Tucker at her post, but on a tall, dark-skinned man leaning against Agent Tucker's balcony. His smile was obscene, his teeth blazing white against the darkness when he lifted a fisted hand, pumping it once in…*victory,* maybe? But what kind of victory? She didn't dare contemplate.

Cocking her ears, she waited for the interior door adjoining her room to Agent Silver's room on her right to burst open. She wasn't supposed to lock it. That was part of the protocol she'd been living under for nearly nine years—and after what had happened at Georgetown, you can bet your bottom dollar she followed the letter of the law to a tee. And surely Agent Silver had heard that awful sound she'd made before her vocal cords quit working. Surely he was two seconds away from racing to her rescue. *Surely…*

But instead of the adjoining door, it was the door to his balcony that skimmed open with a muted *snick.* And it wasn't Agent LaVaughn Silver's big, bald head and black goatee that materialized into the night; it was another smiling, dusky-skinned stranger. He pumped his fist in a salute similar to the other man's, and dread wrapped its black fingers around her throat, threatening to strangle her.

One last chance…

She flicked her attention to the roof of the shopping mall across the street. *Agent Bosco? Tony? Are you there? Is your weapon trained on my attackers?* She waited for the loud report as hot lead left muzzle. One second. Two… Fear buzzed in her ears, sounding like the hive of honeybees she cultivated for the Botanic Garden back in DC. But three seconds…then four seconds ticked by, and the *boom* from the gun never came.

Agent Bosco? Frantically, she searched the wide, flat roof for the last of the three Secret Service agents on duty tonight. But in the next instant, her eyesight faltered and narrowed, turning everything beyond a ten-foot radius into a hazy, befuddling gray.

Then, the drug-induced paralysis that'd frozen her muscles moved to her mind. On the plus side, it meant the fear gripping her so savagely suddenly released its strangling hold, just…*gone.* On the downside, it meant in its place was nothing. No joy. No sorrow. No pity. No pain.

Nothing…

The vast emptiness *should* have been terrifying in and of itself. And there was a part of her—a small, nearly infinitesimal piece of her mind still valiantly fighting off the effects of the narcotic—that understood this, that realized the scope of the trouble she was in. But it wasn't enough. And soon, the wondrously thick cloud of apathy overcame that last tiny vestige of sanity and left her calmly watching herself as if from a distance. Watching as a window-washing platform operated by a shadowy figure dropped into view on the other side of her balcony. Watching as the two thugs who'd smiled and fist-pumped ducked back into the rooms on either side of hers. Watching as the bastard supporting her boneless weight lifted her off her feet and handed her over the ledge to the waiting shadow man, her head and arms lolling as if she were a life-sized rag doll.

In a bleary, unconcerned kind of way, she realized the online chatter picked up by the NSA about the threat of kidnapping was real. It was happening right this very minute. To *her,* not to Caroline, as the reports had suggested. And there was absolutely nothing she could do to stop it…

Nothing she necessarily *wanted* to do to stop it, come to think of it, her detachment from herself so entirely complete. Was she breathing? She couldn't feel her lungs moving, couldn't feel her chest cavity filling with delicious, live-giving oxygen. Was her heart still beating? There was no telltale rush of blood between her ears, no reassuring *lub-dub* of muscle behind her breastbone.

Perhaps she was dying. Or…*dead.* Maybe she wasn't being abducted but had been murdered. And this was an out-of-body experience. *How strange...* She'd never really believed in such things. But if this was death, then—

"Do not worry," the shadow man whispered in her ear, his English clipped and heavily accented. "We will not kill you. You would lose your value."

So…*not* dead, then.

Huh. She should be happy about that. She *knew* she should. But the gray…it was calling to her, beckoning and enticing her to give in. And give in she would. *Why shouldn't I?* She could think of no good reason. And quite honestly, giving in felt…good.

Dan's heart pounded until he felt it in his fingertips… and lower. Because the delectable Agent Penni DePaul had shoved him against the door of his hotel room the second he booted it closed. And now her agile tongue was introducing itself—*well, hey there*—to his in the most mind-numbing fashion.

Soft…that's what she was. Even though she was tall and lean, she was soft in all the right places. In her lovely, flaring hips held tight between his hands. And in her small, round breasts pressed firmly against his chest.

Fresh-smelling…she was that, too. Light and airy and altogether scrumptious, her scent made him harder, hornier than he'd been in…well…a long time. And when he kissed her neck, just below her ear, the taste of her skin was rosewater.

Basically, she was everything he'd been denying himself for the past twenty-two months. She was…*woman.*

A drunk woman? Was it possible he was taking advantage of her?

"How many of those froufrou drinks did you have?" he whispered in her ear.

"Just enough," she giggled, reaching around to grab his ass in order to better rub herself against his hardened length. When he could uncross his eyes, he lifted his head, staring down at her.

Her stance was steady. Her smile was warm. And her pupils were…dilated? He cocked his head and studied her more closely.

"I'm not drunk, Dan," she assured him.

"No?"

"No." She shook her head. "I'm pleasantly buzzed. But a far cry from drunk. So stop being a skootch"—*Skootch?*—"and keep doing exactly what you're doing." Fisting her hand in his hair, she guided his lips back to the junction of her shoulder and throat. *Roger that.* He opened his mouth to taste her gorgeous flesh.

"Mmm," she murmured, and because he took her at her word—and also because he knew drunk, he'd *lived* drunk, and one look told him Penni DePaul was *not* drunk—there was nothing to stop him from lifting his hand to her soft, warm breast. Nothing to stop him from running his thumb over the crest until her little nipple hardened. He started to whisper her name, but in that instant his earlier prophecy came true. He forgot what to call her. Poised on the tip of his tongue was...*Patti...*

He jerked back and let his head fall against the door. It landed with a muted *thud.*

I can't do this. Regardless of what Ozzie and Steady claimed to the contrary, it *was* too soon. The memories of his murdered wife were still clearly written across his mind like chalk on a blackboard, and without the hooch to use as an eraser, he couldn't escape them.

"Dan?" Penni's voice was husky. "Is there...are you okay?"

Ha! Okay? No. He wasn't okay. In fact, he'd probably never be okay again...

He glanced down at the lovely little Secret Service agent. Her smile was soft and hesitant, yet warm...like a low winter sun rising over Lake St. Clair on the east side of Detroit. It made his stomach flip. *Hell's bells*, she deserved more than this, better than him. He told her as much.

A little crease formed between her sleek, arching eyebrows. "What do you mean?"

"I'm not worth your time," he elaborated. "I'm still too fucked up."

"Fucked up about what?" Her big brown eyes were curious…kind. And it was her eyes that'd been doing a number on him since the moment they met, when it was *blammo!* Instant connection. He'd never felt anything like it. Not even with Patti. And, yeah, that made it so much worse.

"You don't know?" How could she not? He thought the word *widower* was stamped across his forehead right beneath the word *alcoholic.*

"No." She shook her head, her eyes softening further, melting into him. Melting *him.*

She really *didn't* know. And it was a relief, in a way. He hated being pitied. On the other hand, it was that much more embarrassing to be standing here, a real-life walking, talking erectile dysfunction commercial.

The thought *God, I need a drink* was immediately followed up by *One day at a time*. And that was progress, he supposed.

"It's just…I've been dealing with some personal stuff recently." And how lame did that sound? Personal stuff? *Jesus.*

"And you can't forget about it?" The way she smashed the words together until they sounded like *fuhgeddaboudit* broadcasted her hometown more loudly than an NYC police siren. "Just for one night?" She nudged her hips against his, and his deflated erection took notice, twitching with renewed interest. *Praise be to heaven*, perhaps he wasn't on the shortlist for Viagra after all.

"I wanna forget about it," he admitted, as much to himself as to her. He wanted to forget about it so he could move on, do his duty by his teammates, do right by his country. Maybe then he could begin to make up for…*everything*. Get over the "toxic shame," as his sponsor called it. That feeling that he *was* a mistake instead of having *made* a mistake. "But, I—"

"You should know I never do this," she interrupted him. "You probably don't believe me. I mean, we've only known each other for three days and here I am trying to jump your bones." She pulled a face. "But the truth is, I've felt a…I guess you'd call it a *connection*…ever since the moment we met." So it wasn't just him. *That* was encouraging. Or terrifying. He couldn't decide which. "All right already. That sounds stupid, doesn't it?"

He thought about telling her *yeah, that's stupid. There's no such thing as love at first sight.* But what they had going here? Lust? Well, that was a horse of a different color. And although he couldn't help but feel disloyal to his wife, to her memory, to the love they'd shared, he also couldn't shake the words he'd heard at his last AA meeting. *It's okay to look back. Just don't stare…*

By God, he'd been staring for nearly two years now. So, was it finally time to peel his eyes away from the past and take a glance into the future? Were Ozzie and Steady right? Could he, *should* he, begin to move on? "It doesn't sound stupid," he finally admitted. "I felt it, too."

Her eyes rounded. "Really? I thought it was just me. Because recently I decided I'm too career-oriented, that I've been letting the job become my life. And I can't help but wonder if some of my best years are behind me. I mean, I'm thirty-*three*." The way she said it, it might as well have been one-hundred-and-three. And what was *with* thirty-three and personal epiphanies, anyway? First Steady. Now Penni? "Which makes me afraid that if I don't start taking advantage of opportunities for real human connection, I'll have blown any chance I have at a future with someone.

"Not that I'm saying I have a future with you," she quickly added, a look of panic flitting across her pretty face. "But I figured it was because I recently decided to start taking chances that I felt this instant, uh, attraction, or connection, or…whatever you want to call it. I figured it was because I'd finally opened myself up to—"

He pressed a finger against her lips. "First of all," he said, smiling down at her, "take a breath. And secondly, has anyone ever told you your accent comes out when you get worked up?" She'd started leaving the *r* sounds off the ends of her words until *wonder* sounded more like *wondah,* and *years* sounded more like *yee-ahs.* And miracle of miracles, his discomfort seemed to drift away in the face of hers. Maybe because he realized he wasn't the only one toting around a heaping helping of emotional baggage. Or maybe because, in that moment, he felt certain of something. Like, the universe or Patti's spirit—although he really didn't believe in any of that—was telling him it was okay to let go. To finally, *finally* let go. A lightness unlike anything he'd experienced in a very long time lifted away a piece, just one tiny piece, but a piece all the same, of the heavy burden he'd been carrying around inside his heart, inside his soul.

"They have," Penni burbled around his finger. "To my eternal dismay."

Okay, and she was adorable. Simply adorable. With

her too-expressive eyes and that little bump on the bridge of her nose…

Everything inside Dan softened at the same time something on the outside of him, something decidedly *south*, hardened. "The Bronx?" he asked, removing his finger.

"Brooklyn." She nodded.

Grinning down at her, delighting in how good he suddenly felt, in how good she felt against him, another AA adage drifted through his mind. *A man can't be content with simply getting by.* And truthfully? That's all he'd been doing since rehab. Getting by.

Ozzie and Steady *were* right. His gentle, loving wife *wouldn't* want him wasting away. She'd want him to move on, to find some semblance of happiness. Some semblance of a *life*. And on his initial attempt to do that, he needed someone kind and understanding. Someone who wouldn't laugh at him if—*heaven forbid*—he burst into tears in the middle of it. Someone who would hold him, comfort him, be patient with him. And Penni DePaul, bless her sweet heart, seemed to fit the bill perfectly.

"That's what I'm gonna call you," he whispered, gently cupping her face in his hands, lowering his lips to hers. "Brooklyn…"

Chapter Three

Abby's world came back to her slowly and in pieces…

First there was smell. *Too* much smell. The dank, salty aroma of dried fish competed with the bloodier scent of freshly butchered meat and the wet, decaying odor of the popular durian fruit. Then there was garlic, pepper, cinnamon…*ugh.* All of it together triggered her gag reflex.

Which made her realize her ears were back online, too. She could hear herself hacking, gasping above the noisy chatter of raised voices and the steady droning of…what was that? The sound was vaguely familiar, reminding her of the time she'd been snowed in during a family ski trip to Colorado.

Generators, maybe? Which would explain the hint of exhaust adding to the bouquet of stomach-churning scents.

Blech! Smells like Chewbacca's burned butt hair. Where the hell am I?

When she opened her eyes, it was to find a world of chaos and color. She appeared to be floating like a lost balloon through an alley that backed up to one of Kuala Lumpur's many night markets. The back sides of multi-hued, tightly spaced booths—which she knew were overloaded with everything from produce, meat, and spices to trinkets and textiles—drifted by on her left. On her right was a labyrinth of alcoves and alleyways filled with the empty carts of the night market's hawkers. And when she glanced up, it was to see the hardened jaws of two men. Tendons and veins bulged in their necks as they struggled under her weight. Okay, so she wasn't floating, she was being carried.

Memories assaulted her…

The pinch of the needle. The body that refused to respond to her commands. Her security detail's perplexing absence and the *presence* of a handful of strange men. The apathy that soon followed…

Well, she could only *wish* for a drop of that apathy now. Because the stark terror was back in full effect, causing her heart to race so fast she was dizzy. Or maybe that was thanks to the remnants of the drug in her system.

"Help me," she croaked, reaching out to a wide-eyed Malaysian woman standing next to an empty cart. Or at least she *tried* to reach out. Her stupid arm weighed in at a cool thousand pounds and didn't do much more than twitch as it dangled from her shoulder socket. And her voice? Heaven help her, it was nothing but an airy whisper.

Still, she'd moved enough, made enough noise, that one of the men glanced down at her. His dark, close-set eyes were fierce, and even in her narco-hazy state she had no trouble reading the cold calculation in them. He looked away to say something to her second abductor. She couldn't understand his words but noted they picked up the pace, breaking into a bumpy, bone-jostling jog. Her head bounced around so much she thought it was a wonder it didn't snap off the end of her neck. Just *crack!* And there it'd go, rolling down the alley.

Although, come to think of it, that particular scenario didn't sound all that bad. At least *then* she'd be free of this terrible paralysis and the mind-numbing terror it evoked.

A few more agonizing seconds passed before they reached their destination—the back of a faded red stall. Her kidnappers parted a slit in the fabric and ducked inside, unceremoniously dumping her into a molded plastic chair. Her arms fell listlessly to the sides, her legs crookedly stretched out in front of her. She couldn't raise her head—like everything else, the muscles in her neck refused to work—but from the corner of her eye, she saw one of the men pull a handful of silk scarves over the front opening of the booth, effectively shutting the three of them inside.

Good God! What now?

And then she wished she hadn't asked. Because one of her kidnappers bent to quickly undo the buttons on her blouse while the other squatted at her feet to attack the laces on the kitten-heel boots she'd purchased specifically for the New Frontiers in Horticulture Convention.

And how ridiculous that all seemed now, her desire to look just so—professional yet stylish—while she gave her speech. How stupid to have worried about her *appearance*, about how the president of the United States' daughter would be *perceived* in this predominantly Muslim country, when there were so many *real* concerns that should've occupied her mind.

Real concerns like abduction. Like something terrible

happening to the tough, loyal people in her protection detail. Like Carlos Soto suddenly reappearing in her life all big and dark and rough, everything she'd ever wanted in a man but couldn't have. Like...*rape*...

The ugly word whispered through her head, causing her heart to crash against her breastbone. It made it hard to breath, hard to hear anything above the whooshing roar of blood between her ears.

"No," she managed to murmur, though her tongue felt like it had swollen to fill her mouth. She wanted to punch. She wanted to kick. She wanted to bite and scratch and scream. But she could do none of that. She could do nothing but sit there, a prisoner inside her own useless body, while these vile men defiled her.

A sob of fear and fury built inside her chest as a thousand horrific images flipped through her mind.

Urgent, ungentle hands...*flip!*

Sweaty, thrusting male bodies...*flip!*

Greedy, wet mouths...*flip!*

The depravity and obscenity of it all caused saliva to pool at the back of her tongue. When she swallowed, it was thick and sticky. But, amazingly, the action enabled her to put some volume behind her next words. "Ssstop it! You b-bastards!" she slurred.

The thrill of succeeding in that one small rebellion was short lived, because the man pulling her blouse from her shoulders slapped her face. *Hard.* White-hot pain burned over the expanse of her cheek and detonated like an atom bomb behind her right eye. Her head whipped to the side where it remained, lolling against her left shoulder.

"Quiet!" he hissed, staring at her with such...

hatred. She had never seen such hatred on the face of a man. Burning tears seeped from the corners of her eyes to trickle across the bridge of her nose and run over her temple.

She loathed the fact that she was crying, detested herself for showing these cowards…these *beasts* one ounce of weakness. But she couldn't stop. Despite her best efforts, the tears kept on coming, soaking the hair at her temple and dripping onto her bare shoulder and chest.

When he reached between her breasts to flick open the front closure of her bra—*No! No, no, no!*—she squeezed her eyes closed and readied herself for the feel of his despicable hands on her flesh, readied herself for the ultimate degradation. But to her utter confusion and relief, it never came.

Instead, an article of clothing was forced over her head, her useless arms manipulated into the long sleeves. She opened her eyes to see the men were dressing her in a black *baju kurung*, a type of conservative, knee-length shirt worn by many of Malaysia's women.

Huh? Why?

But then she forgot to seek the answer to her question when, with a yank and a tug, her trousers slipped from her legs. Hard, hot hands traveled up her bare thighs.

"No!" she managed to yell, only to have a wide, damp palm clamp over her mouth. Sweat seeped between her lips, its bitter, salty taste turning her stomach. She gagged and tried to shake loose the hand. But her feeble movement just resulted in the man digging his fingers and thumb into her face, smashing her cheeks against the rough edges of her teeth until she cried out. *No, don't let them see your pain,* she admonished herself. *It'll only encourage them.*

Of course, on a list of things that were easier said than done, that ranked right near the top. Her nostrils flared wide and her terror ratcheted up another notch when searching fingers curled around the waistband of her panties and tugged. She could smell her abductors, smell the spices they enjoyed in their meals coming through the sweat on their skin, smell the harsh detergent they washed their clothes in. Again, she closed her eyes, determined to block out what was coming next. Poised to disassociate herself from her physical form so that no matter what they did to her *body*, they wouldn't touch her *mind*.

But her eyes flew open, and she blinked her confusion when her panties slipped over her heels only to be replaced by the feel of another garment. She looked down and recognized the straight cut of a traditional Malay skirt as it was pulled over her calves and knees.

Not taking his hand from her mouth, the man standing beside her hooked his free arm around her shoulders and lifted her so that his companion could tug the skirt up and over her naked hips and bottom. Next, a pair of soft-soled shoes—much like the ballet flats she liked to wear around the house—were slipped over her feet.

"I will take my hand from your mouth," Shadow Man said. Now that he'd spoken more words, she remembered his voice from the balcony. "But I warn you, do not scream." He leaned in close, malice shining in his black eyes, his long, thin nose barely an inch from hers. "If you scream, I will have to hurt you again." He gave her cheeks a painful squeeze for emphasis. "Do you understand?"

She was so grateful he wasn't about to rape her—the relief flooding her system so overwhelming it increased her dizziness ten-fold—that she didn't think twice about grunting her acquiescence, blinking rapidly in case he didn't understand.

"Good." He nodded before yanking a scarf from the booth's back wall, deftly wrapping the length of silk around her head. Oh, how she wished she could rub her abused cheeks, but she satisfied herself with watching the second man gather her belongings.

Uh-huh. Just go ahead and hold on to all of that, you son of a motherless goat, she thought with devilish delight. Lamentably, that delight was fleeting, because Henchman Number Two ducked out of the stall with her clothes in hand.

Well, for the love of...

Now how was her Secret Service detail supposed to find her? And then she remembered the three on-duty agents' ominous absences. Did she *have* a Secret Service detail left? These men...these dark, dangerous men seemed to know too much. They'd known which balcony was hers. They'd known where to find and how to take out her protection detail; she prayed they'd only succeeded in incapacitating the agents, because even though she'd only been living and working with this current group for about six months—it was protocol for the agents to remain on a rotation to keep them from becoming too personally attached to their protectee—the thought of anything happening to them was...well... simply unacceptable. And these dark, dangerous men obviously knew about her clothes...

But how?

She didn't have much time to ponder that before the second man reappeared. Empty handed. *Shit on a biscuit!* And even though she'd expected as much, the sight still made her want to cry. *Again.* Of course, she'd be damned if she gave these bastards that satisfaction. *Again.*

A loud banging and some rustling sounded outside the booth. Then the noisy hum of a nearby generator clicked off, quickly followed by another. The market was closing for the night, the vendors folding away their goods and piling their wares into the carts attached to their bicycles or motorbikes, all to be taken home until tomorrow when the grand parade would repeat itself.

Which meant she only had a few minutes to get someone's attention. She opened her mouth. But before she could summon a scream—*screw Shadow Man and his threats*—a third man ducked into the stall.

Some quick words in Malay were exchanged. Shadow Man appeared to be pissed, verbally ripping the arrival a new asshole. That is until New Guy produced a syringe from his pocket. Shadow Man nodded and motioned in her direction. Stalking toward her, New Guy—who looked much like the other two. Dark. Skinny. With hate-filled eyes and nondescript clothes—slapped a bony hand over her lower jaw. His expression was hard, *vicious* as he wrenched her head to the side, exposing her neck beneath the scarf. But before he hit her with the needle, something caught his eye.

She could see his attention move to her hair or… her ear?

Yes! It *was* her ear. How could she have forgotten about the faux diamond studs Carlos had insisted she wear?

"I know you trust your security detail and the protocol they've established implicitly," he told her after slipping into her hotel room with two of his teammates soon after their arrival in Kuala Lumpur. God, he looks good, *she thought.* Grown up. *All the softness of his twenties replaced with one hundred percent pure, hard-bodied* man. Yowza! Hubba-hubba! *And the way he spoke to her? With no nonsense, no hesitation or pause for greeting besides a quick dip of his chin and a flash of that one delectable dimple? It made her feel like it'd been mere days since they last saw each other instead of eight long years.* Familiar, *she guessed was the word. Then again, he'd always felt familiar. Like something she'd somehow subconsciously known was missing in her life...and maybe in her heart, too? "But for my own peace of mind, I want you to wear these."*

He held out his hand. Broad-palmed and long-fingered, with little crescent moons visible in his neatly tended nails, she'd always thought he had the hands of the surgeon he'd considered becoming once upon a time. They were strong, steady...like his nom de guerre*—his war name. And how strange was that? To have gone from a man poised to take the medical community by storm to a man who* literally *stormed into battle?*

A part of her couldn't help but lament the role she'd played in the sudden left turn in his life path. But she couldn't let him see the direction of her thoughts, so she concentrated on the two diamond studs glittering in his grip.

"Oh, Carlos!" She batted her lashes at him and clasped her hands together, playing the part he would expect of her. "You shouldn't have!"

His chin jerked back, his expression startled. "Oh, no. No, they're not what you think."

She made a face. "They're big ol' diamond studs that look like something a rapper would wear. So, I think they're transmitters." When she took the earrings from him, she shivered as her fingertips brushed his warm, calloused palm. What would it be like to feel those hands on my body? *It was a question she'd asked herself a million times over the years.*

"Then they are *what you think," he told her, winking and giving her arm a squeeze before one of his teammates called him away. It was a* friendly *squeeze, like one might give a favorite cousin—though there was no convincing her arm of that; the idiotic thing tingled with awareness. And to her eternal chagrin, she knew that despite the fact she was all grown up now, a woman in every way, Carlos still thought of her as nothing more than a wide-eyed schoolgirl.*

But that's for the best, *she told herself. Though, unfortunately,* herself *wasn't convinced.*

Dragging her eyes away—and, yes, she had to drag *them—from Carlos's broad back...or maybe it was his ass? Okay, so sue her. The man had a great ass...she stared down at the glinting studs in her hand. Why knowing he'd gone out of his way to provide one more level of security should cause butterflies to flutter drunkenly in her belly, she couldn't say. But there they were, the little bastards. Flitting and flapping and making her feel light as air, as if she could float away any minute, and at the same time making her feel a little bit nauseous, like she was two seconds away from tossing her cookies.*

Oh, for the love of… It's time to grow up, Abby. Stop fantasizing about a man you can never have. And while you're at it, get a hold of yourself *and* your damn butterflies!

It was good advice. And she determined then and there to do her best to take it. Unfastening the simple gold hoop earrings she wore, she replaced them with the faux diamonds. Was it her imagination or were they warm with Carlos's body heat?

Okay, and it was official. She was an idiot. An over-estrogenated idiot, and—

A tug on her earlobe brought her crash landing back to the present. The newest arrival to the unholy trio *had* been distracted by her earrings. And now he was covertly removing them, glancing over his shoulder at Shadow Man—who was deep in conversation with Henchman Number Two—as if he didn't fancy the thought of being caught. The syringe was clamped between his snaggly Gargamel teeth so he could use both hands to take out the diamond studs and, oh, how she wished her arms worked. She'd grab that syringe and plunge it straight into his retched, evil eye!

With crazed, nearly hysterical scrutiny, she watched him pocket the earrings. Now her only hope for rescue hinged on whether or not he was accompanying her wherever the hell it was they planned to take her. Because he'd just removed the last thing tying her to the outside world.

Carlos! she thought desperately. *Where are you?*

He had to know she was missing by now, didn't he? He and the rest of the Black Knights as well as her Secret Service unit? They *had* to know!

Once again, the needle slid into the flesh of her neck with nothing more than a small, almost gentle sting. Instantly, the gray was back…clouding her vision, stripping away her sense of smell, stealing her pain and fear in one blood-boiling narcotic rush.

This time she succumbed to the beckoning darkness without a fight, welcoming its cool embrace and blessed oblivion. But right before she slipped unconscious, a random yet familiar thought skittered through her fading mind. *Carlos…could you ever forgive me for what I did?*

Chapter Four

Downy dryer sheets and Palmer's cocoa butter lotion...

Steady remembered thinking back at Georgetown that a young woman whose father was running for the lofty position of president of the United States should smell expensive and untouchable, like French lace and Chanel No. 5. But to the delight of his libido, Abby's clean, fresh scent had always made her seem *eminently* touchable...the girl next door who shopped at the local Walmart, not Barney's.

In nearly a decade, nothing had changed...

And how the hell would he know that, you ask? Well, because, stupid *culo* that he was, earlier today when he was sitting beside her on the sofa in her hotel room, going over the last sit-rep—situation report—with four of her Secret Service agents, he'd leaned close to brush a lock of honey-blond hair behind her ear. He'd wanted to reassure himself that she hadn't removed the transmitters he'd given her now that the conference was officially over. Only instead of scrutinizing her earrings, *bam*! He got hit with a noseful of Downy dryer sheets and Palmer's cocoa butter lotion. All the blood in his brain double-timed it down to his dick, and he could do nothing but blink at her, his mouth hanging open like a guppy, his entire being infused with...*awareness.*

“Carlos?” She turned to him with a pixie’s smile, her brilliant, celadon-colored eyes tilted up at the corners. “Did you swallow a bug or something?” She started pounding him on the back. “Why are you looking at me that way? What is it?”

What is it? Lust, *he thought.* And yearning and longing and…too many memories. *He had to shake himself, clear his throat, and nod at her to leave off already with the… uh…*helpful *back beating. “Just, um…just checking to make sure you’re still wearing the earrings.”*

She touched one of the studs glinting in her ear, her delicate wrist and long, slim fingers mesmerizing him. “Of course I’m still wearing them. I quite enjoy looking like 50 Cent.” She wiggled her eyebrows, then frowned. “Only next time, try adding a big gold chain, will ya? That’ll complete the look and—”

“Just don’t take them off,” he interrupted before she really got on a roll. The woman was too witty for her own good sometimes.

“I won’t,*” she assured him, her expression turning serious. “You told me to wear them, so I will.”*

What else would you do if I told you to? Sí, *it was official. He was a lowdown, dirty-minded horndog. He adjusted his position on the couch, lifting his foot to rest his right ankle on his opposite knee. It was either that or give everybody in the whole damn room a good long gander at the massive stiffy he’d sprung.* Dios! *Talk about a hard time in Steadyville. Pun intended.*

And speaking of…

It was back. His dick was as engorged now as it’d been then. Which really wasn’t any surprise considering he'd paused in front of her room an hour ago on his way to bed and that familiar, sweet scent of hers had seeped under the door only to tunnel up his nose. He thought he'd heard a murmur, or a soft scuffle coming from inside her room, so he'd stood there, head cocked, listening, breathing her in. But when no other noise sounded from behind the door, he'd been forced to move on. To carry her scent with him down the hall and into his own hotel room, into his own bed. Where visions of her soft, pink lips; long, slim legs; and lovely little breasts just big enough to fill his palms had kept him hard enough to cut glass.

"*Hijo de puta!*" he cursed—*sonofabitch*—before reaching beneath the bed sheet and the waistband of his boxers to wrap his fist around his aching erection. Staring into the darkness, watching the faint city lights dance across the ceiling as they spilled in through the gap in the drapes, he stroked himself. Softly at first, and then more forcefully. He stroked himself until his toes curled, his hips arched, and he strained for completion.

How many times over the years had he done this? Jerked himself off while fantasizing that it was Abby's small hands wrapped around him? Abby's hot mouth sucking the head of him—

BOOOOMMM!

An explosion rocked the building, thundering and quaking and rattling the headboard against the wall. Steady felt the percussive effects in his chest. His ears popped. A dozen memories of similar detonations—those he'd lived through as a soldier and operator, and the one that'd killed his beloved sister—buzzed through his brain. But they didn't stop him from hopping out of the bed in an instant and jumping into a pair of jeans. *Damnit!* And neither did they do anything to abate the boner he was still sporting. It was funny what adrenaline did to a man's body. Not so funny was how a hard-on and denim went together about as well as oil and water. Gritting his teeth, he yanked up his zipper and hoped he didn't catch skin in the process. A second later, he nearly wrenched the door from its frame.

Chaos…

He took it in with a glance. Thin smoke filled the hall in a gray film. The overhead lights flickered and failed, plunging the space into momentary darkness before they lit once again. An artistic photo, once displayed on the hallway wall, now lay decimated on the floor, its frame splintered and glass shattered.

"For Chrissakes!" Dan bellowed, and Steady glanced over to find him standing in the doorway of his hotel room wearing nothing but a pair of black Saxx boxer briefs. Besides Abby and her security detail, the Knights were the only other guests on this floor—though technically, and according to the hotel manifest, the three BKI boys were officially booked in rooms one floor below—which was a good thing since Steady had no desire to deal with civilians right now. All he cared about was getting to Abby and getting her the hell out of Dodge. "What the fuck is happening?" Dan yelled.

"Hell if I know!" he barked over his shoulder as he ran toward Abby's room. "Abby, open up!" He pounded on her door. "We need to vacate the building! There's been an explosion!"

Der. As if *that* wasn't obvious. And where the hell

were the Secret Service agents? Why weren't they pouring out of their rooms like ants from an anthill?

"Abby!" A prickle of dark foreboding skittered up his spine when nothing stirred on the other side of the door. "Open up the—"

"Oh, Jesus!" Dan thundered. "Steady, *help*!"

He turned to find Ozzie leaning against the doorjamb of Agent Ledbetter's room, smoke billowing around him in a thin, ominous cloud. But that's not what immediately struck Steady. *Hell no.* What immediately struck him was the blood. It was everywhere. Covering Ozzie's face and naked torso, turning his white boxer shorts an angry crimson, and gushing from between the fingers he used to cover his thigh.

Arterial spray…

Steady knew it in an instant.

"Ah, hell," he whispered hoarsely, his heart having gone nuclear inside the confines of his rib cage as he raced to Ozzie's side. Seriously, he wouldn't be surprised if there were little mushroom clouds puffing out of his ears.

"Lay down, bro," he told his friend, reaching to cover Ozzie's blood-soaked hands with his own. Dan was already there, kneeling on the floor, trying to stymie the flow of life-giving fluid by squeezing Ozzie's thigh above the wound.

"Julia," Ozzie rasped, coughing. The move caused more blood to pulse between their interlaced hands in a rhythmic *spurt, spurt*. It was hot, and its scent filled Steady's nostrils. He would always equate that particular aroma with the delicate path all humans tread between this world and the next, with the awful day his sister died. He'd run into that coffee shop expecting to find something horrible. But the explosion had been so immense there was nothing of her left. Nothing left of *any* of the patrons save for the iron-rich aroma of their blood slicking the remaining surfaces. He'd come to be grateful for that. Grateful that it'd happened so quickly, been so violent, that Rosa hadn't felt a thing. He liked to imagine she'd been sitting there enjoying a coffee, and then…lights out. On to the next plane without a moment of pain or doubt or regret…

"Somebody needs to check and see that Julia—" Ozzie continued, dragging him back to the situation at hand.

"Down!" he bellowed. He didn't have time for Ozzie's chivalry or heroics. If he didn't get a clamp on that bleeder soon, the guy was going to hemorrhage out right here in the doorway.

Ozzie didn't immediately comply, and Steady was forced to stop applying pressure to the wound in order to grab Ozzie's shoulders and swipe his feet out from under him. With Dan's help, he carefully controlled Ozzie's fall. By the time Ozzie was lying on his back, half-in, half-out of the doorway, his skin was ashen.

Too much blood loss. Too much, too fast…

"Move your hands, Ozzie," he instructed firmly, the acrid smoke filling his nose and scratching his lungs. "I need to see."

As if the Fates, those evil bitches, were playing some sort of sick joke, the overhead lights chose that exact moment to flicker again. Steady gritted his teeth, praying to Jesus, Mary, Joseph, and all the saints he could remember from his catechism classes that they didn't go out for good.

Without light to work by, Ozzie was as good as dead. Hell, depending on how badly his best friend's femoral artery was damaged, that might be the case regardless.

No, Dios! Por favor!

From the corner of his eye, Steady saw Penni DePaul emerge from Dan's room clad only in a T-shirt and panties—no real surprise; he'd heard them laughing and giggling and entering Dan's suite not thirty minutes ago. She didn't break stride as she ran toward them. But instead of kneeling to help, she vaulted over them and into Julia's room. He didn't spare her a second glance as he wrestled Ozzie's hands away from his shredded thigh.

"Fuck me," he rasped when he saw what he was dealing with. The front upper half of Ozzie's leg looked like ground beef, the meat and muscle a mess, his femur visible in spots. "Keep pressure above the wound!" he yelled to Dan as he sank his fingers into the horror of Ozzie's ruined thigh. He searched through the heated gore of internal flesh, through gristle, touching bone.

Where are you? Where are—

"Fuuuuuck!" Ozzie screamed, the heel of his uninjured foot beating against the floor when Steady was forced to shove his whole hand under Ozzie's quadriceps muscle toward his groin where the severed femoral artery had retracted. "Steady! Stop!"

"Can't, bro," he grunted, his fingers slipping through blood and tissue, searching, searching... "Gotcha!" he crowed when he found the end of the artery and clamped it between his thumb and forefinger. "Dan! I need a tourniquet!"

"H-holy shit," Dan coughed, staring over Steady's

shoulder. Steady turned to see what'd snagged Dan's attention. Through the thin fog of smoke, he could make out the bed. Or what was left of it, anyway. It'd been blown to smithereens…and Julia Ledbetter along with it. Her partially charred corpse was laying half-on, half-off the smoldering mattress.

"Julia, no!" Agent DePaul cried, her hands covering her mouth as she was wracked by a spate of coughing.

The bomb…er…more like incendiary device—because, after an initial blast of shrapnel, it'd obviously burned hot and fast before instantly putting itself out—had been in Agent Ledbetter's room? It didn't make sense. But Steady didn't have time to dwell on it. "Dan!" he shouted, jolting his teammate out of his temporary shock. "Get my med kit and a belt!" When Dan hesitated, he screamed, "Now!"

Dan jumped to his feet and dashed toward Steady's room.

"You're killing me, Steady!" Ozzie shrieked. "You have to stop!"

"No can do, *hermano*." He gritted his jaw because he knew the horrendous pain Ozzie was suffering. "If I stop, you'll die."

Teardrops leaked from the corners of Ozzie's eyes, streaking the soot on his temples and darkening his blond hair as he thrashed his head from side to side. Steady experienced the prick of sympathetic waterworks behind his eyes. But he couldn't give in to tears. Not only would it do no one any good, but it would also interfere with his ability to do his job. And right now, his job was—

Abby…

Her name whispered through his mind and caused his racing heart to trip over itself.

Abby...

"Agent DePaul!" he bellowed over his shoulder, remembering the code name the Secret Service had assigned to Abby after she graduated from college and took the job at the DC Botanic Garden. "Check on Beekeeper!" But the agent just stood there, staring at Julia's mutilated body. He raised his voice to a booming roar. "DePaul! Secure the Beekeeper!"

She jumped, blinking owlishly before she got a hold of herself. He saw her throat work over a hard swallow. Then she nodded and dug her bare toes into the carpet, sprinting in his direction. He ducked his head, displaced air fluttering his hair as she made like an Olympian and vaulted over him.

He didn't watch her race down the hall, although there was a part of him that wanted to, a part of him that *desperately* needed to see that Abby was safe and sound. For right now though, he had to concentrate everything he had on the task at hand, because his best friend's life could quite easily—and literally—slip through his fingers if he didn't.

"What do I do?" Dan asked breathlessly, dropping Steady's camouflage medical bag to the floor and kneeling beside him in the doorway.

"The belt." Steady fought a cough. The thin smoke made his chest feel full of hot coals. "Wrap it around his leg." He pushed up the bottom edge of Ozzie's blood-soaked boxers so he could point at the lump beneath Ozzie's flesh, high on his thigh, where his fingers were clamping the artery. "And cinch it *tight* above here."

Dan jerked his chin in a nod, then carefully threaded the end of the belt under Ozzie's wrecked leg, snaking it close to his groin. "Tight," Steady emphasized again. "Tight as you can." Dan gritted his teeth and yanked the belt as Ozzie let loose with a shriek guaran-frackin'-teed to haunt Steady for the rest of his life. "Hold him, Dan!" he yelled when Ozzie thrashed. "You have to keep him still!"

Dan threw himself over Ozzie's chest, using his weight to hold Ozzie down. With his free hand, Steady unzipped his medical bag. *Almost there. Almost there.* Madre de Dios, *almost there.* He just needed to find a clamp to put on the end of that artery and then he could start Ozzie on Hemopure, an oxygen-carrying blood substitute produced in South Africa. Even though it had yet to be approved by the FDA, he'd taken to acquiring the stuff from his Recces friend—Recces was the nickname for South Africa's Special Forces Brigade—and packing it in his med kit. It stayed good for up to thirty-six months at room temperature, was compatible with all blood types, and was a wonderful Johnny-on-the-Spot when a transfusion wasn't possible. Like right now…

Unfortunately, before he could find the small plastic case he kept his clamps in, the overhead lights flickered and dimmed…then went out altogether. Instantly the space was plunged into darkness. Deep, dark, impenetrable darkness. *Blinding* darkness…

Shit! Fuck! Sonofabitch!

"Ozzie!" he shouted his friend's name, reaching unseeingly for Ozzie's shoulder. When he found it, he gave it a squeeze. "Ozzie!" he yelled again because the guy continued to struggle against Dan's restraining weight. "You have to be still, *hermano*! I know it hurts! I know it does! But you have to be still so Dan can let go of you. I need him to get a flashlight!"

"Sonofabitch!" Ozzie howled. "I need morphine!"

"Can't give you morphine." He infused his voice with calm, hoping it would help Ozzie do the same. "With the amount of blood you've lost, it could kill you."

"Sonofabitch! Sonofabiiiiiiitch!" Ozzie bellowed again.

"It's mind over matter!" he yelled right back. Okay, so *fuck* calm. How about candor? "Just open up that big brain tank of yours"—besides being the Black Knights' resident lady-killer, Ozzie was also a whiz-kid computer hacker with an IQ big enough to make Einstein envious—"and fill it with some high-octane grin-and-bear it! You hear me? You find a way to be still! Your life depends on it!" And then, just in case candor didn't work, he figured he'd appeal to Ozzie's *machismo*. "Besides, you keep up this prissy shit, and I'm going to have to revoke your membership to Club Dude."

Ozzie moaned, and Steady could hear his gut-wrenching struggle for composure beneath Agent DePaul's repeated pounding on Abby's door and her screams for Abby to "open up!" *Why isn't she opening her door? Is she too frightened?* He'd never figured her for the shrinking violet sort, but—

"He's still," Dan said. Steady's eyes had adjusted to the stygian darkness and could just make out Dan's shape in the dim red light cast by the glowing KELUAR/EXIT sign tacked to the wall above the door to the emergency stairwell. Ozzie was quaking from head to toe, but he was no longer fighting them. Steady had always suspected Ethan "Ozzie" Sykes, despite his constant joking and bad taste in eighties music, was one tough motherfucker. Now he knew it for sure.

"Okay." He nodded. "Now feel around in my bag. There should be a MagLite attached with Velcro to one side."

He could hear his medical gear clanking and clacking as Dan rustled through his duffel, and he tried not to think about the fact that there was no such thing as a sterile field in this particular situation. Then the glaring beam of the flashlight hit him in the face, and he screwed his lids shut to save his eyesight. "*Bueno*, good." He nodded again. "Shine that into the bag so I can find my clamps."

Dan did as instructed, stuffing the MagLite between his teeth so that he could use both hands to hold Steady's duffel wide. Steady located his clamps in an instant and blew out a deep breath. "Cover him again," he told Dan. "This will bark like a bitch in heat."

"Do it, Steady." Ozzie's voice was reedy, thin. "Just do it."

One. Tough. Motherfucker.

"Here goes," he said. Dan threw himself over Ozzie at the same time he shined the light into that awful wound. Steady pushed Ozzie's torn flesh and muscle up with one hand while pulling the artery down with the other. It was a slippery little bastard, but he managed to block out the thought of what would happen if he didn't manage to hang on to it. But there was no way he could block out Ozzie's bloodcurdling wail of sheer, unimaginable agony. It was enough to burst his eardrums, enough to scar his soul.

Finally, *finally*, he had the artery where he needed

it to apply the clamp. Then it was back into his duffel bag for the Hemopure and QuikClot. And, miracle of miracles, the lights chose that moment to come back on.

"Go help Agent DePaul," he told Dan, blinking against the sudden glare. "I've got this now."

Dan nodded and pushed to his feet. Steady watched him sprint down the hall, then immediately turned back to his patient.

Patient...

Jesús Cristo, Ozzie was so much more than that. A trusted teammate. A best friend. A brother really, in every way that mattered. And if he allowed himself to dwell on what he was doing and who he was doing it *to*, he'd probably lose his shit. So, *sí*, his patient...

"Almost finished," he assured Ozzie. "We'll get you to the nearest hospital, and after a little blood transfusion, it'll be all the morphine you can stand. How does that sound, eh, bro?"

"Julia?" Ozzie managed to rasp as he tried to lift his head to peer into the smoky room.

"She's dead." Steady wasn't Willy Wonka. Sugarcoating things wasn't his style.

"*Fuuuuuck.*" Ozzie allowed his head to drop back to the floor, a sob shuddering through him. Steady gave his friend two seconds to mourn before he went back to work on that thigh.

Seven years of higher education and numerous bouts of battlefield triage helped him determine exactly where to shake the QuikClot—a powdery clotting agent—to combat the worst of the remaining bleeding. Ozzie moaned and clenched his bloody fists, but compared to what he'd just been through, the burn of the

QuikClot was child's play. Steady was in the process of hooking up an IV of Hemopure when a loud *bang!* thundered around the space. Instinct had him throwing himself over Ozzie until a double *bang! bang!* made him glance up.

Penni DePaul, weapon in hand, was firing into the locking mechanisms on the doors of her fellow Secret Service agents' rooms. Dan followed behind her, kicking them open. And each time he did, smoke billowed out in a thin but corrosive cloud that wasn't *quite* enough to trigger the hotel's fire suppressant system. That is, if the hotel even *had* a fire suppressant system. In this part of the world, you could never be sure if those sprinkler nozzles attached to the ceiling were functional or just for show.

Regardless, Steady didn't need to look into those rooms to know what was there. The growing smell of charred flesh said it all. It wasn't one explosion that'd rocked him in his bed. It was several small, simultaneous ones. Abby Thompson's security detail was dead or dying. And something inside Steady, something deep and profound, something he wasn't aware existed, shattered with the realization. Was this the abduction scheme they'd been hearing about? Or something far more sinister?

Abby!

He didn't realize he screamed her name aloud until he saw Dan turn in his direction, the man's face a sooty mask of dread. *Oh, Abby, no!*

"I'm firing at your lock, Abby!" Agent DePaul yelled. "If you're in there, move away from the door!"

Steady's skin tried to crawl off his body. He couldn't

draw a full breath. And his heart thundered so loudly he could hear it echoing down the hall. Then he realized it wasn't his heart. It was footsteps. A lot of them…

The door to the emergency stairwell burst open, spewing forth a glut of hotel staff and security at the same time that Penni pulled her trigger. *Bang!* The crowd of new arrivals—hard to believe, but he'd hazard a guess barely two minutes had passed since the explosions rocked the building—dropped to the floor, proned out like a group of sardines, lying side by side as they covered their heads with their hands.

Steady only gave them a cursory glance before turning to watch Dan kick in Abby's door. Dan rushed into the room and Steady's heart proceeded to climb into his throat. Which was strange, because if his heart was in his throat, then what the hell was hurting in his chest, making it feel like he'd had his sternum cracked open by a surgical retractor?

Dan finally reemerged—ten hours later? Twenty? It seemed like an eternity but could have been only a couple of seconds—and his face was ashen, his eyes wild. Steady braced himself for the words he didn't want to hear. The words he'd never be ready to hear. *Oh, sweet heaven! Abby! No!*

But what Dan said was, "She's gone."

Chapter Five

THEY WERE DEAD...

All her colleagues were dead. And much to Penni DePaul's eternal sorrow, she now understood what it meant to be the last man...*woman*...standing. She'd always assumed the phrase had a positive connotation, that it would feel *good* to be the last woman standing. Boy-oh-boy, had she been wrong.

It felt *awful.*

"Those who weren't on duty were killed in their beds. Whoever set the bombs timed them perfectly. They went off thirty minutes after the agents were required to be back in their rooms. Which was just enough time for them to wash their faces, brush their teeth, and snuggle beneath the covers," Dan grumbled into his phone. "And let me be the first to say, those incendiary devices were very effective." *Mad* effective, as people speaking Brooklynese would say, right along with *God help those poor souls.*

Dan and Steady had stood on the roof of the hotel while Ozzie Sykes was loaded into a medevac helicopter. Afterward, a lengthy back-and-forth with hotel security and the local authorities had ended in a somewhat *threatening* call from the U.S. State Department to the head of the Kuala Lumpur police. Once the locals were officially...*dismissed*, Dan and Steady had grabbed her and secluded themselves here, in Steady's room.

Not for nuttin', as her dearly departed father would say, *but I guess diplomatic immunity has it perks.*

Since then, Dan and Steady had made a series of telephone calls while she used Dan's iPad—hers was blown to Kingdom Come thanks to the fact that she'd left it on her now-destroyed hotel bed. And she totally *wasn't* going to think about what might have happened had she not broken protocol, which she'd *never* done before—to locate the signals emitted by the tracking devices sewn into Abby's clothes. *Abby...Abby...* She had to focus on sweet, charming, hilariously funny when it came to colorful curses Abby. Beekeeper. Her charge. Because it was either that or succumb to the mixture of hysteria, remorse, and flat-out *disbelief* bubbling inside her in an evil witch's brew. Unfortunately, the iPad's screen, covered by a digital map of Kuala Lumpur, was lit up like the mother-flippin' Fourth of July sky above the Statue of Liberty.

What the hell does that mean? she wondered. Then answered her own question a second later when tiny alarm bells started ringing in her head. *Most definitely nothing good.*

Dan's next words had her forgetting the task at hand. "The others, the three who were on duty, had their throats slit."

Christ on the cross, as if the shock of seeing her colleagues blown away wasn't bad enough, she'd made the additional, and additionally *horrific*, discovery that Tony, Marcy, and LaVaughn had been summarily executed. Quick and dirty, they'd been left to bleed out at their observation points...

And where was *she* while all this bed-bombing,

throat-slitting was happening, you ask? Forget about it. Because she was across the hall getting her twerk on with the muscle-for-hire hottie who'd reeled her in with his hoohah-igniting eyes and lonely smile.

A sob that was one part shame, two parts regret, and *three* parts guilt threatened at the back of her throat. But she managed to contain it just like she'd managed to contain the fifty others before it. She couldn't afford to break down now.

"HQ says there's a carrier group operating in the South China Sea near Manila," Steady informed Dan after he signed off on his call, "which will save our asses in two very important ways. The first is that—"

"HQ?" she interrupted. "Where is that? And what… or…*who* are you guys *really?*"

And, okay, perhaps that's a question she should have asked before attempting to do the horizontal mambo with one of them. Because the only information she and the rest of her colleagues—her *dead* colleagues, her colleagues who were at this very moment being loaded into body bags…but, no, that was *another* thing she couldn't think about now—had been given about the three beefy guys accompanying them to Malaysia was that they were all former military men whom the president insisted come along to augment security. She'd assumed they, like so many ex–armed forces types, were simply a glorified private bodyguard service. But the swiftness with which that medevac was summoned and the bizarre and timely call from the State Department—not to mention their "HQ" happened to know the highly classified location of the nearest U.S. Navy carrier group—had her internal gyroscope not only wiggling, but swinging from side to side like a stinkin' pendulum.

"Why do you want to know?" Steady asked, a muscle in his jaw twitching a warning.

She didn't heed it. "Call me intrigued," she told him.

"*Sí?* Well, call us classified."

Uh-huh. Okay. So if she wasn't mistaken—and she very much doubted she was—these guys were *other*. And judging by the shuttered looks they were giving her, she figured she knew just what that *other* was.

Black Ops…

Black as in not even the Pentagon controlled them. Black as in the kind of men who operated outside, beneath, and beyond the auspices of international law and order. Black as in folks for whom the phrase *deny all knowledge of your existence* was coined, and then there was its twin, *I could tell you, but then I'd have to kill you.*

She swallowed. "Never mind." Because if there was one thing she knew about shadow operators, it was that the *less* she knew, the better.

Dan sent her a smile she assumed was supposed to be comforting, but a fat lot of good it did her. There was nothing, absolutely *nothing* anyone could do to comfort her right now…*Buck up and keep chicky!* She could almost hear her father's voice in her ear, and she immediately squared her shoulders.

"Once Ozzie is stable"—Steady continued as if she hadn't interrupted. He was stuffing gear into a black backpack with quick, efficient movements—"he'll be transferred from the local emergency facility to the hospital ship accompanying the carrier group. He'll undergo surgery there…which is the first point in our favor because I don't trust these Malaysian sawbones to do what it'll take to save his leg."

"Good," Dan grunted, watching Steady load his pack. Why was he equipping himself? Was the guy planning on a flippin' hike or something? "And I'm sorry you can't be there with him. I know you wanna keep an eye on the medical side of things."

Steady shook his head, the muscles in his broad shoulders flexing. "It is what it is. Besides, right now we have other things to take care of."

"Like finding Abby."

"Exactly," Steady confirmed. "Which brings me to the second point in our favor. That SEAL team tasked with securing the last of the…um…uh"—he snapped a veiled glance in her direction—"*you know whats* from the ocean floor is traveling with the carrier group."

Something was on the ocean floor? Despite the gravity of her current situation, Penni's imagination took flight with the possibilities. A wrecked nuclear submarine, perhaps? Or sunken biological weapons from Syria? Some of the material taken from the al-Assad regime had gone missing from a shipment and—

"They just finished their mission, which means they're gearing up to head our way as we speak," Steady continued. "With flight time and transfer time, I'd say their ETA is approximately"—he glanced at the big black watch on his wrist—"oh-seven-hundred. HQ says you worked beside these men back in the day? That you were pretty good friends with their lieutenant, some guy nicknamed 'The Lion'?"

A smile spread across Dan's face. She tried not

to think about the fact that he'd worn that exact same expression as he loomed over her in bed. "Leo Anderson." Dan dipped his chin. "He's good. All of his men are good. We'll be lucky to have 'em."

"*Bueno*. And hopefully, by the time they get here, we'll have located Abby, scouted the area she's being held in, and have a plan in place for her extraction, eh?"

Which reminded Penni… "Um…guys? I'm not sure how easy that'll be." She pointed a finger at the iPad's screen.

"What do you mean?" Dan's brow puckered.

"According to this, Abby's tracking devices have been scattered all over the city."

Steady stopped loading the backpack to pin her with a hard look. Black Ops… How could she have missed it? It was written all over him. Dan too, for that matter.

Oh, yes indeedie! Just my luck. I go looking for human connection and wind up seducing one of them*! For shit's sake!* Because Black Ops and human connection might as well be antonyms in the wide, wide world of—

Whoa. Okay. So it was difficult not to flinch when Steady stalked toward her. And she did flinch, just a little, when he motioned for her to hand over the iPad with a hard flick of his fingers. The guy's expression was the facial equivalent of a grenade with a loose pin.

Passing him the device, she rubbed the little bump on her nose—it was a nervous tic that, most days, she tried to contain. But *this* was not most days. Evidenced by the fact that Steady cursed like a convict as he studied the iPad's screen. Then he tilted his head from side to side, cracking the vertebrae in his neck, before impatiently handing it back to her. Pulling his iPhone from his pocket, he thumbed it alive. His expression was unreadable as he stepped over to Dan, gesturing at the screen. "What do you think?" he asked.

"Roger that." Dan nodded. "Maybe we're lucky."

"Or maybe we're good."

Huh? *Lucky? Good?* Not necessarily the adjectives she'd use to describe this god-awful situation. But before she could ask what the flippin' hell they were talking about, Steady turned to her. "You're right. Her clothes are scattered to the four winds. So whoever took her knew about the transmitters. I thought that information was classified."

"It *is*," she stressed. "Just like our hotel room numbers were classified. Just like the covert locations we occupy while on duty are classified." *Covert* positions because Abby hated drawing attention to herself, and nothing said *look at me!* like a group of guys and gals in suits standing sentry by her side or beside her door. And since Abby was such a sweetie pie, so kind and generous and flat-out *likeable*, Penni and the rest of the Secret Security agents had gone out of their way to accommodate her need for a bit of normalcy. Unfortunately, covert positions left them alone and vulnerable. Case in point…the slit throats. *Christ!* "Just like this whole *assignment* is classified!" she finished, her voice breaking on a hard edge. Okay, and her hysteria was beginning to bust through to the surface, opening cracks in her demeanor.

"There's a leak or a mole inside the Secret Service," Dan said. The thought was enough to make Penni—already close to blowing chunks—press a hand against her rebelling stomach. "It's either that or…" He glanced sharply at Steady. "You don't think this has anything to do with—"

"I seriously doubt it." Steady was quick to shake his head, and Penni had to bite her tongue to keep from asking who or *what* they were talking about. "How would he have gotten his hands on the Intel from a different department?" Okay, so it was a *who*, a…*he* to be more precise.

"True." Dan nodded. "So, you're thinking total inside job here."

"If I were a betting man," Steady said, "which I am. It's entirely possible that Intel we were given about Caroline being the target was simply a red herring. Used to throw us off the trail."

"Mmph," Dan grunted. "When I spoke to the president, he said no similar attempts have been made to snatch Abby's sister. But they're gonna take her to a secure location anyway." Gonna, wanna, coulda, shoulda…Penni wondered if Dan's penchant for slamming two words together was a Detroit thing or simply a *Dan* thing.

"Good." Steady nodded, having moved back to his position beside the bed. He checked yet another clip before stuffing it into the backpack. And that was five fully loaded magazines by her count. So definitely *not* a hike he was planning. "How did *el Jefe* sound?"

El Jefe? Just how close to the president *were* these guys?

Dan shook his head. "About like you'd think. Pissed. Ready to send in the Army, Navy, Air Force, *and* Marines. Scared even though he was doing his damndest to hide it from me."

Okay, so, *close*. Which meant they were, indeed, blacker than black. Probably the president's very own beck-and-call boys. Years ago, she'd heard rumors about such a group of men. Now she'd wager her entire 401K she was sitting in a room with two of them.

"No ransom demands yet?" Steady asked.

"It's too soon." Dan watched Steady attach a Nalgene water bottle to the outside of his pack with a bungee cord. "I suspect he's gonna hear something when the kidnappers have Abby in a secure location."

Steady glanced at Dan. "But we're going to find her and take them out before that happens. Am I right, *amigo?*"

"Bet your ass." Dan's grin looked like an executioner's right before the ax fell.

Penni couldn't stay quiet a second longer. These guys really knew how to put the *big* in am*big*uous—as in *big,* cryptic A-holes. "How in Christ's name do you propose we do that?" she demanded, pointing again at the iPad's screen for emphasis.

"Simple," Steady said. "While we wait on the SEALs, you and Dan will check each and every one of those signals." He spoke while digging inside a giant camouflage duffel bag, transferring some of its contents into his backpack. "It's possible the kidnappers didn't know where all the transmitters were. Or maybe they allowed her to keep her underwear or shoes. We can't leave any stone unturned."

"Me and Dan?" Penni lifted a brow. "And what will *you* be doing?" *Besides getting ready to start World War III with those five full-to-the-brim clips?*

"I'll be following the *other* set of signals."

"Huh?" Okay, so not her finest retort ever. But,

really, with the horror of her coworkers' deaths, the guilt of being the lone survivor, and the fear of what was happening to Abby all rolled up in a big ol' suffocating lump that was located center stage in her throat, she considered it a win that she was able to form words at all.

Steady zipped the backpack and threaded his tan, tattooed arms through the straps. It occurred to her that at some point—probably when she and Dan excused themselves to slip across the hall and retrieve their clothes, you know…because running around in their skivvies was *so* professional…*not*—he'd cleaned off the blood that'd coated his chest and hands and changed into a pair of camouflage cargo pants, some green lace-up jungle boots, and an army-green tank top. So *he* looked professional. No, come to think of it, that didn't quite capture it. Menacing, maybe? Okay, that was closer. *Threatening…* The word whispered through her head, and she admitted that pretty much summed it up. Carlos "Steady" Soto looked completely, irrefutably, *unmistakably* threatening.

Goose bumps peppered her arms and caused the hairs on the back of her neck to lift, especially when he fixed his piercing black eyes on her again. "I supplied Abby with a set of faux diamond earrings embedded with high-powered transmitters."

"You did? I never heard anything about—"

"That's because I didn't tell you," he cut her off. "I didn't tell any of you."

She narrowed her eyes. "Why?" She let her gaze swing over to Dan. "Did you guys"—she was careful to pronounce the words correctly instead of the instinctive *yous guys* that was poised on the tip of her tongue—"suspect there was a leak even before you got here?"

"Not in so many words," Steady admitted. "It's just that we've been in this business long enough to know it's always best to have a plan B. And most times a plan C and D, too." After that explanation, which was really no explanation at all, he turned to clap a hand on Dan's shoulder. "Okay. I'll call once I figure out whether or not those secondary signals lead to Abby. You do the same if you get lucky here in town, eh?"

"Roger that." Dan dipped his chin curtly. "And speaking of plans C and D, you geeked up?"

Steady tapped the watch on his wrist, nodding. "*Sí.* I put it in when I changed clothes. You?"

Dan pointed a finger toward *his* watch. "Same here."

Huh? What in the flip is—

"Okay." Steady turned toward the door. "All cylinders here, bro. Let's go!"

"Wait a goddamned minute!" she demanded, standing. She was sick and tired of feeling like she was outside the loop on this thing. And, despite her best efforts, her hysteria was beginning to bubble to the surface. "*Where* are you going, exactly?"

"From the current trajectory of the signals coming from the earrings"—Steady walked toward the door. The way he moved, the way he and Dan *both* moved, epitomized the phrase *economy of motion*—"I'm headed up somewhere past the spot where Jesus lost his sandals." He pronounced the word in Spanish, so it sounded like *hey-soos*. And then, before she could ask what the ever-loving hell *that* was supposed to mean, he turned to Dan. "Speaking of… Do me a solid and call back to HQ.

Ask Boss"—the way he said the word, she could tell it began with a capital B—"to send detailed topo maps as well as all the highway, road, and trail maps he can find for the central and northern regions of Malaysia to my cell. I'm itching to follow those signals and don't want to wait to—"

"Say no more." Dan once again pulled his cell phone from his pocket, already dialing a number.

Steady jerked his chin in a quick up-and-down, the guy equivalent of *thanks, bro*, before twisting the doorknob. But before stepping from the room, he hesitated.

"Wazzup?" Dan asked as he lifted the phone to his ear.

Steady's shoulder blades hitched together. "I feel like I'm forgetting something." For a couple of ticks of the clock, he didn't move, remained statue still. Then he shook his head, shrugged, and slipped into the hallway.

She turned to Dan, blinking. "Up past where Jesus lost his sandals? Does that guy ever give a straightforward answer?"

Dan lifted one big shoulder. "That's Steady for you." Then his call went through, and she listened to him quickly relay Steady's request back to their mysterious HQ. Clicking off, he turned back to her. "So, you ready to do this?" He motioned with a broad hand toward the door.

"You bet your ass," she told him, although, truthfully, she wasn't exactly sure. She was reeling from the events of the last hour, all inside out and topsy-turvy. And it was the fact that her head was absolutely spinning that accounted for the tingling sensation in her bicep when he gently grabbed her arm to escort her from the room.

That's my story, and I'm sticking to it...

Chapter Six

The northern Perak region of Malaysia
Seven hours later...

THE RISING SUN BAKED THE DENSE JUNGLE AIR. AND with every breath along the mile hike back to the spot where Steady had hidden the sport bike he'd appropriated off the street in Kuala Lumpur, he felt like he was dragging hot soup into his lungs.

Oh, cry me a river... That was Ozzie's retort the last time Steady complained about the heat while they were slogging through the waterlogged rainforests of Colombia, evading a group of FARC guerrillas bent on introducing the sharp edges of a couple hand-hewn machetes to the blunt parts of his and Ozzie's necks.

Ozzie...*Dios!* His best friend was probably on the operating table right now, and how he *wished* he could be there.

But that was not his mission.

His mission was Abby. And, *saints be praised*, he'd succeeded in his task because he'd found her. Unconscious and tied to a filthy bed—which was bad enough and made him seriously consider going all John Rambo and taking the entire terrorist encampment, plus the twenty-three men occupying the ramshackle huts, by storm—but she was blessedly, wondrously *alive*. So he'd forgo the bloodletting in order to hold his position, keep a weather eye on the kidnappers, and wait for the cavalry to arrive and assist him with her rescue. But in order to do that…

He pulled his cell phone from the side pocket of his cargo pants, checking to see that, *sí*, he still had ten percent battery life and two teensy-weensy bars. Good thing on both counts because the thing he'd forgotten in his haste to get to Abby was his satellite phone. He'd managed to remember the portable charger for his iPhone—which he'd completely used up while downloading the maps and topo charts Boss had emailed him while simultaneously tracking the signals emitted from Abby's earrings—but the sat phone? It was a classic case of head/desk. If there was a desk around this hellaciously hot jungle on which to slam his head, that is. And he suspected it was all thanks, in part, to Abigail Thompson and the fact that she'd been making him forget himself, his name, *everything* since day frackin' one.

The memory rolled over him…

"You know who her father is, right?" he asked his sister as they walked slowly across Georgetown's Healy Lawn toward the South Gatehouse where they were meeting Rosa's brand-spanking-new Mini-Me… otherwise known as her protégé for the next two years while the girl was an undergrad.

Jesús Cristo, *he was happy he hadn't signed on for a similar position. Four semesters playing nursemaid and mother to a snot-nosed teenager sounded like his version of the Seventh Circle of Hell.*

"Of course I know who he is." Rosa slid him a look that questioned the validity of his MCAT scores. The

warm, early autumn wind blew in over the Potomac, playing with the ends of her jet-black ponytail. "I may have spent the last semester with my head buried in advanced pharmacology texts and pulling forty-eight-hour shifts during clinicals, but I wasn't hiding under a rock."

"They say he's poised to win his party's nomination," he continued, throwing an arm around her shoulders. "And if he does, he'll likely take the whole kit and caboodle, which means you'll be mentoring the president's very own daughter."

Onyx-colored eyes exactly matching his own—except for the application of eyeliner and mascara, of course—turned in his direction. "Do you really *think that's escaped me?"*

His chin jerked back as he stopped in the middle of the walk. A young man in a corduroy jacket, Buddy Holly glasses, and carrying a Cordovan-colored shoulder bag mumbled "excuse me" as he darted around them.

"You sly minx," he laughed. "You agreed to the position because *she's poised to be the next first daughter. And how great would a recommendation from POTUS look on job applications, eh?"*

Rosa shrugged and tried to appear innocent. It didn't work. Then her expression changed, became more somber. "Well, there's that and the fact that after having spoken to her on the phone a few times, she seemed like a nice kid. Funny, too. She didn't make my back teeth itch by using the word 'like' ten times in one sentence."

"Like, seriously?" he asked, feigning astonishment. "Like, do you suppose she might become, like, your new BFF? Do you think you'll, like, be invited to the White House for, like, dinners and stuff?"

"Cut it out." Rosa rolled her eyes and threaded her arm through his as they resumed their journey. "You should have applied to be a mentor, too. With our brown skin, we have to take advantage of every opportunity to get a leg up on our East Coast, Hamptons, and Manhattan born-and-bred competition."

"They can get bent." He was never one to worry about the occasional obstacles his race threw in his path. "And besides, I'd suck as a mentor. I have no patience for long-winded explanations."

"And that's *the understatement of the century." She chuckled as they approached the green park benches lined up beside the road that ran through the South Gatehouse. Rosa shook his arm. "Oh, look! There she is!"*

"Where?" he asked, frowning. There were about ten different girls lounging around the grassy expanse and seated on the benches.

"The one bending over that rosebush. She told me botany is a hobby of hers."

Botany as a hobby? Mierda, *this girl sounded like the female equivalent of Steve Urkel.* Did I do that? *If she wore suspenders, he'd happily eat his own dissertation. Although...*

He tilted his head. She did *have quite a nice backside. It was round and firm and—*

Well, of course it's firm, *cara pincha.* She's only eighteen!

But the thought had barely finished skipping through his mind when the short, lithe blond straightened and turned in their direction. The instant she saw Rosa, her face split into a smile. But not just any smile. We're talking a fully weaponized smile. It was enough to lay waste to a man's composure. It certainly laid waste to his...

And now he could only wish *she was the female equivalent of Steve Urkel.* Hell!

"Rosa!" the girl called, shouldering her backpack and jogging toward them. When she was about ten feet away, he watched, dumbfounded, as a pair of crystal-clear eyes—eyes so minty green that for a moment he thought there was no way they could be real—swung in his direction.

Inexplicably, his lace-up boots took root in the path, locking him in place. And since Rosa still had her arm tucked through his, his sudden stop-and-stare forced her to a stumbling halt.

"What the hell?" she grumbled, quickly regaining her footing and glancing at him. "Oh, no. No, no. I recognize that look. Don't even think about it."

"I'm not thinking about anything," he lied straight through his teeth.

"Bullsh—"

"Rosa!" The girl was now standing directly in front of them, beaming at his sister with all the excitement and fervor of an eighteen-year-old. An. Eighteen. Year. Old. *He had the feeling he was going to have to remind himself of that over and over again. "I'm so glad to finally meet you!"*

"Abby." Rosa reached forward to fold the girl in a quick hug. "Are you all settled in your dorm room?"

*"Oh." The girl...*Abby... *actually clapped her hands together. "I am! And guess what? I have a roommate!"*

Rosa chuckled while jamming an elbow into his ribs.

That's when he realized his jaw was hanging open. "And that's a good thing?" his sister asked, affording him the opportunity to reel up his lower mandible.

"It is for me," Abby exclaimed. "With Dad running for office, I was told I'd have to room separately. You know, for security reasons." She waved a hand toward a far tree, and that's when he saw the two women dressed in black pantsuits with matching black sunglasses. Secret Service. And, suddenly, this girl's identity became all too real. It was one thing to know *she was the daughter of the man who was the next prospective president, another thing entirely to have effing* Secret Service *agents staring him in the face. "But I whined and begged, and they eventually caved. So now"—Abby bit her lip—"I'm going to have a* real *college experience!"*

"You may wish you hadn't whined and begged," Rosa said. "My freshman roommate spent the entire year smoking cigarettes, eating SpaghettiOs, and watching reruns of The Big Valley *and* Leave It to Beaver*."*

Abby's nose wrinkled, and he couldn't help but notice what an adorable little button it was. And now he was officially a big ol' pervert.

"Abby," Rosa said, "I'd like you to meet my twin brother."

Rosa motioned to him, the look in her eyes telling him to get his shit together and be quick about it. But no matter how hard he tried, he couldn't seem to make his mouth work. And that was probably a good thing. One, because keeping it closed seemed to hold in the drool. And two, for the life of him, he couldn't remember his own name.

Another elbow landed in his ribs. "He's really not a

mute," Rosa told Abby. "And in case you're wondering, his name is Carlos. Carlos, meet Abigail Thompson."

"Carlos." Abby extended her hand. And there were those eyes again, holding his gaze and doing things to his man parts they had no business doing.

You, sir, *he told himself,* are *stupido.*

"Good to know things haven't changed," he murmured now, shaking away the melancholy and nostalgia the memory always evoked. Rosa…damn he missed her. Had missed her every minute of every day for the last eight years, although the overpowering pain had dulled to a subtle ache. But he couldn't dwell. Not now. Not when he had to concentrate everything he had on Abby's rescue.

Brushing aside the fuzzy pink seedpods of some weird Asian plant, he took a quick look up and down the muddy, rutted logging road that led from what passed as a highway into the jungle and the encampment where Abby was being held. When he satisfied himself that no prying eyes or eavesdropping ears were near, he ducked back into the wet, rich-smelling foliage and punched in Dan's encrypted telephone number. Leaning against the leather seat of the motorcycle, he waited impatiently as the scant cell tower coverage struggled to connect his call.

A couple of clicks and beeps sounded before, without any preamble or salutation, Dan barked, "We're zero-for-zero on the signals here in the city. Her kidnappers took her clothes to a night market and stuffed them into the carts of the hawkers. It was a good trick. It had us running all over God's green Earth and wasted an assload of time, which I suppose was the whole point, aimed at sending any of the Secret Service agents who mighta survived the bombings on a wild goose chase. So, tell me you fared better."

"I've found her," Steady whispered, his chest swelling with relief. It wasn't until that moment, when he actually said the words aloud and knew help was on the way, that he could draw a full breath. A full breath that was pretty much the equivalent of trying to inhale porridge.

Had he mentioned how much he hated the jungle? The heat? The humidity? The mosquitoes the size of Chicago Transit Authority buses? And speak of the devils…he slapped a hand on one of the little fuckers that had the supremely poor sense to try to make a meal out of his forearm.

"Good." Dan's satisfaction was palpable. "Let me just…" Steady could hear a rustling noise and then the tinny, long-distance sound of Dan's next words told him he'd been put on speakerphone. "I can see by the location of your signal that you weren't kidding about it being up past where Jesus lost his sandals. That was one hell of a trip."

Steady nodded and then realized no one but the monkey lounging in a nearby tree and munching on a berry could see his gesture. "*Sí*," he said softly. "And, if I'm not mistaken, we're dealing with the—"

"JI," Dan interrupted. The *Jemaah Islamiyah*, simply known as JI, was an indigenous Islamic terrorist group. They'd claimed responsibility for the Bali, Indonesia, bombing in 2002 that killed two hundred people, as well as the simultaneous 2009 bombings of the J.W. Marriott and the Ritz-Carlton hotels in Jakarta. Known to operate out of Malaysia, they had been growing more and more restive in the last few months. And it looked like they'd just added the abduction of the president's daughter to their résumé.

"How did you know it was the JI?" Steady demanded. Then he answered his own question. "They've called in a ransom, haven't they?"

"Roger that. Supposedly six of their members are being held at a super-max somewhere in Colorado. They want 'em released within twenty-four hours, or they say they're gonna do to Abby what they did to her security detail."

Just the thought had Steady's stomach dropping into his boots. "But we'll have her hell and gone long before then, eh, bro?" An odd silence met his question, and his stomach just went ahead and drilled a hole into the jungle floor. "What is it, Dan? What aren't you telling me?"

"Okay, so before you go getting all bent out of shape, let me assure you our donkey isn't in the ditch. He's teetering on the edge of the road, sure, but he's—"

"Drop the metaphors and get to the point, *cara pincha*."

"I hate it when you call me dirty names in Spanish," Dan declared.

"You're stalling," he accused.

"Fine. Okay. So Leo's SEAL team has been delayed," Dan admitted, by the sounds of it more than a bit reluctantly. "There's one witch's brew of a typhoon blowing in the South China Sea. Ozzie's transport barely made it in before all flights were grounded."

Steady digested the bad news and commented on the good. "But he made it? He's in surgery?"

"Roger Dodger. No worries on that front."

Okay, so that was a bright spot in this otherwise bleak situation. "And the SEAL team? What's their adjusted ETA?"

"The carrier group is steaming for the edge of the storm, but it looks like Leo and his boys won't be here for another six hours minimum."

Steady looked down at his Victorinox Swiss Army Infantry watch. Six more hours of Abby lying on that filthy bed in that smelly hut. Six more hours of her being injected with whatever foul drug he'd seen them administer when he crept, quiet as a *ratón*, into the encampment just as the morning sun was peeking over the eastern horizon. Six more hours when any one of those *hijos de putas* could take it into his fool head to lay a hand on her.

No. Hell, no. It was untenable.

A plan began to form…

"The president is trying to scramble another team," Dan continued, unaware of Steady's racing thoughts, "but it looks like we're simply gonna have to wait. In the meantime, Penni and I will scour through the hotel security footage and try to find out how those bastards were able to place the incendiary devices in the rooms and also how they managed to get the drop on Agents Tucker, Silver, and Bosco. If we find anything, we'll keep poking the hive until we see which bees flight out. And, excuse the mixed metaphors, but maybe one of those bees will lead us to the mole inside the—"

"I'm getting her out," Steady interrupted, holding the phone between his ear and shoulder while digging inside his backpack.

"Huh?"

"I'm Lone Wolf McQuade-ing it. I think that's our best shot."

"Steady..." Dan's tone was full of warning. "Come on, man. Don't do anything stupid."

"It's not stupid. In fact, it may be brilliant. Those JI boys are a sloppy bunch. They're not even keeping watch over her except to slip in occasionally to administer some sort of sedative." And, yes, it'd been *incredibly* difficult for him to leave her there when he realized her guard had no intention of returning to the hut anytime soon. But leave her he had...when he thought help was imminent. Things had just changed. "And besides, aren't you always spouting that AA quote about not letting someone else do your dirty work for you?"

"Uh, that's not AA, man. That's my fellow Michigander and all-around Dirty Harry with a guitar and ponytail, Ted Nugent."

Steady shook his head even though no one could see. Dan had always been proud of his upbringing on the mean streets of Detroit and was known to quote a lot of Eminem and Kid Rock. But now that he was in recovery, when he spouted little truisms, it was hard to tell if he'd picked them up at a meeting or from listening to the ramblings of some Motor City rock star.

"Whatever, *hermano.* The point is, I'll duck in, grab her, duck out, and make for the Thai border before they even know she's gone. It's only fifty miles away. I... uh...*liberated* a Ducati Monster 1200 off the street in KL, and this bad boy"—he patted the seat of the Italian-made motorcycle affectionately—"will make the trip in no time."

The bike didn't have a big, throaty engine or the artistic flash of Ranger, his custom-made Harley chopper back home. But what it lacked in sheer badness, it made up for with full throttle, ball-busting speed. Exactly what he needed right now. And he'd make damned sure the poor schmuck he stole it from was richly compensated.

After he rescued Abby.

"You and I both know the JI won't cross the border since the RTAF"—the Royal Thai Armed Forces—"tend to shoot first and ask questions later when it comes to militants," he added.

"Yeah, but that's fifty miles of open highway," Dan argued. "And that Ducati may be fast, but it's not fast enough to outrun a bullet."

"So I'll stick to the logging roads." His plan continued to evolve as he loaded the extra clips into the various pockets on his cargo pants. "It'll take longer, but the jungle will provide cover. Besides, what's that old saying? Faint hearts never saved fair lady?"

"You've been hanging around Wild Bill too much," Dan said, referring to their BKI teammate who had a penchant for quoting the classics. "And if I remember correctly, it's faint hearts never *won* fair lady. If this plan of yours breaks bad, there won't be—"

"I saw on the maps you had Boss send me that there's a small village right across the border on the south side of the Bang Lang National Park," he interrupted. Now that he'd decided on a strategy, he was itching to get Abby hell and gone from that godforsaken militant campsite. Every minute she remained in the hands of those filthy terrorists was one damned minute too long.

"We'll head there, lie low, and wait for you to come in with that SEAL team or whoever the hell else *el Jefe* manages to scramble to the scene."

"Steady—"

"Oh, and I forgot to mention I somehow neglected to pack my sat phone. Also, my cell battery is about to die, so I'll be going dark. Just follow my signal, and I'll see you when I see you, *amigo*."

"Steady!"

He punched the "end" button on his iPhone and noted he was down to five percent battery life. It didn't matter. Escape and evasion maneuvers didn't lend themselves to friendly phone conversations, anyway.

Taking a deep breath, he turned in the direction of the encampment, one thing and one thing only on his mind. *Save the fair lady.* And if he happened to *win* her, too? Well, that was just gravy…

Chapter Seven

ABBY WOKE UP FOR...*GAH*, IT SEEMED LIKE THE umpteenth time since she was carried from the stall in the night market. She readied herself for another dose of the drug as a traitorous little moan slipped from between her lips. But a couple of seconds passed and...nothing happened. No hot, sweaty hands reached out to roughly expose her neck. No sharp needle pierced her flesh.

And then it occurred to her that she was no longer bouncing around in the back of a covered truck with a handful of dark-skinned, mean-eyed men surrounding her like the other times she'd regained consciousness. Instead, she was blessedly still and lying on something soft and lumpy. When she tried to move, she discovered her muscles were still suffering the effects of the drug and mostly useless. Still, enough of her functions had returned to tell her that her arms and legs were tied spread-eagle. Terror detonated through her system, increasing her heart rate and compressing her lungs. Because it was an awkward position, to say the least. And a *vulnerable* position, to say the most.

Keep calm, she firmly instructed herself when her panic rose to near nuclear levels. *They haven't tried to rape you yet. And maybe, if you're lucky and smart, they won't rape you at all.*

And in keeping with the *smart* part of that little pep talk, she made sure her eyes remained closed when a rustling sound alerted her to the presence of someone to her left. She needed to pretend unconsciousness so she could take stock of her surroundings. *Knowledge is power, right?* And perhaps the right knowledge might afford her the power, not to mention the *opportunity*, to attempt an escape. Not that she didn't trust Carlos, her security team, and her father to do everything they could to find and rescue her. *But the good Lord helps those who help themselves...*

Alrighty, then. Easy does it. Forcing herself to rake in a soft, measured breath, hoping to slow her frantically racing heart, she noted how the dense air filled her lungs and tunneled up her nose. It smelled of wet earth, mildewing fabric, and rotting wood. Okay, so clue number one: she was somewhere hot and humid.

Well, cinnamon-toasted Jesus! That really narrows it down now, doesn't it? Considering all *of Southeast Asia is hot and humid?*

Yep. Moving on...

She cocked her ears and recognized the *whooping* cry of some sort of animal—a gibbon, perhaps?—and the loud *whirring* that could never be mistaken for anything other than the drone of a million industrious insects. Clue number two: she was no longer inside the city limits of Kuala Lumpur. And, for no reason she could name—other than the fact that she was still high on the drug, dehydrated as all get-out, and so scared she was almost hallucinating—the line from *The Wizard of Oz* buzzed through her brain... *Toto, I've a feeling we're not in Kansas anymore...*

Ahem, okay, so back on task.

Unfortunately, she realized the only thing left to

do was open her eyes and take a look around. But the minute she did that, it was likely to be *hello needle* and *bye-bye consciousness.* Which meant she needed to be fast.

So, on the count of three. One, two, th—

"You so much as swallow hard, *cabrón*, and this here knife will shave off the top layer of your Adam's apple."

Abby's eyes flew open. Like, seriously, it was a wonder her eyelids didn't make a *snapping* sound. She realized she was lying on a narrow bed—or cot really—and Shadow Man was standing beside her. Her peripheral vision told her she was inside some sort of rickety wooden hut that was suffering a pretty severe outbreak of moss, but she took in that last bit subconsciously. Because her entire being, her every breath, her very *heart* was focused on Carlos and the flash of his black eyes as he glanced down at her, giving her, of all things, a wink. He was standing behind Shadow Man, holding a glinting blade to the guy's throat, and he had the audacity, or the *cojones,* as he would probably say, to *wink* at her?

"You okay, *neña*?" he whispered, and the smooth sound of his voice, combined with his faint accent and that wonderfully familiar endearment, had her heart racing for a whole new reason.

He came for me! I knew he would!

"Not r-really," she told him, her tongue still thick. "B-but I'll l-live."

"That's my girl." And as if the wink wasn't crazy enough, now he had to gall to flash that smile of his. It deepened the dimple in his left cheek, the one she'd always thought was sweet enough to launch a thousand lady boners—it'd certainly launched a thousand of *hers* and—

Son of a silverback gorilla! Get it together, Abby! You're not out of trouble, yet!

And that was evidenced by the fact that Carlos, never taking the shiny edge of his blade away from Shadow Man's throat—did it make her a heartless shrew to feel a *zing* of delight when she saw a drop of blood?—grabbed the syringe the terrorist had been seconds away from using on her. Shadow Man opened his mouth, probably to call to his compatriots, but in an instant, Carlos twisted his arm behind his back, wrenching it so hard the militant was forced to his tiptoes. Now, the tip of Carlos's blade was digging into the corner of Shadow Man's mouth.

"Ah-ah-ah," he admonished. "Let's not make things worse than they already are. You *do* understand English, don't you, *cabrón*?"

Shadow Man nodded, his eyes swinging wildly. The fear in them was crystal clear and Abby wanted to yell, *Right on! How does it feel to be the one taken hostage? You like that, you evil mothersucker?* Seriously, if karma was real, Shadow Man was due a terrible case of genital warts. Of course, not only would so many words be impossible with her mostly useless tongue, but they'd also be a distraction Carlos didn't need. She satisfied herself with simply watching the terrorist squirm.

And squirm he did. Especially when Carlos whispered in his ear. "That's good that you understand me, *pendejo.* Because while I'm *itching* for a fight—Did I mention I have enough ammunition on me to kill you and your friends every day for the next ten years?—the truth is Abby here isn't much accustomed to gunplay. So, I'll save her ears and delicate sensibilities and simply give *you* a little taste of what you've been giving *her*."

Moving quicker than a Venus flytrap snapping closed on an unsuspecting insect, Steady spun Shadow Man and plunged the syringe into the guy's throat with so much force it was a wonder the needle didn't break in half.

Huzzah! she silently cheered.

"And I'll leave you with this warning," Carlos continued as the militant sagged in his arms. "You try to come after Abby again, and I *will* kill you. That's a promise. I'll put you in the ground so fast you won't have time to make your peace with *Allah*."

Uh... can you say, wow?

Carefully, almost gently, he lowered Shadow Man to the dirt floor of the hut. Then he was by her side, using his knife to cut away her bonds. The blood returned to her hands and feet in a rush of pins and needles. And a second later, *bliss*...

Because she was pulled tight against Carlos's chest and his strong arms were wrapped around her, making her feel safe for the first time in hours. Seriously, she was so happy to see him that had he not been holding her down, she may have levitated up to the hut's grass ceiling. And maybe it was the elation that accounted for the hard shimmy-shake her numb body was now in the middle of completing.

"It's okay, *cariño*," he murmured in her ear, his breath moist against the side of her face. Man, he smelled good. Like native jasmine, faint aftershave, and the open road. Like health and heroics—if heroics had a smell, that is.

Like everything strong and wonderful and capable. "It's okay. I got you, now. I got you."

He was rocking her back and forth, one of his big hands gently patting her back. She noticed something poking into her lower belly, about to cause her full bladder to burst wide open. "Is th-that an extra magazine in y-your pocket?" she asked. "Or are you j-just happy to see me?"

Carlos wrapped his hands around her shoulders and leaned back, staring at her with one dark brow raised. He reached into his hip pocket and pulled out an extra magazine. "Good to see that drug didn't affect your winsome wit."

"Figures about the clip," she feigned a pout. "You always *did* consider me nothing more than a pesky kid sister."

For a moment, he appeared startled and maybe a little bit…*speculative?* But then he shook his head. "Look, we're working on a short clock here. This dickhead's"—he hooked a thumb at Shadow Man's inert form sprawled in the packed dirt—"friends are a few huts over in the middle of breakfast and distracted by some kind of Malaysian soap opera playing on an old tube television. But if he doesn't return soon, they'll send someone to check on him. We need to be long gone by then."

"*We?*" she stressed, her relief taking an instant hit. "As in, you and me? There's not an entire platoon of Rangers waiting for us outside?" And would you look at that? She wasn't stumbling over her words because her tongue was no longer twice its usual size. The drug may be fast-acting, but it was also short-lived. *Praise be to Merlin's beard!*

"That was the original plan." He shoved the clip back into his pocket. "But as you know, shit happens. And now you're stuck with little ol' me."

Well, she could think of many *worse* people to be stuck with. Just about *any*one else was worse when compared to Carlos, in fact. But in the same breath, and not to be ungrateful or anything, she sure would feel better about this little rescue mission if there were fifty or so armed servicemen waiting outside.

"We're going to move QQS." He turned his back to her and pulled her arms around his neck. Standing, he took her weight against his back, then realized the drug's effects still prohibited her from wrapping her legs around his waist.

Yep. She was beginning to get the impression this rescue plan had been made on the fly.

"What's QQS?" she whispered when he sat back down on the bed, supporting her weight as he removed the army-green belt from the loops of his cargo pants.

"Quick, quiet, and small." He pushed up her long skirt and wrapped her legs around his waist so he could cinch his belt tight around her calves. This time when he stood, manacling her wrists over his shoulders with one strong hand and holding his weapon at the ready with the other, she was the human version of a backpack.

To say the position was humiliating would be an understatement. And her complete and utter uselessness infuriated her. Here he was, risking life and limb to save her, and she could do nothing to help him. She wanted to scream. Instead, she turned her head—*hallelujah*, her neck muscles appeared to be working—to murmur in his ear. "In case I forget later, thank you for coming for me."

"Of course." He glanced over his shoulder, his beard stubble rasping deliciously against her lips. "Did you doubt I would?"

"No," she admitted. "Not for one minute." Even though they'd lost touch for so long, she'd always known he wouldn't hesitate to come if she ever called. He'd promised her as much the last day they spoke. And she'd taken comfort in knowing he was out there, somewhere, keeping the world safe, ready to hop-to at the drop of a hat…the most wonderfully loyal, courageous man ever.

The same man she'd foolishly and unforgivably deceived eight years ago…

"Ready?" he asked, adjusting her weight. Thank *God* the stifling heat of Malaysia had put the kibosh on her appetite over the last few days, resulting in a not-unwelcome five-pound weight loss. Because even though Steady was built like a bull, stocky and strong, she didn't suffer under the illusion that carting her around was going to be easy.

"Let's do this," she told him, refusing to acknowledge the fact that her breasts were smashed against his broad back.

"Good girl." He covertly peeked from the rear entrance of the hut before jogging silently toward edge of the clearing.

She bounced lightly with each of his quickened steps, reveling in the feel of him against her, so forceful, so sure, his body a smoothly working machine. She wondered idly why she wasn't still scared out of her head. From the looks and sounds of it, they were a far cry from being out of the woods…er…*jungle?* But it was *Carlos* who'd come for her. *Carlos...*who she was pretty sure was the real-life equivalent of Superman, Batman, and Captain America all rolled into one. Nuclear fallout could be raining from the sky, and if she was by his side...er... on his back?...she was pretty sure she'd feel invincible.

Good girl... His last words whispered through her head as he ducked into the jungle, dodging the slap of wet leaves and jumping over the snaking maze of roots that threatened to trip him.

Good girl? Oh, how she wished that were true. How she wished it could ever possibly be true...

Logging Track 3B
Seventy-five minutes later...

So far, so good...

The hum of the Ducati was reassuring, as was Abby's tightened grip around Steady's waist. They were riding down the devil's own washed-out, rutted, rock-filled hell of a rubber tree logging road, and for the first ten minutes of the harrowing journey, while she'd still been suffering the lingering effects of the sedative, it was just as difficult to keep her on the bike as it was to navigate the frackin' jungle track.

But now they were clipping along at a steady, if decidedly *slow,* pace. No JI goons could be seen in his rearview mirrors—though it was hard to tell exactly, given the fact that the forest encroached from both sides and above. And if his calculations were correct, a half hour or so more should see them entering the lovely kingdom of Thailand.

See, he wished he could call and tell Dan, *sometimes it's* better *to Lone Wolf McQuade things...*

Abby squirmed against his back, interrupting his thoughts and alerting him to the feel of her supple thighs pressed against the outsides of his hips and legs. Which, in turn, immediately focused his attention on her soft breasts—and distended nipples?—grazing his back.

Okay, so who was he kidding? Like he hadn't been keenly aware of *each* of those things since the first moment. Even while worming his way through the dense undergrowth of ferns and vines after escaping the encampment and hiking back to the Ducati, he'd been hard-pressed to concentrate on anything other than the feel of Abby squeezed all nice and tight against him. Abby's soft skin touching his. Abby's sweet smell—even sweaty and bedraggled, she still emanated a soft cloud of dryer sheets and cocoa butter lotion—filling his nose and making his head spin.

That stiffy he hadn't been able to finish off at the hotel was back to doing its best impression of a baseball bat—the *imbécil*. And you want to talk about one of the most pleasurable and uncomfortable rides of his life? It was this one right here. No contest.

"Um... Sorry to say, but I have to pee again," Abby proclaimed from over his shoulder. The poor woman, dehydrated because she'd been unconscious and sweating for hours without so much as a sip of water, had been emptying his hydration bottles one right after the other since the moment she regained control of her arms. They'd already had to stop once to let her stumble into the jungle and relieve herself.

He felt for her. He really did. But he wouldn't rest easy until they crossed that border…

"You're killing me, woman," he called back to her as he throttled down. Coasting to a slow stop, he planted his boots on the earthen road and steadied the bike while she crawled off. Even in the sweltering heat, he missed her sweet warmth all along his back.

"It's a proven fact that we women have smaller bladders than you men," she told him, stumbling slightly. He grabbed her elbow, steadying her. She was still weak, but she was toughing it out just as he'd always known she would. Abigail Thompson might look fragile, but scratch her surface and what you found beneath was one hundred percent pure, brass-balled grit. As if to underscore his thoughts, she added with a smirk, "I think it's to make up for our bigger brains."

He snorted, the wet earth and lush green scents of the jungle tickling his nose. He'd always thought Abby had it all, looks, smarts, charm… But it was her sense of humor he found most attractive.

"Hop to." He shooed her toward the jungle's edge. "I want to make Thailand sometime before next year."

"Thailand?" she asked as she brushed aside the fronds of a humungous fern, disappearing into the forest a second later. It was amazing how the jungle could swallow a person in one verdant bite. *Gulp!* But even though he couldn't see her, he had no trouble hearing her crashing through the undergrowth. She was wearing a traditional straight-cut Malay skirt, and it wasn't exactly made for roughing it in the backcountry.

"*Sí*," he called to her. "How does homemade curry

and a few hours of R&R while we wait on an extraction team sound, eh?"

"Like heaven," she answered, her voice muffled and slightly distant.

Heaven. He knew a little about that. It'd been heaven to hold her in his arms back in that hut and know, no matter what, that he had her and come hell or high water, he wasn't letting her go. Heaven to ride with her these last few miles, to feel her sweet breath huffing against the back of his neck, tickling the fine hairs that grew there.

"Will this extraction team be my Secret Service people?" she called from deep within the bush.

Damnit, he'd known the question was coming and had been wondering how to answer it. Taking a bracing breath, he gave her the truth. "No. It'll likely be *my* people or else some SEAL team or Delta Squad force your father sends in."

"Oh," her voice drifted to him, and he could just make out the hesitation in her tone above the soft purr of the Ducati's engine. She sensed he hadn't told her everything, and he wondered if she'd push the issue. When a few seconds of silence stretched out into an even dozen, he breathed a sigh of relief.

Digging his phone from his hip pocket, he thumbed it on and noticed he had only three percent battery life left and absolutely zero cell coverage. No matter. If he was quick, he could use the maps he'd downloaded, along with his relative speed and trajectory since leaving the JI encampment, to get an approximation of their location.

Pulling up the detailed road atlas, he checked the compass on his watch, did some quick math in his head, and calculated they had roughly ten to twelve miles—as the crow flies—before hitting that border. Unfortunately, the logging trail they were on didn't run due north, so he estimated they'd have to ride another fifteen miles, give or take, before he could finally heave a sigh of relief.

Switching to a different map, he studied the topography surrounding what he figured was their current location and wasn't surprised to see nothing but miles upon miles of jungle split only by the sinuous brown length of a massive river. He'd just brought up another map, this one a hand-drawn reproduction of the Perak region along with the locations of all the tiny villages and native paths that'd been cut through the bush—Boss sure was resourceful when he wanted to be—when his iPhone suddenly decided it'd had enough. Its screen switched to the iconic swirling wheel before it dissolved to black.

But, no problem. It'd held on for long enough to—

A low rumble had his head whipping around. With narrowed eyes, he scanned the road behind him, but he could see no further than five or six yards back. After that, it was nothing but a vast canvas of multihued green.

Switching off the Ducati's engine, he cocked his head, listening…

The steady hum of insects was the equivalent of a dull roar. The squawk of a nearby bird—probably the little one with brilliant plumage perched on the long leaves of a flowering bush—barely competed with the ruckus. Somewhere off to the left, a monkey called. And further still, another answered.

And then…there it was again! The unmistakable sound of a vehicle bouncing down the rutted road toward them.

He was off the bike in an instant.

Now, it was always possible that it was simply a logging truck ambling in their direction. But the good *Madre María* knew he couldn't take any chances. That dickhead JI terrorist seemed the sort who wouldn't take to heart the warning Steady had given him.

Pushing the Ducati off the rutted path, he wheeled the motorcycle a fair distance into the dense foliage. Far enough away so that its chrome components wouldn't catch a stray beam of sunlight, flashing and drawing the attention of whoever was about to motor past them. He covered the bike with a few huge, fanlike leaves he yanked, roots and all, out of the soft forest floor, and whispered, "Abby? Abby, can you hear me? We've got company headed our way." He didn't dare raise his voice, and when she didn't answer, he was left with no recourse but to prowl silently back to the road's edge.

Proning out on the ground, blending into the flora surrounding him, he hoped Abby had either heard his warning or picked up the engine noise coming their way. This would all be for naught if she came tromping out of the jungle for the world to see.

And just in case that happened…

He reached into the holster strapped to his right thigh, removing his Beretta M9. The weapon was a familiar and comforting weight in his hand. *Come on, Abby. Play it smart…*

Then he realized he needn't have worried about her when, a second later, her hand landed softly on his lower back. There she was, lying beside him, pulling the branches of a nearby bush over her for concealment, acting as though she spent every day crawling around jungle floors. Like...*no biggie. Here were are bellied-out with the bugs and reptiles...*

Ay Dios Mio! he admired her.

Raising a finger to his lips, he signaled for quiet. The look she sent him—big eyes and pursed mouth—was all about the *well, duh.*

He felt the tug of a smile as the vehicle lumbered into view. *Damnit!* It was a truck all right. But it wasn't a logging truck. It was the same old-style military vehicle he'd seen parked at the JI encampment. The canvas covering over the bed had been removed, revealing the rig was loaded down with no fewer than ten *Jemaah Islamiyah* militants.

And there was Dickhead—seriously, if a douchebag and an asshole got together and created offspring, it would be this guy—lolling drunkenly in the passenger seat, still feeling the effects of the narcotic, although he'd obviously come out of his stupor pretty quickly. Which was probably due to fact that the dose he'd received was meant for Abby, who was a good thirty pounds lighter. What looked like an AK-47 was perched on the seat beside him. *Go figure.* That Russian special seemed to be the weapon of choice for every guerrilla rebel, rogue military faction, and terrorist regime on the planet. The assault rifle lacked accuracy, sure. But it made up for that by being extremely cheap and frustratingly reliable.

Abby ducked her chin as the vehicle trundled slowly past. They were close enough to feel the ground shake beneath the truck's knobby wheels, to smell the diesel burning in its big engine, to see the whites of the militants' eyes as they scanned the road ahead.

Steady slowed his breathing; his heartbeat followed a

scant second later. It was an old spec-ops trick, a way to effectively control and utilize adrenaline. But Abby had no such training. He could hear her breath catching with each inhale, see the frantic beat of her pulse in her neck when he slid his eyes over to her.

Slowly, carefully, his movements almost imperceptible, he transferred his Beretta to his left hand and threaded the fingers of his right through hers, giving her a reassuring squeeze. She didn't look at him, but she licked her lips. And as silly and inappropriate as it was, the dart of her pink tongue…well…it *did* things to him.

It made his dick twitch, his breath hitch, and his heart skip a beat.

So much for that disciplined spec-ops instruction I received in Ranger School. It might hold up well under a sky raining mortar fire or ducking for cover in the middle of a gun battle, but it was no match for one cute, petite blond.

He got distracted from thoughts of Abby—*thank goodness*—when the clutch on the big vehicle whined as the rig came to a jolting stop not fifteen yards down the road. *Okay,* not *thank goodness.* And as the late, great Amy Winehouse would say, *What kind of fuckery is this?* But he already knew. It was the bad kind. He watched as the JI militants poured out of the back of the truck, swinging the straps of their AKs over their shoulders and intently scanning the black dirt on the road beneath their feet.

Abby's fingers twitched fretfully, squeezing and releasing, squeezing and releasing, but he could do nothing to comfort her. Not when his every fiber was focused on the terrorists. He knew what they sought: the tracks left behind by the Ducati.

Sonofafuckingcocksuckingbitch!

Although, given the poor condition of the logging track, it was always possible they'd be unable to find what they were looking for. He could only hope. Because the alternative—dragging Abby on a madcap journey through a dense Asian jungle filled with tigers and rhinos and snakes, *oh my!*—was too awful to contemplate.

He once more slowed the movement of his lungs, steadied the beat of his heart as one of the men ambled in their direction. With each of the militant's steps, with each drop of sweat that trickled down Steady's spine, his dread grew.

Glancing over his shoulder, he scanned the jungle behind them. Searching…searching…searching for an escape route. *Why did I choose to park the bike there?*

His backpack, with the food rations, iodine pills for purifying water, and medical supplies, was slung around the bike's handlebars. And the bike was parked in the direction of the militants. If he and Abby were forced to make a run for it, they'd be heading directly opposite his equipment and provisions.

Abby curled her fingers so tightly around his, her nails bit into the back of his hand. Carefully, he returned his attention to the road where the terrorist had spotted the tire tracks leading into the jungle. The militant's gaze followed the trail, then seemed to focus right on the place where he and Abby were hiding.

The guy turned and yelled something in Malay to his compatriots. Then he shouldered his weapon and started jogging in their direction.

Steady released the control over his breathing and

heartbeat, released the reins on his adrenaline. It poured through his body, burning his veins, making his muscles twitch. There was a saying in the spec-ops community: "Fear" stands for *fuck everything and run*. Well, by *Dios*, that was exactly the plan.

Jerking Abby to her feet, he swung her around, hissing, "Go!"

Chapter Eight

HAD ABBY REALLY ENTERTAINED THE FOOLISH NOTION that there was nothing that could scare her as long as she had Carlos by her side? Was she *completely* crazy?

Or maybe, at the time, she'd still been experiencing the lulling effects of the sedative. Because, baby, what she was doing right now, sprinting at breakneck speeds through the jungle with armed terrorists hot on her heels? Well, it was straight-up, no-holds-barred *terrifying*. If it was beating any faster, her heart would probably explode. Just, *blam!* And down she'd go.

Speaking of going down…

"Damnit!" Carlos cursed when she tripped over yet *another* vine. Using her hands to keep her skirt pulled up around her hips meant she couldn't employ them to steady herself as she raced through the undergrowth. It was a problem.

Of course, leave it to Carlos to solve it. He jerked her behind the huge trunk of a towering tree. Thrusting his hand between her thighs—*wha?*—he grabbed the back hem of her skirt and pulled it through her legs. Tucking it into her waistband, he yanked the extra material through the newly created leg hole, then brought that up to tuck it into her waistband again. Huh. Well, he'd quite effectively made a pair of poofy shorts. Her long tunic-like top dropped down to bunch above the shorts, and runway ready the new outfit certainly was *not*.

But now was not the time to worry about fashion. Not when a group of militants were scattered through the wet brush behind them, bent on retaking her hostage and killing Carlos…or maybe killing her, too. Shadow Man didn't seem the sort to forgive her for the trouble she was causing him. Quite the contrary, he seemed the sort to take out his frustrations by way of a beheading broadcast worldwide on Al Jazeera.

She shivered despite the heat of the jungle air and the sweat slicking her skin.

Craning her head around the tree trunk, she struggled to see their pursuers. But a field of green was the only thing to meet her searching eyes. Their raised voices told her they were close, and the sudden *rat-a-tat-tat* of automatic weapons fire solidified her belief that they weren't too concerned with recapturing her alive. But, fortunately, it seemed the terrorists didn't quite have a bead on their location.

She sent a prayer of thanks heavenward. *Small miracles and whatnot… Amen!*

"You okay, *neña*?" Carlos whispered, dipping his chin to peer into her eyes.

She gifted him with a classic Kermit the Frog flattened face expression. "You're kidding, right?"

That seemed a good enough answer, because he nodded brusquely before yanking her back into a run. Without the long skirt hampering her movements, she was free as a bird. She veritably sailed over the huge, log-like roots of a tree, landing lightly and never breaking stride. Fear and adrenaline coursed through her system, fueling her to run faster and faster and *faster*.

They blew through the undergrowth, crashing past

bushes and vines, skirting the occasional rock or fallen tree. But when she glanced to her right, she could tell Carlos was tempering his pace to match hers. Sure, his big arms were pumping, his muscled thighs churning, but the controlled twitch of his jaw, not to mention the studied, almost robotic way he analyzed their surroundings, assured her he could be doing all this at a much faster clip.

"This way," he whispered, grabbing her wrist and tugging her to the left. They stumbled onto a tiny trail cut into the forest, and he pushed her in front of him, putting himself between her and the threat at their backs. "Faster!" he encouraged.

Any faster and her poor legs would start pinwheeling Road Runner style. But, by God, she'd give it her best shot. Channeling a little Lauryn Williams, she turned on the afterburners. Leaves slapped at her knees and ankles, beating out a rhythm that matched her racing heart. Her soft-soled shoes pounded into the spongy earth, providing little protection from the occasional seedpod or rock in the path. Yet there was no pain. Later, once the adrenaline subsided, she was sure she'd feel plenty. That is, if she *lived* that long…

"The bridge!" Carlos hissed at her back.

Their path sent them flying directly beneath a band of big-nosed proboscis monkeys. The gang let loose with a string of hacking calls as they scattered higher into the trees. *Son of a mothertrucker!* And *that* was basically a neon sign pointing the militants in their direction. Any minute now the terrorists were going to be on their asses like stink on a Burning Man porta-potty. She renewed her efforts at speed.

"The bridge!" Carlos growled again from behind her. "Do you see it?"

Huh? What bridge?

And then she *did* see it. The jungle to her right opened around a wide, fast-flowing river, the water rumbling and roaring as it tumbled over massive piles of rocks. Spanning that river, about twenty yards downstream, was a feat of human engineering that looked like it'd come straight out of the helicopter rescue scene in the movie *The Deer Hunter*. A series of ropes supported a few rickety boards. To call the structure a "bridge" was pretty charitable. The whole thing looked like it'd blow away in a stiff breeze.

Her lungs hitched when she realized he intended for them to cross it. But, then again, who was *she* to question *him*? He probably spent most of his days doing exactly this while she spent most of her days quietly planting seedlings or laying down mulch.

The bridge it is!

Following the path to the water's edge, slipping and sliding on the loose soil of the embankment, she gritted her teeth as she stepped onto the rudimentary structure's first board. It groaned beneath her weight but, to her utter amazement, held. The rope supports were rough and scratched her palms as she raced and skipped from one set of rotting wooden slats to the next. The river, some twenty feet below, snarled and thrashed and sent up sprays of tea-colored water that turned the boards beneath her feet slick. It smelled like fish and sediment and the promise of a watery death.

"Don't stop," Carlos commanded when, some seconds later, they miraculously made it to the middle of the thing. The whole contraption was swaying violently from side to side, bouncing up and down with each of their footfalls. Abby gripped the rope handrails until her knuckles turned white. One more step and she feared she'd go plunging into the swirling river below.

Thwack! Rat-a-tat-tat!

Alrighty, then! Automatic weapons fire was just what she needed to overcome any second thoughts about continuing her journey. Jumping to the next set of boards, and the ones after that, she ducked when a spray of bullets bit into the river below. The terrorists were fifty yards upstream, letting loose with everything they had and advancing fast.

"Go, go, go!" Carlos yelled, as—*Boom! Boom! Boom!*—he returned fire.

Go? She didn't need to be told twice. She raced across the remaining expanse like one of those Jesus Christ lizards that walk on water. But just when she thought she was home free, the last set of boards disintegrated under her weight.

The sudden shock of losing her footing made it feel as though a million cockroaches raced over her skin. And the blood rushing between her ears outroared the raging river. But, luckily, she had a firm hold on the support ropes on either side of her head. She managed to catch herself before belly-flopping into the river and, swinging Tarzan-style, she landed on the opposite bank with a teeth-clacking *thud.* She fell to one knee but was up like a shot a nanosecond later.

Carlos made landfall right behind her, his big boots sinking three inches into the soft soil. "Take cover!" he yelled. From the corner of her eye, she saw him wrench his knife from the clip attached to his belt loop.

Again, her mama didn't raise no fool. She didn't hesitate to duck into the relative safety of the jungle, positioning herself behind a large tree. The rope supports on one side of the bridge were tied around its trunk and, an instant later, Carlos was there beside her, sawing frantically at the lines as rounds continued to crash into the river not three feet from him. Then a few bit into the dark earth of the embankment.

"Hurry, Carlos," she breathed, even though she knew he couldn't hear her above the thunder of gunfire and the rumble of the river. "Hurry, hurry, hurry..."

She repeated the mantra over and over, her brain buzzing with fear for him. He was partially exposed, and those rounds were getting closer. She'd never forgive herself if—

Snap!

The rope gave way beneath his sharp blade, and one of the supports on the bridge fell loose. He raced to a second attachment on a nearby tree, ducking the spray of bullets as he went. He started slicing at the rope just as a half dozen or so militants made it to the opposite bank. Abby peeked from her cover in time to see them rush onto the expanse of the swaying bridge. They continued to fire wildly despite having to concentrate on crossing the sagging structure. A round bit into the tree she was hiding behind, sending bark flying. She jerked back, digging her nails into the wood until her fingers ached.

"Come on, come on, come on..." A new mantra circled through her overloaded mind, and she watched, heart pounding, breath bated, as Carlos worked.

Tendons and veins bulged in his arms, sweat dampened his forehead and hair, and his jaw gritted so hard she could see the striations of the muscles beneath his face. The man's courage seemed to glow, stitching through him like lightning blazing through the darkness. And like lightning, he was glorious to watch in action.

Then…*Snap! Whack!*

The second rope came loose, causing the third and fourth to take the full weight of the structure. They unraveled a half second later, severing the bridge and sending the militants plunging into the boiling river. Their yells and cries were a welcome sound as she skirted the tree and triumphantly watched them thrash and struggle to remain afloat as the seething current caught them and washed them quickly downstream. *See ya! Wouldn't want to be ya!*

"It's going to be okay now, *neña*," Carlos said from beside her, tilting his head from side to side as if to loosen the muscles in his neck. It was a gesture she recognized from years ago. A kind of tick that would always remind her of the handsome, would-be doctor who'd been the first man to touch her girlish heart. "The bastards who don't drown in the river will have to find another spot to cross. And, according to my maps, there isn't another bridge within a twenty-mile trek on either side of us. We'll be well over the border before they ever set foot on this side of the bank."

His black eyes were fierce, bright with the fire of battle. And while his neck-cracking was wonderfully familiar, that particular gleam in his eye was strangely foreign. It made her realize that *this* was a Carlos she'd never seen before. A warrior. A champion. And although it was a little scary knowing who he was now, *what* he was now, it also stirred something inside her, something that harkened back to prehistoric times and rode along on that pesky double-X chromosome. "But, just in case, let's get a move on, shall we?"

When he began to turn away, she grabbed his wrist. From one second to the next, her fear and tension—and that quick kiss of sexual awareness she felt looking at him standing there all big and bad—was replaced by the weight of her guilt. It dropped atop her shoulders like a thirty-pound bag of fertilizer, and tears she had no business shedding, tears she knew she didn't have *time* to shed, burned behind her eyes.

"Abby?" He lifted a dark brow. "What is it?"

"I almost got you killed." Her voice cracked as the truth of that really set in. "I might *still* get you killed!"

"What are you talking about?"

"If we hadn't stopped so I could pee, none of this—"

And then he made everything so much worse—or better?—when he dragged her against his chest, palming the back of her head so her nose was buried in the soft fabric of his tank top.

"It's not your fault," he crooned. "*Nothing* is your fault."

Oh, if only that were true…

Umar Sungkar was going to kill someone…

Again.

Because it was bad enough he had to suffer the indignity of that stupid American *anak haram*—the word for *bastard* in Malay was so much more satisfying to both think and say—finding his jungle hideout and injecting him with his very own serum. But to make matters worse, five minutes ago he'd heard his men firing recklessly into the foliage!

Didn't they understand the only way to ensure the release of their brethren—of his *brother*—was to keep the woman *alive*? Didn't they realize this time their objective was leverage, not revenge? Was he the *only* one among them with an ounce of brains?

Stupid, uneducated, *blood-hungry* imbeciles! They treated this war he waged against the West as children would treat a game of police and thieves. Something fun and distracting that allowed them to carry around assault rifles, act tough, and frighten people.

He cursed his weakened muscles as he pushed open the truck's passenger-side door and stumbled out. Reaching in behind him, he grabbed the strap of his weapon and dragged it along. What usually felt like an extension of his own arm was suddenly almost too heavy to lift. But lift it he did. After he skirted the vehicle, propping himself against the front bumper, he brought the butt of the Kalashnikov to his shoulder… and waited…

The minutes crept by. And with every one of them, he thought of another reason to put a bullet into the brain of the first of his men to emerge from the bush. He had never suffered fools lightly, evidenced by the fact that, after he regained consciousness, he had been swift to order the execution of Abdullah.

The first slurring words out of his mouth had been a demand to know *how* their encampment could have been found. He had removed the woman's clothes himself, seen to their disposal. And her entire security force should be dead, dying, or severely wounded by the incendiary devices he had placed in their hotel rooms. So *how* had the *anak haram* found them? How? Had they missed something?

Shuffling feet and shaking heads had been the only responses to his questions. And then Abdullah, the young recruit from the Philippines who had been brought into Umar's organization solely for his expertise in the chemical alchemy of creating homemade anesthetics—Umar had needed something strong enough to render the American woman unconscious but not strong enough to risk overdose; her death would gain him nothing—had hesitantly stumbled forward. Digging in his pocket, Abdullah produced two pieces of jewelry.

At first glance, the glittering stones appeared to be diamond earrings. But upon closer inspection, it was clear they were something else entirely.

Transmitters…

Transmitters that had *not* been listed in the file on the president's daughter that Umar had nearly bankrupted himself and his entire extended family to buy.

"C-crush them," he instructed one of his men, watching furiously as the devices were pulverized to dust between two stones.

"We have to run," another of his men had the gall to proclaim. "The Americans must be coming! They must be—"

"Silence!" Umar commanded, thinking, reasoning. "If they were s-sending in their soldiers, we would already be s-surrounded." *Damn that stupid drug and what it has done to my tongue!* "My guess is the man who g-gave her the earrings, the man who had the s-s-supreme arrogance to come here"—*and insult and threaten me*—"was somehow w-w-working alone." It would also explain why the mysterious American had not been listed as part of her protection team and why those damned earrings had not been indexed in the file. An independent security contractor, perhaps? It was the only thing to make sense. "Now, Abdullah," he turned to the young recruit. "Tell me wh-what happened."

Abdullah tearfully admitted to thinking the stones were real and stealing them off the woman at the night market. *After* he'd been late delivering the additional syringes of the serum. You see, the narcotic took precision equipment—equipment that had been delayed by weeks—to make, as well as hours to mix. Abdullah had only had time to cook up one dose before Umar and a handful of his men were forced to depart on the mission to abduct the woman. But Abdullah had assured him there would be many more doses waiting at the night market.

There hadn't been. And the woman had nearly regained enough of her functions to cause Umar real trouble when Abdullah finally appeared.

Now, Umar could have forgiven Abdullah *one* mistake, but two?

It'd been easy enough to order his second-in-command to put a bullet in Abdullah's brainpan. It would be just as easy to do the same now to those of his men who were threatening to ruin all his careful planning…

Such mind-bendingly *careful* planning. There had been finding the desperate hotel maid, paying off the hotel security officer and the men at the window-washing company, bribing the scarf seller at the night market, and the precise timing of the executions and explosions. Not to mention the weeks of misinformation he'd leaked across the Internet to throw the Americans off his trail and point the spotlight on the older sister. All this he had managed to do, to coordinate with the utmost precision because the stars had aligned. Because the American president was due to leave office in a few months and his daughter had dared to allow the horticultural convention to post her scheduled appearance on their website. And all this was about to be ruined by his stupid, overzealous soldiers.

So, yes. He was going to kill someone.

As if *Allah* was listening to his thoughts and granting his wish, Azahari, his second-in-command—his *right-hand man* as the Americans would say—appeared on the edge of the jungle. When he saw Umar aiming his AK-47 directly at his heart, Azahari cocked his head, his eyes narrowing as he lifted his hands.

"What is it, *adik*," Azahari asked, calling him *brother*. "Why do you point your weapon at me?"

"You are *not* my brother," Umar growled, his finger tightening on the trigger. "My brother is rotting away in an American prison cell. And if you have killed that woman, if you have thrown away the only leverage I have—"

"We were not the ones shooting," Azahari interrupted, then lessened the blow of the insult of speaking over Umar by bowing his head in submission. He lifted a hand to include the two men now lined up behind him.

"Then where *are* the ones who were shooting?" Umar demanded, refusing to lower his weapon even though the strain on his drugged muscles was immense. He hoped the young soldiers could not see him shaking. He had learned long ago never to show weakness of any kind. In his world, the weak were used most ruthlessly or killed simply for the pleasure of seeing the satisfying spurt of blood.

"They have been carried downstream," Azahari told him. "They were trying to follow the Americans across the Sedikit bridge when the man cut the supports and sent them falling into the river. Those that survive the current will likely be dragged back to Ipoh."

"Good riddance to bad rubbish," Umar growled in English, spitting on the ground to convey his disgust.

Azahari tilted his head, not understanding.

"There is no equivalent translation," he explained.

Azahari nodded, then motioned to one of the fighters. "If I may," he said, asking Umar's permission.

"Indeed." Umar dipped his chin, finally lowering his weapon.

Noordin, another of his more reliable men, pushed an Italian-made motorcycle out of the undergrowth. Hanging over the handlebars was a black backpack.

"It appears in his haste to escape," Azahari said, "the American left his equipment behind."

A smile tugged at Umar's lips. "So they are alone in the jungle without provisions?"

"It would seem so."

Good. Very good. "Get on the satellite phone. Call the others," he commanded. He had sent half his soldiers eastward, toward the highway, in search of the Americans while he headed west to the logging roads. "Tell them we have located the man and woman. Give them our coordinates and tell them they are to follow us into the jungle. We are going on a hunt."

"But the bridge," Azahari said, "it is useless. We'll have to go back to—"

"Where were you born?" Umar interrupted, anticipation burning through his veins, charring away the last remnants of the drug, allowing him to stand taller, straighter.

"I was…I…" Azahari shook his head, confused by the sudden change in subject.

"Where were you born?" Umar repeated. "Where were you raised? What environment did you grow up in?"

"I…" Azahari glanced over his shoulder at the men behind him, then turned back and shrugged. "Penang," he finally said.

"Ah." Umar nodded. "A city boy, yes?"

Azahari swallowed, nodding hesitantly.

"Well, city boy"—Umar was now smiling in earnest—"lucky for you I was raised in this very jungle. Which means, as the Americans would say, I have more than one or two tricks up my sleeve. All I need is rope and a lot of fishing line. We have both in the truck, do we not?"

Chapter Nine

Steady was going to blame his erection on the adrenaline and not the fact that Abby felt *phenomenal* in his arms. She was so soft. So delicate and feminine and—

Sí, so the adrenaline obviously *wasn't* the culprit here. The culprit was lithe arms, round breasts, sweet breath, and an adorable young girl who, in the last eight years, had turned into a sinfully sexy woman.

He had to adjust his stance. It was either that or she'd feel the hardened length of him pulsing insistently against her hip. *Hello?* he imagined his dick saying. *Even though we barely escaped a group of crazed terrorists, and even though you've never expressed the tiniest bit of interest in me, I'd still like the opportunity to come out and play! So, how 'bout it, eh?*

The male sex organ was an amazing thing in that it actually lived every day in a perpetual state of hope. Which reminded him of the comment she made back in the hut concerning the extra magazine in his pocket or him being happy to see her. Then *that* brought to mind her statement about him never seeing her as anything other than a kid sister.

What was she? Crazy? Or maybe she'd been too naive all those years ago to recognize the signs of ball-busting lust he'd been unable to hide. You know…the cartoonish bulging eyes and the lolling tongue. It'd been inappropriate as hell then, given her age. And it was inappropriate as hell now, given their precarious situation. But regardless of time or place, whenever he was near her, ball-busting lust was *exactly* what he felt. When he looked at her, when he really allowed himself to take in the wonder that was Abigail Thompson, he couldn't help but imagine hot, hungry mouths opening over sweaty, quivering flesh. He couldn't help but fantasize about what it would feel like to—

"Carlos." She pulled back to look at him. Her eyes were bright. Their color two shades lighter than the vibrant jungle around them.

Nobody used his given name anymore. Hell, even *he* now thought of himself as Steady. And it was the sheer novelty of it, of hearing *Carlos* on someone's tongue—on *her* sweet tongue in particular—that accounted for the fact that his body reacted the same way it would had she pressed her lips to his belly. At least that's what he told himself when his scrotum tightened until it was almost painful.

"What, *cariño*?" His heart beat wildly with the thrill of her nearness. Up close like this, he could appreciate how her skin shone with health under a thin dew of sweat. He could count each of the faint freckles smattered across her button nose. He could easily see how her little chin trembled ever so slightly when her eyes darted down to his lips…and held there.

He stilled, every cell in his body coming to a screeching halt. If he were a bird dog, he'd be on point. *Woof!* Was it possible that she—

"If…if I…told you something…" She licked her lips, her tongue flashing pink. *Puta madre!* He may have been on point before, but now his whole body was as tight as a piano wire.

She must have noticed the sudden change in him, because her breath hitched and she quickly glanced into his eyes.

What he saw in her expression struck him dumb. He would have expected chagrin or despair or, hell, even pity. Those were the looks she'd given him when he'd decided to press his luck and seek her out after Rosa's funeral. So the hot, unbridled, *unmistakable* flames of lust glowing in her eyes caught him completely off guard.

Okay, was it possible that here, in the jungle, she didn't care about his pedigree…or lack thereof? Or was it possible the years of separation, or years of maturity, had made her realize that, when it came to the kind of chemistry they had, there was no such thing as being born on the wrong side of the tracks? Did he dare hope? Unlike eight years ago, there was nothing holding him back from giving her the full court press if he thought she might welcome it. She was no longer that naive young girl who needed to be approached gently, carefully. She was a full-grown woman, and if—

She licked her lips again. For one wild and crazy moment, he wondered if it was an invitation. And even if it was, should he risk acting on it?

Okay, that's a question? Of course *you should act on it!* Because maybe, just maybe, it *was* possible to win the fair lady.

Hardly breathing, he lifted his hands to her face, spearing his fingers into her hair at the same time he cupped her sweet jaw between his palms. Lowering his chin, his heart thundering so quickly it would've busted an EKG machine had he been hooked up to one, he watched her swallow jerkily. Then her mouth fell open, and her breaths came more quickly.

Now there was no mistaking *that* for the invitation it was. Especially when she again murmured, "Carlos." His body flashed hot as the sun, his dick doing jumping jacks inside his cargo pants.

"Abby," he whispered against her lips, not kissing her, simply allowing their breaths to mingle, to merge. In and out. In and out. Give and take. Wondering if she'd have second thoughts and stop him. Praying she wouldn't…

And damned if the simplicity of the moment, of sharing the air between them as they stood close, so close, wasn't one of the most erotic things he had ever done. It was so simple, so sweet, and so fucking hot. Passion fizzed through his veins, tightening the skin over his scalp, making him tremble.

Did she feel it? Did she have a clue what she was doing to him?

She must have, because the next instant she moaned. It was a sound of longing…of *yearning*. The age-old cry of woman to man.

He answered it.

Closing his eyes, he did what he'd been dreaming of doing for nearly a decade. And the instant his mouth touched hers, he knew he was a goner. Not just because somehow every single one of his nerve endings had moved to his lips, but also because Abby was everything he'd dreamed she'd be. *More*. Her mouth was soft. So invariably soft and plump and delicious. So delicately feminine. Did he mention soft?

He angled his head to more fully align their lips, and

that's when Abby went and shocked the ever-loving shit out of him. Because he'd always assumed, should she allow him this pleasure, she'd be hesitant, sweet but passive.

Holy hell! She wasn't passive. She was passionate. She wasn't hesitant. She was *hungry!* Stabbing her fingers into his hair, she opened her mouth, plunged her tongue between his teeth, and proceeded to try to eat him alive.

If she succeeds, I'll die a happy man...

I shouldn't be doing this!

It was the second time the thought screamed through Abby's brain. But once again, she chose to ignore it.

Yes, she *shouldn't* be doing this. She shouldn't be kissing Carlos like her life depended on it. She shouldn't be sucking his tongue into her mouth as if the world would end if she didn't. But she'd wanted this for so long. Wanted *him* for so long. And she'd never dreamed he might want her, too. Not in her wildest fantasies could she have imagined smart, sexy Carlos Soto would be interested in *her*.

Yet here he was...his thick fingers speared into her hair, his hard palms framing her face and showing her just what to do, how to kiss him. And every dart of his tongue, each hot glide between her lips might as well have been a wicked lick to the center of her sex. She burned and would have sworn on a stack of bibles she was seconds away from going up in flames. Just *poof!* A human torch...

"Abby," he whispered again before leaving a trail of hungry, hasty kisses across her cheek and back to her ear. "*Dios*, Abby, you taste so good." He sucked her sensitive lobe into his sinfully knowledgeable mouth.

She tasted good? *She* did? No, no. *He* was the one who should be on the menu of the finest restaurant. Because his breath was fresh and warm, and the sweat on his skin when she turned her head to gently sink her teeth into his wrist was sweet and delightful. He was the appetizer, entrée, and dessert all rolled into one wonderfully decadent male feast.

He moaned against her neck when she darted out her tongue, flicking at the pulse beating heavily in his wrist. The sound went all through her, making her nipples tighten, her toes curl, and her womb contract and ache anew. It was a wanton sound. A shameless sound. The sound a man makes when he's mindless and in need of a woman.

She couldn't believe it. Carlos…in need of *her*. Carlos…wanting *her*. She was surrounded by him, overpowered by him. His height. His breadth. His sheer *masculinity*. She reveled in the feel of the muscles in his shoulders, so large her hands couldn't grip the entirety of them when she dug in her fingers to pull him closer, closer… He could never be too close.

"Oh, yes," she breathed—breathed?—no more like *panted* when he opened his mouth over the sensitive spot where her neck met her shoulder. Then he sucked. Hard. And each pull of his lips had her stomach dipping and whirling and tingling as if she was on a roller coaster ride. Her center was an aching void that longed to be filled. Her entire body straining and struggling for release.

How had it all gotten out of hand so quickly? One

minute she was poised to spill her guts despite the vow she'd made to her father to keep their terrible secret. One minute she was on the verge of telling Carlos everything, so he'd know *exactly* whom it was he was risking his life to save. But then the next minute? *Wham!* It was full-on, heart-melting, womb-thrumming foreplay. The kind of foreplay that led to wild, unbridled sex. Sex with a capital *S* and a triple *X*. The nasty kind. The naughty kind. The *delicious* kind.

With an animalistic growl, he deepened their kiss, pushed her hard against the trunk of the tree. Then he took everything up a notch by shoving his thigh between her legs. He moved his hands from her face to her hips, grinding her sex and throbbing clit against the rough fabric of her skirt-turned-shorts.

Her head caught on fire, or at least it felt like it did. And heat exploded through her entire body like the *whoosh* of flames suddenly fueled by kerosene. For a second, she thought she came. She'd never experienced pleasure this painfully intense before. It was strangely orgasmic. Yet…it wasn't.

No. She hadn't come. If she *had*, her body wouldn't still be thrumming, aching, pulsing.

"Kiss me, Carlos." She needed to feel his mouth on hers again. Needed to feed off his desire as she grew hotter, hungrier with every ticking second.

"Show me your tongue," he demanded, and she obliged by opening her mouth. Just a little bit. Just enough for him to see her tongue peeking from between her lips.

A muscle twitched in his jaw, his eyes dark and hot as the jungle at midnight when he focused on her offering.

"Now lick your lips," he rumbled, his voice vibrating all around her.

She never knew it about herself, but she liked it when he went all bossy and demanding. She imagined him forcing her to her knees and telling her to suck and stroke him and—

Holy Moses!

Where had *that* thought come from? She wasn't the submissive sort, was she? At least, she'd never been before. But then neither had she been with *Carlos* before. To be that open, that trusting, she had to have the ultimate faith in her partner.

She'd never had faith in anyone like the faith she had in Carlos…

Doing as he instructed, she slowly ran her tongue over her bottom lip. He made a strangled sound in the back of his throat before ducking his head and claiming her mouth. He sucked on her tongue, doing things with his teeth that made the fire in her blood roar anew. And he continued to grind her sex against his thigh, forcefully but not ungently.

She wanted more. Just a little more…

Bending her knees, she rubbed herself against him. She was getting the fabric on her skirt-turned-shorts wet, and maybe his cargo pants, too. She didn't care.

She needed release. She needed it so badly.

"*Sí, mi vida,*" he growled against her lips. "Ride me."

Dear. *God!* She'd never heard anything so sexy. It was almost enough. Almost enough…

Steady was ready to howl for mercy. He was totally dunzo, sunk, *lost*.

Obliterated by the hungry dart of her tongue into his mouth. Annihilated by the feel of her soft, hot sex grinding against his thigh. Completely consumed by Abby, by all of her wonderfully surprising, wonderfully *wanton* passion. And when her little fingers crept under his tank top, grazing his quivering stomach, searching higher and higher until she skimmed over his twitching pectoral muscles, he figured she'd gone and wrecked his ever-loving mind, too.

His nipples tightened beneath her questing fingers, and he felt her hesitate at the change, her breath sawing from her mouth into his. Then she pinched the buds and he thought his balls would explode. They ached so badly it was a wonder he didn't sink to his knees on the ground, cupping himself.

Somehow, someway this had gotten completely out of hand.

It was supposed to be a kiss. One little kiss. After all, they were in the middle of a jungle filled with wild animals, being sought by a group of armed thugs, and a good number of miles away from the safety of the Thai border. Yet, instead of doing the smart thing and covering those miles as quickly as they could, they were ten seconds away from getting busy against the trunk of a tree.

It was ridiculous. *Ludicrous.*

He couldn't stop…

Especially when Abby reached down to grab his dick, rubbing up and down the throbbing length of him in the same rhythm she undulated her sweet hips against his thigh. *Sweet* Jesús Cristo, this may be the wrong time, but she was certainly the right woman and—

"Oh, *God,*" she rasped, her breath coming hard and fast now. "I'm going to c—"

She didn't finish the sentence. Instead, she threw her head back against the tree, her lovely, damp throat arched delicately, her brilliant eyes squeezed shut in ecstasy. His name moaned from her open mouth, and he watched as the most beautiful woman in the world came unraveled in his arms. Watched as—

A loud *crash* sounded behind them and Steady spun, his weapon ripped from his holster, up and aimed in a split second. All the hot passion roaring through his veins was instantly replaced by the harsh bite of adrenaline. And when he saw what he was drawing down on, his asshole tightened so fast he was surprised the thing didn't whistle. Swearing sharply when Abby's soft-soled shoes scuffled in the dirt as she teetered against his back, he threw an arm behind him to steady her. The puffs of moist air that hit his left tricep were her ragged breaths.

"Merlin's pants!" she cursed, and under normal circumstances he would have barked out a laugh. Abby came up with the most amazing and inventive profanities he'd ever heard. It was one of the things that had immediately endeared her to him. Well, that and her tight little tush. Come on, now. He *was* a red-blooded male, after all. "What the *damn,* Car—"

"Shhh," he hissed. "Don't say another word, Abby. Don't move."

He heard a fainting *ticking* sound as her throat stuck over a swallow. Then she disobeyed him, slowly peeking from behind his back. He knew she'd gotten a good long glance at their current problem when a little *eep* hissed from between her lips and her nails dug into his arm.

You know those wild animals he was contemplating earlier? Well he was eyeball-to-eyeball with one of them.

The *biggest* one of them…

"Okay, Abby," he said softly, making no sudden moves lest he frighten or threaten the big bull elephant standing no more than ten feet away. The animal's ears flared wildly, and its trunk swung back and forth in obvious challenge. He'd always heard the Asian elephant was smaller than the African elephant. But, *Madre de Dios*, this creature looked *huge*. And mean. Definitely *mean.* "We're going to slowly make our way back toward the river bank. And then we're going to run—"

"No," she interrupted him. "We can't run. We have to skirt the tree, hide behind it, and wait."

Wait? Wait for what? "Abby, I don't—"

"*Listen* to me, Carlos. I know what I'm talking about," she growled, and the elephant's eyes rolled until Steady could see the whites. Then it lifted its trunk to trumpet an earsplitting warning, and his heart tried to frackin' Spider-Man its way out of his throat.

How many rounds would it take to bring the bull down?

More than you've got, pendejo. *Much more.* Mierda!

He hesitated a second longer. Every instinct told him to make a run for it. The beast was big, but it was lumbering, *sí*? They could surely outpace it. Then again, Abby was no fool. And if she said she knew what she was talking about, he'd be an idiot not to listen.

"Okay," he whispered, "let's get behind the tree."

And pray to the good Madre Maria *you know what you're doing.*

Slowly, carefully, they began inching their way around the huge trunk. The bull watched them, furiously swinging its head from side to side. Its huge white tusks cut through the foliage with each move, proving how sharp the ivory really was…and how deadly…

When Steady could no longer see the animal, he glanced down at Abby and asked, "What now?"

She looked at him, her mouth squeezed into a thin line. It was hard to believe mere seconds ago she'd had it slung open while in the throes of orgasm. *Dios,* he would have liked to continue watching that. Watching Abby unravel oh-so-completely.

Talk about piss-poor timing. If they happened to survive this encounter with the elephant, he was going to curse the beast to an early grave.

"Like I said," she whispered. "We wait."

And people accused *him* of being reticent with details? "Wait for *what*?" he asked the question aloud this time. But before she could answer, the bull let loose with another eardrum-bursting *baraaaaaag!*

Abby jumped and clutched his biceps. Now it was the whites of *her* eyes he was worried about. She certainly wasn't wearing the expression of a woman who was certain of her decision to hide behind a goddamned tree!

"Wait for *what*, Abby?" he insisted, taking her hands from his arms to squeeze her fingers. There still might be time to make a run for it.

"For him to stop seeing us as a threat, get bored, and wander off." She chewed on her lower lip—that lower lip he'd been in the middle of sucking one minute ago.

Damnit! He had to remind himself once again that their interrupted bout of…uh…whatever you'd call it…heavy petting?…pre-coitus, maybe?…was currently the least of his worries.

The *most* of his worries? Well, those began and ended with the fact that Abby's entire plan hinged on the idea that the elephant would eventually…wait for it…get *bored.*

"Seriously?" he hissed. "We're supposed to rely on the short attention span of a pachyderm? Aren't they *known* for their long memories?"

She made a face at him. He made one right back. She whacked him on the arm. He whacked her—*gently*—right back.

"Stop it," she grumbled.

"*You* stop it," he replied, fighting a smirk. Their playful banter reminded him of how they were together in college. Of how he'd loved to torment her until she slugged him on the arm, which in turn gave him a reason to slug her…but really just *touch* her…in return. Then a shuffling noise told him the elephant had stepped up to the tree, and all his lightheartedness disappeared.

The hairs on the back of his neck twanged a warning. "We should have made a run for it when we had the ch—"

"We *couldn't* have outrun him," she insisted, gulping loudly when snuffling sounded on the other side of the tree.

"And how could you possibly know that?" he demanded in a harsh whisper, his fingers itching for the feel of his weapon. Not that a bullet would do much good should he be forced to use one. It'd likely just piss the animal off.

"When I was studying the effects of rubber tree plantations on the native plant species"—she said, referring to the speech she'd given at the horticulture convention and scooting closer to him when the elephant's trunk appeared directly to their right; they shuffled as a unit two steps to the left to avoid it—"I read a few articles about increased aggression of jungle elephants toward humans."

"Increased aggression?" he growled.

"The articles said that with their loss of habitat, the elephants have started going after farmer's crops. The farmers, in turn, are injuring and sometimes killing the elephants. So now the elephants are charging humans whenever they see them. There have been quite a few deaths. Deaths that could have been avoided had the humans not tried to run. Running only antagonizes the poor creatures. And they're much faster than they look."

Poor creatures? Not exactly how *he* would have described the big bull. Especially when it slammed the flat of its head against the trunk of the tree, causing the entire thing to shimmy and groan. Big heart-shaped leaves rained down from above. Bark snapped as it was cracked loose from wood.

Abby grabbed his shoulders, her eyes flying so wide it was a wonder the things didn't fall right out of her head.

Steady would not have been surprised to see himself wearing a similar expression. "Did these articles happen to mention how *long* it usually takes for the animals to get bored?"

She glanced up at him, wrinkling her nose. "They left that part out."

"*Sí.* Of course they did."

Chapter Ten

SNIFF...WUFFLE...*BARAAAAAAG!*

The elephant was getting frustrated at their continued ability to evade its searching trunk, and Abby could only pray the advice she'd read in those articles was correct. It was bad enough to think of dying at the hands of militants, but getting snuffed out by a pissed-off pachyderm?

PRESIDENT'S DAUGHTER DONE IN BY DUMBO...

Yep, she could see the headlines now. Definitely *not* the most respectable way to go and—

Baraaaaaag! She jumped as another head-splitting trumpet blasted through the humid jungle air. Carlos tightened his arms around her, and she couldn't help but think of what would have happened had the elephant not timed its arrival so precisely.

I mean, what the frickin' sticks was I thinking? Oh, yes. She *hadn't* been thinking. That was the whole problem. She'd simply been playing the part of Slutty McSlutNuggets, attempting to bang the one guy on the face of the planet she had no business banging.

Of course, in her own defense, it was a hard to say *no* to him when she'd been fantasizing about saying *yes* for most of her adult life. And then, as if *that* weren't enough, there was the shock value of the thing. As in, *Carlos Soto* kissing her, caressing her, telling her to ride him and—

She still had trouble believing it. Trouble believing

he'd actually, factually *wanted* her. And, alrighty then, so maybe instead of seeing her as nothing more than that pesky undergrad who followed him and Rosa around like a lost puppy, she had, in fact, grown up in his eyes.

Still, you're an idiot to have let things go so far, she admonished herself, even as she reveled in the feel of being held so tightly against his wide chest that she could hear his heartbeat thudding steadily beneath her ear. She wondered how it was he could remain so calm when they were ten seconds away from being skewered on a set of pointy ivory tusks. But then he moved his leg, just a little, and every thought in her head came to tire-squealing stop.

He was…*hard.*

As in still fully, wonderfully, *largely* erect. Yep, there was no forgetting his rather…er…impressive girth. After all, she'd had her hand wrapped around him not five minutes ago when she'd come. *Come!* And then the afterglow had been cut frustratingly short by the ill-timed arrival of the elephant.

Her fingers twitched against the material of Carlos's tank top, and it was then she realized the stupid appendages were itching to reach down and touch him again. *And maybe this time we'll both be able to get off. Wouldn't that be nice? Wouldn't it?*

No, she admonished herself. *Bad girl. Stupid girl.* Horny *girl... Damnit!*

Glancing up, she raised an eyebrow in question. It was the facial equivalent of *Really? At a time like this?*

He frowned. It caused his delicious dimple to deepen, and her silly womb contracted like he'd stroked a finger into her center. She sighed as she realized there was no going back to the woman she'd been before she knew what it was like to be pleasured by Carlos. To have his lips on her lips. To feel his tongue teasing her tongue. To hear him demanding things that both thrilled and titillated her. To know that he—

"It's the adrenaline," he whispered.

"Huh?"

"Why I'm still hard," he explained. "Adrenaline does that to a man's body. Not that I'm not still terribly excited to have you snuggled tight like this, *belleza*." To prove his point, he pulled her closer, rubbing himself against her hip. She could feel the heat of him through his cargo pants. It was enough to make her light-headed. "And as soon as we get out of this godforsaken jungle, I plan to show you exactly—"

He stopped when the elephant made one final attempt to find them with its trunk. Then the sound of snapping twigs and crackling leaves told them the bull had finally decided to move on.

He gently set her aside and peeked around the tree. But the elephant was now firmly planted at the very back of her mind. Because screaming at the front of her brain were Carlos's words… *As soon as we get out of this godforsaken jungle, I plan to show you exactly…*

What?

She suspected she knew. He planned to show her exactly what they'd missed out on with the arrival of the elephant.

I have to tell him… Sorry, Dad, but it's time to come clean.

"Carlos, I need to t—"

"We're clear." He turned to her, his dark eyes twinkling, his tan face creased in a wide smile that made his white teeth gleam, even in the shade of the canopy. "You were right!" He chuckled before bending to plant a smacking kiss on her lips. "He got bored and wandered off, eh?" He raked a big hand back through his mop of thick, black hair.

She now knew what it was to feel that hair between her fingers, so warm and sleek and alive. And although that last kiss was swift and platonic, try telling that to her lips. The silly things prickled like they'd been stung by a whole hive of bees.

Do it. Do it, now!

"There's something that I need to t—"

"By my estimation, there are at least a dozen or so miles between us and the Thai border. Without my gear, and given the rough terrain, it'll be one hell of a hike." His eyes narrowed as he glanced at his big black watch, then at treetops overhead, and around at the dense, wet undergrowth. It was obvious by the two vertical creases pinching his eyebrows together that he was busy working through the ins and outs of their trip. "If we make sure to stay hydrated and keep up a steady clip, we might just make it by nightfall. Which would be my preference since the jungle is no place to navigate in the dark. And while there is something romantic about the idea of spending the night with you huddled in a slapdash lean-to"—he winked at her—"believe me when I say, the reality is far from sexy. Besides, staying in the jungle might make it difficult for our extraction team to get to us, and it just might give the militants time to catch up."

The militants…

How could she have forgotten about *them*?

Um, probably something to do with Carlos's kisses.

Yep, so those things were hot enough to burn a girl's brain down to ashes. And she was *totally* going to claim that as her excuse. Because…you know…*militants!* Not generally something one filed away under the category of No Big Deal.

"Sorry." He shook his head. "What were you about to say?"

She swallowed and squared her shoulders, briefly closing her eyes in order to bolster her courage. *Frickin' sticks…here goes…*

When she pried open her lids, she did her best to steadily hold his gaze. "There's something we need to talk about," she started, then stopped when his face became an instant mask of inscrutability. The change was so sudden, she frowned, tilting her head.

"You regretting what we just did together?" he asked, a muscle ticking in his jaw, the heat in his black eyes having iced over in under a second.

God, yes! Because if he knew what she'd done eight years ago, he would never deign to touch her, let alone kiss and caress her and whisper hot, demanding words in her ear until he made her come. On the other hand, she couldn't bring herself to lament having allowed herself that one glorious, all-too-brief moment in his arms. Because it would undoubtedly be the only one she ever experienced.

"No," she told him. "That was…" She swallowed, shaking her head, having no words to describe what it had meant to her. She tried another tack. "I'll relive that in my dreams a million times over. You were… It was…" Again words failed her, so she simply shrugged, her expression begging him to understand.

That inscrutable mask of his dissolved into a grin. "*Sí.*" He nodded. "My sentiments exactly."

And it would be so easy to take a couple of steps forward, go up on tiptoe, reclaim his mouth, and forget about coming clean. "Carlos," she began, "what I meant to say is how incredibly sorry I am that—"

"Abby," he interrupted, shaking his head. "Stop apologizing for having to take a leak, *sí*? When a girl's got to go, a girl's got to go. Besides, what's done is done. And if we have any hope of making it out of this jungle alive, we need to focus on what's in front of us, like that Thai border, instead of what's behind us."

Any hope of making it out of this jungle alive...

Focus on what's in front of us...

Alrighty then, so maybe now *wasn't* the time to dish out heaping helpings of truth. Maybe he had enough on his plate without her adding a big ol' spoonful of painful revelations to the mix.

And maybe I'm just a coward...

"Okay." She nodded, forcing herself to swallow the guilt sitting at the back of her throat like a thick slice of *Momordica charantia*, a plant known in these parts as bitter melon. "Let's get a move on." But when she took a step forward, her toe caught on a root, and she was thrown into his arms. "Son of an ingrown butt hair," she grumbled.

"Ha!" Carlos's crack of laughter echoed into the canopy, startling her. "Son of an ingrown butt hair, eh?" With his warm hands on her shoulders, he helped her regain her footing, setting her gently away from him. And now her stupid shoulders were the ones prickling. "That's a new one."

"I try." She twisted her lips and looked down to rearrange her tunic top around the skirt material bunched up around thighs. When she glanced back up, it was to discover a strange look plastered over Carlos's face. Then to her utter consternation, he jumped back and started flailing around like one of those plastic, inflatable air-puppets that dances in front of used car dealerships.

"What's that? What are you doing?" she demanded. "Why are you hopping around like you have ants in your pants?"

"Ants!" he yelped, whacking at his legs as he simultaneously unfastened the holster tied around his thigh. "In my pants!"

For a moment, she simply stood there, blinking at him as he danced around. Then the levity of the situation had her rolling in her lips to keep from grinning. "So that's an actual thing?" Of course, all her humor dissolved when she glanced around to discover that, sure enough, the elephant had disturbed an anthill and the dark red critters were swarming all around them. "Oh, God," she said, then "Oh! Ow!" when one of the little suckers sank its mandibles into her ankle. Hopping on one foot, she slammed her palm down on the impudent pest and ran for the relative safety of the roots of a nearby tree. Jumping on the foot-high, bark-covered log, she watched Carlos bend to untie his jungle boots. For a moment, she was distracted by the quick efficiency of his long fingers. Fingers that had speared deep into her hair. Fingers that had gripped her hips to grind her—

Oh, for the love of Peter Piper's peppers, Abby!

Carlos toed out of his boots, and then—quick as a

whistle—shucked his drawers…er…cargo pants. He stepped out of his boxer shorts a half second later. Buck-naked except for his tank top and green tube socks, he started vigorously shaking both garments as he joined her atop the big root.

Jaw. Slung. Open.

Eyes. Bulging. From. Head.

That was Abby. A caricature of herself. If a blaring sound effect, something like *ah-ooo-gah,* were to blast through the air, she wouldn't be surprised. She tried to close her mouth, and couldn't. She tried to swallow, and couldn't. Blinking worked *slightly* better. She managed to get her eyelids to cooperate once. But then they stuck wide open again like her eyeballs were coated in the syrup she sometimes extracted from the maple trees as a demonstration to tourists who visited the DC Botanic Garden.

One corner of Carlos's mouth quirked as he continued to shake his cargo pants and boxer shorts. "Please tell me you've seen a penis before."

"Y-yes," she rasped. "But I've never see one so… *pretty*." Yep, and maybe she should consider *not* saying the first thing to pop into her head.

His eyebrows pinched together, his grin disappearing. "My penis is *not* pretty," he grumbled, glancing down at the organ in question.

She begged to differ. Because he was thick, long, deeply tan, and still partially erect. And with a plump head and two identical veins running up his length, she'd go so far as to say that, in the world of phallus beauty contests, his could make a run for the money as Mr. Universe.

"If anything," he said, still staring at it, "it's a handsome penis, a *manly* penis."

"Whatever you want to call it"—her voice was a husky parody of its usual timber—"I'm just saying I visually enjoy it." *Gah? Really, Abby? What the frickin' sticks happened to not saying the first thing to pop into your head?*

He glanced up then, and there was no use trying to hide the hunger in her expression. It was plastered so clearly across her face that a man with two glass eyes could see it. To her amazement, she watched his manly, handsome, *pretty* cock swell and rise.

"You keep staring at me like that, *bonita*," his said, his voice all low and rumbling, his accent thick, "and I'll be forced to go against my better judgment and push you back against this tree in order to—"

Her senses came back to her in a rush. There was a very important reason why she couldn't walk over to him, whip off her skirt/shorts, and climb aboard the Latin love train. *Choo-choo!*

"Sorry!" she barked, shaking her head. *Holy ass!* She was dizzy. She lifted a hand to her temple. "I shouldn't be—" She blew out a breath. "I shouldn't have gawked. That was insanely rude of me."

"I don't mind."

She glanced up to find his eyes half-lidded and sparkling. Then movement in her peripheral vision had her gaze once again darting down to his penis. Now the thing was fully engorged, standing almost vertical, and bouncing with every beat of his heart.

Her breath left her lungs in a whooshing rush and for a moment she thought she was going to have to physically reach up and, with thumbs and forefingers, force her eyeballs away from the sheer masculine beauty that was Carlos Soto in his gloriously *aroused* birthday suit. But after a bit of a struggle, she was able to direct her attention to the root beneath her feet.

"Come on now," he teased as he stepped back into his boxer shorts. *For the love of St. Christopher's cane! Hurry up and get 'em on, already!* She was about two seconds away from taking him up on that offer of pushing her back against the tree. And that would be so, *so* bad. For many reasons. "Surely you're not shy after what we just did together."

"I'm not shy." She decided to play the *logic* card. It was the only thing she had in her deck that was worth anything. "I just think we shouldn't press our luck. Let's cross the Thai border, catch a ride with that extraction team, and then we can talk about..." *what happened* "...whatever."

"Probably for the best." His tone was amused. Although she didn't lift her gaze from the pattern of brown bark winding beneath her black flats, she could hear him slipping on his pants and then hopping from the root to retrieve his jungle boots and holster. The subtle *clanking* sound of a jostled handgun told her he'd re-strapped the latter to his thigh. And for the first time in what felt like an eternity, she was able to draw a full breath.

She'd done it. She'd resisted him. And it was as if she'd run a marathon. She was completely and thoroughly depleted.

"You ready?" he asked.

No. Not in the slightest. "Of course." She forced a smile.

"Good girl."

God, *why* did he have to keep saying that?

"Tell me why you planted those bombs!" Dan thundered, slamming his hands down on the little circular table and glaring at the blubbering hotel maid with so much fire in his eyes Penni thought it was a wonder the woman's hair didn't ignite. Just *whoosh!* "Tell me how you knew which rooms to put 'em in!"

Penni curled her fingers under the seat of her chair as Dan's voice echoed around the cramped storage space the hotel manager had allowed them to turn into an interrogation chamber. The hotel's security director had called in sick to work, and the only surveillance footage the manager had known how to access was that from the elevators. But it had been enough. Because after spending a couple of hours combing through the previous day's archived digital recordings, they happened to come across footage of a maid, the very maid seated across from them now, as she exited the elevators onto the twenty-third floor, *their* floor.

Under normal circumstances, this would not have been strange. But the Secret Service eschewed housekeeping services because number one, it was a breach in security, and number two, by their very nature they were a private, reclusive lot. And given both of those factors, upon arrival they'd made it abundantly clear to the hotel that there was to be *no staff allowed on floor twenty-three.*

And, okay, was it conceivable the maid had not been informed of that particular protocol? *Hello?* Of course, it was. Mistakes were always a possibility when the human factor was involved. But what were the odds she just *happened* to stumble onto their floor the one time *all* of them had been on duty while Abby gave her speech?

Most definitely slim to none, Penni figured. And Dan had wholeheartedly agreed. When they showed the footage to the hotel manager, and after yet *another* call from the U.S. State Department, the blubbering maid had been handed over to them, apron, wheeled cart, and all.

So here she was. The culprit. The fiend. The *monster.* This small, slightly pudgy, middle-aged woman with her hair twisted up in a bun was the whole reason Penni could barely breathe for the crush of sorrow and guilt. This weeping, wailing, dark-skinned stranger had taken the lives of Penni's friends and colleagues with nothing more than a universal room key, a set of cheap timers, a few pounds of accelerant and shrapnel, and some duct tape. *Uh-huh,* Penni had taken a peek at what remained of the incendiary devices, and though she was no expert, she could tell they'd been rudimentary.

And effective…just as Dan had said. Mad, *mad* effective. *Christ on the cross!*

"Tell me!" Dan demanded again.

The woman just sat there bawling her eyes out and shaking her head.

"Check her cart," Dan grumbled, tipping his chin toward the wheeled contraption. "Maybe there's something in there that'll help loosen her tongue."

Penni figured that fell under the heading of *Yeah, right*. "Dollars to doughnuts she was smart enough to clean out any evidence before she started today's shift," she said. Then, "But what the hey, it's worth a try."

Standing, she walked to the cart. Ignoring the weighty lethargy of her tired limbs, she dug through various cleaning apparatuses and dirty room service breakfast trays until she came to a half-used roll of duct tape. "Well, would you look at that? I guess I gave her too much credit, huh?"

And, *oh!* How she wanted to turn and hurl that roll of tape at the maid's head. But by gritting her teeth so hard she was pretty sure she heard enamel crack, she managed to simply lift it and brandish it in front of the woman's nose.

She took no joy in the rounding of the maid's eyes, no pleasure in the look of dawning realization on her face. Because all Penni felt in that moment was pure, undiluted rage. And since there weren't enough vile words in the English language to accurately convey the ferocity of her feelings, she let her expression do the talking for her. *Yes, you are totally busted, you crazy, vicious, murdering bitch!*

Babbling in Malay, the maid plunged her hands below the table, reaching for something.

Penni dropped the tape in a flash. It fell onto the tabletop with a *thunk* just as she pulled her weapon and aimed it at the woman's head. For the first time in her life, she knew what the phrase *killing rage* truly meant. It took everything she had not to squeeze that trigger. Dragging in a deep breath of the tear- and sweat-soaked air inside the tiny room, she saw that Dan had beat her to the mark. The barrel of his Ruger P90 was pressed securely to the woman's left temple.

"No! No English!" The maid wailed, choking as she

raised her hands and began waving around something that was the approximate size and shape of a postcard.

"What is it?" Penni asked, her voice breathless and thready. Her throat was scoured raw as New Jersey Turnpike road rash from the tears she continued to gulp down. *Stay tough, kiddo.* Her father's familiar advice whispered through her head and bolstered her resolve. Putting some steel in her spine *and* her tone, she demanded again, "What does she have?"

Never lowering his weapon, Dan wrenched the object away from the maid, glancing at it. Instantly, his blond eyebrows formed a deep vee and Penni's stomach turned one quick flip like the time she'd ridden the Coney Island Cyclone. She could tell by his expression that she wasn't going to like whatever it was he thrust in her direction.

Holstering her weapon—Dan seemed to have everything well in hand, and her faith that her itchy trigger finger would continue to obey her was running out—she took the card and slowly, still scowling at the woman, allowed her gaze to drop.

Well… flippin' hell…

It wasn't a postcard. It was a photograph. A photograph of a black-eyed boy, probably no more than eight or nine, who was obviously suffering the effects of some sort of degenerative disease. His arms and legs were heartbreakingly skinny, his naked chest a xylophone of ribs, and his sunken eyes were nothing but dark pits inside his tragically angelic face.

"Jaya!" the woman wailed, pointing to the photo. "Jaya!" she moaned again, followed by a string of words in Malay that Penni didn't begin to understand.

"We need a translator," she told Dan, grabbing her chair and carefully lowering herself into it. She'd never in her life experienced this kind of exhaustion. Oh, wait. Yes, she had. In the days following her father's death. Once again, she was forced to swallow the spiky lump of tears that tried to strangle her. *Most definitely New Jersey road rash…* "We could call the embassy and ask them to—"

"No." He shook his head. Shoving his weapon into the waistband of his jeans, he held out his hands, palms down, and patted the air: the universal signal for the woman to calm down. It didn't work. The maid continued to cry and wring her hands so hard Penni wondered how she didn't snap off a finger.

"What do you mean *no*?" she demanded, scowling. Her ability to control her emotions was slipping, and slipping *fast.* It was bad enough that her colleagues' deaths had already taken a baseball bat to her professional composure and left it bleeding out in the street. But ever since Dan informed her that Steady had made a play at rescuing Abby—*all on his own!*—and was even now headed north to Thailand, she'd been teetering on the edge of full-on panic attack.

When he didn't immediately answer her, she snapped, "Okay, lookie here, Danny Boy. I don't know what it is about me that makes you think I'm a wilting lily, ready and willing to sit by while you and Mr. Fly-By-the-Seat-of-His-Pants run this show. But I'm telling you right now that I want…" She frantically shook her head. "No. I don't want. I *demand* a plan. So what is it? If we're not calling the embassy for an interpreter, what the hell *are* we doing?"

And by the look on Dan's face, she realized some of her panic had come across in that little diatribe. Blowing out a blustery breath, she squared her shoulders and deliberately wrapped her fingers around the Styrofoam cup of coffee Dan had placed on the table in front of her when they first entered the little room. But she didn't raise the cup to her lips. The coffee inside was black, which she loathed. But that was her fault. She'd forgotten when she told Dan to make it a "regular" that most of the country equated "regular" with "black" as opposed to the liberal amounts of cream and sugar that made up an NYC "regular." Still, just the ceremony of holding the warm cup between her hands managed to calm her. A little.

"The president doesn't wanna involve the embassy if he doesn't have to," Dan said after having patiently watched her get her sorry self back under some semblance of control. "He's trying to keep this as quiet as possible. In fact, he'd prefer it if Abby was already back in our custody before the press gets word of her abduction. And keeping a lid on this will be nearly impossible if we start hauling in a bunch of outside help."

"And speaking of," she said. "Is he aware Steady is currently, right at this very minute, in the middle of a solo rescue attempt?" She couldn't stress the word *solo* in *solo rescue attempt* enough. *For Christ's sake!*

"He is." Dan nodded. "He's being kept apprised of Steady and Abby's position and northward trajectory by my HQ."

She'd learned that when he and Steady were talking about "geeking up," they were really referring to the tracking chips they'd both implanted in their wristwatches. Talk about state-of-the-art accessories. Not that she should be all that surprised. Because, if she'd guessed correctly, they *were* the commander in chief's very own gang of merry current and/or former military men.

"Since you brought it up," she said, her first order of business being Abby, always Abby, "are they still en route to the border?"

"At last check," Dan assured her. "And as soon as the SEAL team gets here, they'll fly over and pick 'em up."

"Which means another unit couldn't be mustered on such short notice." She wished this suckass day would just *end* already. Wished Abby was back with her safe and sound so she could hide herself away somewhere and give in to the grief clawing inside her chest. "The president has to be beside himself with worry."

Dan shrugged. "He trusts Steady to get the job done. As for…"

She stopped listening after his first sentence because she wanted to yell, *Oh, for the love of—it's not like you guys are superheroes or anything!*

Or maybe they were. Because that's obviously how POTUS was treating them. She tilted her head, trying to see if Dan was sporting an invisible cape.

"…but I know someone who can translate for us. Someone I can trust to get it right and not paraphrase or lose something in the translation. And someone who won't breathe a word to the press."

"Who is he?" She lifted a brow. "And how do we get him here?"

"It's a *her*. And she's not coming here. We're gonna call her."

Not waiting for her acquiescence to the plan—*so what else is new?*—he reached into his pocket and extracted his cell phone.

Turning his back on her and the still-blubbering maid, he punched in a number before lifting the device to his ear. When Bertha Bomber continued to sob and wail, he frowned over his shoulder and plugged a finger in his opposite ear. "Hey, Rock," she heard him say after a moment. "I need Vanessa. She around?" A couple more seconds passed, then, "Hey, beautiful. How's your Malay?"

Beautiful? *Beautiful?* Uh-huh, Penni was pretty sure if she squinted, she'd catch a glimpse of a green-eyed monster sitting atop her left shoulder. Which proved how far off her rocker she'd fallen. She had no claim over Dan. She *wanted* no claim over Dan. But try explaining that to her new emerald-eyed friend.

"Excellent," Dan said into his receiver, turning to smile and wink at her.

When she smiled back, he cocked his head, his expression faltering. Obviously she'd flashed too many teeth. More snarl than smile.

"Penni"—he took the phone away from his ear to switch it over to speaker—"I'd like you to meet Vanessa Cordero. Vanessa is a comm specialist extraordinaire."

A low, husky voice, like what Penni imagined phone-sex operators might use, sounded from the device. "Hello, Penni."

The monster on her shoulder doubled in size.

"Hiya, Vanessa," she ground out, feeling terrible because the name sort of stuck in the back of her throat. *One* almost *sexual encounter with the guy and suddenly you're all Glenn Close in* Fatal Attraction. *Could you* be *any more of a penis-wrinkle, Penni?*

"Rock," Dan said, "you still on the line, too?"

"*Oui, mon frere,*" a deep, melodic baritone slid through the phone's speaker. "I'm here."

"Good." Dan nodded, glancing at her. "So you're also talking with Rock Babineaux. He's a bony-assed Cajun who happens to be a leading expert in interrogation techniques. I'm hoping these two, working together, can pry some information out of our…uh…far-from-friendly *friend* here." He jerked his chin toward the maid.

"I take exception to the bony-assed comment." That smooth voice echoed through the little room, sounding like a late-night radio host.

One corner of Dan's mouth twitched, a light entering his eyes that couldn't be mistaken for anything other than the gleam of camaraderie. Dan and this Rock guy were obviously friends. Friends and coworkers and—*Zoink!* Penni's green-eyed pal blipped out of existence. Gone so fast she wondered if he'd ever really been there at all or if she'd simply imagined him, her mind struggling for anything with which to occupy itself, since every time it turned toward thoughts of her colleagues, she damn near hyperventilated.

Like now…

She concentrated everything she had on not letting the tears prickling behind her burning eyes fall. She *couldn't* let them fall. Because once she started, she figured she might not be able to stop for a full week.

One second stretched into two. Two became three. And then she lost count. Time seemed to warp and expand like the taffy she'd seen pulled on the machines in the confectionary shops along the boardwalk as a kid. In fact, she was so lost in herself, so lost in simply taking one breath after another, that she jumped, the legs of her chair scraping against the floor tile, when Dan laid a warm, heavy hand on her shoulder.

"You don't hafta stay in here for this," he assured her. "We can handle the—"

"No," she cut him off, raking in a slow, measured breath to make up for the twenty shallow, fast ones she'd taken. Christ, she was losing it, becoming completely unhinged. Unconsciously, she lifted a finger and quickly ran it over the little bump on her nose. It grounded her…a little. "I need to hear what she has to say for herself." She tilted her chin toward Bertha Bomber. "I *want* to hear what she has to say. I owe it to Abby. I owe it to…the others."

Chapter Eleven

"I DON'T UNDERSTAND WHAT THOSE SHITBIRD militants—what did you call them?" Abby asked, then grumbled under her breath when a low-hanging branch slapped her on the arm after Steady brushed by it. He glanced back to make sure she wasn't hurt, then scolded himself for not being more careful.

They'd been slogging through the undergrowth for over an hour, and it had to be hell on her. She'd already been physically drained from the drug coupled with lack of food, and that was before the energy-sucking heat and humidity of the jungle had a chance to go to work. But she was a trooper if he ever saw one. And, *Dios*, he admired her for it. Admired her and craved her and damned if he could think of anything other than the hot, hungry gleam in her eye when she'd stared at his penis.

As if the silly thing knew he was thinking about it—or else it, too, was simply remembering the expression on her face—it twitched behind the fly of his cargo pants. *Bueno.* Because the only thing worse than sporting a stiffy while riding through miles of potholed logging trails, was sporting one while hiking and hacking through the jungle.

Uh…so, *what* had she asked again? And then he remembered. "They're called the *Jemaah Islamiyah,* or JI for short." He stepped over a gigantic, snaking root and pushed aside the slick leaves of a large bush so Abby could easily pass by without tripping. When she wasn't looking, he surreptitiously reached down to adjust himself into a more comfortable—and less chafing—position.

"Yep." She lithely hopped over the root. "The JI. That's right." The excess material bunched around the tops of her legs made her slim thighs look almost skinny. It highlighted how small she actually was, and made every protective instinct he had stand up and howl like his father had done every New Year's Eve after a couple shots of top-shelf Puerto Rican rum. "But I don't understand what they hoped to gain by kidnapping me. My father has always said he doesn't negotiate with terrorists for anything. Not for friends, not for family, not for all the tea in China or oil in Saudi Arabia."

"But that was before he was due to leave office in a few months," Steady told her. "It's harder to stick to your guns when it really *is* your baby girl's neck on the chopping block, and you know you'll never have to run for office again, so what's the harm in going back on your campaign promises."

Her expression turned contemplative as he slid by her to resume his place as trailblazer. His arm inadvertently touched hers, and the *zing* of awareness that detonated through his system did nothing to dissuade his erection. *Mierda!* He checked the compass on his watch to make sure they were still heading due north. Baseball bat of a stiffy aside, it was easy, *too* easy, to get turned around in the jungle. And as dead tired as he knew Abby was, he'd be damned if he made her take one step more than was needed. Not to mention the fact that that last map check had indicated a due north trajectory would land them directly in the middle of the Bang Lang National Park, only a few hundred yards from the little town he was aiming for.

"I hadn't thought of it like that," she said to his back. Then, "And speaking of Dad leaving office, what will happen to Black Knights Inc. when he does? I mean, you're *his* group, right? He's the one who founded you guys?"

"Technically, it was the head of the JCs, Navy General Pete Fuller, who rubber-stamped the inception of BKI," he told her, glancing over his shoulder with a raised brow. "And how do you know so much about all that anyway? I would think our existence was something your father kept close to his vest. In fact, until about a year ago, even the DOD had no idea we existed."

Had his head not been turned, he would have missed the fleeting look of…what was that expression exactly? He couldn't be sure, but it looked remarkably close to guilt dancing across her face. He stopped in his tracks, which caused her to slam into his back. "Son of a blue-balled biscuit eater!" she snarled. "What's with the air brakes all of a sudden?"

He really, *really* liked the feel of her pressed against his back—and as soon as they made it out of this god-forsaken jungle he was going to make sure he pressed her against his *front*; that is, if she still wanted him once they were back in the real world; please *Dios*, yes—but that didn't stop him from taking a step back in order to turn and fully face her. "First off"—he had trouble controlling his smirk—"I'm trying to imagine what a blue-balled biscuit eater looks like. Maybe a guy holding his nads in one hand and a Pillsbury buttermilk biscuit dripping with grape jelly in the other?"

She shrugged, fighting a smile. "That's it in a nutshell."

"And secondly…" Now his smirk was nowhere to be found, though his hard-on was still firmly in place; *yippee!* "What aren't you telling me? Because in case you didn't know it, *cariño*, you have a terrible poker face. And I figure you better spill the beans about whatever it is you're—"

He stopped mid-sentence when her eyes focused behind him before bugging out as if she were, quite literally, trying to shit the proverbial brick. His M9 was in his hand, his finger poised on the trigger before he finished spinning around. And then there he was, drawing down on…

Huh. It appeared to be an Oompa Loompa with a massive 'fro. Even though Steady wasn't overly tall by American standards—he topped out at just under six feet—he towered above the man standing in front of him. The little wrinkly guy—no telling his age; he could have been anywhere from fifty to a hundred and fifty—was wearing an oversized Tweety Bird T-shirt and a pair of crazily printed trousers. He was shoeless, and that hairdo? Well, that hairdo was enough to make Samuel L. Jackson's character in *Pulp Fiction* slap him a high five. *Be cool, Honey Bunny!*

"Put it away." Abby laid a soft hand on his forearm. "This man won't harm us."

"*Sí.* That's pretty obvious," he agreed. "Because unless this dude plans to bite our ankles, I can't see how he poses much of a threat." Holstering his weapon, he tilted his head at the guy who continued to stand there, eyeing them curiously.

"Hello." Abby bobbed her head in a friendly greeting.

"Hello," said the little Oompa Loompa... Okay, so Steady had to stop thinking of him in those terms. His skin wasn't orange like the guys in the film, but a dark, mahogany brown like much of the country's population. Of course, that's where the similarities stopped. Because his flat, wide facial features made him look less Asian and more Aboriginal Australian. And what were the odds he spoke English? *Praise be!* But also...*wince.*

"Hi." Steady extended his hand for a shake. "First of all, I'm sorry about the ankle-biting comment. That was...uh...my bad. And, secondly, can you tell us approximately how far we are from the border to Thailand?" Because a mile or two error in the calculations he'd made back on the logging trail could mean the difference between them making the border before sundown or having to make camp for the night.

Mr. Tweety Bird...that was only *slightly* better...stared at his offered hand, his brow knitted with confusion.

"I doubt he speaks English," Abby said.

"What?" Steady's chin jerked back. "But he just said *hello*."

"Hello is the universal greeting in multiracial Malaysia," she told him, nodding to the diminutive man.

"And how in the hell would you know that?"

"Because of all those art—"

"Articles you read," he finished for her. "Got it." And maybe he should have looked into doing more research on Peninsular Malaysia before he agreed to take this gig. Then again, tromping through the jungle hadn't exactly been on the agenda, soooo...yeah.

Abby clasped her hands together as if to pray. Then

she dipped her head in a gesture of respect. "Orang Asli?" she asked, keeping a warm smile firmly in place.

Señor Snazzy Pants...*sí, that's the one*...nodded, cracking a wide grin that revealed a boatload of missing teeth. Those that remained were brown and stubby. Obviously the man didn't end each day with a quick scrub of Colgate.

"What did you ask him?" Steady murmured to Abby, mirroring her gesture. Hey, if it caused Señor Snazzy Pants to smile—even though Steady could have gone his whole life without getting a peek into that toothless maw—he figured it wouldn't hurt to follow her lead.

"The Orang Asli are the original people of Malaysia. They're tribal, and prefer to remain mostly cut off from civilization."

"Except when it comes to shopping for T-shirts, obviously."

She twisted her lips. "He probably received that from a charitable donation or something. The Orang Asli make their living from the jungle. But with the cities growing by leaps and bounds and the forests being cut back, they're becoming more and more marginalized, and more and more dependent on the government for assistance."

"How many articles about Malaysia did you read?" he asked her.

"Enough."

"I'll say."

Señor Snazzy Pants said something that sounded like a sneeze followed by the name of a syrup used to induce vomiting. "Atchoo ipecac!" He gestured wildly.

"What did he say?" Steady asked from the corner of his mouth, keeping a wary eye on the animated little guy.

Abby turned and planted her hands on her hips. "I read a few articles." She frowned at him. "I didn't learn the different dialects for the whole frickin' country. *Sheesh.*"

"Well, you seem to know everything *else*," he said in his own defense.

"Atchoo ipecac!" Señor SP said again, strolling forward to grab Abby's arm.

"Whoa there, *compadre*." Steady's senses instantly went from high alert to code red. "Hands off the woman."

The little guy didn't need to speak English to recognize the warning in Steady's tone. He lifted his gnarled, aged hand from Abby's arm and bowed his head in acknowledgment, smiling that toothless smile. Then he raised his fingers to his mouth and pantomimed taking a bite of something.

"I think he wants to give us food."

"*Sí*," he agreed. "Without reading a single article, I was able to piece that one together all by myself."

She frowned, swatting his arm.

He swatted her—*gently*—right back.

"Stop it," she said.

"*You* stop it." He had to bite the inside of his cheek to keep from laughing.

Señor SP turned into the undergrowth, gesturing for them to follow.

"Can we go with him?" she asked, and damned if Steady could ignore the note of hope in her voice. She hadn't complained once since they started out on this humid, airless hike, but he'd heard her stomach growling like it was trying to gnaw its way through her backbone. "I-I'm *really* hungry. And I could use a break. And there's a good chance—"

"How do you know he's not working for the JI?"

Her head tipped back and to the side. "Well, because the Orang Asli aren't interested in political affiliations or terrorist pursuits. They're a peaceful people. Probably stems from the fact that they're a matriarchal society." She nudged him. "*See* what putting women in charge will get you?"

"You mean besides ridiculous T-shirts and big hair?"

She swatted his arm again.

He swatted her back.

"Stop it," she hissed.

"*You* stop it," he repeated, his stomach muscles twitching with repressed laughter.

For a moment, they just stood there, smirking at one another, the years of separation having melted away. Then she shook her head, frowning. "But seriously. What use would the JI have for them? The Orang Asli have no weapons, no money, and no military training."

"Not to mention the fact that they're seriously vertically challenged."

Abby glanced over at Señor SP. "I'm not sure that's true," she lowered her voice to a conspiratorial whisper. "I think they're actually a pretty average height for the region. This guy is just particularly…uh…petite."

"Why are you whispering?" he asked. "He can't understand you."

Her chin jerked back. "Whatever," she huffed. "Can we go with him, or what?"

Steady weighed his options. On the one hand, Abby had yet to steer him wrong. So his instincts told him to trust her on this occasion, too. On the other hand, he really, *really* wanted to cross that border. He wouldn't rest easy until they were safe and sound in Thailand.

Then again, they might not *make* that border without getting some food in her. For all her grit and bravado, the dark circles under her eyes—not to mention the sunken look to her cheeks—told him she was getting very close to reaching the end of her rope. Even Señor SP seemed to understand that, because he glanced back at Abby, frowned, and motioned again for them to follow him, once again pantomiming taking a bite of something.

Hue puta! His decision was made. "All right," he said. "Let's go get some food, eh? But I warn you, if he makes me eat a grub worm, I'm never forgiving you. I've managed to go my whole career without noshing on creepy crawly things, and it's a trend I'd like to see continue."

Some of the guys he'd trained and worked with over the years took great pride in their ability to make a meal out of just about anything they stumbled across. Grass, bugs, fungi, *moss*. But Steady's background in medicine gave him a natural aversion to things abounding with bacteria or loaded with weird unprocessed chemicals. And his beliefs were solidified the time he watched a fellow Ranger who ate a bad mushroom hallucinate for six hours straight. The wild-eyed dude had pulled a knife on his fellow soldiers, threatening to cut off everyone's balls—not something *any* man took lightly, but particularly not a group of beefed-up GIs—and the result had been that the guy came out of his delirium to find himself hog-tied by a bunch of carabiners and bungee cords, and with a length of duct tape slapped over his mouth.

"The Orang Asli don't eat grub worms, silly." She

nodded and motioned for Señor SP to lead the way. "Their diet consists of fish, rice, and fruit."

"And you know this because?" he asked.

She grinned over her shoulder at him. Weaponized. There was no other way to describe that smile of hers. It gave his heart a workout harder than any PT—physical training—he'd ever had to do in Ranger School. "Because of those art—"

"Articles you read," he finished for her again. "Of course."

She nodded and turned away, and all he could think was Ay Dios mio, *I sure do like her.*

Then again, *like* seemed like such a vapid term for the warm, fuzzy, *relentless* feelings she provoked in him.

Could it be love? The question seemed to come from nowhere. But, miracle of miracles, and contrary to what he would have expected, it didn't fill him with dread.

Huh. Will you look at that? Was it possible he was falling in love with her? Or…maybe he already *had* fallen in love with her? All those years ago? The good Lord knew he'd never held a torch for any woman as long as he'd held one for her.

Watching the determined swing of her arms and the dogged way she followed Señor SP, he let the idea percolate like the healing tinctures he'd practiced making back in med school…and enjoyed the resulting warmth that spread inside his chest.

Chapter Twelve

"Jaya is her son," Vanessa's voice, pinging from satellite to satellite, took a split second to reach them. Dan glanced over at Penni, not surprised to see all the color still drained from her face. She'd been pale as the frosted doughnuts his fellow teammate and friend, Ace, liked to buy from the bakery down the block from BKI headquarters in Chicago. The dude was addicted to pastries. And, back in the dark days—that's how Dan termed the twelve months he'd lived as hammered shit—Ace had tried to get him hooked on the sweet culinary treats as opposed to the whiskey he'd swilled by the gallon jug.

It hadn't worked, of course. Sugar was no substitute for high-octane grain alcohol when it came to staying obliterated for twenty-four hours a day, seven days a week. But Dan gave the guy massive points for trying.

"Penni." He drew her attention away from the maid. Her brown eyes were wide and glassy, revealing how exhausted she was. And the bloodshot red tinting the whites was evidence of the tears she refused to shed. She was one tough cookie. He'd give her that. Because if all *his* friends had suddenly and brutally been taken out, he'd probably be blubbering like a goddamned baby, not sitting there all ramrod straight and quietly stoic. "We really can handle the rest of this interview if you'd rather not hear—"

"No." She shook her head. "I-I'm okay." The ends of her dark ponytail slipped over her shoulder, and for a moment he was reminded of how lovely she had looked with her sleek, chocolate-colored hair fanned out across his pillow. How sultry and soft her mouth had been as she watched him slip on the condom Ozzie shoved in his pocket before leaving the dance floor with Julia on his arm—the condom he had *not* had the chance to use, since the incendiary devices exploded a split second later. Still, Ozzie's last words whispered through his head. *Yo, man. This is just in case you start thinking with your downstairs brain instead of your upstairs brain.* And for all the shit he dished Ozzie, and all the shit Ozzie dished him right back, it killed him to think of the guy losing his leg. The job was *everything* to Ozzie, and if he couldn't do it…

Dan squashed the thought before he could finish it.

"I'm serious, Dan," she insisted when he'd been quietly staring at her for too long. "I'm fine. Really."

And, yeah, he suspected she was trying to convince herself more than she was trying to convince him. "If you're sure?"

She nodded again, the movement a little odd and jerky. And when she lifted a finger, running it quickly down the bridge of her nose—something he'd noticed she did when she was feeling particularly vulnerable—he decided not to press her. "Okay." He dipped his chin and turned back to the phone lying faceup on the table. "Go on, Vanessa. What's wrong with Jaya and what the hell does he hafta do with her planting the bombs?"

For nearly twenty minutes, Vanessa—taking her cues from Rock on which questions to ask and in what order—had conversed in Malay via the open line with the wailing maid. And little by little, the woman had settled down. Now she was slumped in her chair, her head bowed, her tears silently falling onto the white apron tied around her waist. Dan experienced a twinge of sympathy and also a twinge of foreboding. He could tell by Vanessa's tone that whatever she'd discovered, it wasn't anything he'd want to write home about.

"First of all," she said, "her name is Irdina, and she's a single parent. Her husband died in a trucking accident six months ago, right around the time Jaya was diagnosed with a treatable form of leukemia." Dan glanced down at the photo lying atop the table. That poor, emaciated little body. Those soulful, suffering black eyes. His stomach turned over, and his diaphragm decided to become a steel vice, squeezing his lungs into his throat. From the corner of his eye, he thought he saw Penni's lower lip tremble. "The doctors told her Jaya had an eighty percent chance of survival if he received the right therapy, but Irdina didn't have the money for it. So she took the job at the hotel. Unfortunately, she has yet to save enough to start his treatment and in the meantime Jaya has taken a turn for the worse."

"Lemme guess," Dan said. "She was suddenly approached by someone working for the JI. And this someone offered her the money she so desperately needed in exchange for one teeny, tiny favor. In order to save her son, she just had to tape some explosives beneath the beds of a few Americans."

"To make a long story short," Vanessa concurred. "But Irdina swears she didn't know they were bombs."

Dan snorted. "Come on. Didn't she see the wires

attached to electronic timers? What the hell *else* would they've been?"

"She's poor and uneducated," Vanessa said. "And I may not be as fluent in Malay as I am in some other languages, but I'm still good enough to pick up on the sound of bullshit when I hear it. I think she's telling the truth."

"You okay, *mon cheri*?" Rock's voice drifted over the open line, and Dan could picture the man brushing Vanessa's ink-black hair over her shoulder. The love those two shared was as obvious as the noses on their faces. And for some reason, Dan's eyes were pulled over to Penni. The muscle twitching beside her pinched mouth made his heart ache.

"I'm fine, Rock." Vanessa's whispered words drifted over the airwaves. "It's so sad. So unbearably sad."

And, yeah. That was it in a nutshell.

Still staring at Penni, he admitted, not for the first time, that he hadn't a clue what to do with her, *for* her. Did he go with his gut and take her in his arms? Did he leave her alone to courageously endure? What did she want from him? What did she *need* from him?

Her statue-like stillness, her stubborn silence offered him no direction. And for a few moments, the only sound to break the tense quiet of the storage room was Irdina's soft sniffle and the hard rumble of a cat's purr rolling over the open phone line.

Peanut, the fat, mangy tom who was the Knights' unofficial mascot, always seemed to know when one of the women was unhappy. The feline offered comfort by way of curling his rotund self upon whoever's lap and starting his engine. Obviously, he'd seen Vanessa's distress and was proving true to form.

Shit a brick! If the maid had been a fanatical believer in the JI cause, it would've been so easy to hate her, so easy to hand her over to the Malaysian authorities. But Irdina wasn't a terrorist bent on the downfall of all the infidels. She was simply a mother. A terrified, frantic mother who was willing to do anything she could to rescue her son from the savage jaws of illness. It was a goddamned Charlie Foxtrot if ever there was one. Dan scrubbed a hand back through his hair, trying, quite unsuccessfully, to swallow the lump in his throat.

I need a drink.

One day at a time...

"How do you say 'I'm sorry' in Malay?" Penni suddenly asked, her shoulders slumped down so low Dan figured she'd need a hydraulic hoist to lift them up again.

Do I go to her? Do I not?

He was still waffling, still ignoring the AA advice that went a little something like *quit slackin' and make shit happen*, when Vanessa rattled off a string of syllables. Listening intently, Penni nodded and reached across the table to lay a gentle hand on Irdina's arm. The maid glanced up, her face tear-streaked and swollen. Tapping a finger on Jaya's photo, Penni repeated the syllables just as Vanessa had said them. Irdina's face caved in on itself, and she lifted her hands to cover her eyes, wailing anew.

"I have to—" Penni's voice hitched as she quickly pushed back from the little table. Her chair tipped over, hitting the tile floor with a loud *crack!* Then she was racing for the door.

Cock and balls! He'd been wondering when that would happen. Because for the last several hours she'd borne a striking resemblance to a suitcase nuke waiting to go *boom!*

"Hey guys," he directed his voice toward the face-up phone, wincing when the door to the storage room slammed shut. The shelves stacked with stainless-steel coffee urns and rows of cups rattled with the impact. "I'm gonna need you two to find out how Irdina knew which beds to plant those incendiary devices under, because I suspect she had direction from someone here at the hotel. In the meantime, I'm gonna go after Penni. I need to make sure she's okay." *Make some shit happen, indeed.*

"*Oui*, *mon ami*," Rock answered after a beat, once Dan's cell signal had pinged to the other side of the globe and back. "But what if she decides to make a run for it—"

"We're standing in a storage room just off a conference room," he interrupted, understanding Rock's confusion and concern before he finished the sentence. "Both can be locked from the outside." He reached into his pocket to remove the universal keycard the hotel manager had given him.

"Right," Rock said, but Dan was already opening the door, pulling it closed and securing it behind him.

"Penni!" he called. She was halfway across the vacant conference room, making a beeline for the hallway. Her ponytail flew out behind her as her long legs ate up the distance. "Penni, wait!"

She ignored him as she slammed out of the room. And the choked sob that drifted back to him hit his ears like a percussion grenade. He jettisoned after her, skirting the conference table and hopping over the trash can sitting beside a coffee service cart. Quickly pulling the door closed behind him, he scarcely registered the faint *clicking* sound of its automatic lock. Turning, he saw Penni disappear into the women's bathroom.

Jogging down the deserted hallway—obviously the hotel manager had made good on Dan's demands for privacy—he tried to think of what he could possibly say to Penni to bring her some small measure of comfort in this goddamned pisser of a situation. Unfortunately, like Eminem would say, *I come from Detroit where it's rough, and I'm not a smooth talker.* But when he wrenched open the door to the ladies' room only to have her instantly hurl herself into his arms, her nose buried in his neck, her hot tears wetting the fabric of his T-shirt, he realized no words were necessary.

Penni DePaul simply needed to be held. And, by God, he could certainly do that…

The river roared and thrashed over the rocks as Umar hung onto the rope he had strung across the watery expanse using an ancient technique his grandfather taught him. It basically consisted of attaching one end of the sturdy rope to a leader line, in this case some fishing filament, which was itself attached to native seedpod that was capable of floating atop water. Using a quickly constructed slingshot made of vines and palm bark, he sent the seed with the fishing line attached flying across the raging river. After a couple of failed attempts, the seed finally sailed over his target…the thick limb of a tree. Then, just as it'd done when his grandfather showed him how to do it twenty years ago, the weight of the seed caused it to fall to the ground, roll down the opposite bank, and plop into the water.

Then came the tricky part…

By carefully and patiently tugging, and subsequently letting out more and more slack in the lead line, Umar was able to make the seedpod dance across to their side of the river before it was washed too far downstream and he ran out of fishing filament. Then it was a small matter of sliding down the slippery bank without falling in, fetching the seed from the clutches of the seething water, and reeling in the line. Since the rope was attached to its opposite end, by reeling in the line, it forced the rope across the river, over the branch, and back to them. He finished the task by tying the two ends of the rope around the trunk of a tree. And, as the Americans would say, *bingo!* He and his men could now forge the volatile river by inching their way across the rope like silkworms. And even though the complicated maneuver had given his prey a head start of nearly two hours, it was far better than having to trudge the twenty or so miles down the trail to the next bridge.

Dropping to the ground after having tested that the rope would hold his weight, he dusted off his hands and turned to catch Azahari and Noordin exchange a look.

"You do not think it sturdy enough?" he asked his men, narrowing his eyes. Though he was no longer feeling the effects of the serum, it had left him overly tired, in turn making him overly irritable. Then again, his poor mood could simply be a result of knowing his months of careful planning—not to mention the small fortune he had spent—might all be for naught. And that his chances of ever seeing his brother again were slipping farther and farther from his grasp with each passing minute and each additional step that *anak haram* and the woman took toward the Thai border.

"It is not that," Azahari assured him, reaching forward to lay a hand on his shoulder.

Umar looked down at the offending appendage. Then glanced at Azahari, lifting his brow.

Azahari quickly removed his fingers, and Umar secretly smiled when the man's throat worked over a quick, uncomfortable swallow. *Yes. You are walking the knife's edge with me.* Turning, he made sure to include the other men in the threat shining from his eyes. *You all are.*

Only when his two soldiers bowed their heads in submission did he glance back to Azahari. "Then what is it?"

"It is the jungle," Azahari admitted. "It is filled with tigers and elephants. Did you not hear one trumpeting earlier?"

"Yes. I heard." Umar once again narrowed his eyes. "What of it?"

"There are stories of people being killed by—"

"It is not the jungle you should fear," Umar warned, stepping close to Azahari. He hated that the man was taller than him, forcing him to lift his chin. But what Umar lacked in height, he made up for in intelligence and ruthlessness. Azahari would do well to remember that.

"We are not afraid," Noordin was quick to assure him. "And we will not fail you, Umar."

Azahari nodded vigorously in agreement. "Noordin speaks the truth. But, still, would it not be better to wait for the others to arrive? They should be here in less than half an hour. And we will be safer in numbers should we happen upon—"

"No," Umar silenced him with one word, his hand slicing through the air. *Fools.* To be afraid of the jungle like children. And, yes, he understood that most of his men had been born and raised in cities—where some of the more dogmatic mosques had schooled them to hate and revile the West—but still, that was no excuse for their infantile fear of the bush. Did they not see what he had just accomplished? Did they not understand the jungle was *his* turf? "We will not wait. We will not allow the Americans to gain another minute of ground ahead of us. The others will simply have to catch up." He could tell by Azahari's expression that the man wanted to say more. "What is it?" he demanded, growing more impatient with each ticking second.

"The others will be hesitant to follow," Azahari said, his Adam's apple bobbing in the column of his throat. "Not only do they fear the jungle, but they fear the RTAF. This close to the Thai border—"

Umar had reached his wit's end. Grabbing Azahari's shirt in a fist, he snarled into the man's face. "They *will* follow. Or, by Allah, I will find them when this is all done and I will kill them myself." Stepping back, he pointed an angry finger at the rucksack slung over Noordin's shoulder. "Get on the satellite phone and tell them as much." When Noordin hesitated, he screamed, "Now!"

Noordin fumbled with the pack, extracting the large, clumsy satellite phone and dialing the number. After he chokingly relayed Umar's message, he nodded vigorously. "It is done. They will follow as soon as they arrive."

Of course they would. They knew he did not make empty threats. “Good.” He nodded smugly. Then he turned to Azahari and pointed to the rope. “You first.”

Chapter Thirteen

The Orang Asli village of Semaq Ulu
Ten miles from the border of Thailand

"These things are delicious," Abby enthused, a growing pile of rambutan skins and seeds forming at her feet. Rambutan was a red fruit about the size of a small plum. Its thick outer coat was covered in fine, green hairs—not at all an attractive sight, really. Though she was not going to complain over a lack of aesthetics when the little buggers tasted like manna straight from heaven.

Sitting on a wicker stool in the middle of the village—which consisted of around fifteen bamboo huts constructed high atop stilts and covered with dried palm-leaf roofs—she was amazed to find the tiny piece of furniture was wonderfully comfy. Then again, given the ache of her tired bones and the fatigue in her sore muscles, a bed of nails would've probably felt like a goose down comforter.

Carlos lounged to her left on an identical stool, doing a better job of remembering his table manners. He reached over to wipe a drop of rambutan juice from her chin, and the pad of his calloused thumb felt deliciously abrasive. It highlighted the fact that even though he had the beautiful hands of a surgeon, they were also the seasoned, battle-roughened hands of a soldier. *Yum!* And, *grrr.*

Because now that he'd made it clear he returned her unbridled feelings of…okay…let's just call it what it was…*lust*, keeping him at arms' length was going to be just that much more difficult. And she *had* to keep him at arms' length. If she didn't, she wasn't sure she'd have the courage to tell him what she'd done. And seeing him again after all these years, seeing how brave and selfless he was, had convinced her she *must* come clean. Carlos deserved the truth.

Shaking away her tumultuous thoughts—there'd be plenty of time for them later—she glanced to her right where Yonus, a young Orang Asli man, was sitting on a third stool. The moment they had pushed out of the jungle, the old guy who found them—an elder she'd come to understand was named Mamat—walked them straight up to Yonus. And after a flurry of words in that oddly staccato-sounding dialect, Yonus had shocked the ever-lovin' shitpickle out of them by welcoming them to the village in the most pristine English she'd ever heard. We're talking Queen Elizabeth couldn't have done any better. Then again, maybe she shouldn't have been all that surprised. You know, considering Yonus was wearing a Polo shirt, Levi's, and Clarks flip-flops, as opposed to the brightly printed tunics and trousers sported proudly by the other male villagers.

Long story short, apparently Yonus, orphaned at a young age and sponsored by a missionary group, had received an education outside the tribe. He'd gone to college in Johor, learning English and Malay, and was now working as an advocate for the Orang Asli people all over the country. And luckily—the good Lord knew they were due some luck—he was visiting this particular village on this particular day.

A couple of bowls of sticky rice and a fat bunch of rambutans later, and Abby figured she might survive long enough to make it to Thailand.

"I am so glad you like them." Yonus motioned toward the rambutans.

"Like them? I'd like to be alone with them," she enthused.

Yonus grinned down at his flip-flops. "There is a joke amongst the Orang Asli when it comes these fruits."

"What's that?" she asked, noshing on another juicy morsel, willing her body to absorb the calories and give her a welcome boost. As soon as they left here, it was going to be ten more grueling miles of monkey calls and tiger roars and big, slithering snakes. Ten more torturous miles of clinging vines and tripping roots and air so thick it made her feel like she was drowning anytime she sucked in an exhausted yawn.

"They say they resemble a grown man's..." he gestured vaguely toward the fly of his Levi's..."nether bits."

Carlos chuckled, using his fingernail to split the skin on another rambutan, revealing the glistening white meat inside. "Sort of gives credence to that whole twig and berries euphemism, eh?"

Abby glanced down at the two fuzzy balls in her palm and realized they *did* sort of resemble a man's testicles. Except for the green hairs, of course. *Maybe the Hulk's testicles? But those would be bigger, right?* She frowned and shook her head, wondering at her own sanity that she should be sitting here in the middle of the jungle contemplating the size of the Hulk's balls. Then again, the heat was known to do strange things to people. "But what they lack in visual appeal on the *outside*," she told the men, pushing away all notions of irradiated superheroes and their *nether bits*, "they more than make up for with sweet deliciousness on the *inside*."

Yonus and Carlos exchanged a look.

"Oh, for the love of—" she harrumphed. "Why is the male brain always in the gutter?"

Yonus's grin widened, his face splitting around a mouthful of gleaming teeth. "Brain in the gutter." He pronounced the words very precisely in that strange English/Malay/Orang Asli accent of his. "I like that phrase very well, indeed. It is very illustrative, yes?"

Abby rolled her eyes at him before turning to smile at the little girl, no more than four or five years old, who lifted a lock of blond hair from her shoulder. Since their arrival in the village, Abby had been the center of attention. The adults, more hesitant, had remained some distance away, simply standing and staring. But the children had been circling her, occasionally touching her, and keeping up a constant stream of excited chatter.

"They have never seen green eyes or yellow hair before," Yonus told her. "Having you here is like having a unicorn in the village."

"Oooh." She grinned. "I *like* that. A unicorn, huh?"

"So what am I?" Carlos feigned a frown. "Chump change?"

Yonus laughed. "I do not know this phrase. *Chump change.* But I can gather its meaning." He tilted his head as if to study Carlos. "And I would say you are not exactly chump change, but neither are you exactly a unicorn. Black hair and black eyes they have seen plenty."

"Hmph," Carlos grunted, popping the white ball of fruit into his mouth.

"So tell me, my new friends," Yonus said, "how it is you came to be so lost in the jungle?"

And, just like that, all the sweet simplicity of the moment was shattered. The nearby stream no longer babbled quite so happily. The children's laughter didn't seem quite so gay. And the rays of the hot sun beaming down on them didn't feel quite so benevolent. With that one simple question, Abby was reminded that out there, somewhere, a group of terrorists stalked her. It was time for her and Carlos to be on their way.

"We were riding our motorcycle to Thailand when we ran out of gas," Carlos was quick to explain. "We had decided to get off the highway and onto an old logging trail, not realizing there would be no villages or towns around where we could fill our tank. We would've called for help, but..." He lifted his iPhone from his hip pocket, punching the button and showing Yonus the screen with the glowing empty battery symbol and the little Harry Potter-esque lightning bolt. Then he shrugged and feigned a sheepish grin. "I guess we weren't all that prepared when we left our hotel this morning."

Wow. And will you look at that? The man obviously missed his calling. With that gorgeous face and those acting chops, he should've graced the silver screen.

Yonus pursed his lips, glancing at the weapon strapped to Carlos's thigh, then over at Abby. "You look familiar to me. Why is that?"

Well, hmm, perhaps because she was the youngest daughter of the president of the frickin' United States.

Although, in accordance with her father's wishes and her own, she had remained mostly out of the limelight, only allowing the press to film or photograph her on the very rarest of occasions. Still, her face *did* get the occasional airplay.

Having no idea what she was going to say, but deciding that taking a page from Carlos's book and winging it was better, and far less suspicious, than sitting there like a mute, she cleared her throat. "I suppose I have one of those faces, you know? All-American. You've probably seen a hundred girls who look just like me on Coca-Cola commercials." *And, huh. That didn't sound half bad, did it? Booyah!*

Her celebration didn't last long when Yonus's frowned deepened. *Okay, maybe not such a slam dunk after all.* She opened her mouth to elaborate, but Yonus beat her to the punch by shrugging and waving a hand through the air. She suspected he wasn't really buying their explanations, but neither did it look like he was going to press them further. She wondered if he assumed they were part of the heroin trade that was so lucrative in this part of the world and, as such, had decided it was better not to ask too many more questions. Considering drug offenses were punishable by death, the locals tended to avoid the illegal enterprise at all costs.

And on that note, she started to thank him for the hospitality and to tell him they were going to continue on their journey when the little girl tugged on her hair again, leaning in to jabber something in her ear. She glanced at the wild-haired cherub, then frowned when she noticed the girl rubbing her eyes. Upon closer inspection, the thin layer of fluid coating the conjunctiva surfaces looked milky.

"What's wrong with her eyes?" she asked.

Yonus glanced at the little girl, making a face of regret. "It is an illness that runs in her family," he explained. "In the elderly, like her grandmother, it sometimes causes blindness."

Abby may not have finished her premed degree, but she didn't for one minute think this was some sort of genetic mutation. "Carlos," she said, turning to him, "will you look at her eyes?"

Carlos dropped a bunch of rambutans, dusted off his hands, and slid her a speaking glance. It said, *it's time for us to get the hell out of here.*

Her expression and the subtle little tilt of her head toward the girl replied, *well, duh, but first...the girl.*

He sighed and turned to crook a finger at the child. The scamp immediately grabbed Abby's arm in a death grip, adamantly shaking her head. Abby couldn't really blame the little girl for her fear. Carlos pretty much looked the part he played. Big, mean, and threatening. Especially with those black tattoos running along the insides of his forearms and peeking from the back collar of his tank top.

Taking the sweet bit of adorableness onto her lap, she nodded and leaned over to pat Carlos's muscular shoulder, showing the girl without using words, *see, he's a super nice guy.* "Will you explain to her that Carlos is a doctor?" she asked Yonus.

"Are you?" Yonus turned to Carlos, his surprise evident both in his tone and his face.

"*Sí.* In a manner of speaking," Carlos admitted,

leaning toward the girl who was wriggling on Abby's lap. The minute he got close, the little cherub went as still as the large gray stones the villagers had used to line the stream's edge.

Yonus uttered a string of incomprehensible syllables to the little girl, and Abby twisted to the side to see if she understood what Yonus was telling her. Those big, black eyes blinked a couple of times before that cute chin tilted up and down in a jerky nod.

Carefully, gently, Carlos pressed her eyelids wide. Abby could feel the girl stop breathing, every muscle in her tiny body quivering like a jungle leaf during the height of monsoon season.

"Quickly, Carlos," she whispered. "She's about to bolt."

"Just a second more."

"And it would probably help matters if you weren't wearing a frown that says you munch on little girls for an afternoon snack."

He looked at her, pulling a face, so she flattened her expression. One corner of his mouth twitched. This time he smiled at the girl before bending close to peer into her eyes.

Slowly, hesitantly, the girl raised her arm and pressed a timid finger into his dimple, proving the damned thing was irresistible to anything with ovaries. She squirmed and giggled with delight when Carlos winked at her before quickly turning his head to kiss the tip of her little digit.

Right on, sister, Abby thought, *I know just how you feel.*

"Bacterial infection," he murmured, sitting back. "Not river blindness."

She waited for him to go on, but it quickly became apparent he had no intention to.

"Carlos," she admonished him, "would you care to elaborate?"

He grumbled something under his breath.

She raised an eyebrow.

He pursed his lips.

She lifted her remaining eyebrow.

Sighing, he said in a harried rush, "I don't see the telltale nodules on her upper lids. And considering it runs in her family and isn't present throughout the entire village, I'd say it's spread through repeated contact with infected persons and their belongings, or perhaps it *is* some sort of genetic predisposition to that specific type of infection. But it is definitely not caused by the bite of the black fly, which is how river blindness is contracted. Besides, river blindness is rare in this part of the world."

"See," she chided him. "Now was that so hard?"

"Not hard," he insisted. "And not necessary. I'd already summed it up with five words. Bacterial infection. Not river blindness."

"You're impossible," she told him, unable to contain her affectionate smile.

"*Sí*," he admitted, giving her a wink. "Which is one of the many reasons you love me."

Everything inside Abby went perfectly still. Luckily, Carlos didn't notice the effect that one simple phrase had on her because he turned to Yonus. "Can I see someone else in her family who has it?"

Yonus nodded and called something over his shoulder to the group of adults standing beside the thick bamboo stilts supporting the village's central structure.

When he turned back to them, his expression was contemplative. Obviously, he was having a difficult time figuring them out. Possible drug runners who also practiced medicine?

Offering Yonus what she hoped was an innocent smile, she turned her attention to the group of adults, watching as heads swiveled toward a woman in an orange and pink printed dress that resembled some sort of elaborate sarong. With hesitant steps and pie-plate eyes, the woman slowly emerged from the center of the group. The first thing Abby noticed about her, besides the lovely tilt to her dark eyebrows, was that she had a beautiful orchid in her charming riot of frizzy black hair. An *Arundina graminifolia* by the looks of it. And Abby should know. She'd been trying to breed one with exactly those deep, rich colors for nearly two years now.

Just goes to show, Mother Nature is a better horticulturist than me. Not that she'd ever imagined otherwise.

The woman dragged her feet, making the journey over to them in record-breaking time. Seriously, Abby was considering submitting her name to Guinness under the category of Slowest Snail-like Pace Ever! But eventually she completed the journey, smiling hesitantly when Carlos stood from the stool.

"Will you ask her if it's okay for me to touch her face?" Carlos asked Yonus.

Yonus translated Carlos's request. The woman nodded shyly, causing the petals on that glorious orchid to quiver. Abby watched Carlos hold the woman's top lids wide and couldn't help but admire the gentle way he tilted her face toward the beam of yellow sun slicing through the gathering clouds overhead. Rain was coming. Abby could smell it in the air, feel it in the uptick of the sticky, oppressive heat.

"Definitely bacterial." He clasped his hands together, nodding his thanks to the woman for allowing him to examine her.

Orchid Lady repeated the gesture before turning, lifting her skirts, and running back to the group of adults. *Now she hurries?* "She needs antibiotic eye drops," Abby told Yonus, bouncing the little girl on her knee until she giggled. "They *both* do. The whole family probably does."

Yonus was already shaking his head. "They will not venture into town to visit a doctor. And even if they would, I doubt they would willingly put something that comes out of a plastic bottle into their eyes. They distrust things that are not natural to the jungle."

Natural to the jungle...

And just like that, inspiration struck Abby. "Okay, so say I could show them a plant that if they pound the leaves into a poultice and put it over their eyes while they sleep at night, it could cure them of this infection? It will take longer than the eye drops, of course. Perhaps a few weeks to a few months depending on how bad their case is. But, if used consistently, I'd say it has a pretty good chance of keeping them from going blind."

"What're you talking about, Abby?" Carlos asked, his black brows pulled low. The little girl took one look at his scowling face and made a squeaking sound like she'd spotted the boogeyman. She hopped from Abby's lap to run over to the group of children who'd grown bored with Abby's appearance and were now playing some sort of game down by the stream.

I guess even unicorns lose their luster after a while…

"I saw a patch of *Sida rhombifolia* somewhere back there in the jungle." She hooked a thumb over her shoulder. When Carlos continued to frown at her, she shook her head, reminding herself that even though he was schooled in medicine, he wasn't aware of the names of the plants that provided the extracts for so many of today's modern cures. "It's sometimes referred to as Queensland hemp or Indian hemp, though it's not really in the hemp family at all."

"Is there a point to this lesson in botany?" he asked.

This is the part where, had he been sitting beside her, she would lean over and smack him on the shoulder, telling him to *stop it.* Then *he* would take a swipe at her and say, *no,* you *stop it.* Which would then have them grinning at each other.

"*Yes*, there's a point to it," she told him, making a face. "*Sida rhombifolia* has incredibly high antimicrobial and antibacterial properties. It can be used to treat any number of infections including, I would suspect, whatever type of infection that little girl and her family are suffering from."

Carlos glanced toward the jungle, a muscle ticking in the hard line of his jaw. Yep, she knew the smart thing to do would be to immediately resume their journey north. But she couldn't stand the thought of that sweet little girl losing her eyesight when the solution was so easy and growing right in her own backyard.

"Pardon me," Yonus said. "But could you tell me what plant you are speaking of?"

Eagerly, Abby turned to the young man. "Its leaves almost look like that of the mint plant, but it has these little yellow flowers. It grows to about this high," she held her hand up to her chin.

Yonus nodded, relaying her description to the group of adults. A flurry of discussion commenced within the crowd, then Mamat stepped forward, bowing.

"Mamat says he knows of which plant you speak," Yonus told her.

Yep, *this* was a headline she liked much better: PRESIDENT'S DAUGHTER CURES MALAYSIAN VILLAGE OF BLINDNESS! And how wonderful would it be if something good were to come from her abduction? Something worthy of the sacrifices and risks Carlos had taken on her behalf? She needed, more than she was willing to admit, one thing, *anything*, that she could look back on and be proud of.

"Right on!" She jumped from the stool, clapping her hands and stepping forward to slug Carlos on the arm. "How awesome is this? We're like…frickin' Doctors Without Borders here!"

He nodded, his expression that of a man resigned to forgo the start of their journey. The soldier in him needed to make that Thai border with all haste. But the doctor in him couldn't leave that little girl and her family behind to suffer when there was something they could do to help. "Have I ever told you how much you amaze me, *neña*? How proud I am of the woman you've become?" His deep voice reminded her of the rhythmic purr of a big jungle cat.

"Oh, stop it," she told him, dramatically fluttering her eyes and simpering. "My poor, swollen ego can only take so much."

He chuckled and caught her chin between his thumb

and forefinger, giving her head an affectionate shake. The key word here was *affectionate.*

Damnit! It was obvious now that Carlos liked her. That he *trusted* her. And the good Lord knew he shouldn't.

The smile she bestowed on him was sunny. But inside, that familiar dark pain reared its ugly head…

Chapter Fourteen

"I wanted to h-hate her," Penni cried against Dan's shoulder. She knew she was covering him in tears, and probably some snot, too—*gross*—but she couldn't stop the grief that poured from her in torrential, soul-sucking waves. "I w-wanted to—"

"I know, baby," Dan crooned, hugging her tight. So tight she could barely breath. And yet, it still wasn't tight enough. She wanted to crawl inside his big, strong body and hide. Hide from the pain and guilt that had been eating her alive since she saw what had been done to her friends. Hide from the fear that she would ultimately fail in her duty to see Abby safe and sound once again. Hide from the awful truth of Irdina and Jaya and the desperate inequality that existed in this cruel world. Just hide, hide, *hide!*

And it was so despicably cowardly of her. She was disgusted with herself, disgusted with her weakness. This was not the woman her father had raised, this woman who was having an emotional meltdown of Sicilian proportions. And if he could see her now, he'd be appalled. *She* was appalled. But the tears…

The tears wouldn't stop. Because there was too much shit, and she hadn't come equipped with enough shovels.

"I know," Dan soothed again, running a hand over her ponytail to cup the back of her neck. His palm was warm and rough. And it served to remind her of why she was the only one of Abby's security detail left alive. It served to remind her of where she'd been and what she'd been doing when her whole world was torn apart. "It's okay to cry. It's okay to grieve."

She pushed back from him, wiping a hand under her nose. "No." She shook her head. "It's *not* okay to cry. Not yet. There's still so much left to do, and I have to keep—"

She gasped when he lifted his hands to firmly grasp her head. Lowering his chin until he was looking out at her from under the heavy ridge of his scowling blond eyebrows, he gave her a little shake. "Stop it, Penni," he commanded. "You stop it right now. In the last few hours you've been braver, *stronger*, than anyone I've ever known. So for chrissakes, it's okay to just take a minute here. Besides, hasn't anyone ever told you that control is just an illusion?"

Uh-huh. As a matter of fact they had. Her twenty-years sober uncle liked to repeat that mantra anytime life's sugar turned to shit.

She stilled in Dan's embrace, searching his pretty green eyes and saw…pain…and understanding… and other things she couldn't quite put her finger on. Something inside her shifted. Just a little. But it was enough. Because it occurred to her right then and there that she may not be able to crawl inside him and hide away from the world, but there was another way to forget. For a while…

Stepping forward, she pressed herself close, going up on tiptoe to seal their mouths. His lips were so soft and warm, his breath even warmer when it hitched as she forced her tongue between his teeth. He tensed for a second, one tiny second, then he groaned and wrapped his arms around her, spinning her until her back slammed against the door to the bathroom. And, just like that, the unbearable sadness made way for lust. The intolerable hurt moved aside for hunger.

And, hello? *This* was what she needed. Not tears. Not sorrow and regret and second-guessing. Escape. Physical escape. Mental escape. Emotional escape. If she could just for bit, just for a while, get away from it all, she might be able to wrestle herself back under control. She might be able to do her duty. Do what was right and honorable and worthy of the title of Secret Service agent. Make proud the man who'd taught her how to be a warrior, how to be a champion. Honor the friends she'd lost this day.

"Make love to me," she whispered against Dan's neck between a string of hard, biting kisses. She lifted a leg, hooking her heel behind his knee. He was gratifyingly hard when she rubbed herself against him, and her body answered with a swift rush of marvelous liquid heat.

"Brooklyn...*Jesus*," he groaned, flattening his wide palm beside her head as she gently bit his earlobe. She loved the nickname he'd given her, loved that he only used it when they were on the brink of intimacy.

With his free hand, he gripped her hip, giving it a squeeze before sliding his hot palm down the length of her thigh until he reached the crook of her knee. Lifting her leg high around his waist, he more fully aligned their bodies. And this time when he stroked forward, rubbing against her, it was as if the material separating their sexes had melted away. She could feel the length of him graze her distended clitoris. The subtle ache that had been building between her thighs exploded into a painful coil of tension.

She reached down to attack the buttons on his jeans, her fingers trembling as first one, then another, and then another popped open. When the front of his fly gaped wide, she shoved her hand inside his black boxer briefs, gripping the heated, rock-hard length of him, remembering how violently red, how hugely swollen and painful his erection had looked right before he slid on the condom.

"Brooklyn," he gasped, his head falling back on his shoulders, the big veins running on either side of his neck standing out like garden hoses. "We shouldn't… *Holy shit*, that feels good."

"Mmm," she hummed, keeping one hand inside his pants, pulling, petting, stroking, as she used the other to undo the button on her trousers. Her zipper made a soft *scriiiitching* sound that was barely audible above their heavy, gasping breaths. Lowering her leg, she toed out of her shoes. It was a pity she had to release the steely length of him in order to grab the waistband of her pants and panties and push them down her thighs. But she was rewarded for that small sacrifice when, after stepping out of the puddle of clothing, she discovered both of Dan's hands were now planted on the door beside her head. His chest rose and fell in huge, hungry breaths. His eyes glowed with a lust so hot it was like gasoline to the fire already burning in her blood.

"Make love to me," she said again, wrapping her arms around his shoulders, going up on tiptoe to realign their bodies. "Make me forget just for a little while."

A frenzied muscled ticked in his jaw, his lips flattening

into a thin line. "Brooklyn, you have no idea how much I wanna do exactly that. But I don't have a condom."

She shook her head. All this talk was allowing some of that terrible pain to creep back in, some of that spirit-crushing despair to seep into the mortar she'd used to quickly build up a wall around her grief. "Forget about it," she told him, shoving his jeans and boxers down his thighs until his erection sprang free. "I don't care..."

Steady watched Abby scoop some of the goop she'd made from that hemp-plant-that-wasn't-really-a-hemp-plant off a palm leaf. She mimicked sticking it to her eyes while Yonus translated for the people of the village. "And then, you press this to your face like this and go to sleep for the night. It will make the infection..." She wrinkled her button nose, glancing at Yonus. "Does that translate? The word *infection*?"

"I'm calling it the eyesight stealer." Yonus shrugged.

Abby nodded. "I like that even better," she said, before continuing to demonstrate. "So it will keep the eyesight stealer from...well"—she shrugged her shoulders—"stealing your eyesight."

Steady glanced at the dark faces around him once Yonus had fallen silent in his translation. He didn't need to speak the language to know the Orang Asli were eager to give Abby's remedy a try. One man stuck his finger into the goo and lifted it to his nose, inhaling deeply. His expression was intrigued as he offered his finger to the rest of the villagers.

Steady had to roll in his lips to keep from chuckling as a dozen dark heads leaned in to give the paste the ol' sniff test. But when he looked over at Abby standing in the middle of them, her skin dewed with sweat and her pale green eyes bright with enthusiasm, all his laughter died. Because in that instant everything, *everything*, suddenly became clear. Cut-glass clear. Mountain rain clear. As if he'd been clocked in the skull with a two-by-four of crystal-clear truth.

He *loved* her.

"Abby…" Her name was on his lips before he could call it back. He didn't know why. All he knew was that he needed to say it.

"I know." She laughed when one of the women of the tribe timidly touched a lock of her hair. "We need to be on our way. I know."

Sí. They probably did. For many reasons, not the least of which was that he was itching to find a pay phone or a landline or even an electrical outlet with which to juice up his iPhone. He needed to call back to HQ to see if they had a status update on Ozzie. His best friend's situation had been a constant presence in the back of his mind. But…that wasn't what he meant. He meant… "Abby…"

And there it was again. Her name. Slipping from between his lips of its own accord. And each time he said it, it rang inside him like a promise…like a prayer. Which made sense since the good *Madre Maria* knew he was tempted to fall at her feet as a penitent, pledging to worship her forever.

"Okay, Carl—" Her words cut off the instant she looked into his face. No surprise, really. Considering some of what he was feeling had to be plastered there. I mean, he was thunderstruck. Awestruck. Dumbstruck. Every kind of *struck* you can imagine.

He waited breathlessly for her response to the love in his eyes, to the adoration scrawled across his face as if he'd written it there with a big black Sharpie. But then he realized his expression couldn't be all that obvious when she said, "Oh, what the hedge cutter's ass? Are you sick or something? Was it the rambutans?"

Hedge cutter's ass? Oh, Abby. Sweet, wonderful, hilarious *Abby...*

And just like that, the laughter was back. This time, he didn't try to contain it. This time he let loose with it. Let it echo up into the roiling, cloud-filled sky. Let it fill his chest, and warm his heart.

He loved her!

If it wouldn't have scared the ever-loving crap out of the villagers, he would have shouted it to the world. Roared it through the jungle like a lion. And fuck the fact that he was a *maldito bori* and she was the president's daughter. Fuck the right side of the tracks versus the wrong side of the tracks. Fuck everything that had ever kept them apart in the past or threatened to keep them apart in the future. Because he *loved* her. And, by *Dios*, if it took him moving heaven and earth to have her, that's exactly what he'd do!

As if the universe knew and understood the weight of the pledge he'd made, the boiling clouds chose that second to rip open. Rain surged from the sky in a deafening roar, drenching him in an instant. He continued to laugh, lifting his arms wide as he let the downpour wash away the last remaining vestiges of the hurt he'd felt when Abby rejected him eight years ago. Let it wash away any lingering doubt that she would reject him again.

He was hers. And she was his. And she had to *see* that. She had to *know* that.

With one last bellow of unfettered delight, he lowered his arms and his chin. Rain sluiced off his face in sheets, running into his eyes. But he had no trouble seeing the shocked, wary expressions of the villagers. They probably thought he'd lost his mind. Flipped his lid. Gone clean crazy. And, in a way, he had. Because from one second to the next, he'd fallen crazy, head-over-heels in love.

A bolt of lightning crashed overhead, cleaving the angry clouds in two and casting the tiny village in harsh, white light. The tart smell of electricity burned through the air, and somewhere in the distance a monkey screeched out a frightened call. Then it was as if a spell had broken. The villagers jumped and scattered, climbing up ladders to run inside their high-built huts. The children screamed with glee as they raced in from the stream's edge, scampering up the latticework built beneath their bamboo homes to disappear inside. And Abby...well, Abby stood there in the deluge, gaping at him.

And, yes, she, too, probably suspected some of his screws had come loose. And maybe he was proving her right by grabbing her wrist and jerking her forward. Maybe he *had* gone stark-raving mad. But the truth of the matter was he didn't give a rat's...uh...hedge cutter's ass. Because he *loved* her. And, *hue puta,* he wasn't going to go one more second without letting her know it.

"Carl—"

But that's all she managed before he threw his arms around her, lifting her feet from the waterlogged ground and dipping his head to hungrily claim her mouth. Since it was already gaping open in a little *O* of surprise, it made it that much easier to slide his tongue inside. He tasted her, savored her, drank in her surprise and bewilderment, and gave back promises of devotion and tenderness. She was so sweet, so pure. Her breath candied by the lingering juice of the rambutans. And despite the fact that he'd filled his belly, he was ravenous. Starving. So hungry for her that he probably would have laid her down right there in the mud and the muck, showed her with his hands and mouth and body all the things he felt for her, had not an incessant tapping on his shoulder forced him to lift his head.

"What is it?" he growled, a little surprised to see Yonus standing in the rain beside them. He'd completely forgotten the man existed.

"You should take shelter in the ceremonial hut!" Yonus yelled above the violent *crack* of another bolt of lightning. The rain had drenched the man's jeans, darkening the material and causing them to hang heavily on his thin frame. He was pointing to the central structure at their backs. "I will go take refuge with the family next door"—he hooked a thumb over his shoulder—"and come for you once the storm has passed! My truck is parked on a logging road about a mile away! I can drive you to a petrol station and then take you back to your motorcycle!"

And suddenly Steady remembered why laying Abby down in the mud and the muck was out of the question. Because it was time for them to be on their way toward the safety of the Thai border. Well *past* time for them to be on their way.

Flicking a harried look toward the edge of the village where the jungle grew thick and green, blinking away the rain that ran into his eyes, he tried to imagine dragging Abby through the undergrowth in the middle of this torrential downpour. She could do it, he knew. Hell, the wonderful woman had proved she could do almost anything. But was that really their best option?

Lifting his wrist, he checked the time, doing some quick calculations. Afternoon storms here tended to be violent and fleeting. Lasting no more than an hour or two. So, even if he decided to take off and haul Abby through the worst of the drencher, they still wouldn't be able to make better time than simply staying here, waiting out the storm, and taking Yonus up on his offer of a ride. Though, unbeknownst to the young Orang Asli man, he wouldn't be carting them back to the Ducati, but rather the remaining ten miles to Thailand.

Glancing down at Abby, he was charmed to discover she looked like a drowned kitten. Her hair was plastered to her head, her eyes blinking against the pouring rain, and her succulent little mouth was back to forming the perfect *O. Jesús Cristo!* Did she have any idea what a temptation she was? Probably not. But, if things went his way, he was just about to show her.

"It's a deal!" he yelled to Yonus.

Chapter Fifteen

"WHAT THE FRICKIN' STICKS HAS GOTTEN INTO YOU, Carlos?" Abby demanded incredulously, plopping down on the palm-leaf mat spread across the floor of the little ceremonial hut. "Is rain some kind of aphrodisiac for you or something?" she asked while twisting the water out of her sodden hair. "What's with kissing the bejeezus out of me right there in the center of the village, in the middle of a torrential downpour, with our new buddy Yonus playing the part of the unwitting voyeur?" *And FYI, your mouth should come with its own warning label: Caution! These lips have been known to melt ovaries!*

And as if all those things she mentioned weren't odd enough by themselves, there was the nutty way he'd thrown his head back, laughing up at the rain like he was...well...Gene frickin' Kelly or something. Seriously, had there been a lamppost nearby, she wouldn't have been all that surprised to see him gaily swinging himself around it. She couldn't help but wonder if he'd contracted some sort of weird, psychedelic jungle fever.

She eyed him askance when he dropped down beside her, running his big hands over his face, sluicing the water from the black stubble darkening his jaw. He lowered his fingers, and she wasn't all that surprised to find him grinning at her. Obviously, whatever jungle fever he'd contracted wasn't the sweating/chills/vomiting kind, but the deliriously happy/laughing manically kind.

And then there was the stupid, adorable, *tempting* dimple.

"Don't you know by now, *mi vida*," he chuckled, the low sound reverberating inside her chest—Was it her imagination, or had his voice dropped an octave while his accent thickened into patented Latin Lover mode?—"that *everything*, given the right context, is an aphrodisiac to a man?"

Yep. So it *wasn't* her imagination. Rolling her eyes—and trying with all her might to ignore the sudden burst of flames that ignited low in her belly—she opened her mouth to remind him that now was not the time and this was definitely not the place, when another flash of lightning blazed overhead. It created a strobe effect through the paper-thin spaces between the poles of bamboo that made up the walls of the hut. And a second later, the accompanying *crash* of thunder rattled the entire structure. The rain hammering against the leafy roof reminded her of the time her father had taken the family on a trip to see Yosemite Falls. And all of it combined seemed to highlight the fact that this little hut had become their island in the storm, a private oasis cutting them off from the rest of the world.

Emphasis on the word *private*.

And given the hot look in his eyes right now, that could prove to be very dangerous. She may have managed to resist him and his damned dimple and his pretty penis once, but she didn't trust herself to be able to do it again.

Not the time or the place, remember? Yep. She *did* remember. But did he? Once again, she tried to remind him of the fact. But this time she was thwarted not by the lightning, but by Carlos himself. He suddenly leaned over, lifting her damp hair off her neck.

"You have a tattoo," he said like it was an accusation.

Jesus, Mary, and Joe Cocker! She hadn't been thinking when she'd wrung out her hair. The deep-red rose inked near her hairline was something she'd never meant him to see.

Thinking fast, she said the first thing to pop into her head. "Well, so do you. A *lot* of tattoos. And I've been meaning to ask you what they say."

When he dropped her hair to hold out his wide hands, palms up so that the intricate black scroll on the insides of his flexing forearms was visible, she heaved a sigh of relief. She'd distracted him from asking her about the symbolism of her tattoo. And that was good. Just as now was not the time or place for kisses and hot Latin looks, neither was it the time or place for her confession. When they were home, when they were safe, when he could walk away from her and never look back, *that's* when she'd tell him.

And forget the fact that her stomach hollowed out at the mere thought.

"This one"—he pointed to the words in Spanish sketched into his right arm—"says, 'Mess with the best.'"

"Mess with the best?" She lifted an intrigued eyebrow.

"*Sí.*" He nodded, his dark, wet hair curling across his forehead. A drop of crystalline water glinted near his temple, and she was tempted to reach up and brush it away. "And this one says, 'Die like the rest.'"

Mess with the best, die like the rest...

Her jaw unhinged as a shiver of awareness and... wariness...skittered across her nerve endings. When she looked into his eyes, into those deep, black eyes fringed by those thick, dark lashes, she didn't see the handsome, happy-go-lucky medical student she'd known back in college. Instead she saw the man he'd grown into. The hardened soldier, the…take-no-prisoners, no-guts-no-glory *warrior* who'd taken his place. And not for the first time since he dropped back into her life, she couldn't help but feel a bit of remorse. Because he never would have *become* this man, this hard-assed, battle-scarred man, if not for—

"It's an Army Ranger slogan," he told her, reaching over to give her a friendly nudge. The place where his elbow gently connected with her upper arm was suddenly hypersensitive. "Makes me seem tougher than I really am."

"I seriously doubt that." In the last few days, and more specifically, in the last few hours, he'd proved to be the toughest sonofagun she'd ever met, which just made him that much harder to resist. I mean, what woman *wouldn't* want to throw herself into the arms of a man who was a real-life doctor turned soldier—and when the moment called for it—turned sex god?

Ride me…

Those two simple words echoed through her head until goose bumps erupted over every inch of her flesh. When she raked in a deep breath, she fancied she could smell the rain on his skin, the gun black he used to clean his weapon, and the lingering hint of the open road mixed with the jungle's wet foliage.

Shaking her head to scatter her thoughts, she pointed to the edges of the black tattoo on his back. It peeked from the armholes and the collar of his tank top, giving her intriguing hints of what might lie beneath. "And that one?" she asked.

For a moment he regarded her quietly, his eyes like lasers cutting through the dim light inside the hut. Outside, the rain continued to pound. Inside, her heart did the same, clattering against her ribs like the wooden wind chimes she'd installed in a tree back at the DC Botanic Garden. Something in his face made her eyebrows pinch together.

"You don't have to show me," she hastily added, "if you don't w-w-w..."

Her words stuttered to a stop because he reached over his head, grabbed a handful of wet, army-green cotton in a fist, and whipped his tank top off. Tossing it aside, it landed on the floor of the hut with a gentle *splat*.

Sweet son of a monkey's uncle...

The man was just so...*pretty*. And, no, there was no other way to describe him. Because his skin was impossibly smooth and tan. His shoulders were impossibly wide and muscled. His pecs were impossibly defined around his flat, brown nipples. His stomach was impossibly corded and ripped. And then there was that line of black hair...trailing from his navel down into his camouflage cargo pants.

In short, he should *not* have wasted time on a medical degree or in Army Ranger training. Instead, he should have been a Calvin Klein underwear model. Either that or the subject for anatomy textbooks.

Even the raised white ridge of scar tissue cutting across his bicep and the jagged red line of skin puckered on his flank didn't seem to detract from the overall... well...*prettiness* of him. Although she'd already learned her lesson about using *that* word in conjunction with any of his body parts.

She bit her tongue when he turned to show her the monster tattoo stretching across his broad back from shoulder to shoulder and from below his neck to the small of his waist. Of course, with the thing clamped between her teeth, it was a wonder she didn't chew it clean off. Because the ink was equal parts fascinating and terrifying.

In deep, impenetrable black, a screaming skull with the coils of a fat serpent slithering from its gaping mouth sat atop two crossed machine guns. An Army Ranger cap had been drawn onto the bony skull, Carlos's battalion number scrawled across a tattered patch above the bill. A huge knife seemed to skewer the skeletal face under its chin. And surrounding it all was a set of intricately drawn angel's wings. They worked to soften and offset the harshness of the skull and weapons. And the feathers...they looked so real she would not have been shocked had they fluttered in the breeze drifting in under the flap of burlap covering the door to the hut. Again in Spanish, winding beneath the whole thing, was a string of beautifully scrolled words.

"Wh-what does it say?" she asked. Her voice sounded like she'd been swallowing cactus needles. But she was so riveted, so...*moved* by the artwork, it was a wonder she could speak at all.

"Rangers lead the way," he told her, glancing over his shoulder.

And, yes, she'd known when he joined the Army eight years ago that he wouldn't be content to stay back behind the front lines. She'd known even then that when he decided to leave the green lawns of Georgetown behind, he was doing so with every intention of jumping into the fray and *leading the way*.

How she'd wanted to save him from all of that. How she *tried* to save him from all of that.

When she forced her gaze away from the intricate details of his tattoo, she discovered his eyes on her, his expression unreadable. She tilted her head, wondering what he was thinking. But then he flexed his shoulders and the wings along his back seeming to expand. She couldn't help herself.

Lifting her hand, she ran a tentative finger over one of those elaborate feathers. His tough, smooth flesh quivered beneath her touch, and she was keenly aware of how warm he was. How solid. How…*near*.

Suddenly, it was as if all the air had been sucked from the room. She couldn't draw a breath.

"You hate it, don't you?" he asked quietly, turning so they were once again face-to-face, stretching his long legs out in front of him and crossing them at the ankles. He planted his hands behind him, leaning back. His expression was hard, his black eyes flinty.

"Hate it?" she managed to suck in enough oxygen to ask. "Hate what? Your tattoo?"

He nodded, a muscle ticking beneath the stubble of his jaw.

"H-how could I hate it, Carlos? It's *beautiful*. And fierce. Just like you."

And there she'd gone again. Basically telling him he was pretty…

But this time he didn't call her on it. His Adam's apple bobbed in the column of his throat as he sat there, watching her with hooded eyes. When he finally did speak, his voice barely audible above the rumble of thunder overhead, his words bewildered her. "It shows how different we are."

Wha? "What do you mean?" Different how? Besides the obvious, of course. Because he was strong and brave and beautiful. And she was weak and cowardly and… well…on a good day she could maybe pass for *cute*.

"You're the well-to-do politician's daughter who went to private schools and summer camps. And I'm the son of immigrants who barely had two pennies to rub together. I bet the men you date aren't covered in tattoos."

She frowned, shaking her head. "First of all, I rarely date. Being the president's daughter tends to draw out the crazies or the power-hungry. And I could do without either in my life, thank you very much. And secondly, what's this all about, Carlos?"

"It's about the day of Rosa's funeral when I came to your hotel room," he ground out, quickly glancing down at the mat beneath them. She'd seen something that was heartrendingly close to pain in his eyes in that split second before he turned away. "It's about me needing you, and you rejecting me and sending me packing."

The silence that followed that announcement was so loud it was almost deafening. And Abby's throat was instantly sore, thick with unshed tears.

He'd *needed* her? Big, tough, beautiful Carlos Soto had *needed* her?

The memory of that soul-sucking day flashed through her mind…

"Abby!"

The sound of her name and the pounding of a heavy fist on the hotel door had her scampering from atop the bed where she'd been sprawled for the last hour, crying her eyes out until all her mascara had run onto the pristine white pillowcase. Wiping one hand under her nose and the other beneath her leaking eyes, she straightened the lines of her black dress—which she planned to burn *at the first opportunity—and glanced around the room looking for...what? Escape? Did she think it was possible to grow a set of wings and fly from the tenth floor window?*

She stilled, her breath sawing from her lungs as she looked past the balcony doors and into the bright, unwavering sun of the Miami afternoon. The thought held a speck, the tiniest, smallest, oh-so-infinitesimal kernel of temptation. If she jumped, it would all be over. She wouldn't have to live with the terrible knowledge that a woman she'd grown to love like a sister was dead. If she jumped, she wouldn't have to open that door and lie straight to the hurting, anguished face of the man she'd come to adore with all her broken, shattered heart. If she jumped—

"Abby! Dios! *Tell them it's okay to let me in!" Carlos's voice thundered again, making her flinch, making her realize how scary and how cowardly her thoughts had become. Of* course *she couldn't jump. Jumping solved nothing. Jumping didn't turn back time or lift Rosa from the grave. It didn't change the fact that the coffin they'd lowered into the cold, dark ground beside the final resting places of Rosa's parents had been mostly empty; a symbolic gesture more than an actual vessel for Rosa's scant earthly remains.* Holy hell, *it was all so horrific. So horrific and so*

unbearable. But maybe if she opened that door and told Carlos the truth—

You can't tell him the truth. *Her father's voice rang inside her pounding skull.* It won't do anybody any good, and it could possibly do my chances of election a whole lot of bad.

"Come on, Mitchell," she could hear Carlos cajole. "You know me. You know I—"

"Miss Thompson," Agent Mitchell called through the door, his low voice booming like a bass drum and abrading her already frayed nerves. In that moment, she couldn't help but wish all of this, the agents, the stupid election, the awful destruction a nineteen-year-old college student could cause with one ill-timed text, would just go away. "I can have him escorted from the premises if you—"

"No!" she screamed, racing across the room. "Don't do that!" She threw open the door.

And then, there he was. Carlos. So smart. So sweet. So handsome in his suit and undone tie. So... everything a young girl dreamed about.

For months she'd hoped he would see her as more than the slightly troublesome, sometimes funny teenager who hung on his sister's every word. For months she'd wished he would see her as the kind of full-grown woman she'd been desperately trying to become. The kind of woman worthy of the attention of someone like him.

But now she thanked her lucky stars he'd never come to think of her as anything more than a kid, his twin sister's sarcastic little protégé. Because if he felt for her even half of what she felt for him, it would make the lie she'd agreed to tell just that much more terrible.

"Abby." He pushed passed the two men in black suits and shoulder holsters positioned on either side of her hotel door. Years… If her father won the election, she would have to suffer years more—at least four and possibly eight—of this complete and utter lack of privacy.

For a moment, she considered throwing it all away. If she confessed to Carlos, if she confessed to the world, *perhaps her father wouldn't win and then everything, her* life, *could go back to normal. She'd never wanted any of this anyway…*

For a second, the idea, the temptation, *took hold, making her heart race with the possibilities. But in the next breath, she knew she couldn't ruin her father's dream, destroy everything he'd worked for his entire life. It wouldn't be fair to him. It wouldn't be fair to her mother, who'd spent long, exhausting hours on the campaign trail, giving speeches and living on greasy roadside food. It wouldn't be fair to Caroline, who was riding on their father's coattails to possibly win a seat in the House of Representatives.*

"I didn't know where else to go," Carlos said as she nodded to her security detail and closed the door. "With our parents gone—" He suddenly stopped and ran a hand back through his hair, choking. That sound… that defeated sound coming from the throat of a man who'd always seemed invincible, had tears welling and spilling freely down her cheeks. Her chest burned like she'd swallowed a handful of poison sumac. "Thank the good Madre Maria *they didn't live long enough to see this day. To see her… empty," he husked the words, "casket lowered into the ground."*

To keep from reaching out to him, she gripped her

hands so tightly in front of her that her short nails threatened to draw blood. Touching him was out of the question. She had no right.

"None of our friends loved her like you did." He turned to her, his brilliant black eyes full of tears. "That's why I had to come. Because you're the only one who can understand what I'm—"

A sob cut him off before he could finish. And that's when he reached for her. Dear God! *He pulled her to him, wrapping his arms around her as he laid his cheek atop her head and cried. Carlos was crying! She could feel his hot tears seeping into her hair, feel his big body shake with the enormity of his grief. And how long had she waited to be taken into his embrace? How long had she dreamed of holding him close and placing her head against his chest?*

But it was never meant to be like this. Never like this…

"Carlos." She tried to pull back even though it was the last thing she wanted. If she were to die right here, wrapped up in him, it would be fine by her. In fact, a part of her wished for it. Then the pain would stop. "I can't—"

His arms tightened, keeping her close. Oh, the glorious torture of it. Of breathing him in. Of hearing his heart hammer so solidly against her ear. Of knowing that he'd shove her away in a nanosecond if he knew what—

"I'm dropping out," he confessed. "I'm joining the Army. I need to make sure those—"

"No." This time she was successful in pushing out of his arms. "Carlos, no! You're a doctor! A wonderful *doctor. Don't throw that away. Rosa"—the woman's name stuck in her throat as if she'd tried to*

swallow a whole grapefruit in one gulp—"wouldn't want you to—"

"It's done." He wiped a hand under his nose. His tan face was splotchy from crying, the whites of his eyes an angry, heartrending red. "I need an outlet for all this violence inside me."

She grabbed his forearms in a desperate grip. "We're at war! You could be killed!" The thought was untenable. Intolerable.

"Come here." He reached for her again. "Hold me, Abby."

She wrenched herself from his grip, her heart beating frantically. She could maybe—the jury was still out—live with Rosa's blood on her hands. But Carlos's? No. No! "Call the dean," she begged him. "He'll let you back into the program. He'll let you finish your rotations, and—"

"My decision is made," he told her. "Now, come here. I want you to—"

"No, Carlos."

He lifted a brow, shaking his head in confusion. "What? I don't underst—"

"I need you to... to go. I have to..." Call her father or... or the dean. Something! *She shook her head, begging him with her eyes.*

His chin jerked back a second before his expression hardened. "I see."

Did he?

"Okay, then..." He swallowed, his throat seeming to have trouble with the maneuver. "So, I guess I... I guess I'll be seeing you."

"What?" Why did that sound like a final farewell? "Wait! I—"

When he turned to her, the smile on his face was the saddest thing she'd ever seen. It hit her with the force of a wrecking ball and she nearly doubled over with the impact of it. "I do *understand, Abby," he assured her. "But even though..." he trailed off, swallowing again as he reached for the door. "Just... if you ever need me... don't hesitate to call, okay?"*

And then, just like that, he was gone. Never to be seen again until a few days ago. Though he'd always remained a constant in her thoughts, in her heart, in her *life,* seeing as how that was the deal she'd struck with her father. *You promise to keep an eye on Carlos and let me know of any change in his circumstances, and I promise to keep living the lie.*

And, oh! How she'd *hated* her father for tossing Carlos out of the frying pan of the Rangers once his stint with the Army was up and into the fire of Black Knights Inc. She'd threatened to go to Carlos and tell him the truth, but her father had assured her it had been Carlos's decision. He could have finished medical school. He could have joined the Secret Service. He'd *chosen* the Black Knights. *Chosen* them of his own free will because that's the life he apparently wanted. And so she'd held her tongue. Again.

When she lifted her eyes to his now, it took everything she had to stop her hot tears from spilling over her lower lids. Despite the warm, humid air inside the hut, she was cold. Cold through and through. Down to her bones. Down to her soul.

"I didn't reject you that day," she whispered, shivering. "I swear I didn't. I sent you away because I had to call my father, call the dean, call whoever would listen to me and whoever might have the power to persuade you not to join the Army."

His brows pulled together, his frown smoothing away his dimple. "So *that's* why they both tried to talk me down? I always wondered why either of them would take an interest in me."

"But nothing would dissuade you." She shook her head. "You were so stubborn. So determined."

"I was hungry for retribution," he admitted. "I wanted to make those cowardly *hijos de putas* who killed my sister—and all the other evil men in the world—pay for what they'd done."

"And have you?" she asked, searching his face, not allowing herself to focus on the fact that she herself fell into the category of one of those cowardly *hijos de putas*. "Did the battles in Fallujah or Lashkagar or Sangin or all the missions you've been on with the Black Knights quench your thirst for vengeance?"

He tilted his head. It was strange that, at a time like this, she should notice the crystalline drop of water that hung from the lobe of his left ear. It slowly coalesced and fell to the mat and she found herself watching its journey. Then her gaze was riveted to his face when, with narrowed eyes, he asked, "How do you know about those battles? Those missions?"

And shit on stick. She'd just outed herself. "I—" She had to stop and take a deep breath. There were those smells again, the rain on his skin, the gun black. "I made my father promise to keep tabs on you. I made him promise to tell me when something important happened in your life."

For a moment, he didn't move, simply continued to watch her with searching intensity. Then he jerked his chin in a nod. "Well that explains the look on your face back in the jungle when I asked how you knew about the Black Knights," he said, his stern expression sliding into one of contemplation. "But why? Why would you do that?"

"Because losing Rosa"—even after all these years it was still difficult to say the woman's name—"nearly killed me. I couldn't bear the thought of losing you, too. I had to make sure you were alive. I had to know that you hadn't died out there on the battlefield. I had to *know*. It was the only way I could stay sane."

"But I never knew"—he shook his head—"I meant anything more to you than a fleeting acquaintance. I suspected you loved Rosa." Good Lord, more than he'd ever know. "But I didn't think you—"

"I *adored* you," she told him. She had no pride left. No shame. "I adored everything about you. The very ground you walked on. Which is why I had to make sure I hadn't lost you, too."

And just as it'd done all those years ago in that hotel room, his throat seemed to stick over a swallow. He was no longer lounging back on his hands, his legs stretched out in front of him. Now he was sitting forward, his black eyes drilling into her as surely as that pesky woodpecker continued to drill holes into her favorite sycamore tree back in DC. She almost winced under the sharp force of his gaze.

"And now?" he asked, his voice hoarse.

She knew what he was after. And considering all the years of lying, she felt it only right, only *fair*, that she give him this one irrefutable truth. "Oh, Carlos. I *still* adore you."

Chapter Sixteen

Had Steady ever felt such unfettered joy? Had he ever known such unmitigated bliss? It was like he'd taken a hand grenade of happiness to the chest, his heart blown wide open. And, *sí*, for a moment there, and despite what he'd told himself standing out in the rain, he'd allowed old hurts, old insecurities to seep in. But Abby…wonderful, delightful, beautiful Abby had obliterated all his self-doubt with four little words.

I still adore you…

His instincts took over before he formed another thought. Grabbing her wrist, he pulled her into his lap, cradling her against him, holding her as close as he'd always dreamed. Overwhelmed with the desire to get closer still. As close as a man and woman could possibly be… "Abby," he whispered her name, peppering her face with kisses. He drank the tears from her skin, reveling in their salty sweetness on his tongue. "Oh, Abby, I've always adored you, too, *cariño.* From the first day I met you, you're all I could think about. *Dios,* how I wanted you. It drove me mad."

He wasn't aware she'd been squirming, struggling in his embrace, until she suddenly stilled, going stiff as the scalpels back in his duffel bag. He lifted his head to look down at her, not surprised to find her eyes wide. But the fragile, volatile expression on her face gave him pause. "What is it, *neña*?"

"Y-you *wanted* me? All those years ago, you w-w…" She didn't go on, simply shook her head in disbelief. He smiled down at her, loving the way her wet hair curled around her face. Loving the faint pink color of her makeup-free lips. Loving how her long lashes turned from dark brown near her lids to blond up at the tips. Loving *her*.

"Of course I did," he told her, bending to kiss her nose. "You were like this delightful, spritely, incandescent thing capable of lighting up the whole world. I was a moth to your flame, Abby. Surely you knew that."

And he was accused of being reticent with details? Well, how about *them* details? He'd damn near waxed poetic! *Hooah!*

She shook her head. Then, in consternation, he watched her face crumble before she buried her nose into his bare chest.

"Hey, now," he murmured, rocking her from side to side, patting her narrow back, taking pleasure in her smallness, in her nearness. "What's this all ab—"

That's all he managed before she pushed back to look at him, her green eyes puffy and swollen, the tip of her nose shiny. The poor woman was a mess, no joke. And, at the same time, he'd never seen her looking more beautiful.

"I didn't know." She shook her head. "Why didn't you ever *say* anything?"

"You were so young, Abby. *Too* young. And even if that wasn't the case, I was a nobody. And you were the soon-to-be president's daughter."

"Why do you keep saying that like it's a *thing*?"

And although he didn't think it was possible to love her any more, those simple, heartfelt words had the warmth in his chest, the joy in his heart expanding tenfold. "Because, to most people, it *is* a thing."

"You're crazy," she insisted, catching her bottom lip between her teeth. His teeth itched to do the same. Catch that plump piece of flesh between them before he reintroduced his tongue to hers. "If anything, *you* were… *are*… the one who's too good for *me*."

His crack of laughter competed with the rumble of the deluge pounding on the roof. "Oh, Abby." He buried his face in her neck, inhaling the delightful aromas of cocoa butter lotion, dryer sheets, and clean, clear jungle rain. "Only you could possibly believe that." And, then, the idiot in his pants finally took notice of the fact that her skirt-covered bottom was pressing down on it. A telltale rush of blood surged to his groin.

His thoughts instantly turned from the past to the present. From old hurts and misunderstandings to new possibilities. He loved her. She admitted to adoring him—which wasn't exactly the same as dropping the L-bomb, but it was close, right? *Right.* And the storm was probably going to rage for at least another hour. So he had a minimum of sixty minutes to finally, *finally* do the things to her in reality that he'd been doing to her in his fantasies for nearly a decade.

It wasn't going to be enough. Not nearly enough. But it was a start. And for now, it'd have to do. He turned his face slightly, whispering in her ear, "I wanted you Abby. I wanted you then. I want you now. Let me have you."

~

Abby's body thrilled at his nearness, at his hot breath whispering in her ear. But her heart ached with sadness.

Oh, how she *wished* she could give him what he wanted. But, if she let him have her without him first knowing what had happened, her *part* in what had happened, it would be another deception. And she was finished with lies. Finished with secrets.

She'd wanted to wait. Wait until they were somewhere safe. Somewhere he wouldn't think twice about heading for the door and leaving her behind. But, unfortunately, the time for her confession had come…

"Carlos," she whispered, her breath shuddering when he flicked his tongue into her ear. Her toes curled at the warm, wet intrusion. Her sex throbbing when her mind conjured up the image of him sticking it somewhere much more intimate. "There's something you need to know about—Oh, *God!*"

His hand had traveled under her tunic. His big, callused fingers finding her nipple and pinching gently. She felt that caress from her breast all the way down to her clitoris. The little bundle of nerves tingled violently with every skillful pluck of his fingers.

No. No! She couldn't give in to the pleasure he pressed on her, to the hot demand of his mouth when his lips landed atop hers. She turned her head, panting. Dizzy. "There's something I have to tell you, something you have to know."

"Not now, Abby," he groaned, taking her hand and placing it over his distended fly. She'd felt the twitch of his big thigh muscles beneath her bottom, noticed the subtle trembling of his solid arms around her, but that was nothing compared to the throb of his hardened length against her palm. So big. So hot. So tempting. It took everything she had not to curl her fingers around him. "I want you too badly." He bit the flesh over her throat, his teeth a gentle, stinging reminder of the power he kept in check. Her breath huffed from her lungs in a stuttering exhale. Her brain went fuzzy with passion, with pleasure. "I've wanted you for too long. I need you to let me—"

"But you wouldn't want me if—"

"God, Abby," he implored her, flipping her onto her back against the mat, wedging his hips between her thighs and stroking against her. Her eyes crossed and threatened to roll back in her head. "Please, *please.* Let me have you. Let me show you all the things I've been dreaming of showing you since you were eighteen."

Sonofa—! This man. This man was *killing* her. And in that moment, for one split second, she allowed herself to revel in her own glorious death.

"B-but the—" she began, only to lose her words on a gasp as he stroked forward again. The cotton of her skirt was deliciously abrasive, damp from the deluge and from her body's excitement.

"Don't worry," he said between kisses against her throat. "We have a while. Long enough, I think. And the rain will drown out our cries."

Their cries…

Holy cannoli! Just the thought of Carlos throwing his head back, crying out her name as an orgasm burst through him, as he poured his lust inside her, made her blood pop and fizz like it was carbonated.

"I hurt, Abby," he breathed against her lips. She opened her eyes to find him looming over her, his palms braced on either side of her head, his shoulders bulging with the strain of holding himself aloft. Black hair fell across his forehead and his midnight eyes sparkled in the dim light, imploring her even more than his words. "I hurt so badly from wanting you. Let me have you."

And in that moment she knew she'd give him anything. She may hate herself later, and he would *certainly* hate her later. But right here and right now she would let him have, let him *take*, anything he wanted. Swallowing down the ache at the back of her throat, refusing to let the tears pricking behind her eyes fall, she wrapped her arms around his neck, and pulled his mouth down to hers, whispering against his lips, "Okay, Carlos. Take me…"

The celebration that occurred inside Steady's head was the equivalent of New Year's Eve, the Fourth of July, and Mardi Gras all rolled into one. Because Abby had just agreed to let him have her. Not forever, mind you. But for right now. And after he made love to her, he figured her agreeing to forever was just around the corner.

Not to blow his own whistle or anything—especially when he was *sooo* looking forward to having her blow it for him; come on, he was a guy, after all—but he was good at this. He'd spent a lot of years and a lot of time practicing, and it dawned on him that it'd all been in preparation for this moment right here. Those previous women, those one-night stands he'd thought were simply outlets for his nervous energy or ways to pass the time, had really been training for this. When he'd finally take Abby in his arms and make her his own, mind, body, and soul.

And though there were probably some women who wouldn't appreciate his gratitude, he sent out a silent thanks to every lovely *mamacita* who'd taken the time to teach him the infinite wonders of the female body. From the dark-eyed girl who pulled him behind the bleachers his sophomore year of high school to the brown-skinned beauty in Marrakesh who showed him how to accurately find a woman's G-spot. He praised them all for their generous tutelage. Because now he could spend the rest of his life giving pleasure to one woman. The woman of his heart…

And speaking of the woman of his heart, the kiss she pressed on him was wet and sweet. A little bit tentative and so fucking hot he almost forgot his manners—and all the lessons he'd learned—and stripped that wet skirt from her hips so he could plunge into her, balls deep.

But he managed to rein himself in…just barely. And when he lowered some of his weight atop her, when he wrapped his arm under her head to provide a pillow, he realized how perfectly she fit him. *Sí*, she was small in comparison, but her hips were womanly, creating a soft cradle for his. Her breasts were supple, providing the ideal cushion for his heavy chest. And her legs…

Sweet Jesús Cristo! Had there ever been a sexier pair of gams than Abby's? If so, he'd never seen them. Because her calves were slim yet muscular and her ankles impossibly delicate. She bent her knees, squeezing his hips with her thighs and tucking her feet on the insides of his knees to better align their bodies…their sexes.

He could feel her wet heat all the way through both sets of material. And he'd always been a little controlling in the bedroom, but her overt femininity made him want to pound his chest like Tarzan and pound his cock into her soft, giving body over and over and *over* again! *Mierda!*

There went those reins again. Slipping…

Okay, okay, deep breaths.

Then again, deep breaths were a bit hard to accomplish with her agile tongue darting hungrily in and out of his mouth. With her industrious hands smoothing over his back to squeeze his ass. With her rubbing herself against him until his eyes crossed and his toes curled inside his jungle boots.

So first things first, he had to slow things down. Manacling her wrists in one hand, he pinned her arms above her head. "Slowly," he instructed, lessening the frenzied fervor of the kiss, gently nipping at the corners of her delicious lips.

"Carlos," she panted, and he pulled back to see her cheeks flushed with passion, her eyes half-lidded and pleading. "Please, I—"

"Slowly," he repeated. "Very slowly, Abby, I want you to open your mouth and offer me your tongue." There was just something about seeing her do that. Probably because she'd had a habit of licking her lips back in college that'd driven him absolutely wild—and given him a million nut-tightening fantasies of her turning to offer him a taste.

Her eyes widened. She swallowed. And then he could feel her tremble beneath him as her sweet-tasting breath huffed against his chin, tickling him, delighting him. His hardened length thudded heavily, begging to be set free. But he resisted—just barely—the urge to reach down and undo his fly so he could rub himself against the inside of her silky thigh.

He watched avidly as her pupils dilated and her moistened lips parted, revealing the pink enchantment that was her little tongue. A surge of new blood rushed to his groin, taking everything up a notch.

"Good girl," he said before dipping his chin. He tasted her offering, gently sucking the delicate tip of her tongue into his mouth. She moaned, writhing beneath him, bucking her hips, seeking more pleasure, more stimulation. And he would give it to her. Soon. But first…

"Shhh, *cariño*," he soothed against her lips. "We will get where you need to go. But we will take our time, no?" And he couldn't help but notice the inflections he used, his accent, tended to thicken when he was being ridden hard by lust.

And, *Dios,* he'd never been ridden this hard. Because his love for Abby, his complete and total adoration of her, made everything that much more urgent, that much more…*poignant*. Which meant he was all the more determined to make this time, this first time they were together, as memorable, as *pleasurable* as possible.

Carefully, with infinite care, he showed her what could be accomplished with teeth and lips and tongue. He showed her all the different ways to suck and lick, to give pleasure and to take. He didn't know how many minutes passed. And the truth was, he would have been happy to spend the rest of eternity simply kissing her. But the way she was moving beneath him, so sinuously, so urgently, he knew she was desperate for the next step.

Breaking the seal of their lips had her moaning with frustration. "It's okay, *mi vida*," he said against her throat, sucking on her pulse point again and grinning in masculine approval when it caused her hips to buck beneath him. He lowered more of his weight atop her in order to keep her from rubbing herself to completion. Because the first time she came, it was going to be with his fingers inside her…or maybe his tongue. He hadn't decided which.

"Carlos," she cried. "God, I *ache!*"

"I know," he told her. "I ache, too. But *bueno*. It's good, no? The more it hurts right now, the better it will feel when I finally put myself inside you. You want me inside you, don't you?"

"Yes," she panted. "Yes. Please. Right now. I can't stand it."

"You *can* stand it," he assured her, reaching down to grab the hem of her tunic top. Slowly, so infinitely slowly, he pulled the garment up her body, watching as inch after inch of smooth, creamy flesh was revealed. Then, when the backs of his fingers brushed the soft, warm undersides of her breasts, he quickly whipped the shirt over her head. Bunching the tunic in a ball, he shoved it under her neck. Then he resecured her wrists in one hand, pulling her arms back above her head.

The wonderful woman had taken the opportunity of her shirt removal to leave little claw marks down his spine. And his dick came damn close to exploding as a result. If he was going to do this the right way, the way he wanted, he couldn't have her hands on him. It was too much temptation. Too much stimulation. And he was already so close to the edge.

"You can stand it," he said again. "Because it's what I want. And though you don't know it, it's what you want, too."

"You're a domineering bastard when it comes to this, aren't you?" she snarled, her chest rising and falling with each rapid breath. He looked down at the wonder he'd uncovered, at Abby's small, pale breasts. At her tiny pink nipples. And he nearly lost his mind. She was even more beautiful than he imagined. Even more delicately feminine.

"I am," he admitted, ducking his chin to gently suck one delectable bud into his mouth. She gasped and arched her back into a supple bow. The maneuver had her pelvis rubbing the tip of his cock, squeezing it delightfully against her pubic bone. "And you love it," he finished, taking the distended nub between his teeth to flick it with his tongue.

On the one hand she tasted like an angel, ethereal and exquisite. Like something from a dream. On the other hand, her flavor was that of a flesh-and-blood woman. Her skin was salty with sweat, sweet with lotion, and so damned hot it was a wonder it didn't singe his tongue. But regardless of whether or not she was corporeal or celestial, the truth was, he'd found heaven…

Chapter Seventeen

THE HARD LENGTH OF CARLOS INSIDE THOSE ass-hugging cargo pants was a rod of stimulation against the top of Abby's sex, a hot shaft that promised both temptation and satisfaction. She wanted that satisfaction right now, two minutes ago. But Carlos was almost dictatorial in his need to be the one to set the pace. And something inside Abby, something she'd never known was there, thrilled at his autocratic demands. Thrilled at the orders falling from his lips and the way he held her captive to his wants, his desires, all the while feeding her longing, fueling her lust higher and higher and *higher.*

She'd never wanted anything this badly before. Never *needed* anything this badly before. And it hurt her almost as much as it excited her.

"I'm going to take off that skirt now," he told her, her nipple popping free of his lips. His mouth was so hot the humid air inside the hut was almost cool against her tender, distended peak.

This is really happening. I'm really about to have all my fantasies come to life. I'm really about to make love to Carlos. She couldn't believe it!

And that niggle of doubt at the back of her head? That little voice that whispered she shouldn't be doing this? That he'd despise her more for it in the end? Well, it was silenced when he pushed up to his knees, letting go of her wrists to grab the waistband of her skirt.

Damn, but the man was pretty. Yes, *pretty.* There was just no other way to describe the way his dark skin glowed under the sheen of rain and sweat. The way his black eyes were like lasers inside the dimness of the hut. His heavy chest muscles and corded stomach muscles bunched and flexed as he slowly, ever so slowly pulled the wet skirt from her legs. Carelessly tossing it aside, he peeled the soft-soled shoes from her feet and dropped them to the mat. When her heels landed on the dried palm leaf, his position between her thighs kept her legs splayed and her sex… *Oh, God!*

Embarrassment or shyness or…*something* along those lines had her face flushing hot. She lifted her arms, ready to cover herself, but he stopped her.

"No, *bonita,*" he rasped, his deep voice heavy with desire as he caught her wrists in a firm grasp. Leaning over her, his warm chest brushing against her distended, aching nipples, he once against placed her hands behind her head. "You will keep them here for me, *sí*?" And, as if to lessen the demand in his tone, he placed a gentle kiss on her mouth. His day's growth of beard stubble was wonderfully abrasive against her lips. "I want to look at you. I want to *see* you."

She swallowed, nodding jerkily as he pushed back to his knees, doing just as he said he would. Slowly, so excruciatingly slowly, his gaze traveled down the length of her body. Past the quick rise and fall of her breasts, past the hollowed quiver of her stomach, to the place where she burned and ached.

His nostrils flared, and every inch of Abby's skin flushed with a deep blush. She'd never had a man look at her. Not like this. Not so openly. She couldn't stand it. She was too exposed, too vulnerable. And he was too…*intense*.

Covering her face with her hands, she whimpered his name.

"Don't be shy, *cariño*." He nudged her hands away. She bit her lip when she saw his eyes sparkling above her, his cheeks flushed pink with the heat of his desire. "Don't you know how beautiful you are?"

She shook her head. She'd wasn't beautiful. Cute, perhaps. But never beautiful. And that place on her body, her most intimate place, was never something—

"Oh, sweet heavens!" she cried when he reached down to spread her labia, pressing the rough pad of his thumb into the hard knot of nerves at the top of her sex.

"You are gorgeous." His eyes watched what his fingers were doing. "So pink. So plump and wet for me." His voice was solemn, almost reverent, as if he were worshiping her. And when his middle finger stroked into her like rough velvet, abrading the tender nerve endings that had been screaming for sensation, the good Lord knew she felt like a goddess. Powerful and divine. Her body having become a glorious instrument of pure pleasure.

"C-Carlos," she panted when he stroked her. Just that one thick finger. In and out. In and out. Until she thought she'd go crazy.

"*Sí, mi vida*," he growled, a muscle ticking in his jaw, his chest rising and falling heavily, telling her that he was enjoying this as much as she. "Tell me how it feels."

"So good," she rasped, lifting her hips so he could go deeper. "It feels so good."

"And this?" he asked as he slowly, gently forced another finger inside her, stretching her, filling her.

"Uhnn," she whimpered, her heart pounding, her lungs struggling to remember to breathe when every single synapse in her brain was focused on Carlos and the intense pleasure he inflicted on her body. "Yesss," she managed to hiss after a second. "Please, Carlos."

"Please, Carlos, what?" he asked, placing the pad of thumb on her clit and slowly caressing it in a tight, circular motion.

Abby was surprised she didn't spontaneously combust. Her blood was running so hot. Every inch of her skin was on fire. And her sex, where he stimulated her so well, was blazing like a furnace. "Please, make me come. I need you to—"

"Not yet," he grumbled, stroking her one last time before pulling his fingers from her.

She couldn't help herself, she growled her frustration as she clenched around the void his fingers had left behind.

"Shhh," he crooned, scooting back and going down on his belly on the mat. When she lifted her head, she saw his face no more than a few inches from her sex. But he wasn't returning her gaze. Oh, no. Once again, his attention was focused solely on the center of her, where she was, as he'd said, so pink and plump and wet. Only this time there was no embarrassment. Because the hot, yearning look in his eyes was impossible to miss. As was the hunger. And when he licked his lips like a man about to feast, her head dropped back to floor.

Sweet Jesus! He was so much hotter than she'd ever imagined he would be. So much more demanding and...*knowledgeable.*

Knowledgeable, oh, most certainly. Because when

he pressed his lips to her, he didn't hesitate or fumble like the few men she'd been with before. He didn't lap or stab at her clit with the point of his tongue. Heavens no. He simply wrapped his lips around the distended bud, pressed the flat of his raspy tongue against her, and licked up and down. Slowly and gently at first. Then more forcefully.

Son of biscuit. She was going to come. If he'd only add a finger inside her to what he was already doing with his mouth, that is. She was close. So wonderfully, frustratingly close. And she had to fight herself not to beg him for more, not to beg him to lick harder, lick faster. Because it seemed like every time she asked him for more, he punished her—the most decadent, erotic punishment—by slowing everything down. And that was, like, the sexiest catch-22 ever, wasn't it? Because that arrogant way he took control made her that much hotter, that much wetter, that much achier.

Holy Jeez! It was torture! Divine, sublime torture…

"Carlos," she couldn't stop his name from slipping from between her lips. "God, yes. That feels good."

He hummed his approval against her, and the added stimulus had her bare toes curling. Then her breath caught in the back of her throat, her arms lifting of their own accord so she could bury her hands in the sleek, warm riot of his black hair, when he slid first one, then a second finger inside her. He pumped twice, stretching her intimate flesh until he seated his fingers to the last knuckles.

She gasped. The pleasure was so intense she lost track of time and place. She had no idea where she was, no clue how long his sexual assault went on, how many minutes had passed since he'd begun her…*education.* All she knew was, if he kept that up, it was going to be over soon. And while one part of her lamented that, another part of her—a much stronger part—yearned for it. She needed release so badly. She hurt so—

"Oh, God!" she cried. Because right at that moment he curled his fingers in a come-hither motion inside her, caressing some hidden patch of nerves she'd never known existed. And like the lightning that blazed through the paper-thin cracks of the hut, she exploded…

Steady had never tasted anything as sweet as Abby's release. Salty and sexy, her flavor was one hundred percent pure, healthy woman. As she bucked and heaved, her nails digging into his scalp, the prick of pain just added to his pleasure, making his dick pulse heavily. And he'd never heard anything sexier than his name on her lips. She said it over and over again as her inner walls clamped and released his fingers so forcefully they ground his knuckles together.

Continuing to stroke and lick, he drank her in. Her essence, her passion. He consumed her until his senses were overcome, his entire being overwhelmed. And as the last remnants of orgasm rolled through her, he was tempted to rip open his fly, grab the base of his dick, and thrust inside that fiery slick body of hers. Just stroke and rut and screw until his own climax burst from him.

But…that would come later. Because no matter how much he might be tempted to assuage the ache in his balls, the painful stretch of his dick, he had other fantasies to fulfill. Fantasies of showing Abby more of the things he'd learned. Fantasies of taking her up that mountain of pleasure again and holding her there. Making her beg him to let her take the leap.

When her inner muscles stopped spasming, he slowly, carefully slid his fingers from her. A growl rumbled through his chest when, at the last moment, her body clenched around the tips of his digits. As if her sex didn't want him to go.

"*Jesús Cristo*, Abby," he breathed, placing a kiss to the tiny, baby-soft patch of trimmed blond hair at the top of her sex, then moving to plant one on the inside of her silky thigh. He breathed deep the musky aroma of sexy, sated woman as the rain continued to pound on the roof, keeping them cocooned inside the dry safety of the hut. "You're even hotter than I imagined."

She didn't answer him as he climbed up her body, leaving a trail of open-mouthed kisses along the way. One to her hip where her bone stretched her delicate skin tight. One to her cute oval belly button. One to her right breast that had her breath catching at the back of her throat. One to her left that had her moaning and fisting her hands tighter in his hair. And the last one he placed on her slack mouth.

Grinning against her lips, he reveled in his power over her, his ability to give her the kind of pleasure that left her dazed and disoriented. Then, holding himself above her, he watched her eyes slowly open. Her pupils were so dilated he could barely make out the misty green of her irises. Then the lovely, adorable, *sexy* woman caught her lower lip between her teeth and grinned.

"That was..." She cleared her throat, shaking her head as she continued to catch her breath. "It was just...*wow*."

Oh, Abby. Delightful, delectable Abby. "I'd say that about sums it up," he chuckled before resealing their lips.

Her tongue met his eagerly yet lazily. And since he'd become a man, since the moment he realized sex didn't have to be hot and heavy and *over* in a few minutes, he'd come to like this part the best. When his lover was sated and languorous. When she was soft and fulfilled. Because the beautiful thing about a woman's body was that it didn't need time to recover like a man's did. But the *challenge* was figuring out how to bring her back up, push her higher, past the pinnacle once again.

The good Madre Maria *knows I love a good challenge...*

And he figured with Abby he'd start with her nipples. He'd noticed how sensitive they were. How caressing them made her back bow and her neck arch. He hadn't spent much time on them earlier because he could tell fondling them, licking them made her too hot too quickly. And he'd wanted to draw out her orgasmic torture that first time. But now, *now* he figured it was the perfect opportunity to give them the attention they deserved.

Gently pulling his mouth from hers, he peppered her throat and chest with kisses before lazily catching her left nipple between his teeth. And as he'd expected, she gasped. Her back curving, a lovely little moan sounding in her throat.

With infinite, hard-won patience he suckled her, licking and laving and biting first one hard, pebbled peak, and then the next. Soon she was writhing beneath him, her breaths coming fast and hot, and had he still been sixteen, he would have pumped a fist. He was right. Abby's delicate breasts were the key to her libido.

Thank *Dios*! Because he was on fire, so horny his patience was quickly fraying. And before he lost control completely, before he allowed himself the ultimate pleasure of sinking into her little body, there was one more thing he wanted from her. One more thing he *needed* from her to make all of his fantasies come true.

Loving the sucking sound her nipple made as it popped free of his lips, he pushed to his knees, going to work on his belt and thigh holster. Carefully laying his weapon to the side, and not so carefully tossing his belt away, he stood to unlace his boots and shuck his cargo pants and boxers. Abby watched it all with soft, sparkling eyes. And when he towered above her, completely naked, he saw her swallow involuntarily.

Chuckling, he reached down to pull her to her knees. Grabbing the base of his dick in one hand, he softly slid the other into the hair on the back of her head.

"Suck me, Abby," he told her. "I want to feel your lips and tongue on me."

Authority in the bedroom was a core part of him, and though he'd shown her plenty over the last little while, he wondered how she'd react to this salacious demand. Would it be too much? He held his breath and waited.

Thank goodness, he didn't have to wait long. She gave him an answer when she sucked her bottom lip between her teeth, her chest rising rapidly, her eyes dropping hungrily to the rampant thrust of his cock.

Relief and love and joy burst inside him. Because she *liked* this side of him. More than liked it if the hot blush on her cheeks, the way her thighs quivered, was anything to go by. In fact, he would go so far as to say she *loved* it. Which meant, as he'd always subconsciously suspected, she was perfect for him. The perfect mix of bold willingness to match his gentle brand of dominance.

He watched, his testicles aching, as she leaned forward. Only instead of taking him into her mouth, she kissed the raised ridge of the scar on his flank. The muscles of his stomach rippled in response and he groaned, tightening his fist in her hair.

"Do it, Abby," he hissed, so close to the brink he could hardly stand it, hardly keep his knees from buckling beneath him.

Her green eyes glittered up at him. Then she parted her pink lips and flicked out her tongue to taste him.

"*Dios*," he rasped, clenching his jaw so tight it was a wonder he didn't shatter a molar. And when she closed her soft mouth over his swollen, aching head, he knew he'd just experienced rapture. He also knew he wouldn't last much longer.

Carlos smelled like sex and man. His shaft delicious and salty as Abby's lips stretched to accommodate his girth. She used her tongue to bathe the swollen head of him. And for what seemed like just a few seconds, he allowed her to give him pleasure. To look up and find his dark eyes blazing as he watched her suckle him. To see that big muscle in his jaw ticking frantically.

Then he pulled himself from her mouth and she frowned. His chuckle was more of a rasp when he saw her pout. Shaking his head, his beautiful naked chest working like bellows, he said, "Not this time. Next time you can finish me that way. But this time I want to come with you."

Her blood was rivers of fire burning through her veins. And that ache Carlos so expertly satisfied earlier had returned with a vengeance. Although she would not have thought it possible, she was hungrier for him now, hurting more for him now, than she had been before they started. And she figured that was because *now* she knew exactly what sort of pleasure he could give her.

"Lay back, Abby. Spread your legs for me," he said, his voice barely above a growl. "I'm going to make love to you now."

"Yes," she whispered, doing as he instructed, laying back on the mat and spreading her legs so he could kneel between them. The tan skin on his flanks looked so dark in contrast to the paleness of her thighs. "Yes, Carlos," she said again when he leaned forward to brace his hands beside her shoulders.

He drank his name from her lips with a kiss, his tongue plunging deep, stroking forcefully. Then he stilled, pulling back.

"What?" she breathed, lifting her head to nip his jaw. With her ankles hooked behind his knees, she could slide her slick channel up and down the hot, raging length of him. And his plump head felt wonderful against her swollen clit. "What is it?" she managed, even though talking, *thinking,* was difficult when she was so close to orgasm.

"I don't have a condom," he groaned, pressing his forehead to hers. "Please tell me you're on the pill."

"No." She pulled his mouth back to hers. "But the timing is okay. We should be fine." And even though she knew it was a stupid risk to take despite the fact that she was pretty sure what she'd told him was true—she wasn't in the fertile phase of her cycle—she couldn't make herself care. And, yes, that was everyone's favorite excuse for not using birth control, wasn't it? And, yes, she was now the official poster child for irresponsibility. But right now she didn't give a rat's ass that she was a cliché or that the repercussions of her decision could be disastrous. Right now she just...*wanted*.

"If you're sure?" he said between hot, hungry kisses. She could feel his urgency, his hunger as if it were her own. He needed this as much as she did.

"I'm sure," she breathed against his lips. And this time, *she* was the one to make the demand. "Put your cock in me."

He hesitated a second more, seeming to war with himself. Then something inside him broke. With a curse, he reached down to grab the base of his erection, angling it toward her opening. And even though she was so wet and ready for him, the fact remained, he was big. And the head of him stretched her, straining the capacity of her flesh.

She didn't care. Planting her feet flat on the mat, she thrust her hips up at him, sending his shaft a few inches inside her. It was *bliss!* And at the same time, not nearly enough. She growled her frustration.

"Slow. Go slow, Abby," he told her gruffly before reclaiming her lips. His tongue delved and retreated inside her mouth with the same rhythm his hardness slid and stroked into her body. It took a few tries, a couple of forceful glides and retreats before he finally seated himself to the hilt.

Then, dear God, she was so completely full of him. His girth stretched her inner walls to their limits, and she would swear she could feel his heartbeat in the hard, steady pulse of his shaft.

"You okay?" he asked against her mouth, his breath sawing from his lungs into hers.

"God, yes," she managed, amazed she was able to speak when she was absolutely overcome with aching, sexual sensation, poised right on the brink.

He ducked his chin then, glancing down to the place where their two bodies joined.

"Jesús Cristo," he breathed. "Look at us, Abby."

She lifted her head and saw his neatly trimmed, jet-black pubic hair in harsh contrast to her sandy blond curls. The deep flush of his penis, his tan skin stretched tight and shining with her essence, was in stark opposition to the pink of her most intimate flesh.

"We're beautiful together," he husked.

"We are." She smiled, letting her head drop back to the mat. *So beautiful.*

And with that, with those two words, he began to move. Slowly at first. So infinitely slowly, his shaft rubbing deliciously along screaming, aching nerve endings. Then, as her womb pulsed, as she clawed his back, he picked up the pace. His hips pistoning as he strained toward his own release.

She bucked against him, with him, matching his thrusts. And she rose up, up, *up*. Reaching. Climbing. Until…*climax*. It burst through her like an atom bomb.

"Yes, Abby!" he bellowed. "Yes, *neña*! Take me with you!"

And even through the head-spinning, pulse-pounding rapture of her own orgasm, she was able to squeeze her inner muscles around him. It drove her own pleasure up a notch and, at the same time, milked Carlos's release from him. She felt the hot rush of his seed fill her when he threw his head back, crying her name.

Chapter Eighteen

"CHRISSAKES," DAN SAID, BLOWING LIKE A BULL, HIS hands planted against the bathroom door on either side of Penni's head. No matter how he struggled to pull in oxygen, he couldn't seem to catch his breath. It didn't help that she was staring at him with those dark, luminous eyes and—

"Yo!" A voice from the past sounded on the other side of the door, causing Penni to squeal and duck under his arm. She retrieved her trousers, panties, and shoes in one frantic scoop as a hard fist landed on the wood. *Bam!* Dan bent to hastily jerk on his jeans and briefs. "You in there, Dan The Motor City Madman?"

Hell's bells, how long had it been since he heard *that* nickname? Not since he said *sayonara* to the Teams and joined Boss in building BKI.

"Anderson?" he called, quickly buttoning his fly.

"Yeah, man. The hotel manager said you'd be down here in a storage room, but we stopped when we heard noises comin' from the ladies' john. Everything okay in there?"

Okay? Well, that was debatable. He decided to ignore the question and instead went with one of his own. "Holy shit, dude. I didn't expect you guys for another three or four hours."

"Lucky for you," Leo Anderson replied, his deep chuckle muffled by the door, "we happen to know a pilot insane enough to take off in that hellacious crapper of a squall. You remember Romeo, right?"

Dan glanced over his shoulder to find Penni smoothing her hair back into her ponytail. She'd managed to pull off some sort of crazy, phone booth, superhero-esque redressing. Because not only were her trousers zipped, her shirttail neatly tucked into her waistband, but her shoes were back on, too. *Huh. Impressive.* Did the Secret Service practice fire-drill appareling or something? If so, he needed to ask her for some pointers.

"You've got a little mascara..." he whispered, indicating the skin beneath her left eye and *not* allowing his gaze to ping down to her ass when she spun to face the bathroom mirror. She licked her finger and scrubbed the makeup away. And, yeah, so maybe he gave her tight little booty the briefest, teeniest of glances before turning back to throw open the door.

"Of *course* I remember Romeo." He flashed a grin he hoped hid the fact that he'd been half-naked and rubbing up against the lovely Agent DePaul barely thirty seconds ago. "How could I forget the guy who flew that old decrepit Huey in a series of crazy eights just for shits and giggles?"

Seven men in jungle fatigues who ranged in size, shape, and coloring stood on the other side of the bathroom door. And one look at their familiar faces as their eyes skipped over his shoulder to Penni told him he hadn't quite succeeded in pulling off that whole *nothing to see here; just go about your business* shtick. Their expressions varied from minor curiosity to smirking insight.

Well, shit on a stick.

But speaking of familiar faces, he experienced a fleeting pinch of…*hmm*…he guessed the best word to describe it would be *nostalgia.* Because Lieutenant Leo "The Lion" Anderson and his group of SEALs had that squinty-eyed, shaggy look that said they'd recently been or were about to go on a mission to a part of the world where the women wore burkas and Americans were considered enemy number one. The same type of place where an overabundance of body hair gave them a sort of camouflage within the local population.

Not that working for Black Knights Inc. didn't come with its own perks in the form of covert missions to the globe's most notorious jungles and deserts. But since BKI was the darkest of the dark operators within the United States, Dan's jobs tended be looser, his objectives less defined than the cut-and-dried sorties routinely carried out by the military. And it was that simplicity—if balls-to-the-wall raids, assaults, rescues, and offenses could ever be called *simple*—that he found himself missing right now.

Then again, maybe he was merely feeling sentimental for a happier time. A time when he thought himself indestructible. When life was nothing but adventure and intrigue. When his wife was still alive.

His wife…

And, *sonofabastard*, that brought him back around to Penni and—

"Speaking of shits and giggles, if I remember correctly," Romeo said, his speculative gaze swinging away from Penni to land on him, "I was the one doing the giggling. And LT here"—he slung an arm around Leo's shoulders—"was the one doing the shitting. Of his pants, that is."

Leo's mouth curved down in a frown as he shrugged off Romeo's arm. "What's this?" he drawled, lifting his middle finger toward Romeo. "Why, it's my ass-hole antenna. I'm happy to report you're comin' in loud and clear."

"Oooh, good one, LT," Romeo said, referring to Leo's rank of lieutenant. "That earns you one of these." He pointed to his toothy grin. It blazed white against his swarthy face and close-cropped black beard. And right now, with the fatigues and the facial hair, Spiro "Romeo" Delgado looked like the Navy SEAL he was. But if Dan's memory served, when Romeo was clean shaven, he could give Steady some serious competition for the title of World's Most Successful Latin Lady-killer.

"How many times do I have to tell you," Leo harrumphed, popping his gum and pulling his always-present Ray-Ban aviator sunglasses from his face and hooking one earpiece over the collar of his army-green T-shirt, "that pirate smile of yours only works on those of us who possess a pair of ovaries."

"Not true," Michael "Mad Dog" Wainwright spoke up from his position leaning against the door jamb. When he grinned, it caused the scraggly brown whiskers of his beard to poke out every which way. "Remember the little blond-haired guy in that rundown cantina in Monterrey? He was bound and determined to make Romeo change his religion. And after six shots of tequila, I think Romeo was prepared to let him try."

"Oh, that's right," Leo smirked and turned back to Dan. "In case you were unaware, let me be the first to tell you that Romeo's penchant toward painted-on jeans and skin products makes him the equivalent of homosexual fly paper." His Deep South accent seemed to draw out the last three words until they were about twenty syllables long.

"You guys say that like it's a bad thing." Romeo made a face. "But I take it as the ultimate compliment that I'm irresistible to both sexes."

"You're only irresistible because people tend to judge books by their covers," Mad Dog retorted. "And your pretty cover disguises the fact that you're one chromosome away from being a kumquat."

"I'd rather be a pretty kumquat from fabulous L.A.," replied Romeo, "than an ugly Italian mutt from Atlantic City. And *zing*!" He winked. "You just got hit with my truth beam. Tell me something, Mad Dog. Are you blinded by it?"

"Tell *me* something, Romeo. Do you huff glue? Because it's the only thing that could explain your idiocy."

"Has anyone ever informed you that the Venn diagram of things that make up your personality and things that are annoying is a circle?" When Mad Dog's chin jerked back, Romeo grinned in victory. "How's *that* for idiocy? And you tried to liken *me* to a kumquat? Let me guess, all that grease you guidos put in your hair stunted the growth of your brain cells."

"Better to be a guido than a cholo."

"Oh, why don't you go over in the corner and play your own skin flute," Romeo said, his tongue planted firmly in his cheek. It'd been Dan's experience that spec-ops boys liked nothing better than to feed each other several servings of shit each day. And while being a crackerjack shot or good with a knife in CQB—close quarters battle—was highly revered, having a rapier wit was what really earned a guy top billing within a group.

"I think I might," Mad Dog was quick to reply. "And with a hog as big as mine—"

"Will you guys cut the shit?" Leo said. "I haven't set eyes on this bastard for over six years." He grabbed Dan's shoulder in a tight grip. "Come here, Dan Man. Let me get my mitts on ya."

And then, in typical guy fashion, the SEALs descended on Dan. He was crushed in a round of manly back-slapping bear hugs that left him wheezing. Mad Dog was the last of his former colleagues to whack him affectionately on the back. And while doing that, he was growling lowly in Dan's ear, "I was sorry as hell to hear about your wife, man. And what happened to you afterward. But I'm glad to see you're back on the horse."

"Thanks," Dan hissed, "but I'm not back on *anything*."

Mad Dog chuckled, continuing to hold him close and whispering, "Whatever you say. And speaking of lies, you sonofabitch! I knew you and Boss weren't really leaving the SEALs to settle down and build custom motorcycles. But, fuck me sideways, POTUS's very own League of Extraordinary Gentlemen? I thought that was only a rumor."

And for anybody keeping score, that's one more group of folks who now know exactly what I am and who I work for.

In the last couple of years, for one reason or another, the list of people "in the know" about Black Knights Inc. had expanded beyond the president and his Joint Chiefs of Staff to include just about every alphabet-soup government agency housed under that behemoth known as the Department of Defense. And Dan wasn't sure if BKI being forced from the clandestine closet would prove to be a boon or a boon*doggle*. As far as he could figure, for right now the jury was still out.

Of course, the one person who *wasn't* privy to the true nature of his affiliation—though he was sure she had her suspicions—was Penni.

When Mad Dog pushed him away, he cleared his throat and flicked a meaningful glance in her direction. "Those rumors are unconfirmed," he said from the corner of his mouth.

Mad Dog's expression blanked in an instant. And, *damn*, Dan wouldn't want to go up against the guy in a cutthroat game of poker, that's for sure. "Coming in loud and clear." Mad Dog nodded.

"Penni"—Dan turned, motioning for her to join them—"come let me make some introductions."

"Are you sure it's safe?" She waved a hand in front of her face and wore a soft grin Dan knew was all for show. The woman had just experienced a long-overdue emotional meltdown followed by…well…a few minutes of insanity. Which he wasn't going to think about unless he wanted to sport the world's most painful boner.

"Safe? What do you mean?" he asked.

"With so much testosterone floating around, it's like I'm standing inside of a testicle. And I'm afraid of what getting any closer to the source will do to my eggs. They might spontaneously fertilize or something."

Before Dan could think up a response to *that* bit of unexpected witticism, he got distracted by Romeo's crack of laughter as it echoed against the acoustic tiles on the ceiling. "Ah, the lovely Agent Penelope DePaul,"

Romeo said, stepping forward to offer his hand. "Your file didn't say anything about your wonderful sense of humor. And the picture the Secret Service has of you doesn't do you a bit of justice, *querida*."

When Penni reached forward for a handshake, Romeo caught her hand between both of his. Dan could tell she bit the inside of her cheek when the devilish, dark-eyed bastard lifted her fingers to his lips.

Whoa. What?

The tips of his ears were burning like he was jealous or something. But that was impossible. He and Penni were…well…they weren't *anything*. So maybe he was imagining that weird fire in his blood. Or maybe it had just been a very long day.

That's gotta be it.

Still, he couldn't stop himself from reaching out to jerk Penni away from Romeo and pull her next to his side. "Penni, you've already met Spiro Delgado, known as Romeo. I'm sure you can guess how he came by *that* name." He frowned at the man. "But I wanna introduce to you to the guys from my former SEAL team. And even though they're lowly Alpha platoon—I was with Bravo, by the way—try your best not to hold that against 'em."

He went around the group, making the introductions, and by the time he'd finished, Penni looked a little dazed. Dan didn't know if it was all the new names and nicknames, the fact that Leo's team was a handsome bunch—the fuckers—or that she was working on zero sleep. He was hoping for the latter.

"So," Leo said, scratching his brownish-blond beard. "Now that *that's* out of the way, how 'bout you tell us where, when, and *how* we're supposed to evac the president's lovely young daughter..."

"Mmm," Abby hummed when Carlos stretched like a cat. He was absolutely glorious in his nudity...and completely unabashed. He even reached down to absently caress his flaccid penis where it lolled lazily against his thigh.

"Mmm?" he asked, releasing himself to tuck one hand beneath his head and reach for her with the other. She went to him willingly. And with his strong arm holding her close to his side, her cheek resting on his broad chest, she could almost pretend it was possible for her to be like this with him forever. To be *his* forever.

"Yes, mmm." She ran her finger around one of his flat, brown nipples. "That's the sound a woman makes when she's completely sated."

His chuckle sounded particularly low and rumbly beneath her ear. "Say it isn't so. Not *completely* sated, anyway. Because I have much more in store for you. In fact, it's best you prepare yourself now for a full week of Steady lovin' once we return stateside. I've got some time off coming to me."

She ignored the sharp pain that sliced through her at the thought of what their return stateside would mean and instead latched on to the first change of subject that came to mind. "How did you get the nickname Steady? Is it because you're so brave and courageous and reliable in the field?"

"Ha! I wish. That'd be so much cooler." He was drawing little circles on her shoulder with his index finger.

And even though the hut had to be pushing ninety degrees with ninety percent humidity, his soft touch made her shiver. "No, I picked up that name back in Ranger School during a live-fire drill. A young petty officer caught a round to the right lung, and it looked like he was going to suffocate on the blood and air filling his chest cavity long before the ambulance arrived. So I had to do an emergency thoracentesis there in the field."

He stopped caressing her shoulder, lifting his chin to glance down at her. "I keep forgetting you didn't finish medical school. Do you know what a thoracentesis is?"

"A pleural tap. Where you cut into the pleural space in the chest in order to release the air or fluid that's building up."

"*Sí.*" He nodded before dropping his head back atop his hand. "So, anyway, I grabbed my Swiss Army knife, unfolded the reamer tool from the case, found a space between the kid's ribs, and jabbed that blade deep. I had to use somebody's ballpoint pen casing to keep the wound open so the blood and air could continue to drain until the medics arrived."

"And let me guess," she finished for him. "You were steady as a rock through it all."

"So I was told," he said, and she could feel him shake his head. "I find that hard to believe considering I was scared shitless the entire time."

"You?" She pushed up on her arm to stare down at him, smiling. "Scared? I don't believe it."

"Believe it, little *neña.* That was the first time I ever operated on someone outside a clinical setting and without a whole slew of experienced doctors on hand to correct my fuck-ups if I made any."

Planting her elbow on the mat, she cupped her cheek in her hand, narrowing her eyes.

"What?" he asked, a line appearing between his dark brows. "What's that look for? What are you thinking?"

"Do you ever regret not becoming a surgeon?" And even though she tried to keep her tone light, she held her breath for his answer.

"Nah," he said almost instantly. She covertly blew out a relieved breath. *Thank God I don't have* that *to add to my guilt.* "I mean, while I'm not happy *why* I decided to join the Army, I *am* happy with the life I've led. I've seen and done amazing things. I've been to some incredible places and have had more adventures than you can ever imagine. And there are a thousand adventures still to come." Yes. She could see how that would appeal to someone like him. "Plus, I get to call some of the fiercest, bravest, smartest warriors on the planet my friends. All and all, I'd say that's a pretty sweet existence."

"You don't know how *glad* I am to hear you say you feel that way," she told him.

He cocked his chin, narrowing his eyes. "Why do I get the impression I'm missing something?"

She shook her head. Too much more of that and the terrible poker face—*non*-poker face?—he'd accused her of having was going to give her away. "No. It's nothing. I'm just really happy things turned out okay for you."

"And you, Abby?" he asked. "Are you sorry you didn't become a doctor?" His eyes were still narrowed and speculative, like he was seeing far more than she wanted him to. Which he probably was.

She dropped her head back to his chest to avoid his penetrating black gaze. They were tap dancing—*clickety-clack*—all around a subject she'd decided to dodge until they got back to safety. And because of that, for a brief second she considered prevaricating. But then she thought *No, I'll be damned if I lie to him about one more thing*. So, she admitted, "It's not that I didn't become a doctor; it's that I *couldn't* become a doctor."

"What?" He stilled beneath her. "Why?"

"After the..." She had to lick her lips. "After the bombing, I...I couldn't stand the sight of blood. Every time I picked up a scalpel to do a dissection, I had a panic attack or passed out. Like, *blam!*" She snapped her fingers as punctuation. "Seriously down for the count. My therapist diagnosed me with post-traumatic stress disorder."

But in all honesty, she'd always figured it was more post-traumatic *guilt* disorder. When she saw a drop of blood, she was instantly reminded of the bombing victims and the blood that had speckled the scene that horrible day. And even now, eight years later, just talking about it had the memory threatening to overcome her. She could feel the horror of it, the terror of it wrapping a ghostly hand around her throat. And a sudden rush of sorrow filled her chest until breathing became a labor.

"Hell, Abby," he whispered, hugging her tight. "I'm so sorry. I had no idea."

Oh, no. No, no, no. "Don't you *dare* be sorry," she told him fiercely. "You have absolutely *nothing* to be sorry for."

And despite her best efforts, hot tears burned behind her nose. And they were the insistent kind. The *persistent* kind. *Oh, God! I can't stop them!* It was like when she was a little girl and Veronica Wachowski pushed her down on the playground and called her a gangly, green-eyed goblin. Her whole second-grade class had been watching, and in spite of her savage desire to act tough, to act like her tailbone and her feelings weren't hurt, she'd been unable to stop the tears that flooded her eyes.

So she did the only thing she could: She gave herself a *reason* to cry. One he wouldn't find suspicious. "And since we're on the subject of sorry," she quickly added, dismayed to hear her voice crack, "I think it's time you told me what happened to my security detail. Why you were forced to come up here all alone."

She hadn't missed that strange...*something* that had entered his tone back there in the jungle when she asked who would be meeting them over the border in Thailand. Although, quite honestly, she'd been doing her damndest to avoid it. Because niggling at the back of her brain like a colony of termites was the suspicion that she wasn't going to like whatever he told her. And, sure enough, she'd been right to put off the inevitable when his big chest rose on a huge, indrawn breath a second before his words plunged into her heart like a giant pair of hedge clippers.

"They're dead, Abby. All except Agent DePaul."

Oh...*God!* It was worse, even, than she'd feared. She'd been prepared for incapacitation or injuries, but...but *this*? And now she didn't need an excuse for her tears, the explosive waterworks were in earnest. She choked on them as she pushed up on her elbow to stare down at him, disbelief and remorse nearly suffocating her.

"H-how?" she asked, then wished she hadn't when he

described, in clipped, no-bullshit terms, the brutal deaths of the Secret Service agents.

"Sweet *Jesus*!" she wheezed when he was finished. "Not again!"

"Abby." He tried to pull her into his arms, but she refused to let him, refused to be comforted when six more people were dead because of her. "This doesn't fall to you, *cariño*. Wait…what do you mean *not again*? Has something like this happened before?"

She realized her mistake. "I-I can't…I don't…No. No, I can't believe it. I can't believe I've lost them, too," she finally managed, shaking her head.

His expression cleared, and this time when he wrapped his big hand behind her head to pull her dripping face down to his chest, she let him. Lord forgive her, but she needed him right now. Needed his warmth, his strength, his support.

Six dead…

"Shh, shh, *neña*," he crooned, running his wide-palmed hand over her hair as she gnashed her teeth and soaked his chest. "You have to know this wasn't your fault. You didn't do anything wrong. And those agents were well aware of the risks they faced when they joined the Secret Service."

Yes, maybe she hadn't done anything wrong *this time*, but she couldn't help but feel responsible. Those agents never would have been in Malaysia, in the same realm with a skinny bunch of bloodthirsty terrorists, if not for her. Marcy Tucker, LaVaughn Silver, Tony Bosco, and the others would still be here if she'd only—

"You're breaking my fucking heart, Abby." He

grabbed her shoulders and pulled her completely atop him so he could wrap both arms securely around her. Her knees fell to either side of his narrow hips, scraping against the mat. "But it's okay, *mi vida*." He lifted her chin with his thumb and forefinger to pepper her wet face with gentle kisses. "It's okay to cry. I'll kiss each tear away."

Only when he was holding her like this, loving her like this, the last thing she wanted to do was cry. In a blinding flash of clarity that seemed to coincide with a blaze of lightning through the hut's walls, she realized this was it. These few moments, right here, right now, were all they had left. The rain would let up soon and their time together as friends, as lovers, would end with the fury of the storm.

I'm not ready for that. Not yet. Not yet…

And despite the soul-sucking pain and grief slicing into her chest like a garden spade, she was determined to make one more beautiful memory. One that would last her a lifetime. "Make love to me again," she whispered before claiming his lips in a deep, penetrating kiss. She could taste the salt from her tears mixing with the sweetness of the rambutans and her own flavor on his tongue.

He stilled beneath her, hesitating, even as his tongue eagerly met hers stroke for stroke.

"Touch me, Carlos," she husked. "I need to feel your hands on me again."

"*Dios*," he growled, his hands sliding from her back to her bottom, the calluses on his palms deliciously scratchy. He grew hard in an instant. His plump plumb-shaped head pulsing insistently against her lower belly.

"Yes," she breathed into his mouth, bracing one hand

above his shoulder and using the other to reach down between them. The thick base of his cock filled her hand as she angled him toward her opening. And when the searing head of him penetrated her, filled her, stretched her, she watched him grit his jaw and arch his neck.

The move revealed his lovely Adam's apple and the thickness of his carotid arteries beating heavily with excitement. She couldn't help herself. She took a small, nipping bite of his toned, tan neck while simultaneously forcing his thick, solid length deeper inside her. All the way. Until she was impaled. Until she was full. Until she was stretched to the absolute limit.

"Cristo!" he grunted, grabbing her hips at the same time he reclaimed her mouth, sucking her tongue between his lips. Then, as if he could only allow her the freedom of control for so long, he ground her against him, forcing her hips back and forth, sliding himself deep and hard, rubbing her clitoris into an aching frenzy. "Ride me, Abby," he groaned. "Ride me until I come deep inside you."

She did as instructed. And all the while, tears leaked from her eyes because the world was a terrible place, because her people were dead, because this was it. It was all over. This was the last time she'd be with Carlos and—

Like a shot, she crested the peak and was instantly flung over the edge. She cried out from the intense, soul-shaking pleasure shooting through her body and from the heavy, heartbreaking sorrow squeezing her heart. With a grunt of victory, Carlos followed her into the abyss, pouring himself into her, sealing them together one final time.

And then, moments later, just as they were catching their breath, just as the last tremors of completion rippled through the place where they remained joined, the rain stopped as it had started…in an instant.

Chapter Nineteen

Penni listened with half an ear to the low drawl—uh, Dan had said the guy's name was Rock, right?—sounding through the speakers of the iPhone. It still sat atop the little table inside the storage-closet-turned-interrogation-chamber. And, yes indeedie. She knew she should be paying attention to the information he was giving them with not only a *whole* ear, but *both* ears. Unfortunately, she was too distracted—and *mortified*—by her recent behavior in the ladies' room, not to mention the seven huge, handsome…eight if you counted Dan, which she *totally* did…soldiers occupying the tight space with her.

The place was awash with the smells of spent aviation fuel, various aftershaves, and healthy, hulking males. And she thought maybe, if she tilted her head just so and squinted her eyes a tiny bit, she might actually be able to see the testosterone floating around in the dense, humid air.

If it was like walking around in a testicle before, then this *is like—*

"…Irdina says she saw the hotel's security director talking to the same *Jemaah Islamiyah* militant who offered to give her the money for Jaya's treatments," Rock said. And, okay, so *that* got her attention. And as *another* Rock, a far more *famous* Rock, was wont to say, she could totally smell what he was cooking.

Dan could too, if the fierce frown on his face was anything to go by. "And surprise, surprise. The asswipe called in sick today."

"He's probably on the next flight to Dubai," the tall, sandy-haired SEAL named Leo surmised. "If he hasn't already fled to another non-extradition treaty country, that is," he added in a drawn-out drawl, his brownish-blond beard twitching with the movement of his heavy jaw muscles as he vigorously chewed on a piece of gum.

"And FYI," Rock's smooth Cajun-country accent sounded again through the phone's speaker. "We lost Steady's signal a while ago. The jungle canopy and a crap-ton of cloud cover over the region created too much interference, and the satellite couldn't compensate. It happens. We weren't all that worried initially. But the storm passed, and we've been able to pick up his signal again. It's showing he's hell and gone off the logging road. He seems to be on foot and currently near some sort of small clearing. Our best guess given the sat imagery is it's a native village of some sort."

"What the fuck?" Dan growled, running a hand through his hair.

As if on cue, the seven SEALs began checking their weapons. The loud *clanks* and *shnicks* as clips were slid from the butts of handguns and knives were pulled from ballistic nylon sheaths were particularly loud in the little room. Irdina began to cry again, her soft wailing muffled by the shaking hands she used to cover her face.

"It could be nothing," Rock continued, as the hair rippling over Penni's arms told another story. "Maybe he ran out of gas, or maybe he was being tailed and needed to lose them by hoofing it through the bush."

"Can you use the satellite's infrared to see if it looks like he's been followed?" she was quick to ask, figuring if they could track Steady from a little signal emitted by a device that could fit inside his watch, then that satellite Rock mentioned more than likely came equipped with all the latest bells and whistles in the ever-changing arena of spy technology.

"No can do," the drawling man said. "The ambient temperature of the jungle is too hot to use infrared. Basically the whole damned place is glowing like a human body."

"Last Intel we received before we left the carrier group," Leo added, "is that he was some fifty miles from the Thai border. What's his approximate location now?"

"Somewhere closer to ten miles south of it," Rock replied.

Penni's level of concern escalated exponentially. It was bad enough that delicate, diminutive Abby Thompson was off traipsing through a snake-infested jungle. Worse still was not knowing *why* she and Steady had been forced to abandon the motorcycle. A heavy foreboding settled in her stomach like a dense hunk of that rye bread her father used to buy from the Jewish bakery up on Atlantic Avenue in Boerum Hill.

"How can my team get hooked up to track his signal?" Leo asked. "Just in case communications between us and those of you stateside get hinky."

"Give me the numbers for your cell phones," Rock replied. "I'll send y'all the application software from the NSA's secret server. It'll take a couple of minutes to download the app and to establish your secure connection. But once that's done, y'all should be able to bypass the satellite link if it proves unreliable and instead track Steady's signal through the local cell towers when he's within the coverage zone. Which means, hopefully, you'll have a far better time keeping up with him than we've had."

"That's pretty slick," one of the SEALs whose name she'd forgotten said.

"Membership has its rewards," Rock replied. "Okay, I'm ready. Give me those digits, *mes amis*."

As Leo and his men rattled off their cell numbers, Dan turned to her. "We got a couple options here," he said, his expression hard, almost…malevolent.

"Which are?"

"We can go with Leo and his team to pick up Steady and Abby, or we can stay here and try to catch that security director on the off chance he hasn't already flown the coop."

"And on the off chance he actually knows something," she added. "He could be like Irdina here"—she flicked a hand toward the poor, sniffling woman—"and be nothing more than a dupe and a patsy."

"But what if he's not?" Dan's eyes were twin orbs of green fire in the shadow of his face. "What if he can tell us how the hell those JI militants knew the covert locations of the agents on duty? What if he can tell us how they knew about the tracking devices sewn into Abby's clothes? What if he knows who the mole is? Isn't it worth our time to try to find out?"

She made a face. "Hello? When you put it like that…"

"Good." He nodded, throwing an arm around her shoulders like it was the most natural thing in the world. She ignored what his fingers brushing against the bare skin on her arm did to her stomach. "It's decided then. Leo?" He turned toward the man. "While you and the boys go superhero yourselves a rescue, Penni and I are gonna attempt to track down the hotel's security director. See if he can answer some questions that have been troubling us about this whole goddamned clusterfuck from the very beginning."

"Ten-four." Leo dipped his chin and shoved his smartphone into the breast pocket of his military-grade T-shirt. "It'll take us..." He looked down at the thick, plastic watch on his trim wrist, then over at the swarthy, flirtatious man aptly nicknamed Romeo. "What do you figure, Delgado? Sixty minutes, give or take, to make the flight?"

"I'd say more like seventy or seventy-five," Romeo replied, punching a finger onto the screen of his own cell phone before sliding it into the hip pocket of his jungle fatigues. His expression was so serious it was hard to fathom he was the same man who'd been grinning so cheerily while slinging insults at his teammates not more than ten minutes ago. "We have to swing by the airport and refuel the helo before heading out, so we'll be at the mercy of the Malay ground crew there. But according to JSOC"—Joint Special Operations Command—"they know we're coming and are ready for us. It should be a quick turnaround."

"*Hooah* then, boys." Dan lifted his free hand to bump knuckles with the SEALs as they filed past him toward the door. "Keep your heads on swivel out there."

"Or as we say in Brooklyn," she added, "keep chicky."

"We never do it any other way," Leo said as he slid by them.

And then, just like that, Penni was once again alone with Dan. *Uh-oh.* Well…and Irdina. *Whew.* Which reminded her. "What are we going to do about *her*?" She frowned toward the woman who sat slouched in the chair, no longer attempting to meet their eyes.

"Hell's bells." Dan ran a hand back through his hair again.

"I guess we could always turn her over to the local authorities," she suggested.

"Negative." Dan shook his head. "I say we get her some food, some water, make sure someone from the social services department—if there's an equivalent department here, that is—looks after Jaya. And leave her here until someone from our side decides what to do with her. I don't trust the locals. They'll either let her get away scot-free or else brutally punish her for bringing this international goatfuck down on their heads. And I'm thinking something more in the middle of those two would be better suited to the crime."

"Okay." She nodded.

"In the meantime, you and I need to find the manager and get whatever information he has on that security director. Starting with a home address." Again she nodded. "And Penni?"

"What?"

"If you wanna talk about what happened back in the bathr—"

She shook her head, ducking out from under the comforting, *distracting* weight of his arm. "No. Let's chalk it up to grief mixed with exhaustion and idiocy, and leave it at that. At least for right now."

For a moment he just stood there, so tall, so strong, his hard expression unreadable. Then he shrugged, nodding, and she blew out a relieved breath.

She'd said *at least for right now.* But if she had her way, they'd *never* speak of it. Though…*Christ on the cross*, she'd always remember what she'd so foolishly asked him to do…

"The rain has washed away their tracks," Noordin complained, his whining tone traveling from the end of Umar's spine up his vertebral column to detonate at the base of his skull. When he turned, he found Noordin's face was still dripping from the hard deluge they had trudged through for nearly an hour. Then again, it was possible that was not rain but sweat. With the passing of the storm and the baking of the sun, the humidity in the air was almost palpable. Those who were unused to the oppressiveness of the jungle, like Noordin, tended to disintegrate into soggy, disgusting messes.

"We should wait for the others to arrive," Noordin continued, swatting at a mosquito. The man was too miserable to heed the warning glinting in Umar's eyes. *The fool.* "During the last call on the satellite phone, they said they are only thirty minutes behind us. If we delay until there are more of us, then we can spread out to search. It will be easier than fumbling around in circles in the middle of this hot—"

"Do you value your life?" Umar asked, tilting his head. Although the expression he donned was curious, the edge in his voice alerted Noordin to the precariousness of his situation. Umar could tolerate many things.

Bellyaching, as the American's called it, was not one of them.

Noordin gulped as a muscle near his eye twitched fitfully. "Of course."

"Then you will close your mouth and refrain from speaking until I give you leave to do so. Do you understand?"

Noordin nodded vigorously, the other two men carefully keeping their eyes trained on the narrow jungle path lest they incur any residual spillover from his wrath.

"Good then." He turned to point out a bush with a couple of crushed leaves near its base. "And, yes, the rain did obscure their path. But only if you do not know what to look for. You see there?"

The three men bobbed their heads obediently but didn't say a word. Umar fought a smile. It had taken him years to engender this kind of fear in his subordinates. Years of maneuvering and fighting and killing. But it had all been worth it for moments like these. Moments when he could wield his superiority and power without ever having to touch the weapon slung over his shoulder.

Leaning forward, he pushed back the branches on the shrub, revealing the small footprints on the ground beneath. The plant's leaves had protected the imprints from the fury of the storm. "As you can see, we are still on the correct path, and—"

The shrieking laugh of a child somewhere nearby cut him off. He cocked his head, listening…

There it was again!

"Follow me," he hissed, breaking into a jog. Winding his way through the undergrowth, he hopped over twisting roots and dodged snaking vines. His men were not nearly as dexterous. In fact, he was pretty sure the quiet curse and muted *thud* he heard was Azahari falling to the ground behind him. He did not turn to check. Instead, he skidded to a stop at the edge of a clearing. One look at the crude little village cut into the middle of the jungle told him immediately what he was dealing with.

Orang Asli, the backward forest dwellers of Malaysia. The types of tribal people he considered barely better than the monkeys hanging in the trees. Poor. Dirty. *Ignorant.*

His lip curled as he grabbed the strap of his Kalashnikov, effortlessly lifting the weapon to his shoulder. The butt was a familiar pressure. The trigger rubbed smooth by the continual presence of his finger. "Azahari and Noordin, you two will come with me. You"—he turned to the third man—"will stay back here and provide a lookout."

Stepping from the clearing, weapon raised, he slunk into the center of the village where a circle of wicker stools sat empty. A group of children laughed and danced in the hazy air down by a stream while the adults gathered in a small, defoliated gap in the nearby forest. Down on their knees, the women were busy spreading wet rice onto mats—which they would later pull out into the sun to dry—and the men were kicked back against the trunks of trees, smiling and talking, cracking a joke here and there if the occasional burst of laughter was anything to go by.

Simpletons, Umar thought with disgust before loudly clearing his throat.

Twenty pairs of wide, terrified eyes turned in

his direction. The men pushed away from the trees, the women scrambled to their feet. "Where are the Americans?" he demanded in Malay, making sure his tone adequately conveyed his intent to kill them all should they refuse to answer. "I know they came through here. Where are they? Which direction did they go?"

North toward the border was a given. But whether the *anak haram* and the woman continued on a straight trajectory through the jungle or whether they decided to take an easier, yet more circuitous route on one of the logging paths was key. This close to Thailand, he could not afford to guess. Catching them before they crossed over was already going to be a very close thing.

"Answer me, you smelly, witless pigs!" he bellowed, taking a few menacing steps forward, feeling Noordin and Azahari shadow his every move. The barrels of their machine guns were a welcome sight in his peripheral vision. "Answer me!" he screamed again.

The women shrank back upon his advance, crying out in alarm as the men arranged themselves in front of them in what Umar figured was supposed to be a wall of opposition.

What? Do they think they can glare me to death? It was almost laughable. And if he had not been in such a hurry, he might have allowed himself a good chuckle. But the clock was ticking…

He opened his mouth to make another demand when the frightened cry of a child caused one of the women to push past the screen of men. Tears streaming down her face, the ugly little shrew yelled something in that ridiculous, clipped language of hers to the little girl running toward her.

Noordin swung his weapon in the child's direction, and that was more than the woman could stand. She broke away from the group of adults and raced for the girl. But Umar was on her in an instant, catching her by the arm and using her own momentum to jerk her off her feet. He smiled with glee at the grunting *whoosh* of air that pushed from her lungs when he slammed her spine into the ground. From the corner of his eye, he could see the other adults shuffling anxiously, though stupidity and terror—and the fact that Azahari kept them pinned beneath the evil black eye of his AK-47—stopped them from interfering. Placing one foot on the woman's abdomen, her stomach muscles quivered beneath the tread of his boot when he pointed his machine gun straight between her eyes.

"Where are the Americans?" he asked. This time, he kept his voice low. So only she could hear. "You may not speak Malay, but you understand that word. *Americans*," he stressed.

She shook her head, causing the orchid stuck in her ridiculous mess of fuzzy black hair to quiver. Crying pitifully, she babbled something he did not begin to understand. Rolling his eyes, his patience having frayed to near nothing, he turned to Noordin. "Grab the girl," he instructed. "Maybe *that* will encourage this bitch to grow a few more brain cells."

Noordin did as he was told, swooping down on the little girl and lifting her into his arms despite her banshee shrieks and violent flailing. Azahari stepped up to Umar. "I do not think she understands, *adik*," he said. "I do not think any of them do."

"She understands enough," he growled, hauling the

woman to her feet and shoving the barrel of his AK under her chin. "Place the girl on the ground, Noordin," he said when the man stopped next to them. For the life of him, he couldn't remember why he had been so annoyed with Noordin, who followed orders so very, *very* well. "And be careful to keep the end of your weapon in contact with the child's head."

Noordin completed the maneuver succinctly. The little girl stood still as stone, despite the hiccupping cries that shook her little chest. In that respect, she was much like her…*mother?* Umar tilted his head to look into the woman's face. Hmm. It was hard to tell. All the Orang Asli looked alike to him. Moon-round faces and wide, smashed features. *Repugnant.*

"Now." He motioned with his chin toward the child. "Where are the *Americans?*"

The woman didn't hesitate this time. Lifting her arm, she pointed toward the northwest side of the clearing. Umar turned in the direction of her extended finger, squinting his eyes, trying to remember if there was another logging trail in that direction.

"Go see if she is telling the truth!" he yelled over his shoulder to his man waiting in the bush. From the corner of his eye, he watched his foot soldier break from the jungle and jog to the edge of the village. For a couple of interminable seconds, the man walked around, checking for tracks.

"Yes!" he finally called excitedly, and Umar's pulse leapt. "There are footprints in the mud. Definitely a pair of Western-style shoes alongside imprints from the soft-soled slippers the woman is wearing!"

"Now, was that so hard?" Umar smiled down at the

woman, loving the way she shrank away from him. Loving the absolute terror in her eyes.

Shoving her away, he instructed Noordin to do the same with the girl. Then, keeping their weapons trained on the villagers—who just continued to stand there like slack-jawed imbeciles—they backed toward the edge of the jungle.

"Keep drawing down on them," he told his men as he slung the strap of his machine gun over his shoulder so he, too, could inspect the tracks. Squatting, he noted the deep impressions left in the mud. "These were left after the storm, when the ground was soft," he muttered, as much to his men as to himself. "Which means we are not far behind…"

Chapter Twenty

"I MAY HAVE BEEN MISTAKEN ABOUT THE DISTANCE TO my truck," Yonus said. "I am now thinking it was more like two miles from the village."

Steady grinned at the young man's back. "That's okay," he called. The guy was about ten yards out in front of him and Abby, due to their slower pace. Abby's gams may be world-class, but they were also lacking a bit when it came to vertical inches. "When hitching a ride, beggars can't be choosers. But I have to ask you, *hermano*, does this truck of yours come equipped with four-wheel drive?"

Because the rain had turned the entire region into a big bowl of muck. And their hike from the village through the drenched, dripping jungle had been slow going from the start. Unfortunately, their progress had become *more* snail-like since they made it to the logging trail. The mud atop the rutted road was three inches thick and slick as snot. Which forced them to trudge awkwardly alongside the shoulder where the footing was more stable, and far more uneven.

"Of course it has four-wheel drive. What do you take me for?" Yonus turned to flash them a quick smile. It was the exact same expression he'd given them after they crawled down the ladder from the ceremonial hut once the storm passed. Now, just as then, Steady couldn't help but wonder if perhaps he and Abby's…

uh…*activities*—and corresponding cries of ecstasy. *Dios!* Just thinking about that made him semi-hard and achy again—hadn't been completely drowned out by the roar of the raging squall.

"I take you for a lifesaver," he called, putting a little jiggle and swivel in his step to covertly adjust himself into a more comfortable position.

"It is my pleasure, my friends." Yonus dipped his chin before turning back to continue up the trail.

Steady glanced over at Abby, expecting to see her grinning after Yonus. The guy's smile was the infectious sort, after all. But instead he found her frowning, her brow puckered with two vertical lines. "You okay?" he asked, reaching over to brush her fingers, trying not to think about what it was like to have that small hand wrapped around his cock or cupping his balls. *Oh, and great. That did* nothing *for my semi.* "Do we need to stop and take a break?"

"No." She shook her head, instantly smoothing away her frown. "No. I was just thinking about…" She trailed off, shrugging.

"Your security detail," he finished for her, careful to keep his voice low so Yonus couldn't hear.

She dipped her chin and made a face. "Among other things. They were good people. Brave people. They didn't deserve what happened to them."

"Well of course they didn't. But there was nothing you could have done to stop what happened. You know that, eh?" When she didn't immediately answer, he caught her hand, jerking her to a stop. The sun, dappling through the tree limbs that were trying so desperately to bridge the gap over the logging road, shone down on her golden hair, creating a halo effect that took his breath away. He braced himself for the one-two punch of her eyes.

But she didn't meet his gaze, instead staring at the hollow in his throat like it was a rare species of flower or something else she might find equally fascinating. He was forced to grab her adorable chin between his thumb and forefinger, gently forcing it up. "You *do* know that, right?" he demanded.

Sighing, she pointed to her head. "I know it here." Then she placed her hand over her tunic, above her left breast. "But *this* part of me remains unconvinced."

And, *sí*, he knew all about that. He'd seen and done things in the Rangers and working for BKI that were easy to rationalize in his mind, but not so easy to accept in his heart. "That part is *always* trickier. But you know how you make their sacrifice worth it?"

She blinked at him. "No. How?"

"By living. By loving. By laughing. Their job was to make sure you were always around to do all three. And you honor them anytime you do."

One corner of her mouth pulled back. "You know, I used to think you missed your calling to be a Calvin Klein underwear model by going to med school and then joining the army. But now I think you should have studied to be a psychiatrist. You may not say much, Carlos Soto." She reached forward to place her hand over his heart, and he wondered if she could feel that it beat only for her. "But when you *do* say something, it tends to be the right thing."

"And that's what I've been trying to tell everyone for *years*." He made a face, grabbing her fingers and lifting them to his lips. Then, "A Calvin Klein underwear model? As my mother used to say, *Dios no lo quiera.* Heaven forbid."

She laughed, and the sound was like church bells ringing.

"That's better." He winked at her before turning to continue after Yonus.

For a few moments they hiked in silence, letting the humming, buzzing, screeching chorus of the forest sing them a tune. And for the first time in probably…well, *ever*…he discovered himself not necessarily *enjoying* the jungle, but not exactly *hating* it either. It was still hot as hell. The humidity was still so high it'd likely bust a hygrometer. The frackin' mosquitoes were still as big as city buses. But Abby was by his side. And not too long ago she'd given him the kind of sex that made his head spin, his heart ache, and his dick swell and pound inside his pants with the need for more. *Much* more.

He wondered what Boss would say to him taking off for a week or so once they got back stateside, when a florescent-green bird with bright-blue feathers on its chest buzzed by him. The brilliantly plumed fowl was hot on the trail of a fuchsia-colored dragonfly that darted and dipped as it raced toward the safety of the jungle on the opposite side of the logging road.

He smiled after the pair despite the fact that they were locked in a deadly game of cat and mouse…uh…bird and dragonfly? And that's when he realized he was… *happy*. He was still itching to make it over the Thai border. Still concerned with who might be the mole. Still scared to death for Ozzie. But all those things played second fiddle to the fact that Abby adored him. She *adored* him!

"What are you smiling about?" she asked, dragging him from his thoughts. Then her gaze pinged down to the fly of his cargo pants, where he was still semi-erect. "Never mind." She rolled her eyes. "Of course that's what's behind that goofy grin. What else would it be?"

It was so good to hear her sling a gibe that he refrained from reaching over to throw an arm around her shoulders and smack a kiss on her soft, wonderful lips. Instead, he decided to play along. "And what's that supposed to mean?" he asked, narrowing his eyes in mock warning.

"That as a gender, your minds, when not occupied with the task of making war somewhere, are usually either filled with thoughts of sex, beer, or the latest baseball scores."

"That's not true," he informed her, lifting his nose haughtily.

"It's not?" she asked.

"*No*. Most times we're thinking about all three at once."

Snorting, she nudged him with her elbow. He, of course, nudged her right back.

"Stop it," she told him, feigning a frown.

"*You* stop it," he retorted. And now the grin he wore had nothing to do with thoughts of sex. Instead, his mind was filled with love.

"Gah!" She shook her head, mistaking his expression. "And there's that grin again."

"Don't act like you don't like it." He wiggled his eyebrows at her, slowly giving her a wink. "Because I know for a *fact* that you do."

"And why would you possibly be suffering under that delusion?"

"Because Rosa told me you once told *her* that my smile was the sweetest you'd ever seen. And that my dimple should be outlawed." And you had better believe that had stayed with him through the years. There'd been times when he thought he wouldn't make it out of this battle or live through that mission that he closed his eyes and relived the memory of the day his sister fed him that delicious little nugget, imagining Abby's adorable face as she confessed.

He expected her to hit back with one of her patented jabs. So watching her face blanch and then crumble caught him completely off guard. "Ah, hell. I didn't mean to—"

"No." She shook her head, lifting a hand to stop him. "Please don't apologize for anything. Really."

Back in the hut, he'd noticed she had a difficult time talking about his sister. And the question of *why* she was still mourning Rosa so vigorously bothered him. It'd been eight years. His own grief had mellowed from a sharp, searing pain that nearly brought him to his knees to a soft, blunt kind of remorse that was almost wistful in its melancholy.

Yes, he missed Rosa like crazy. And there wasn't a day that went by when he didn't think of her and wish she was still by his side, still giving him shit, and still holding the fact that she was a full two minutes older than him over his head. But he'd managed to move on with his life, move past his sorrow to a place where he could look back with laughter and love on the time he'd spent with her.

Why hadn't Abby done the same?

"Seriously." She ran a hand under her nose. "Don't mind me. It's just been a really long day, and I'm feeling—"

"There it is!" Yonus called back to them. He pointed up the road. And though the jungle did its best to obscure their view, faint red taillight covers and the silver glint of a back bumper were visible.

"If that isn't a sight for sore eyes"—Steady slung an arm around Abby's shoulders and gave her a squeeze—"I don't know what is. Can I get an amen?"

"A-frickin'-men," she replied, forcing a smile to her lips, and lengthening her stride. She seemed content to drop their conversation, and he didn't dare push her to finish whatever it was she'd been about to say.

They joined Yonus and were barely thirty yards from the truck when the familiar *crack* of igniting gunpowder sounded a second before a round bit into the ground near their feet. The hairs on Steady's scalp lifted so fast and high it was a wonder they didn't jettison off his head. He reached for his Beretta as another loud, malicious *crack* echoed through the jungle at the same time a bullet nicked his upper arm. Pain bit into him with sharp, jagged teeth, but he gave it barely a fleeting thought.

"Get down!" he yelled to Yonus who was standing beside the road, eyes wide, face slack in shock. "Stay low and make for the tree line!"

And then, wrapping both arms around Abby, keeping her in front of him so that his body was between her and the shooter, he heeded his own advice. Two bounding steps brought them to the relative safety of the jungle's edge. After securing her behind the huge trunk of a tree—and after a quick look assured him she was unharmed—he thumbed off his safety and prepared to let the bullets fly…

"Okay, so this *should* be the place." Penni leaned against the front bumper of one of the big, black SUVs the Secret Service had rented to use as transport to and from the airport. Dan was propped beside her, arms crossed, watching as she glanced down at the piece of paper on which the hotel manager had scrawled the security director's address. When she looked over at him, she pulled a face. "I mean, this *has* to be the place."

"You sure?" he asked as she folded the slip and tucked it into the front pocket of her austere black slacks before pushing away from the vehicle to stand on the side of the street. Until today, until seeing how the material draped around her long, slim legs while delicately cupping her heart-shaped derriere, he would've sworn there was no way a pair of pants like that could ever be made to look sexy. But, man, he did not mind in the least that Penelope DePaul had proved him wrong. Ozzie called her a tall drink of Secret Service agent, and he couldn't disagree.

"Considering I thought the other two houses we checked were the right ones," she frowned, "the answer to your question is *no*. I'm not sure. But if your friend Vanessa translated what that lady at the last place said, the address we're looking for is the *blue* house at the end of *Jalan Putra*. This *should* be Jalan Putra and *that* is definitely a blue house."

She pointed to a bright-azure structure built atop a

crumbling gray slab. The tiny house had a rusting tin roof and three poured cement steps leading up to a scratched wooden door. Bright-green curtains fluttered in its two open windows and a clothesline with an array of apparel flapping in the gentle breeze was strung from the side of the structure to a nearby light pole. A multi-hued rooster strutted his stuff in the front yard, shaking his tail feathers at the drab-colored hen who ignored him as she pecked in the dirt. *Typical.*

All in all, to call the place decidedly *low*-tech would be an understatement. Which was why it was weird to glance over the roofline and see the incredibly *high*-tech, almost futuristic-looking Petronas Towers looming in the near distance.

"But seeing as how there aren't any house numbers anywhere and half the street signs are missing," she continued, rubbing an impatient finger down the bridge of her nose, "I wouldn't be at all surprised if we find ourselves zero for three."

Her frustration was palpable, and Dan couldn't blame her. They'd driven around in circles through this neighborhood only to knock on two wrong doors. And since no one spoke English, he'd had to call back to HQ to elicit Vanessa's help in translating their questions to the locals so that they could try to figure out where the hell they were and where the hell they *should* be.

It had eaten up a lot of time. And every minute that ticked by was one more minute the hotel's security director could use to make his escape. Even so, it was good to see Penni focused on something other than simply trying her damndest to keep from falling apart.

Because, quite honestly, watching her struggle to do that had been…well…*awful*. And then when she *had* finally broken, when she pulled him into the bathroom and went up on tiptoe to claim his mouth, when she asked him to make love to her despite the fact he didn't have a condom, when she—

"Hey." Penni grabbed his elbow, pulling him from his thoughts. "Isn't that the guy we're looking for?"

He followed the line of her extended finger to see a man with a plastic grocery bag in each hand meandering down the road toward them. The guy's eyes were focused on his footing on the uneven pavement, and Dan agreed. He looked remarkably similar the employee photo the hotel manager had showed them earlier.

"Could be," he murmured, putting his hand behind his waist to grab the butt of his Ruger P90. It sat nestled at the small of his back, so familiar he sometimes forgot it was there and fell asleep wearing it. "This guy coming has the same face-shape. The same tall, skinny build. Same black hair and skin tone. Then again, that describes the majority of the population."

As the man ambled closer, a little spurt of adrenaline zipped through Dan's veins, heightening his senses, coaxing to life the hard-hitting Navy SEAL who still lived inside him even though he'd spent a year doing his best to drown the fucker. Suddenly the sound of the hen's gentle clucks were amplified, and the humid air pressing against the exposed skin along his arms and face was like a wet, silken sheet.

Jesus, he'd *missed* this feeling when he'd been nose-first in a bottle. This feeling of awareness. Of anticipation. Of…*readiness*.

"That's him for sure," Penni whispered at the exact same moment he came to a similar conclusion.

"Rajen Musa!" he called the man's name.

Startled, Rajen skidded to a stop in the middle of the rutted street. And then—*holy fuck!*—he dropped his bags, turned on his heels, and straight-up *bolted*.

"Christ!" Penni hissed as that spurt of adrenaline turned into a full-on fireman's hose.

His weapon was out in an instant, aimed, and ready to fire. "Stop!" he yelled as he beat feet after the scumbag with Penni hot on his heels. The soles of her flat dress shoes slapped against the pavement with a rhythmic *thwack, thwack.* "Stop! Or I'll shoot you dead!"

Not really. He needed to ask the asswipe some questions first. But a round to the knee wasn't out of the question. His finger tightened on his trigger as he poured more effort into eating up the distance Rajen was trying to put between them. Too bad for Rajen that once he'd gotten through the hell of detox, he'd stuck himself on a treadmill, working his way up from a slow, one-mile jog to a fast, five-mile sprint. There were still some things he was struggling to get back after his year of drunken self-destruction, but speed and agility weren't on the list.

"I'll do it!" he warned again, pulling away from Penni and halving the distance to his target. "And I know you understand me, motherfucker! Your boss told me you speak English!" But it was obvious the bastard wasn't going to heed his threat, and up ahead the city grew dense, a rabbit's warren of alleyways and cramped buildings vying for space. Taking aim, his legs still pumping and closing the gap, he pulled the trigger. *Bam!* The Ruger belched out a .45 caliber bullet at over a thousand feet per second. And *down* went the security director.

From the bloom of blood Dan glimpsed on the lower half of the guy's khaki-colored trousers, he'd missed Rajen's knee by two or three inches, nicking the side of his calf. But it was enough. The dude wasn't going anywhere.

Five more thundering steps brought him to the man's side. Rajen was now sitting in the middle of the street, grabbing his injured leg and wailing. Like, seriously, *wailing*. He could give Irdina some stiff competition in terms of tear production and loud, hiccupping cries.

"Rajen Musa," he said, his chest rising and falling with the effort to suck in the dense, wet air. The smoky smell of spent gunpowder filled his nose and mouth, its taste tart on his tongue. Pointing the Ruger at the security director's head, he continued, "You shoulda left the country when you had the chance."

"No!" Rajen cried, rocking slightly. Deep crimson blood coated his hands as he squeezed his leg. "No! I know nothing! I am innocent!"

"Innocent men don't…" Penni—who'd just caught up to them—bent at the waist, blowing hard. "Run," she finished.

"No, no, no." Rajen shook his head, his face shiny with tears. "Whatever they did, I had no part. I-I just gave them room numbers th-they ask for and…and access key to s-s-stairwell. Nothing more. Nothing *more!*" he wailed, his accent so thick it was difficult to make out his words. "I swear."

Dan glanced at Penni as she straightened, still trying to catch her breath. "You believe him?" he asked.

He could tell by her expression that she wasn't sure, but

she was a bright bulb. And she'd read his intention correctly. "Not for an instant." She shook her head vehemently.

"I swear," Rajen insisted again, grabbing the leg of Dan's jeans with a bloody hand. "They found me and—"

"*Who* found you?" he demanded, not allowing the barrel of his weapon to waiver from its position an inch from the man's temple.

"I do not know name," Rajen insisted, and Dan tilted his head, making sure his expression hardened further. Rajen's voice fell to a terrified, pain-filled whimper. "I promise I do not know. I only know he *Jemaah Islamiyah.* He offer me much money to give him room numbers of Americans coming to…uh…uh"—Dan watched the man's desperate expression edge toward panic as he searched for the correct word—"flower assembly." Flower assembly? Oh, horticultural convention. Yeah, close enough. "He no tell me his plans. Just tell me find room numbers and give access key." He shook Dan's pant leg as a small puddle of blood formed on the ground beneath his injured calf. "Please, I speak truth."

"How did this man, this *Jemaah Islamiyah* militant," he snarled the words, "know where to find the agents on duty? The one on the balcony and the one across the street on the roof of the shopping mall? That had *nothing* to do with room numbers or—"

"I know not what you say!" Rajen screamed, more tears welling in his eyes, and was that? Yeah, the dude had a serious amount of snot running over his lips. Dan's own lips curled. "I know nothing of—"

"How did they know about the transmitters in Abby's clothes!" he bellowed, pressing the barrel of his weapon tight against Rajen's head.

"I know not!" the security director's voice screeched loud and high enough to send a flock of pigeons that had alighted on one of the gazillion overhead wires strung across the city, into noisy flight.

"Then why did you—"

But that's all he managed because Penni interrupted him by yelling, "Go back inside your homes!" He found her gripping her service weapon with both hands and turning in a slow circle, keeping her eyes trained on the people who had begun slipping from their houses to investigate the commotion. "We are American authorities!" She shifted her Glock to one hand so she could reach for her Secret Service badge with the other, flashing her credentials to the growing crowd. "This man is a terrorist!"

"No! No terrorist!" Rajen cried, hiccupping and releasing Dan to once again place both hands around his injured leg.

A few murmurs rippled through those gathered even as more people slowly emerged from homes, backyards, and the narrow alleys running between the houses.

"I don't think they understand you," Dan whispered. "And even if they do, I don't think that badge of yours holds much water with 'em." The twanging hairs on the back of his neck told him they might be about to find themselves in a world of trouble. The kind that happened when a crowd turned into a mob. Tension vibrated through the air, and he was reminded of the time he accidently stumbled into a notoriously gang-violent neighborhood back in good ol' Detroit Rock City. Just like back then, he thought, *This could get real bad, real quick.* "Penni, get the car."

"Uh-huh." She nodded, swallowing. "I think you're right."

He watched her break into a run toward the SUV, keeping an eye on one particular guy who was stalking up the street toward them. To say the dude's expression was unfriendly would be like calling a great white shark unfriendly.

"No. Fuck, no," he whispered to himself, well versed in how quickly things could turn violent in a situation like this. "If you didn't know what their plans were, if you're so innocent," he continued to question Rajen because, holy shit, if Penni didn't get that vehicle back to him PDQ he might be fighting off half the population of Kuala Lumpur and miss his chance to ask the man anything else, "then why did you run when you saw us? Why did you call in sick to work today?"

Rajen, too frightened and too preoccupied by his own pain to recognize the volatility of his environment—and just how close he might be to obtaining his freedom—answered tearfully, "I call in sick because the man, he tell me to. When I say I the only one to know how to get footage from hotel cameras, he say *that good. That may help slow authorities down.* And then he offer me more money to stay home today."

Shit ten thousand bricks! This was turning into a CCF. A classic clusterfuck. "And you ran when you saw us because?" he prompted, narrowing his eyes at the man who was still advancing in their direction. He shook his head, the universal signal for *you want no part of this, buddy.* Unfortunately, the guy didn't agree. He just kept on coming. And the crowd…it was beginning to vibrate, to hum with disapproval. In short: the natives were growing restless. Dan's heart beat out a rapid *lub-dub*, his every cell focusing as he readied himself to take his Ruger away from Rajen's head so he could point it elsewhere. He figured he'd start with Mr. Looking for a Fight.

"B-because you look like Americans. I gave room numbers of Americans to *Jemaah Islamiyah*. I scared! I in trouble!"

"Sure, sure." Dan nodded, the hairs on his arms alerting him to the fact that he was sitting in the middle of a lit powder keg, and things were about tens second away from blowing the hell up. "So *not* so innocent are you, Rajen? You knew the JI wouldn't use that information you gave 'em for anything good."

"But I—"

Whatever Rajen was about to say was drowned out by the sound of the big engine on the SUV roaring to life up the street. The squeal of tires followed a half second later.

"Come on, Mr. Musa," he said, bending to grab the security director's collar in one hand—careful to simultaneously keep hold of his P90; yeah, you better believe it—while wrapping the other around the guy's waistband. "You're coming with us."

"No!" Rajen yelled, struggling in his grip. And that's all it took for the crowd to ignite. All at once, two dozen individuals, tall, short, fat, small, young, and old began advancing in Dan's direction. But Penni, bless her, was quicker than the mob. The SUV lurched to a stop beside him, the rear passenger-side door swinging open. With a heave and a toss, he lobbed Rajen into the bucket seat, diving in after the guy and yelling, "Get us outta here!"

Penni didn't hesitate. She stepped on the gas, working through the gears like a classic Motown speed racer as the big vehicle fishtailed its way down the block.

"You get anything more from him?" she called over her shoulder after a bit.

"Only that you were right. He's just as much of a dupe as Irdina. He'll be useless in helping us found out who the mole is."

"Mother-flippin' hell!" she hissed, taking the next corner on two wheels and proving she was skilled at far more than just kissing.

"Yeah," he said. "I couldn't have said it better myself."

Chapter Twenty-one

"What the frickin' sticks?" Abby breathed, her heart trying to beat through her rib cage. "Who's shooting at us?"

"I told that sorry *cara pincha* I would kill him if he tried to come after you again," he growled, his upper lip curled back in a snarl. "Fucker obviously has a death wish."

Fucker, aka Shadow Man…

She swallowed. How had the JI leader possibly managed to forge the river with the bridge down? The current was too fast to swim across, and surely there hadn't been a handy-dandy motorboat lying around the jungle. Then again, given the ingenuity he'd displayed in carrying out her abduction, he'd proved himself nothing if not resourceful. "Are you sure it's him?" she wheezed.

Carlos paused while pushing the clip back into his weapon after checking to make sure it was full. "Who else would it be?"

"Good point," she admitted, turning to see Yonus standing between two of the huge brown roots of the jungle giant growing next to the one she and Carlos were hiding behind. He was flattened face-first against the mammoth trunk, his arms spread, his fingers desperately gripping the bark like he was afraid the thing might suddenly decide to fly away.

"What is h-happening?" he asked, his voice low and raspy, yet perfectly audible given the two loud, obnoxious gun blasts had resulted in an eerie, almost malevolent silence descending over the jungle. The buzzing insects, chirping birds, and calling monkeys were quiet, as if they knew lives were hanging in the balance and waited breathlessly to see what the outcome would be.

"We're being targeted by JI militants," she said, sorry as hell to see the sweet young man dragged into her own personal shitstorm. *And add one* more *item to my long list of Things to Feel Awful About.* Luckily, Carlos was standing next to her, no doubt formulating some sort of brilliant, super-secret spy-guy plan to foil the militants.

"But Carlos here is a special operations warrior," she added. "He's like Superman, Batman, and Captain America all rolled into one."

"That may be pushing things," Carlos muttered, taking a peek from behind the trunk, only to duck back quickly when a loud *pop* and a *whiz* sounded right before a bullet slammed into the road in front of them.

Yonus tried licking his lips. But the way his tongue stuck told her he had that whole high-noon, desert-dry mouth thing going on. Weird how terror and confusion had that effect on the human body. "I th-thought you said he was a doctor," he hissed.

"He's that, too," she assured him, comforted, despite their current predicament, by the feel of Carlos's back muscles flexing against the fingers she'd tucked into his waistband. "A man of many talents."

The whites of Yonus's eyes blazed in the dark shade of the overhead canopy, and it was obvious he didn't share her confidence that Carlos would be able to get them out of their current predicament alive. But that's only because he didn't *know* Carlos. If he did, he'd know that Shadow Man was a few minutes away from being turned into crap on a cracker.

"What do the *Jemaah Islamiyah* want with both of you?" Yonus asked, his chest rising and falling with rapid-fire breaths.

"Not Carlos," she whispered. "Just me."

"What do they want with *you?*"

"Leverage," she said, taking a page from Carlos's Book on Brevity.

Yonus frowned. "How could they possibly use you as leverage?"

"Because I'm the daughter of the president of the United States." I mean, she figured it was only fair Yonus knew *exactly* what he'd gotten involved in.

"Oh, no," he husked, but didn't have time to elaborate because right then, Shadow Man called out from his hiding spot.

"Give us the woman and no one has to die!"

Alrighty then. Sure. And where had she heard *that* before? Oh, yes. It was a line in every B-rate thriller movie. The kind where everyone—or *nearly* everyone—ended up dead by the closing credits regardless of any promises made by the villain.

"The only one who'll be dying here, *pendejo,*" Carlos called back, "is you and any rat-faced fucker you brought with you!"

Rat-faced? Hmmm. All right, so given Shadow Man's beady black eyes and long, skinny nose, she could maybe see the resemblance.

"Your one gun," Shadow Man retorted, a hint of arrogance in his tone, "against my four!"

A second passed. Then two. "Did he really just give away how many men he has with him?" Carlos whispered incredulously, almost to himself.

"And I have more men coming!" Shadow Man quickly added, forcing Abby to wonder if that was the truth or if he'd simply realized his mistake and was looking for a way to cover it. "Send out the woman now, and no one gets hurt!"

Carlos listened to the response with his head cocked in such a way that she knew he was busy getting a bead on Shadow Man's location. *See*...straight up superhero stuff. "I don't believe you!" he yelled back. "You already tried to kill her by the river! You were shooting at us with everything you had!" Again he cocked his head, waiting for the response.

"A mistake made by my overzealous compatriots, I assure you!"

"And when you took a shot at her now?"

"Not her!" Shadow Man called. "You! You know as well as I that the woman is no good to me dead! Just send her out!"

She swallowed, curling her fingers more tightly around his waistband. He glanced over his shoulder. "Don't worry, *cariño*. I'll get you out of this."

"I know," she whispered, trusting him implicitly. She lifted a hand to squeeze his arm reassuringly. He needed all his wits focused on the terrorists, not worrying about whether or not she was about to disintegrate into a puddle of terrified goo around his jungle boots. "I know you will, and I—Oh my God! You're hit!"

Her hand came away from his arm wet with warm, sticky blood. And when she glanced down, she saw it dripping from his fingers, speckling the big roots of the tree snaking beneath their feet. Just like that, the world titled on it axis. And then, as if that wasn't bad enough, it spun crazily in its orbit. She squeezed her eyes shut.

So much for not turning into a puddle of goo around his jungle boots. She knew from experience that what came next was something straight out of a Pitbull featuring Ke$ha song. She was going down. Although, as far as she could figure, no one was yelling, "Timber!"

Chewbacca's flying shit, Abby! Don't do this now! But no matter how she gritted her teeth and clenched her fists, little flashes of white strobed behind her eyelids, the precursor to lights-out.

"Abby." Carlos grabbed her arm, giving her a little shake. "Take a breath. It's nothing. Just a nick, eh?"

Yep…just a nick. With a *lot* of blood.

No! She wouldn't pass out. She *couldn't* pass out. She might be the damsel in distress. But by God, she refused to act it. Concentrating everything she had on remaining vertical, she planted her hands on her hips and forced great gulps of air past her constricted throat and into her lungs. Oxygen rushed to her brain in a dizzying *whoosh*, and the forest instantly stopped doing its best impression of a merry-go-round. Although, when she opened her eyes, little specs of light were still flashing in her peripheral vision.

Not exactly great. But better.

Not daring to glance down at Carlos's wounded arm, she grabbed the hem of her tunic and raised the material to her teeth. Finding a seam, she bit down hard, and yanked. A long strand of cotton tore free, and the curious quiet of the jungle caused the subsequent *riiiiiip* to sound ridiculously loud. Before she could think about what she was doing—and have another go at performing the ol' Pitbull/Ke$ha *timber* maneuver—she wound the material around Carlos's bicep. Doing her best to tie it off without really ever taking a good, long gander at the furrow of shredded flesh that leaked long streaks of—*gulp; Oh, God!*—blood down his forearm.

"You okay, *mi vida*?" he asked when she lifted her hand to her head.

"Yep." She nodded vigorously. Too vigorously obviously when the jungle did another slow tilt. *Gah!* "Sorry. I'm no good around blood anymore."

Just don't look down at his arm. Just don't look down at his arm. Just don't look—

"No worries," he told her. "I've cut myself worse shaving." And if *that* was true, the man definitely needed a new razor. "But thanks for the field dress—"

"Uh, I hate to interrupt," Yonus said politely, as if it were every day he found himself smack dab in the middle of a Mexican standoff. *Malaysian standoff?* "But I think someone is trying to sneak up on us. I saw a flash of movement over…over there." He pointed.

Carlos's chin swiveled in the direction of Yonus's finger. Then, "Stay with her," he told the young man. "As long as you do, you'll be safe. You heard him. They won't kill her. They need her alive."

"Wait." She grabbed his arm—his *uninjured* arm; *don't look down, don't look down*. "You can't go out there by yourself."

"Trust me." He chucked her on the chin. And then he did it again. He frickin' *winked* at her. She opened her mouth to tell him they needed to have a serious discussion about which circumstances were and were *not* appropriate for winking, but he cut her off. "I do this kind of thing all the time." And with that, he pulled that deadly sharp knife from the clip on his waistband and disappeared into the undergrowth behind them.

Yep, he might do this kind of thing all the time, but he'd never done it for *her*. To protect *her*. And for the first time since they made that madcap dash across that rickety bridge, she considered the possibility that Carlos could very well die while trying to spirit her across the border to Thailand.

No. God, no. Don't let that happen. And although she'd gotten pretty good at praying over the years—mostly for Carlos—the pact she made at the moment with the big man upstairs would have her down on her knees every single night for the rest of her days...

Steady flattened himself behind a tree less than twenty yards away from Yonus and Abby and waited...

Yonus was right. Someone *was* trying to flank them. Fortunately, whatever else this JI asshole was, stealthy he was *not*. Steady could hear each of his footfalls disturbing the debris littering the forest floor. And every time he moved a little closer, the clip attaching his AK-47 to its strap clanked quietly. The man obviously hadn't learned the trick of wrapping the harness around his wrist and arm. That little maneuver both kept the weapon attached to the body should the shooter lose his grip and also kept the accoutrements from jangling against one another.

And thank you, Ranger School, he thought as he listened intently to every subtle rustle, every tiny *clink* that told him his target crept closer and closer.

As it had the tendency to do when a person's life was nearing its end, time seemed to slow and stretch. Each of Steady's heartbeats took an infinity, each of his breaths lasted a millennia. And during this strange time without time, he took the opportunity to clear his mind, clear his heart, wipe clean his soul. In an instant, he became nothing but a blank slate. A thing. A machine. A *soldier.* One without feeling, without regret, and without remorse.

It was a practice he'd learned very early in his stint with the Army when facing an enemy down the length of his sights or head-on in hand-to-hand combat. Because as a doctor, he was trained to protect life, to *save* life. But as a Ranger and a spec-ops warrior, he was often tasked with just the opposite, dispatching life with swift and oftentimes brutal precision. So in order to do that, in order to keep his true self from hesitating and giving his adversary an opportunity to get the upper hand, he'd learned to turn off, empty out, let go of Steady and simply…*act.*

The tree against his back was rough. The air in the jungle hung heavy with the scent of wet foliage and exotic flowers. And the sweat slicking his skin ran down his temples and the groove of his spine. But he sensed none of it. His entire being was focused on one and only one thing. His target. And, then, it was time…

The militant crept by him, crouched low and advancing slowing. Steady slid out from his position behind the tree and slunk onto the heels of the terrorist like the dark specter of death he was. One hand grabbed the man's perspiration-damp forehead as the other expertly pulled his knife across the guy's throat. Flesh, muscle, tendon, and vein gave way to the impossible sharpness of his blade. And a soft, surprised gurgle was the only sound to breach the silence of the forest.

Steady held the dying terrorist against him for a brief moment as the man's lifeblood quickly drained from him. Then he carefully, gently lowered the body to the ground. Which is when he spied the man's small backpack. Quickly unzipping the main pouch, he pulled out an old, plastic satellite phone the relative size and shape—and *weight*—of two bricks. Punching in the number for BKI headquarters, he crossed his fingers for a connection. But a double beep told him the damn thing's battery had run out. *Hell.* Tossing the useless piece of equipment aside, he grabbed the strap of the AK and slung the machine gun over his shoulder—in a situation like this, a man could never have too many weapons.

Without a backward glance, he stalked in the direction of the one he loved, and thought, without guilt or apology, *One down. Three to go...*

Abby was so relieved to see Carlos materialize from the foliage it took everything she had not to run to him. Of course, along with the fact that exposing herself in any way would be beyond stupid, there was the dark, deadly gleam in his eye, the hard clench of his jaw, and the way he wiped his blade against the front of his cargo pants, leaving behind a—*holy shitpickle*—dark, wet stain that helped to keep her rooted to the spot.

Blood…

She didn't need to be told what had happened out there in the eerie green screen of the jungle. One look at him and the newly acquired machine gun slung over his shoulder and she knew the whole story. He had killed. For her. And as grateful as she was that he was walking toward her, so big, so tough, so very capable, a part of her couldn't help but regret the fact that he'd been forced to take a life in her name.

Why did so many have to die? *And when will it all stop?*

Her treasonous lower lip threatened to tremble, so she clamped it hard between her teeth. And the tears pricking behind her eyes she quickly, angrily blinked away. She couldn't have him mistaking her expression of sadness for condemnation or disapproval. That was so far from the truth. He was everything fine and good and brave. So when he took a position beside her—his heat radiating out to her like gentle fingers—she didn't hesitate to meet his gaze straight on. "Is it taken care of?" she asked, keeping her voice neutral.

He dipped his chin once, a muscle tightening in his jaw.

"Good." She raked in a deep breath. "So what's next?"

She thought she saw his eyes clear, just a little. And if she wasn't mistaken his shoulders relaxed the tiniest bit. But instead of answering her, he turned and yelled in the direction of the logging road, "In case you were wondering, you're down one man! And if my math is right, now it's your three guns to my two!"

A muffled bark of rage came from across the road some distance behind them. Further along, Shadow Man hissed something in Malay, obviously a command for whoever was moving in their direction to keep quiet. Abby watched as Carlos glanced quickly around the tree, calculating range and scope and probably a whole slew of other variables she couldn't possibly comprehend.

After a couple of seconds, Shadow Man called back, "I still like my odds!"

"Which just proves what a fucking idiot you really are!" It was obvious Carlos was taunting the guy, and Abby could only assume he was trying to force Shadow Man into acting irrationally. Or else he was simply trying to keep track of everyone's location. She didn't have time to ask him which one it was because he turned to Yonus, whispering, "They're trying to get ahead of us, likely to keep us from making a break for the truck. Which is why we need to move. Now!"

With one hand gripping his pistol, and the other wrapped around her arm, he pulled her away from the tree and deeper into the undergrowth. She glanced over her shoulder to see Yonus hesitate. And just as she was about to tell Carlos they had to wait, they couldn't leave the young man behind, Yonus gulped and dashed toward them. He caught up just before they slid out of sight.

Darting from tree to tree, the three of them quietly jumped over roots and slapped aside creeping plants that tried to snag their arms and legs as they paralleled the logging road. And all the while, Carlos led the way just as the tattoo scrawled across his back said he would. Ever-ready, ever-steady, and ever-*deadly.*

Which he proved when a terrorist jumped out at them from behind a large bush. Abby couldn't hold back the scream that tore from her throat when a machine gun pointed straight at Carlos's chest. But she didn't have time to do more than that. Thank goodness Carlos's reflexes were quicker than hers. Before the man could squeeze off a round, Carlos booted the weapon from the militant's hand with a roundhouse kick that would've made Jackie Chan proud.

For a couple of seconds, the two men stood there, facing each other, both blowing like they'd run a race.

"Don't do it," Carlos hissed when the guy reached for the knife on his belt.

Yonus yelled something in Malay. Probably *stop* or *no!* But the JI goon didn't heed his warning. With a snarl and a demon yell, the skinny terrorist launched himself at Carlos, his silver blade glinting in the dappled light, his free hand curved into a claw.

No, no, no!

Abby bent to pick up the dropped machine gun, surprised by its weight and the warmth of the trigger's metal against her finger. But she didn't have time to straighten or aim when a loud *boom* echoed into the treetops. She lifted her gaze to see Carlos's pistol faintly smoking and the terrorist crumpled on the ground in a heap of dirty clothes and mahogany skin.

Again, Carlos's tattoos had proved correct. The JI militant had messed with the best and he'd died like the rest. She shook her head, swallowing. It was so senseless. All this killing. All this…*dying*.

"Don't look," Carlos warned, turning to offer her a hand up. With a brief glance—and you can bet your bottom dollar it was only the *briefest* of glances—she noted the deep-red blood that had snaked and dripped from around his fingers was dried to a crusty brown.

Good. That's good. Because it meant her slapdash field dressing had stopped his bleeding.

"I wasn't planning on it," she gulped, allowing him to pull her to her feet.

"Did you hear that, you motherfucker?" Carlos tilted his head back, yelling into the canopy. "Now I have three weapons to your two! You want to keep playing this game?"

Silence met his call. And that was somehow worse than the sound of Shadow Man's wretched voice.

"He's moving in," Carlos whispered, taking the machine gun from her hands and slinging it over his shoulder to join the one already hanging there. A chill of foreboding snaked up her spine as he continued, "Let's go! QQS!"

Abby didn't bother to enlighten Yonus as to what the letters stood for. She figured he got the general gist. And a few more seconds of dodging and jumping and running brought them to the edge of the tree line, directly beside Yonus's Chevy pickup truck circa 1960-something. Rust had eaten away at the edges of its wheel wells. There was a massive crack snaking across its rear window. And the paint was an odd mix of faded yellow and primer. But the big, knobby wheels looked new. And it'd made the trip out here from the highway, so Abby was crossing her fingers it would make the trip back.

"Okay." Carlos glanced left and right. Then he stared straight at Yonus—*poor* Yonus who'd suddenly found himself stuck in the middle of some deadly international tomfuckery. The guy probably wished he'd stayed in bed this morning. "I'll step out, lay down covering fire, and you and Abby hop in the truck. Once you're in with the engine running, I'll jump in the back."

Now hold the mothertrucking phone. "Wait a minute," she hissed, her heart going from a wild jog to a full-on sprint. *This* was the grand plan she'd been giving him so much credit for? "You can't just step out in the open. You'll be shooting blind while basically wearing a big ol' bull's-eye on your chest."

"It's the only way."

"No." She shook her head, holding up a hand she discovered was shaking. "No, it's not. We could come up with something else, and I—"

"You have your keys ready?" he asked Yonus, completely ignoring her.

"Yes." Yonus lifted the ring and the keys attached to it jangled quietly. In the continuing quiet of the jungle, they sounded like the frickin' bells of Notre Dame chiming the hour…and giving away their position.

She winced, making a face, but undo noise was currently the least of her worries. "Damnit, Carlos. This isn't—"

"If things go sideways"—he interrupted again, his black eyes boring into her with enough force to bring her to her knees. Luckily, blood was the *only* kryptonite to her Superman. Pushy, courageous, *idiotic* men she was completely immune to. Well, at least outside of the bedroom—"I don't want you playing the hero, *mi vida*. You make a run for that border just as quick as you can."

Uh, yep… And she would file that under Hell No.

"If things go *sideways?*" she stressed. "See, you think

this plan is just as crazy as I do." She grabbed his arm, giving it a shake, growing more and more desperate with each passing second. Desperate and scared. No, desperate and *terrified.* Her pulse pounded through her veins, burning like it was full of weed killer, and her brain buzzed like she'd wrapped it in a string of outdoor electric lights and flipped the switch. "So there has to be another way to—"

"Abby," he stopped her with a finger on her lips. "This is our chance. And by the way, I love you."

Um…*wha?*

Had she heard him correctly? Surely not, because in what world did those six words ever go together? *By the way* belonged in sentences that ended with *I forgot to fold the clothes in the dryer* or *your mother called to see if you wanted to go to brunch next Sunday. By the way* did *not* go with the words *I love you.*

But before she had time to dig a finger in her ear and ask him to repeat himself, he bent to press a quick kiss to her lips, his warm breath so sweet she almost wept. Then the brave, beautiful sonofabitch raised his sidearm, shouldered one of the machine guns, and stepped out into the road…

Chapter Twenty-two

Steady laid on the Kalashnikov's trigger and sawed a continuous arc of hot lead across the jungle and road behind the beat-up pickup truck. Globs of mud jumped from the surface of the logging track, bark splintered on the trees, and leaves ripped to shreds under his steady barrage. The constant *rat-a-tat-tat* of the rusty Russian special was a deafening roar. Luckily, he'd learned long ago to ignore the distracting thunder of gunfire and concentrate instead on the task at hand.

"Now!" he yelled over his shoulder to Yonus and Abby. "Go now!"

He didn't see them emerge from the brush, too preoccupied with dropping the weapon when the clip ran dry and quickly shouldering the remaining AK. But he could feel them race into the open. His heightened senses telling him they'd left the tree line as surely as if he'd seen them with his own two eyes. And that was more than enough impetus to have him squeezing the trigger, gritting his teeth against the bruising pressure of each recoil, and raining a Rambo-style path of destruction in a violent arc down the road in what he *hoped* was the direction of the remaining terrorists.

Was he scared to stand out in the open when he wasn't sure where the enemy was? The quick answer was *no*. He was a spec-ops soldier, a strange breed of man who'd lived and worked so close to the edge that life-and-death situations no longer engendered in him the usual—some would say *sane*—emotional response.

But the thought of Abby catching a stray round? *Dios mio.* Now *that* filled him with the kind of terror he hadn't experienced since his very first combat mission. Or, quite honestly, maybe *ever.* Never before had he had so much to lose. When he'd joined the Rangers, his parents had already been dead for five years, he'd just put his twin sister in the ground, and the one girl he wanted more than his next breath had soundly rejected him—or so he'd thought at the time.

But now?

Now he had so *much* ahead of him. In the midst of the chaos, he could see it so clearly. A big, white wedding—if Abby would have him. And a whole passel of kids—if she'd have them. A lifetime of loving and laughing and teasing and screwing. And it was the fear of losing it all to one misplaced bullet that made him dizzy with relief when he heard the truck's passenger-side door groan open a second before the big engine turned over with a choked growl.

Okay, on to step two...

The second AK spit forth its final bullet, and he dropped it to the muddy road at his feet. Squeezing the trigger on his M9 with focused precision—*Boom! Boom! Boom!*—he aimed each bullet at the trees he figured the militants were most likely to be hunkered behind. And all the while he backed toward the truck's tailgate.

He was maybe five feet from the vehicle when he saw movement in his peripheral vision...just a second too late. He felt the gaping black hole of the Kalashnikov's barrel focus on his head before he had a chance to position himself to return fire. And in that split second, he had time for a million regrets. Starting with him not being around to call in the weekly order to have fresh flowers put on Rosa's grave, and ending with him never hearing Abby tell him she loved him. With a sense of sad acceptance, he braced himself for the *crack* of the bullet—the last thing he'd ever hear. But instead, the faint and wonderfully familiar *click* of a jammed weapon sounded instead.

Sonofa—

He spun in an instant, his finger tightening on his trigger, but not before the terrorist standing on the side of the road grabbed the barrel of his AK and swung the entire weapon baseball bat–style, like he was frackin' Babe Ruth or something. A blast of white-hot pain rocketed up Steady's arm when the metal of the machine gun met the bones of his hand. He cursed as the Beretta flew from his fingers and landed some distance away in the muck and mire. He had no time to make a grab for his Applegate-Fairbairn tactical blade before the JI *culo* launched himself in the air, grabbing his shoulders, and knocking them both to the ground.

His breath *whooshed* from his lungs on impact with the roadway, stars spinning crazily in front of his eyes when his skull bounced off the track. But he still had enough wherewithal to dodge the blow aimed for his face—*motherfucker!*—as he landed one of his own against the man's ribs. The terrorist groaned but didn't do much else. Steady didn't exactly have a good angle. And then the two of them devolved into a writhing mass of arms and legs, both vying for position, both screaming and grunting, both trying for the knife still attached to his belt.

"Go, Yonus!" he managed to bellow as hate-filled eyes and gritted teeth filled his vision. The man reached back to try for another blow, but he caught the asshole's flying fist right before it connected with his nose. Then…*fuck!* The militant managed to rip his knife from its sheath.

"Go, go, go!" he yelled as he used both hands to grab the asswipe's wrist. He fought against the weight bearing the blade down on him, his biceps burning, his tendons popping. The tip of the knife kissed the skin of his stomach, threatening to sink into his gut. And in that moment, he knew it could go either way. "Go, Yonus! Leave me!" he roared as adrenaline fueled him to fight harder. Fight smarter. Adrenaline and love. Because if he didn't come out the victor here, at least he'd die knowing Abby had gotten away.

That is if Yonus would just Get. The. Fuck. Out. Of. Here!

He thought he heard Abby screaming his name as Yonus *finally—gracias a Dios*—did as he was told. The truck's tires spun and kicked up mud in an earthy-smelling spray. It covered him in a cool, slick film, spattering across his face and the face of his assailant. Neither of them paid it any mind as they fought and spit and kicked. With a grunt and a heave, he managed to flip the terrorist onto his back. And for the first time, *he* was the one with the upper hand.

"Carlos!" This time he was certain he could hear Abby screeching through the truck's open window, her voice thick with tears as the vehicle fishtailed down the road. "No, Yonus! Stop!"

Don't you dare stop, Yonus, he thought as he gritted his teeth, squeezing the militant's wrist with every ounce of strength he had, growling his fury and his fear until he could feel the man's bones rubbing against one another. The terrorist yelped under the assault, his fingers loosening around the knife's handle.

Steady didn't hesitate. Wrenching the blade from the man's grip, he spun it neatly around on the flat of his palm, curled his fingers over the hardened nylon grip, and plunged the entire stainless steel length between the militant's ribs at an upward angle. The tip of the knife pierced through the man's pericardial sac and sliced straight into his beating heart. He was dead in an instant. His arms falling away and landing in the muck on the roadway with a couple of muted *splats*.

"Damn." Steady raked in giant gulps of oxygen, both in relief and disbelief. That'd been a very close thing. *Too* fuckin' close.

Yanking his knife free, barely noticing the sickening sucking sound it made upon retreat, he used the back of his wrist to wipe some of the dripping mud from his eyes. His heart raced so fast he had to fight to slow it, had to force himself to take steady, measured breaths even though his lungs longed to work like bellows. And despite his muscles aching and burning with spent adrenaline, he managed to push up to his knees, straddling the lifeless body of the terrorist.

A quick glance told him the truck was still barreling down the road toward safety. *Bueno*. Because according to his count, there was still one JI goon—aka Dickhead—left to dispatch. He was in the process of getting his feet under him, his eyes scanning the roadway in search of his Beretta, when something up the way caught his eye.

Holy fuuuuuuck! He watched in disbelief as the passenger-side door on Yonus's truck flew open a second before Abby threw herself from the moving vehicle. And so much for calming his racing heart, the organ felt like it exploded inside his chest. He was surprised it didn't take him to his knees again.

"No!" he roared, terror shooting through his system like a poisonous drug as Yonus slammed on the brakes, the truck sliding in a slow arc that ended when the vehicle slid off the side of the road and rocked to a stop. "Oh, *Dios!* Abby!"

But after a couple of bumpy rolls, the brave, stubborn, *crazy* woman hopped to her feet like a stuntman. And now she was running toward him, screaming his name. She looked like she'd been dipped in chocolate she was so completely covered in mud. And for one brief moment all he could do was stand there and stare. She was so beautiful. And *fierce.*

His love for her filled him anew, filled him to bursting. His love and his fear, because—

He didn't have time to finish the thought when the hairs along the back of his neck twanged out a warning. Which was why he wasn't surprised to hear Dickhead yell, "Don't move!"

Abby skidded to a stop in the middle of the road, slipping and going down on one knee. She was a full twenty yards up the way, but he could still see the whites of her wide eyes blazing through the mud covering her face.

Oh, Abby, he briefly squeezed his eyelids shut, desperation and despair warring for supremacy inside him. *Why didn't you leave when you had the chance,* mi vida*?*

But he knew the answer. The wonderful woman was

selfless and courageous. And damn her for it. Because he'd *won*. He'd seen her headed for safety, and that was all that mattered. But then she had to go and be all… well…*Abby*-like, and now he was back to square one.

He glanced over his shoulder and sure enough, there was Dickhead, crouched low along the side of the road and advancing quickly in his direction. His shoulder blades itched where Dickhead's AK was focused, and turning forward he calculated the distance to his Beretta, wondering how good of a shot Dickhead was and if the guy would be able to kill him before he had a chance to reclaim his weapon, take aim, and bring the fucker down.

He liked his chances, he decided. Because even *if* Dickhead managed to mortally wound him, surely he could live long enough to return the favor. *Surely.*

Taking a deep breath, he swallowed and dug the toe of his jungle boot deep into the mud atop the road, searching for solid ground and the traction it provided. His muscles coiled and shivered with readiness. But just before he pushed off, just before he launched himself toward his pistol, a deep muttering sounded overhead and he tilted his chin to see the canopy swaying violently.

What the—

Six combat-ready soldiers fast-roped in from above. And his relief was so overwhelming he nearly crowed a welcome. They hit the ground as a unit, unclipped, and aimed their M4s in the direction of Dickhead, who—no surprise—was already busting ass toward the tree line.

Sí. *If the sight of six fully geared-up U.S. spec-ops boys doesn't put the fear of* Allah *into a man, then nothing will…*

"You call for the cavalry?" one of the soldiers yelled above the sound of the chopper's rotors beating through the dense air overhead. His face was covered in camouflage paint, his aviator sunglasses nearly obscured by his floppy jungle boonie hat.

And just call Steady Mr. Noodle Legs. Because first he stumbled, and then he decided *screw it* and went ahead and allowed himself to fall to his knees. "*Sí*." He grinned, the need to laugh bubbling inside him. He stifled it. Figured the guy would think he'd lost his marbles if he let loose with it. "I sure am happy to see you boys."

"Happy to be here," the soldier replied. Then he motioned with his bearded chin toward the jungle. "Approximate number of unfriendlies out there?" Were these the Navy SEALs Dan had spoken of, the ones who'd fought side by side with a handful of BKI operators back in the day? Steady would bet a dime to a dollar they were. They had that scruffy, barely leashed, and fully locked-and-loaded SEAL look about them. *Hooah!*

"Just one," he said. "But if he was telling the truth, there could be more headed this way."

"Ten-four," Boonie Hat said. Then, with a series of hand gestures, he commanded his team to spread out into the jungle.

Steady didn't watch them go. Because right at that moment, Abby appeared in front of him. She slipped down to her knees, her arms thrown around his neck, her sweet lips peppering his muddy cheeks with even muddier kisses. And then, in true Abby form, she pulled back, her tears having left wet trails through the muck on her face. "You egg-sucking asshole!" she snarled.

"If you *ever* try to do anything like that again, sacrifice yourself, I swear I'll kill you myself!"

Umar could not *believe* it! All his hard work, all his planning, all the money he had paid to all those people had come to nothing. *Nothing!* His brother was still rotting away in a cell. And here *he* was running through the jungle with a squad of American soldiers hot on his heels. His only hope for escape was if somehow, someway, through the grace of *Allah*, his remaining men made it to him before he could be captured…or killed. Those soldiers had looked *more* than capable of the latter, although it was definitely the former he feared most.

He sent up a silent prayer as he vaulted over a low-lying bush and ran smack into a wall of hanging vines. Growling his frustration, slapping the clinging plants away, he managed to free himself and immediately broke into another headlong sprint.

Distance… Distance… He needed distance…

Because if he was being quite honest with himself, the chances of his men finding him were slim to none. The satellite phone had lost power before he could call in his last set of coordinates, and unless his fighters had heard the gunfire, they could very well be headed in the wrong direction. And if they *had* heard the gunfire? Well, it was not assured they would come to investigate. To say the majority of his men were unreliable was an understatement at best.

Rage and fear fueled him quickly through the undergrowth, his heart pounding, his breaths labored. There had been a small ravine some distance back, yes? And perhaps if he could make it there, he could duck into one of the narrow rock alcoves, cover himself with foliage, and hide. Perhaps if he could—

The sound of a stick crunching beneath a quickened step directly to his left had him ducking behind a tree. His chest burned like he had swallowed fire. His skin crawled like he had fallen into a bowl of maggots. *No, no, no!* This was not how it was supposed to end for him. He was a warrior of Islam, a jihadist who had so much more to accomplish! This could not be!

Snap! Crack!

He held his breath and tightened his finger on the trigger of his Kalashnikov. But just as he was prepared to jump from behind the tree and fire, the cool barrel of deadly weapon kissed his temple. His heart and his lungs stopped functioning, causing his head to spin with dizziness.

"Don't move," a deep, growling American voice advised. From the corner of his eye, he could see the soldier staring down the gun's sights at him. Blue eyes the color of the Oriental magpie-robin that used to nest outside his boyhood home, brooked no argument. But in that moment, Umar knew what he had to do. He would not end up like his brother. He would not allow himself to be taken only to spend the rest of his days behind bars. Better to die a martyr for the cause.

Quickly angling the AK's barrel beneath his chin, he closed his eyes and offered his soul to eternity. But before he could pull the trigger, his weapon was yanked from his hands by the blue-eyed soldier drawing down on him. He roared his fury just as another tall, brutal-looking commando materialized from behind a bush in front of him. The man was covered in camouflage…except for a pair of sunglasses that seemed to mock Umar because he could see his terrified reflection in them.

"Now normally," the man said, cradling his weapon in one arm while scratching the blond beard covering the lower half of his face with his free hand, "me and Mad Dog"—he dipped his chin toward the soldier holding Umar hostage—"and the rest of the boys wouldn't hesitate to just go ahead and let you eat a bullet." And, as if on cue, four more soldiers emerged from the undergrowth, quiet as ghosts. "But as it happens, there are some folks back in the States who are just *itchin'* to ask you a few questions."

"Noooo!" he yelled in English, spittle flying from his lips, his vocal cords flaying until his scream ended in a reedy whisper that sounded far too much like surrender…

Chapter Twenty-three

20,000 feet above Washington, DC
Fifteen hours later...

Penni leaned over her armrest, glancing down the cabin aisle of the private luxury jet to check on Abby. In the way any loving father whose daughter had been abducted and subsequently rescued would do, President Thompson had insisted Abby, in his words, "be brought home with all immediate haste." So the SEALs had flown her and Steady straight from the jungle to the Kuala Lumpur airport before taking off again with their hostage/kidnapper and the poor, terrified Good Samaritan Abby and Steady had met in the jungle in tow. She and Dan had been waiting to hustle the couple onboard the hastily chartered Gulfstream G650, no stops, no detours, and no pause to pick up their belongings from the hotel. Just wheels-up and get the hell home ASAP.

When POTUS gives an order, we follow it to a T, Dan said after Penni asked whether or not they should let Abby and Steady hit the showers in one of the airport's lounges before climbing onboard the high-tech aircraft. *And we do not deviate,* he'd finished, shooting her a meaningful look.

And so they hadn't. Deviated, that is. But Abby didn't seem to mind that she was still covered head to toe in dry, crusty mud. She was conked out in a seat four rows back, having fallen asleep less than ten minutes into the flight and having barely stirred since—even when they stopped to refuel in Beijing.

Penni was glad for it. Sleep, and its amazing recuperative powers, was the best thing for the poor woman after everything she'd been through.

Turning back around, she blew out a deep breath. Fifteen more minutes and they'd touch down in DC. There, she'd hand off the job of Abby's security to the freshly showered, bright-eyed, bushy-tailed Secret Service agents who were no doubt waiting to whisk the woman away. And then *she* could crawl under the covers back in her apartment and get some sleep. Probably *cry* herself to sleep, if she was being honest. She could feel the effects of the last two days, all the shock and the trauma, waiting for an outlet.

Like the kind of outlet you were looking for in the ladies' room? a little voice whispered.

No, she answered angrily. *Nothing like that. I just need to indulge in a good old-fashioned bawl-a-thon in the privacy of my own home. That's all. And then, maybe, I can start—*

"You didn't get any sleep?" Dan asked, stretching and yawning in the seat across the aisle. The muscles in his shoulders bulged into hard balls when he lifted his arms over his head. His T-shirt rode up the tiniest bit, just enough to reveal the light brown love trail that led from his belly button into the waistband of his jeans.

Hello! Her blood stirred at the sight, but she studiously ignored it. "I already fell down on the job of protecting Abby once," she told him. "I'll be damned if I do it again. I'll get some sleep once I'm officially released from duty."

Dan tilted his head, one corner of his luscious mouth quirked. "Tell me something, Agent DePaul. Were you always this tough?"

Tough? *Tough?* If he knew even a *fraction* of what was going on inside her, the turmoil of her emotions, the absolute *last* thing he'd think her was tough. "Growing up on the mean streets of Brooklyn with a police officer for a father pretty much ensures a backbone of steel."

But even steel has a melting point. And she had just about reached hers. *Christ,* she couldn't wait to get off this plane.

"Cop for a father, huh?" he asked, rubbing two fingers under his chin. The stubble on his face rasped against his knuckles, and his expression said he was poised to question her further about her past.

Because he was actually interested? Or because he felt somehow obligated to ask?

Either way, it doesn't matter. As soon as we're on the ground, he'll go his way and I'll go mine. After all, *she* was looking for human connection, and *he* was a black-ops warrior… So, no. There was no need for them to break into that whole let's-get-to-know-each-other song and dance. Besides, for whatever reason—call it insanity or accelerated attachment due to the crisis they'd been through together—it was going to be hard enough saying good-bye to him. Throw in a touching little heart-to-heart right here at the end, and it might turn mad impossible.

"He worked the same beat for nearly thirty years," she said, then quickly changed the subject. "So, I just got off the phone with my superior. He said agents from the U.S. embassy in Kuala Lumpur have picked up both Rajen and Irdina, and they're sending someone to look after little Jaya. The decision has been made to cover the cost for Jaya's treatment while they're trying to determine what, if anything, should be done with Irdina."

"That's good." Dan nodded. "And as it should be."

Penni agreed. "If ever I doubted Uncle Sam could be magnanimous, that little bit of news restored my faith in him."

Dan smiled, and she had to look away so he wouldn't see what that expression did to her insides. "Like any powerful man," he mused, "ol' Uncle can be equal parts brutal and kind."

"Mmm." She nodded noncommittally, figuring he'd know better than most.

"And Rajen? Our illustrious hotel security director? What's to become of him?"

Unconsciously fiddling with the buttons on her blouse, she said, "He underwent additional questioning once his wound had been patched up. But according to my superior, he's as much of a dupe as we thought. They're coordinating with the Malaysian government on how to handle his punishment."

Dan nodded, and she glanced over to find him letting loose with another massive yawn. "So that leaves?" he asked around a noisy exhale.

"Yonus Amani," she said, "the young man who tried to help Abby and Steady escape the JI's clutches. He's been debriefed. And my boss didn't come right out and say it, but I get the feeling he's been paid a pretty impressive sum to keep his mouth shut about anything and everything he saw out there in the jungle."

"Good for him." Dan nodded and one corner of his mouth quirked. "He deserves every red cent."

Penni nodded. "Which brings us to Umar Sungkar." Just saying the man's name made her lip curl. "Initial reports say he's a nasty piece of work. A fanatical militant through and through. My supervisor didn't know the exact location, but Umar is being transferred to what I can only assume is one of our black sites to undergo more vigorous…uh…questioning about where he got his Intel." And by questioning, she meant interrogative techniques that skated very close to the lines international laws had established more than sixty years ago. And that was the *brutal* side of Uncle Sam that Dan had spoken of.

"You mean one of the black sites that traitor Winterfield *didn't* disclose to the press?" Dan asked, his expression having gone from tired and lazy to hard and vicious in an instant.

For a couple of months now, the whole country had been reeling from the documents leaked by one former CIA agent named Luke Winterfield. It was all over the news, day and night, the exact locations of the safe houses, interrogation sites, and catch-all bolt-holes the U.S. kept throughout the world. And anyone who had ever held a position of affluence in either party, or who had worked in a classified post within the government, felt betrayed by the man's perfidy. Although there were some, mostly in the civilian sector, who lauded Winterfield for exposing the locations of those super-secret international facilities. *Those* people declared—quite loudly, usually—that it was only right they should know everything their government was up to.

And she would go ahead and label that No Stinkin' Way. The world didn't run on rainbows and glitter and unicorn farts. And in every corner of the globe, there were bad men ready and willing to do bad things. And the only way to catch them before they did those things was to have people who operated in the dark—people like Dan—and to maintain places, secret places, *special* places where those people who operated in the dark could take those bad men should the need arise.

"I mean exactly one of those." She nodded, pretty sure her expression mirrored Dan's. "Winterfield couldn't have known the locations of all them, right?"

Something...*strange* flashed across his handsome face.

"What?" she asked, cocking her head. "Do you know something I don't?"

He was quick to shrug. Maybe too quick. "I just think if a guy is gonna sell out his country in one area, there's not a lot stopping him from doing it in *all* areas."

"Hmm." She nodded, getting the distinct feeling he wasn't telling her the whole story. Her mind flashed back to Steady's hotel room and the cryptic "he" the two guys had briefly discussed when trying to determine who the mole might be and where he might have come from. "You don't think it's possible *Winterfield* was the one to give Umar his information, do you? I mean, how would he have come across that Intel? The Secret Service doesn't usually have dick to do with the CIA. Separation of powers and interests and whatnot."

"I guess we'll hafta wait and see what they get from the guy," Dan mused. Then, "So what'll you do now?"

"What do you mean?"

"I mean, once you get back to DC?"

Uh, non sequitor anyone? Anyone? Bueller? But she didn't call him on it. "Well, after eighteen or so hours of sleep, I'll do exactly what my father taught me to do." She clenched her hands into fists to keep from reaching up to rub her nose. She'd noticed anytime she did that, Dan cocked his head and narrowed his eyes at her. "I'll get right back to work." What she left off the end of that sentence was *and try with all my might to forget about you.*

He nodded, his lips twisting.

What's that look for? She didn't think she wanted to know. Especially when he opened his mouth. Closed it. Then opened it again before hesitating.

All right already. Here it comes.

And right on cue. "I know you said you didn't wanna talk about—"

"Still don't." She raised a hand, cutting him off.

He looked like he was inclined to argue, but the captain came over the intercom telling them they'd begun their initial descent into Reagan International Airport, and the moment was lost…

Abby cracked a lid, peeking over at Carlos in the seat next to her. *Huh. I thought super-secret black-ops warriors were supposed to hop-to from a dead sleep at the slightest rustle.* But even the captain's announcement wasn't enough to stir Carlos. His head was thrown back against the window, his mud-crusted arms crossed over his filthy tank top, his legs stretched across the aisle where the toe of his left jungle boot touched the brace on her seat. The quick-and-dirty field dressing the SEALs had applied to his frickin' *bullet wound*—scratch or not, it was still a frickin' *bullet wound*!—stood out in sharp white contrast to his dark, swarthy skin.

He looked awful. And wonderful. And so damn heroic. Which made sense considering that's exactly what he was. A hero. *Her* hero. She could not *believe* he'd been willing to sacrifice himself for her.

Oh, wait…

Yes, she could. Because that's exactly the kind of man he was. And that was the whole reason she'd been feigning sleep for nearly fifteen hours. She couldn't bring herself to face him and all his gallantry and courage and…love?

Just as it'd being doing the whole plane ride, her heart fluttered and flitted around inside her chest like that group of sphinx moths that had moved through the Botanic Garden last May. And like those moths—who had died when a late-season frost set in—she worried the sorry organ wouldn't survive what was coming next.

Had he told her he loved her right before he walked out into the middle of that logging road? Sitting there, eyes closed, not moving, barely breathing, she'd replayed the scene in her mind's eye time and again. *This is our only chance,* he'd said, following that up with, *And by the way…*what? It had *sounded* like *I love you.* But no matter how often she rehashed it, she couldn't believe it.

I misheard him, right? It's the only thing that makes sense.

After all, they hadn't seen each other in *eight years.*

And great sex—the most amazing, mind-bending, soul-shredding sex—aside, they were still virtual strangers.

Except we're not...

The truth was, she knew everything about him. The important things anyway. That he was gallant and loyal and true. Funny and so wonderfully smart-alecky when he wanted to be. And he knew her, too. Because despite that one thing, that one unforgiveable thing, she was still the same young woman he'd teased and tormented, laughed and joked with.

So maybe it *was* possible he loved her. For heavens to Betsy's sake, twenty-four hours ago she'd thought it unimaginable he could actually *want* her, see her as anything but that naive young girl she'd been. And look how wrong she'd been about *that*.

Her mind jumped back to the hot, humid hut. To salacious words whispered in her ear. To hard hands stroking her trembling flesh, and soft lips teasing and tormenting her as he thrust the long, thick length of himself inside. So deeply. So forcefully. So—

She shook away the memory when a rush of liquid heat pulsed between her thighs. *Back to the question at hand.* The question of whether or not it was possible Carlos might actually be in love with her. Because she sure as shit loved *him*. Loved him with every breath she took, every move she made, every bond she...

Holy ass, and now she was channeling an old Sting song. No, no. That was back when Sting was still with the Police, right? And...what the leaping lizard dung did any of *that* matter? Except to prove how exhausted, how flat-out bone-tired she was. Her brain was mush, her synapses firing out a bunch of nonsensical...uh...

lizard dung. Oh, and lookie! They were obviously stuck in a loop, too.

Good. Great. Gah!

She shifted, her elbow aching where it was pressed against the armrest. And just like that, Carlos's eyes flew open. He hadn't flinched when the captain's voice boomed over the intercom, hadn't stirred when the plane started its descent and the pressure inside the cabin caused her ears to pop. But the instant she moved... *bam!* He was awake. Dark, sparkling, completely lucid eyes focused on her.

"Good morning, *neña.*" His mouth curved into a slow, sexy grin. She had to look away.

Glancing out the window, she noted how the sinking sun cast a golden glow over the city below, shining over the Capitol building and the Washington Monument. It bathed their white exteriors in a rosy pink hue. She should be happy to be home. But for the life of her, she could take no comfort in the familiar sights. Because the end of her time with Carlos was quickly approaching.

"I think it's more like good *evening,*" she said, apropos of nothing.

"Mmm." He stretched, lifting his arms above his head and yawning mightily before pushing into a seated position. Tilting his head from side to side, the little *snapping* sounds of his vertebrae were heartbreakingly familiar. And he was so frickin' beautiful. So wonderful and fierce and kind and...*perfect.* And hers. At least he had been for a little while. But that was all about to change. Just as soon as she told him the truth about Rosa.

Which was *another* reason she'd been feigning sleep. She'd wanted...no...she'd *needed* a few more hours to gather her courage, to gather her wits, to try to find the right words to tell him—

The plane dipped, beginning its slow, lazy turn as the pilot aligned it with the runway. "*Mierda.* Are we here already? Did I sleep the whole way?"

"You needed it," she said. "You deserved it."

"Mmm," he hummed again, then reached over to touch her wrist.

She turned her hand palm-up to lace her fingers through his. His skin was so amazingly warm, roughened by calluses, and deeply tan compared to her own pale flesh. *This is probably the last time I'll ever touch him*, she realized. And, closing her eyes, she tried to burn the memory into her brain.

Then after a few more rare, wonderful moments, she told herself, *It's time to stop being a coward.*

"C-Carlos," she began, swallowing because his name was barely a whisper, inaudible above the loud throb of the jet engines as they throttled back for landing. But he was turned sideways in his seat, his temple pressed against the headrest, staring at her. So he saw her lips move.

Lifting his head, his mouth quirked. "What is it, Abby?"

Come on. Come on. Don't chicken out! "There's s-something I want to t-tell you," she managed with a little more volume.

His smile softened. His expression becoming sympathetic, almost…understanding. "I think I know what it is."

Her heart went from fluttering wildly to a dead stop. All the blood drained from her head. "You do?"

"*Sí.*" He winked. "You want to tell me you love me,

too." He reached over to push a crunchy, mud-caked lock of hair behind her ear.

So she *hadn't* misheard him back in the jungle. He *had* said he loved her. Carlos Soto…the doctor, the soldier, the *hero* loved…*her*…

And just like that, all the horror, all the pain, all the lies and heartbreak could no longer be held at bay. They rushed through her as surely and unstoppably as a stream filled to overflowing by spring rain. She burst into tears in an instant, her sobs wracking her body until she thought it was a wonder she didn't snap in two. Oh, if *only* that was what she needed to tell him. If *only* it could be that simple.

"Shh, *mi vida,*" he crooned. "Don't cry. Don't cry. You're turning all the dirt on your face back into mud."

She couldn't help herself. She reached across the aisle and threw her arms around his neck, pulling him close until they were both leaning over their armrests. "Oh, Carlos," she whispered, choking. "Can you ever forgive me?" Her brain buzzed. Her skin crawled. And her chest felt like she'd sliced it open with a rusty shovel. And even though he was filthy, he still smelled good. Like healthy sweat, like clean jungle earth and big, wonderful man. She breathed deep through her tormented tears, knowing this was the last time she'd be this close to him.

"There's nothing to forgive. You didn't mean to get yourself kidnapped," he said, completely misunderstanding her.

"No." She pushed back. She wished her tears weren't blurring her vision. She wanted to look at his handsome face and see him clearly one more time, one more time while he still loved her. "That's not it."

"Then what is it?" he asked, a little vertical line appearing between his brows.

She opened her mouth, but, try as she might, she couldn't force the words out.

His scowl deepened. "Whatever it is," he said, pushing back a few strands of muddy hair that'd fallen over her forehead, "you can tell me. You can tell me anything. I love you, *neña*."

She closed her eyes against the burn of tears. "You shouldn't," she whispered over the whine of the engines, over the soft *thunking* sound of the wheels lowering in preparation for landing.

"What?" He raised his voice to be heard above the noise. "Why?"

She opened her eyes as the plane touched down with a hard *bump*. The jet's engines screamed in reverse, the flaps straining against the atmosphere outside. And for a couple of seconds as the aircraft fought against its own momentum, she simply held his confused gaze, a hand braced against the seat in front of her. Then they slowed and turned off the tarmac, taxiing toward the hanger. And she finally spoke the truth she'd kept secret for eight long years. "Because I killed your sister..."

Chapter Twenty-four

Black Knights Inc. Headquarters
Chicago, Illinois
2 days later...

"Where's this firecracker of a wife I've been hearin' so much about, Boss?" Leo Anderson asked, stopping to rub a hand over the leather seat of one of the custom motorcycles parked against the shop's soaring, brightly painted, three-story brick wall. He hummed his approval of its soft texture.

Lt. Leo Anderson and his team were on their way to their next assignment: something to do with a mounting brouhaha at an American embassy in Pakistan. But as Michael "Mad Dog" Wainwright had said upon their arrival outside the big wrought-iron gates that surrounded the old menthol cigarette factory and various outbuildings that made up BKI's headquarters, "We had to come see with our own beady eyes what all this super-secret, private government defense firm fuss is about first."

And so Steady, Dan, and Boss had been showing Leo and his Alpha platoon boys around the warehouse space for the last twenty minutes. After Boss—BKI's founder, head honcho, and a former SEAL teammate to Leo and the guys—had set them back on their feet following a manly round of back-slapping bear hugs and obligatory jokes told at each other's expense, that is. Both of the latter being pretty much par for the course between any group of men who had lived and fought together for years.

They had started the tour with the third-floor bedrooms, where those BKI boys still living on site—Steady included—managed to catch some Z's between missions and when Becky, the all-around superstar bike builder and woman Leo had asked about, didn't have them down in the shop, grinding metal or installing break lines. Then they had moved to the second floor, the heart of the operation, where the many offices, conference room, and state-of-the-art electronics belied the true nature of their work. And, now, finally, they stood on the shop floor, where all the custom motorcycles were made and where the civilian front for Black Knights Inc. began and ended its domination.

Put together, the place was a sight to behold. Underscored by Leo's low whistle when he stood at the second-floor railing, taking it all in, including the newly painted UH-60 Black Hawk helicopter with its red BKI logo visible through the windows on the huge garage doors at the opposite end of the shop. The helicopter was ostensibly used to promote the custom bike business—*sí,* just go ahead and insert an eye roll of disbelief there. But in reality, that logo peeled off in an instant, turning that badass war bird back into…well…a badass war bird.

"She's out buying a leg of lamb to cook up for Angel's homecoming tomorrow," Boss said, motioning them over to the next custom bike and ripping Steady from his thoughts.

"Angel?" Leo asked, squatting to look at the bike.

"You don't know him." Boss waved a hand of dismissal. "But the long and short of it is, he joined us a couple of years ago, happens to be Jewish, and for reasons beyond me, my wife has since made it her mission in life to learn how to cook kosher. With varying degrees of success, I can assure you." He made a face that caused the scar cutting up from the corner of his lip to pucker, and Steady found himself smirking. He loved Becky Knight, née Becky Reichert, to death. And the woman was many things. However, a kosher chef she most definitely was *not*.

"As for the rest of the crew," Boss continued, "they're out on missions or else otherwise occupied with family matters. In fact, I don't know if you guys have heard, but that asshat Jake 'The Snake' Sommers had the gall to up and marry my baby sister and put a bun in her oven. They're at the doctor's office right now getting a final ultrasound before she's due at the end of the month."

Leo hooted as he pushed to a stand. "I *had* heard they finally tied the knot. When Snake left the Teams, he was hell bent on gettin' her back. It was all he talked about. And, don't kill me for this"—he winced when Boss scowled at him—"but I always kinda thought those two belonged together."

"Unfortunately"—Boss was unable to hold on to his severe expression. His mouth curved into a lopsided grin—"I did too."

"Well, as this Angel fellow would probably say"—Leo slapped Boss on the back—"*mazel tov*. And speaking of glad tidings, what have you heard on your injured man, the one still back with the carrier group? Anything?"

Boss's smile disappeared. And just like it had the moment Steady laid eyes on that gruesome wound on Ozzie's thigh, just as it had every time he'd checked on his best friend's status since, his heart sank like a stone. And if he ever got his hands on Umar Sungkar, he vowed to tear the guy so many new assholes, he wouldn't be able to remember which one was the original.

"He kept his leg," Boss said. "And as soon as he's stable for travel, he'll be transported back here."

"That's good." Leo nodded, whistling again when they moved to the next bike and he saw the intricate, chrome wheels whose spokes were a series of chains woven around five-point stars. The motorcycle, aptly named Ranger, was Steady's pride and joy, a nod to his time in the Army. And every time he looked at the glistening green camo paint covering the fenders and gas tank, or the killer front forks truncating in brass .50 caliber bullets, or the chrome battery box that was stamped with the Ranger motto—Rangers Lead the Way—he felt a punch of pride. Then there was the exhaust: three twisting, twining, glistening pipes that put out a roaring rumble that was the audio equivalent of a full-on, body-shaking orgasm.

Not that *all* the bikes at Black Knights Inc. weren't hardcore, mind you. They were. But Ranger? Ranger was one badass mofo.

"Shit yeah. We'll be glad to have him home," Boss continued, running an agitated hand back through his thick crop of dark hair. "But as of right now, we're not sure what his combat status will be."

Ethan "Ozzie" Sykes had months of PT—physical therapy—ahead of him. And even then, it wasn't a given he'd ever be mission ready again. The kinds of jobs they were required to do for the president and his JCs demanded the utmost in physical fitness. A gimp leg was pretty much a career killer.

Mierda.

And Ozzie knew it, too. The few times Steady had managed to get through to him via satellite phone, he'd heard it in the man's voice. The despair, the desperation, the…*fear.*

"Fuckin'-A." Mad Dog shook his head. "That sucks." And Steady figured that was putting it in the mildest of terms. "And it always seems to happen to the best of us, doesn't it?"

This time Steady was the one to answer. "*Sí.* If by the *best of us,* you really mean *all of us.* I don't know one guy who's quit because he wanted to. Injury seems to be the way we all go out eventually." Which was just one of the tough truths about being a million-dollar, government-trained, spec-ops warrior. Once Uncle Sam turned a man into a machine of destruction, it was hard…no, not *hard*…it was damn near *impossible* for him to be anything else.

"But not us. Right, LT?" the SEAL nicknamed Romeo said, turning to Leo. "After this last mission in Pakistan, we're out."

"The hell you say." Boss's big jaw jerked back like Romeo had socked him on the chin.

"It's true." Leo grinned, crossing his arms over his chest and nodding. He unhooked his aviator sunglasses from the collar of his gray T-shirt and slid them onto his face with dramatic flair. Then he wiggled his eyebrows until they bounced above the mirrored lenses.

"We're buggin' out, boys. Kissin' the Teams good-bye and headin' down to the Keys to take over my family's salvage business...and do a little treasure huntin'."

"Wait, treasure as in *pirate* treasure?" Dan said, his tone and the smirk on his lips broadcasting just how hilarious he found this idea to be. "Pirate treasure as in *argh!*" He closed one eye to indicate the thing might be missing and covered with a patch.

"Yuck it up, asshole," Leo told him. "You won't be laughin' when—"

Boss's cell phone came to life in the front pocket of his jeans. "Excuse me for one sec," he said after pulling it out and glancing at the screen. Steady could tell by the look on his face that the president was on the horn. Boss's mouth always pinched in a certain way, his eyebrows nearly touching over the top of his nose when POTUS called.

"Hey"—he jogged after Boss, who'd started toward the metal staircase that led up to the second floor—"tell him he better start answering my frackin' phone calls!"

Boss frowned back at him, waving him off. But Steady thrust out his chin, sending Boss a look that very succinctly conveyed, *I'm not fucking around.*

After Abby dropped her bomb, he'd sat there, staring, blinking at her in dumbfounded disbelief for all of about ten seconds. But that's all it had taken for the door on the jet's fuselage to burst open and admit a glut of Secret Service agents. The suit-wearing throng had immediately gathered Abby and Agent DePaul up, bustling them off the aircraft before he had the chance to ask Abby what the *hell* she'd meant by that statement. *Because I killed your sister...*

Huh? I mean, *what the ever-loving huh?*

She hadn't killed Rosa. A *terrorist* had killed Rosa. End of story.

He'd tried to go after her, but one of the SS agents had placed a firm hand in the middle of his chest, shaking his head. "That's a negative on leaving the aircraft," the guy had said. "The press has gotten wind of Miss Thompson's abduction, and they're waiting on the tarmac. As such, the president insists you remain onboard during refueling. The pilot already has the go ahead to drop both you and you're…uh… *compatriot*," this was the part where Dan had glanced back at him, raising a brow and mouthing *compatriot*, "back in Chicago."

And even though every single one of Steady's instincts had been screaming at him to go after the woman he loved and demand she explain herself, the fact of the matter was, he couldn't risk the presence of the press. Black Knights Inc. may have been forced from the closet, its operators' identities revealed to the DOD and some of its subordinate agencies, but they could never, repeat *never*, divulge themselves to the civilian press. Doing so would be the equivalent of a death knell, ringing in the end of the BKI's clandestine operational capabilities.

And so, good little soldier that he was, he'd stayed aboard the jet, allowing himself to be ferried back to Chicago where he'd immediately begun leaving messages for Abby.

But given she was being hounded by reporters seeking the inside scoop on her recent ordeal, it was no big surprise she'd had her cell phone disconnected. Which had left him no other recourse but to leave a half dozen messages for *el Jefe* himself, insisting on an explanation for Abby's outburst.

So far? Radio silence. On all fronts. And for the last two days he couldn't escape the feeling that he was pushing a wheelbarrow full of shit up a very steep hill.

He crossed his arms, shaking his head when Boss stopped near the foot of the staircase, turning to shoo him away. "Fuck no," he said. "I'm not moving until he agrees to answer my questions." He'd already decided when he awoke this morning that he was giving everyone twenty-four more hours to start talking, or he was mounting up on Ranger, roaring his way to Washington, and demanding an audience.

Boss rolled his eyes, then said into the phone, "I don't know if you're aware, sir. But the Alpha platoon boys are here with us." He listened for a little while longer before, "Yes, sir. Just wanted to make sure you were okay with their presence here." Then he reached out to slam his hand over the big red button above the ten-drawer rolling toolbox behind him.

A loud *beep, beep, beep* similar to the reversing sound made by the small forklift truck they kept onsite for moving the larger of their machinery around echoed through the expanse of the shop, bouncing off the soaring leaded glass windows. A red light beside the staircase blinked out a warning, and Steady lifted a brow, a question without words. Boss nodded, answering him in the same vein before clicking off his phone and sliding it back into his hip pocket.

"What the fuck?" Leo Anderson breathed as one entire twelve-foot by twelve-foot section of bricks on the far wall punched out and slid to the left, rolling noisily against the metal tracks. Within seconds, the big motor operating the door—the thing was known to be unreliable, but today it seemed to be working just fine—finished its task and the secret tunnel that ran from Black Knights Inc. under the north branch of the nearby Chicago River to a similar hidden access point in a parking garage two blocks west was revealed.

The SEALs shuffled closer to the yawning black hole as a unit. Then, "Holy shit!" Leo laughed, whipping off his sunglasses and glancing over at Boss as the shop filled with the smells of damp concrete and stale, fishy air. "Who the hell do ya think you are? Batman or somethin'?"

"Or something." Boss winked, turning to watch as a yellow wash of headlights appeared in the tunnel. "You know as well as I do, guys in our line of work often have need for an extra bolt-hole. Plus it's a fucking handy-dandy little thing to have onsite when, say, the president of the United States wants to make a covert visit."

Now it was Leo's turn to whisper, "The hell you say."

Boss nodded, then turned to watch a lumbering black SUV pull out of the mouth of the tunnel. After the vehicle rocked to a stop, all four doors opened simultaneously. From the front seats poured two guys in off-the-rack suits and slicked down Don Draper haircuts—Secret Service. From the back emerged President Thompson and Navy General Pete Fuller, the head of the Joint Chiefs. Both men were dressed in the civilian garb of jeans and polo shirts. But there was absolutely no mistaking who they were.

President Thompson had a full head of silver hair that the press liked to say made him look *trustworthy*, and a confident smile that had won over the hearts of Americans not once, but twice. And Pete Fuller? Well, *he* had a buzz cut that would do any drill sergeant proud. And when you added that to the perpetual scowl he wore, a person was almost *forced* to both fear and respect the guy in equal measure.

Steady hid a grin when the SEALs snapped to attention, their hands stiffly lifted to their heads in salute, their chests puffed out like a bunch of peacocks.

"At ease, gentlemen," General Fuller said after returning their salutes.

Leo and the rest of the Alpha platoon boys lowered their hands only to formally lace them behind their backs, spreading their feet and keeping their eyes straight ahead in the standard military pose. *Sí*, it'd taken Steady a while to get over that particular bit of training after he'd joined BKI and began seeing the president and the general on a fairly regular basis. He'd finally stopped the day the general told him, "Cut that shit out, will you, Soto? I'm saluted so often, I'm developing tennis elbow in my right arm. And you standing there, staring straight ahead, not meeting my eyes, makes my asshole pucker."

Pete Fuller had a way with words. No doubt.

"Welcome back to BKI, General. Mr. President." Boss stepped forward to shake both men's hands. Steady did the same, lifting a brow at the leader of the free world.

"I wanted to tell you again how much I'm indebted to you for saving my daughter," the president said, pumping his fist. *Sí, sí*. But that's *not* what he wanted to hear from the man. Then President Thompson leaned in close, his expensive aftershave tunneling up Steady's nose. "And I received your messages. You're right. You deserve an explanation. But first, we need to deal with another issue."

And *that's* what Steady had been waiting to hear. The relief that poured through him was nearly enough to bring him to his knees. Regardless of the hard-assed front he'd been wearing these last couple of days, the truth was he'd been beside himself with worry. Worry for Abby and how she was dealing with the press. Every news headline had been some mishmash of the words "President" and "Daughter" and "Abducted." Worry over *why* in the world she'd think *she* was the one responsible for Rosa's death—he didn't even entertain the possibility that it might be true; not Abby, not sweet, wouldn't-harm-a-flea Abby, not the woman he loved both heart and soul. Worry over whether or not she loved *him. I mean, she never came out and said it.* And perhaps she'd let him take her in that hot jungle hut not due to love, but due to some grossly false assumption that she somehow owed him because of her confusion surrounding his sister's death.

"...obvious the scope of Winterfield's thievery is far greater than anything we or the CIA ever imagined," the president was saying, and Steady joined the group that had gathered near the motorcycles. He shot Boss a wide-eyed look then let his gaze slip over to the SEALs who were standing by, listening intently.

The general caught his expression. "It's okay, Soto. Given that these boys were responsible for securing the nukes, it's only fair they know exactly what we're dealing with here."

The nukes...

What the press didn't know, what *no* one knew, was that the CIA had discovered weeks ago that their rogue agent's betrayal didn't begin and end with the revelation of the locations of the black sites. There'd been a big to-do involving a terrorist group, a couple of old marine sonar specialists, the Black Knights, and the coordinates of the handful of missing pre– and post–World War II nuclear weapons sitting at the bottoms of the world's oceans that had occurred as a direct result of Winterfield selling classified information on the black market. Leo and his men had been working tirelessly to retrieve the decades-old warheads from their watery graves ever since. And everyone had hoped that when they pulled the last weapon from the depths of the South China Sea, it would be the end of Luke Winterfield's treasonous activities.

Apparently not. *Hue puta!*

"Understood." He nodded, then shook his head. "And sorry, I'm coming in a little late." He turned to the president. "Are you saying Winterfield was the one who supplied Umar Sungkar with the Intel on Abby's security detail and their protocols?" His thoughts pinged back to his hotel room in Kuala Lumpur when he and Dan had been quick to disregard the possibility because it'd seemed so far-fetched.

It *still* seemed far-fetched.

"According to Umar's confession," General Fuller said. "The man claims Winterfield contacted him about Abby's scheduled trip to Malaysia, offering him the Intel he'd need to carry out her abduction in exchange for the not insignificant sum of one million U.S. dollars."

"Sonofa*bitch*," Leo cursed, scratching at the beard covering the lower half of his face. "First that fucker reveals our nation's black sites to the world. Then he deals in missin' nuclear weapons. And now this?"

"So it would seem," General Fuller concurred.

"The man needs to be taken out." Boss's massive jaw sawed back and forth. On a good day, Boss had a face only his mother—or his wife, Becky—could love. And today was definitely *not* a good day. His expression was the facial equivalent of a disembowelment.

"Indeed he does," General Fuller agreed. "But not before we know how much more information he stole and who he's since sold it to. Which is where you guys come in."

"You'd like us to work with the Company on capturing him?" Dan asked. The newspapers claimed the former CIA agent had moved to a Central American country with no extradition treaty with the U.S. But the truth was, Winterfield seemed to have fallen off the face of the planet. And for weeks now, the hunt for the traitor had been the CIA's *numero uno* objective.

"Something like that," General Fuller said. "We want BKI to find him and grab him *before* the CIA can."

Steady exchanged another quick look with Boss. And that soft rustling sound he heard was the SEALs shuffling just the tiniest bit in surprise. The only reason the president and the JCs would tap the Black Knights for this job was if they didn't trust the Central Intelligence Agency.

Fucking hell! This Winterfield debacle kept getting bigger and bigger every frackin' day.

"I'll go after him," Dan volunteered quietly, and

Boss shot him a sharp look. "Hey," he shrugged, "if I'm jumping back into the mission pool, I might as well start at the deep end."

President Thompson glanced from Dan to Boss and then over to the general. "I'm fine with that as long as Pete and Boss sign off."

"You sure you're ready?" Boss asked Dan, his concerned frown causing the scar cutting through his eyebrow to pucker and turn an angry pink.

Dan didn't hesitate to meet Boss's eye. "Ready as I'll ever be."

Good for you, Dan Man. Good for you.

Boss lifted his chin in a jerky nod, and Steady figured there was a lump in the big man's throat, just like there was a lump in his. The good *Madre Maria* knew it'd been hard as hell to watch Dan fall apart. But it was a beautiful thing to see the guy picking up the pieces and putting himself back together again.

"Good." The president clapped a hand on the general's shoulder. "I'll let Pete talk you guys through some of the logistics." Then he turned to Steady. "While he's doing that, I have a personal matter to discuss with Soto here…"

Chapter Twenty-five

Abigail Thompson's Townhouse
Georgetown, Washington, DC
Seven hours later...

"Miss Thompson, you have a visitor," Agent... what was his name? *Gah!* Abby felt awful that she couldn't remember...called from the doorway at the top of the stairs leading from her kitchen to her basement family room.

For two days now, she'd been sequestered inside her house. Supposedly "recovering" from her ordeal. But in reality, the White House had insisted she stay hidden away until the media's feeding frenzy died down. Although, truthfully, she figured the press secretary really wanted to be the one to steer the conversation, make the story into whatever he felt was most palatable to the American public and most beneficial to her father's image.

So what else is new?

But, you know what? It was all good. Because the last thing she wanted was a bunch of cameras and microphones shoved in her face. On the other hand, she *was* getting lonely holed up all by herself, no one to talk to save her mother or her sister. And only when they managed, amidst the chaos of their busy schedules, to spare Abby a quick phone call—via her new, encrypted cell phone, of course. *Ugh.* Would she *ever* get to live like a normal person again?

No, she realized. *Probably not.*

In fact, she wasn't sure she *could* after all these years, entrenched as she was in "the machine," knowing what she did about how the world worked. Sort of like Carlos after he'd finished his tour with the Rangers. He hadn't been able to meld back into society, not after everything he'd seen and done. Not after he'd been turned into a *warrior.*

Carlos…How many times had she—

"Miss Thompson?" Agent—*Sonofabiscuit!* What was his name?—called again.

"Who is it?" she yelled back, thumbing the pause button on the remote for her DVR. The screen on her television froze on an image of *Modern Family*'s Cam and Mitchell. The two men were sitting in their living room, doing one of their hilarious interviews in front of the camera. She'd been spinning episode after episode all day, needing something to take her mind off the horror of what had happened to those six brave souls who'd gone with her to Malaysia. To take her mind off all the terrible, *terrifying* things she'd seen in the jungle. To take her mind off the man she loved and what he must think of her now that he knew the truth.

"It's President Thompson," the agent called down. "And…a Mr.…"

She could hear the rumble of male voices as the agent asked for the man's identity.

"Abby?" her father's voice boomed down the stairs. "Are you decent? I'm coming down."

Was she *decent?* "What the frickin' sticks, Daddy!" she grumbled loudly, pushing up from the cushy comfort of her cream-colored sofa. "I've got a house full of Secret Service agents. *Of course* I'm decent!"

Well, if you considered yoga pants paired with a sports bra and a tank top decent. Which she totally did. *A woman should be able to lounge around her own home in comfy clothes. Am I right? Or am I right?*

She rounded the sofa as her father appeared at the bottom of the stairs, a pair of long, jean-clad legs visible on the treads behind him. As her mystery guest continued to descend, her heart leapt. Above the legs appeared a trim waist…and then a broad chest encased in a tight black T-shirt sporting the Black Knights Inc. Custom Motorcycles logo…and then…

She had to grab the back of the sofa, her nails sinking deep into the plush fabric. "C-Carlos?" she squeaked, her hand jumping to her throat. She could feel her pulse racing beneath her thumb, which might explain why she was suddenly so dizzy. Or maybe the room really was spinning? Was that possible?

She knew her father walked over to her. She knew he wrapped his arms around her, hugging her tight. She knew he planted a kiss on her temple. But she only had eyes for Carlos, standing there on the last step, his face so…*unreadable.*

What is he doing here? Why is he with my father?

Upon landing in DC two days ago—*Holy Moses*, really? Just two days?—the first thing she'd said to her father was *I told Carlos the truth. He deserved to hear it. And I couldn't live with the lie anymore.*

She didn't know what she'd expected him to say. Probably something along the lines of *we had a deal* or *but you promised.* Instead, he'd simply nodded and pulled her into his arms, kissing her temple like he was doing now. Only then, he'd begun to cry. Deep, wrenching sobs. It was the first time in her life her tough, take-no-prisoners politician father had broken down around her. Which meant, of course, that she'd turned into a big ol' bawl-bag, too. And as they stood there, sobbing in each other's arms, they hadn't spoken another word about Carlos and her broken promise.

"Biscuit," he whispered now, using the nickname the family had given her as a baby, "can you ever forgive me?"

Whoa. *Wha—?*

That was enough to rip her eyes away from Carlos. She pushed back, searching her father's face. Sometimes when she looked at him, all she saw was the president of the United States. But there were other times, like now, when he was just Dad. "F-forgive you for what?"

"For making you keep that secret when it ate you up inside," he said, his hands squeezing her shoulders. "For not seeing that, for all these years you've been blaming *yourself* for what happened to Rosa. You told Soto it was your fault? Oh, Biscuit"—he shook his head, his expression the picture of sorrow—"how could you ever think that?" Her eyes filled with tears, her nostrils flaring. "Don't you know that if one of us shoulders any blame, it's me?"

One hot drop spilled over her lid, leaving a burning trail down her right cheek. No. *No.* "B-but *I* was the one who sent that text message," she insisted, her chin trembling, feeling the crushing regret of her mistake as strongly in this moment as she had eight years ago. "I was the one who—"

"No." He shook her, just a little, just enough to stop her mid-sentence. "*No*, Abigail," he swore firmly, his tone having turned harsh, authoritative. And *there* was the president of the United States. "You're blameless here." He pulled her in close again, hugging her tight. "Oh, baby girl, you're so blameless."

No, she wasn't!

Now it wasn't one hot tear, but a dozen that slipped from her eyes, soaking her father's red polo shirt. She shook her head, her throat so full she couldn't argue. But in her head she was screaming.

"But if you don't believe me, maybe you'll believe him." He let go of her to gesture over to Carlos, who was standing at the foot of the steps, his hands tucked into the front pockets of his jeans, his chin dipped down as if he'd lowered his eyes in an attempt to give them a bit of privacy. But now he was staring at them from beneath his eyebrows.

She gulped, shaking her head again. Oh, how she *wished* what her father was saying was true. How she *wished* it!

Then he turned back to her, bending to kiss her cheek and whisper, "And just so you know, I approve."

"Wha—?" she managed to croak, running a hand under her leaking nose. She was no longer shaking her head in denial; she was shaking it in bewilderment. *Approve of what?* But before she could ask him, he straightened and headed for the stairs, stopping to quickly pump Carlos's hand. Then he jogged up the carpeted treads with the quick, confident steps that only the leader of the free world could pull off. A second later, a muted *snick* told her he'd closed the door behind him.

Oh, sweet Peter, Paul, and Mary. And now she was alone with the man she loved more than life itself, the man whose sister she'd—

"It doesn't represent your love of gardening and all things botanical, does it?" Carlos asked, lifting his chin but remaining rooted over there by the stairs. He looked good. A little tired, but clean-shaven and freshly showered and…so handsome she could barely catch her breath. Or maybe that was because her nose was all stuffed up from the Niagara Falls' worth of tears stacked behind it.

"H-huh?" she stuttered, completely taken aback, completely confused. Those were *not* the first words she'd expected to hear from him should he ever deign to be in her presence again.

"The tattoo on the back of your neck," he said, rocking slightly on his heels. "The rose. It doesn't have anything to do with your profession."

Of its own volition, her hand jumped to cover the ink on the back of her neck, visible because she had her hair pulled into a sloppy ponytail. "M-my tattoo?"

"*Sí.*" He nodded. And then, *oh, jumping Jesus!* He started stalking in her direction.

One step. Two. Three in that lazy, loose-hipped walk of his. She stopped counting when he was close enough for her to feel his heat, smell the soap on his skin, hear the low murmuring sound he made deep in his chest when he removed her hand. His palm was so warm, so deliciously familiar. And his touch brought back a thousand wonderful, painful memories. She closed her eyes, and two more fat tears raced down her cheeks.

"Just as I thought," he said, having bent to study her tattoo. His hot breath puffed against the back of her neck causing every inch of her skin to erupt in goose bumps. "I didn't get a good look at it in the hut, but I wondered if this twining bit of vines running up beside the rose spelled something."

She opened her eyes, her breath sawing from her lungs on a noisy exhale. He was right. It *did* spell something. It spelled...*Rosa.*

"It w-was a way for me to p-pay tribute to her," she admitted. "For years afterward, whenever I would smile or laugh or whistle or get lost in a movie, I would feel awful. Like I'd forgotten about her, even if it was only for those few minutes. And so I..." she had to swallow as more tears threatened to choke her. "I got her name tattooed on my neck. A daily reminder of her, the woman I loved like a sister. The woman I k—"

The hand he still had wrapped around her wrist tightened. "Don't say that again," he warned. She sucked in a breath, her eyes snapping up to his face. It was still so... *unreadable.* "I don't want to hear you take the blame for Rosa's death ever again."

"B-but—"

"I know what happened. Your father told me everything on the flight from Chicago. And how awesome is Air Force One, by the way?"

She didn't hear his question; she was so focused on the first two things he'd said. He *couldn't* know what happened. If he did, he'd know she *was* to blame.

"Carlos," she whispered. He heart was raw and burning, like a papercut doused in rubbing alcohol. I mean, really, was she going to have to take him through it, step-by-step? Wasn't it enough that—

"So, then let's move on to another matter." He slid

his hand down to lace his fingers through hers. It was so unexpected, so simultaneously wonderful and awful that she had to lean against the back of the couch or risk a very ungraceful ass-plant straight into the carpet.

"No," she told him, sniffling. "No, we can't move on. Not until you tell me *exactly* what my father told you."

His chin jerked back, his brow furrowing. "He told me what really happened with the bombing." His tone was all about the *well, duh.*

Some of her tears dried up as she frowned at him. "This is one instance where you need to go into detail. *Please.*"

He smiled down at her then, shaking his head. "*Dios.* You people and your need for details."

And it was a good thing she was already leaning on the sofa, because that smile, directed at her when she never thought she'd see it again, would have brought her to her knees otherwise. "I'm serious," she told him.

"So am I." He was still grinning.

"Stop it, Carlos," she said. But he continued to stand there, *killing* her with that smile, with that dimple. "I mean it," she stressed. "Stop it." And maybe it was habit—because she had no right to touch him, much less slug him—but she used her free hand to swipe at his arm.

"*You* stop it," he told her, tapping her shoulder in retaliation.

And, oh, *God!* It was so wonderful and so…so *awful!* She buried her face in her hands and that was all she wrote. The waterworks had totally and irreversibly burst the dam.

Steady looked down at the bowed head and trembling shoulders of the woman he loved. His heart felt too huge and too hot for the confines of his chest. She was just so sweet. *Too* sweet. Taking on the responsibility and guilt of…*Jesús Cristo*…it seemed like the whole frackin' world. Well, that stopped. *Now.*

He pulled her into his arms and, delight that she was, she struggled. For an instant. Which caused him to tighten his hold. Then, surrendering as only Abby could, so softly, so gently, she wrapped her arms around his waist, squeezing him tight, sobbing into the cotton of his T-shirt.

"Shh, *cariño*," he murmured, laying his cheek atop her head, breathing deep the smell of Downy dryer sheets and Palmer's cocoa butter lotion. His dick twitched with interest at both her nearness and those ever-captivating smells, but he told the stupid prick—*literal* prick; *ha!*—that now was not the time. Now was the time to prove to her, once and for all, that she was *not* the one to blame for his sister's death.

Being careful to keep his voice low, soothing, he recounted the details her father had given him. "I know the bombing of the coffee shop wasn't coincidental, that the explosion was really meant for you." Her arms loosened slightly, and he pressed her closer in response. "I know the terrorists knew you'd be at the coffee shop because they hacked into your cell phone and intercepted a text message you sent to my sister, telling her the time and the place to meet you. I know they targeted you specifically to try to make a point to your father, because he'd always been so vocal in his vow to go after extremists with the full might of the American military should he ever become president." Her trembling had softened, her sobs reduced to sniffles as she listened. "And I know your father and his party decided to keep the truth of all of that under wraps, out of the press, because they thought it would hurt his chances of winning the election. Because they thought the American public, in light of the incident, would view his outspokenness as a giant *come and get me* to terrorists the world over." Her little fingers bunched the material of his shirt into fists. "I know the only reason you were saved from sharing Rosa's fate was because you were running late. And I know"—he ran a hand over her ponytail, reveling in the silkiness of her hair—"that your father made you promise to tell me none of this."

She pushed back from him, her face a soggy, beautiful mess. "Did you *also* know that my Secret Service agents had warned me about sending specifics in my text messages?" she demanded. "And that I just…*forgot* and did it anyway?"

He cupped her jaw in both hands and used his thumbs to brush the tears from her soft cheeks. "You were a busy college student doing what every busy college student does. It *wasn't* your fault, Abby. It just *wasn't.*"

"How can you *say* that?" she implored on a harsh whisper. "If only I'd—"

Poor little *neña.* Poor little wrong-headed *neña.* "Do you blame your father for speaking out so harshly against extremism?" he interrupted.

She swallowed, drawing his attention to the lovely length of her neck. Even red and splotchy, it still tempted him, made his lips itch to bend down and taste her sweet flesh. "N-no," she said. "Of course not."

"Do you blame Rosa for not catching the fact that you'd forgotten about not sending out personal info by text?" he asked, moving his hands along her jaw until he could softly massage the back of her neck with the tips of his fingers. She was wound tight as the tough little stainless steel springs used in craniofacial reconstruction surgery. "Your security detail debriefed her, debriefed us *both*, about what protocols to use when corresponding with you. So…is it *her* fault?"

"No." She shook her head jerkily, her voice barely a whisper. Then, more forcefully, she said, "*No.* Of course it wasn't Rosa's fault. How could you—"

"Then whose fault was it?" he asked gently, still holding her lovely jaw in his hands. "Where does the buck stop, Abby? Who is ultimately responsible for Rosa's death that day?"

Something happened then. Her eyes widened and she stopped breathing. Some people liked to call it an "aha" moment. Steady leaned more toward the phrase "lightbulbing it."

"Who killed Rosa?" he prompted again.

"Th-the…" She stopped to lick her lips, and the pink dart of her tongue worked on him the way the smell of a frying T-bone worked on a hound. Suddenly, he was ravenous. But instead of bending down to claim her unconscious offering, he simply adjusted his stance to better accommodate the erection now straining against his fly. "The terrorists," she finally managed, her lower lip quivering.

"*Sí.*" He smiled down at the comprehension in her eyes, at the hesitant joy as the guilt she'd been misguidedly carrying around all those years lifted away. "Just like the blame for those deaths in Malaysia falls squarely on the JI's shoulders. You, Abby…" He used his thumbs to brush away the remnants of her tears. "*You* are innocent."

She sucked in a breath, shaking her head as if she were struggling with the revelation. But struggle or no, she *did* understand. *Finally.* And now that they'd worked through that, he had a very important…the *most* important…question to ask her.

With his heart full of love, and hope no doubt shining in his eyes, he laid it all on the line. "Do you love me, *mi vida*?"

Overwhelmed. Elated. Hesitant. *Dizzy*…

Abby felt all those things as her heart beat wildly and her thoughts spun crazily. But the moment Carlos asked that question, *the* question, everything inside her screeched to a stop. Seriously, it was as if every single one of her cells applied the brakes at once and trillions of tiny *errrts* sounded between her ears.

Did she love him? Did she love *him?* What was he? Crazy? *Of course* she loved him!

But when she searched his face, his uncertainty was shining like a neon sign. "Oh, Carlos." She tightened her arms around his waist. Was that…? Yep. The man was fully, beautifully, largely erect. Bless him. A surge of warmth bloomed in her womb, and her nipples tightened as a result. "I've always loved you. Since the first day I met you and every day since. You're the one. You've *always* been the one. Don't you know that?"

And she wouldn't have believed it if she hadn't seen it with her own eyes, but Carlos's firm jaw trembled and one lone tear leaked from the corner of his left eye. She knew in that moment that whoever coined the phrase *and the truth shall set you free* had only gotten it half right. Because it was the truth and *love* that had finally broken the bonds of doubt, guilt, and sorrow shackling her heart.

"That's good," he said choking a little on emotion and quickly dashing away the teardrop. Then his expression turned devilish. And when he smiled, the sight of his dimple, his *beloved* dimple, instantly had her blood running hot. "Now"—he put his hands on her waist and pulled her close until there was no mistaking the insistent throbbing of his erection—"show me your tongue..."

Acknowledgments

It should be no big surprise at this point that the first round of thanks goes to my husband. Sweetheart, being married to me means you have to deal with my over-caffeinated deadline hijinks, my neurotic mid-manuscript meltdowns, and my questionable hygiene during debut week. But you do it beautifully. With that cute, dimpled smile on your face. And I can't thank you enough for that. XO!

I also have to give a shout-out to my badass agent, Nicole Resciniti. Nic, you've expertly guided me (and sometimes dragged me kicking and screaming *wink*) through this minefield known as publishing. I wouldn't have done any of this without you. I *couldn't* have done any of this without you. A million and one thanks for your steadfast support and counsel.

Next up, my thanks go out the two editors who have made the Black Knights Inc. series what it is today. Leah Hultenschmidt, you took a newbie author and through hard work, sweat, and a few tears (hopefully all mine) you made me into a bestseller. There aren't enough words in the English language to describe how grateful I am to you for that. And Deb Werksman, you were forced to take on the role of pinch hitter. But, baby, you stepped up to the plate, straightened your ball cap, and swung for the frickin' fences. I hope we write dozens of books together.

And I can't forget Penni DePaul, real-life author, Facebook friend, and unwavering fan of Black Knights Inc. Thank you so much for championing this series, Penni. And thank you so much for lending me the use of your name! I hope the character does you justice in some small way.

And last but certainly not least, a resounding *thank you* to our fighting men and women, those in uniform and those out of uniform. You protect our freedom and way of life so we all have the chance to live the American Dream.

About the Author

Julie Ann Walker is the *New York Times* and *USA Today* bestselling author of the Black Knights Inc. romantic suspense series. She is prone to spouting movie quotes and song lyrics. She'll never say no to sharing a glass of wine or going for a long walk. She prefers impromptu travel over the scheduled kind, and she takes her coffee with milk. You can find her on her bicycle along the lakeshore in Chicago or blasting away at her keyboard, trying to wrangle her capricious imagination into submission. For more information, please visit www.julieannwalker.com or follow her on Facebook www.facebook.com/jawalkerauthor and/or Twitter @JAWalkerAuthor.

In Rides Trouble

Black Knights Inc.

by Julie Ann Walker

Trouble never looked so good...

Rebel with a cause

Becky "Rebel" Reichert never actually goes looking for trouble. It just has a tendency to find her. Like the day Frank Knight showed up her door, wanting to use her motorcycle shop as a cover for his elite special ops team. But Becky prides herself on being able to hang with the big boys—she can weld, drive, and shoot just as well as any of them.

Man with a mission

Munitions, missiles, and mayhem are Frank's way of life. The last thing the ex-SEAL wants is for one brash blonde to come within fifty feet of anything that goes boom. Yet it's just his rotten luck when she ends up in a hostage situation at sea. Come hell or high water, he will get her back—whether she says she needs him or not.

Praise for *Hell on Wheels*:

"Edgy, alpha, and downright HOT, the Black Knights Inc. will steal your breath...and your heart!"
—*Catherine Mann,* USA Today *bestselling author*

For more Black Knights Inc., visit:

www.sourcebooks.com

Rev It Up

Black Knights Inc.

by Julie Ann Walker

He's the heartbreaker she left behind...

Jake "the Snake" Sommers earned his SEAL codename by striking quickly and quietly—and with lethal force. That's also how he broke Michelle Carter's heart. It was the only way to keep her safe—from himself. Four long years later, Jake is determined to get a second chance. But to steal back into Michelle's loving arms, Jake is going to have to prove he can take things slow. Real slow...

Michelle Carter has never forgiven Jake for being so cliché as to "love her and leave her." But when her brother, head of the Black Knights elite ops agency, pisses off the wrong mobster, she must do the unimaginable: place her life in Jake's hands. No matter what they call him, this man is far from cold-blooded. And once he's wrapped around her heart, he'll never let her go...

Praise for *Hell on Wheels*:

"Edgy, alpha, and downright HOT, the Black Knights Inc. will steal your breath...and your heart!"

—*Catherine Mann,* USA Today *bestselling author*

For more Black Knights Inc., visit:

www.sourcebooks.com

Born Wild

Black Knights Inc.

by Julie Ann Walker

New York Times and *USA Today* Bestselling Author

Tick...Tick...

"Wild" Bill Reichert knows a thing or two about explosives. The ex-Navy SEAL can practically rig a bomb blindfolded. But there's no way to diffuse the inevitable fireworks the day Eve Edens walks back into his life, asking for help.

Boom!

Eve doesn't know what to do when the Chicago police won't believe someone is out to hurt her. The only place to turn is Black Knights Inc.—after all, no one is better at protection that the covert special-ops team. Yet there's also no one better at getting her all turned on than Bill Reichert. She has a feeling this is one blast from the past that could backfire big-time.

"Drama, danger, and sexual tension... Romantic suspense at its best." —*Night Owl Reviews* Reviewer Top Pick, 5 Stars

Hell for Leather

Black Knights Inc.

by Julie Ann Walker

New York Times and *USA Today* Bestselling Author

Unlimited Drive

Only a crisis could persuade Delilah Fairchild to abandon her beloved biker bar, let alone ask Black Knights Inc. operator Bryan "Mac" McMillan for help. But her uncle has vanished into thin air, and sexy, surly Mac has the connections to help her find him. What the big, blue-eyed Texan has against her is a mystery…but when the bullets start to fly, Mac becomes her only hope of survival, and her only chance of finding her uncle alive.

Unstoppable Passion

Mac knows a thing or two about beautiful women—mainly that they can't be trusted. Throw in a ticking clock, a deadly terrorist, and some missing nuclear weapons, and a man just might find himself on the wrong end of the gun. But facing down danger with Delilah is one passion-filled thrill ride…

"The heat between the hero and heroine is hotter than a firecracker lit on both ends… Readers are in for one hell of ride!" —*RT Book Reviews*, 4.5 Stars

The Night Is Mine

by M.L. Buchman

NAME: Emily Beale

RANK: Captain

MISSION: Fly undercover to prevent the assassination of the First Lady, posing as her executive pilot

NAME: Mark Henderson, code name Viper

RANK: Major

MISSION: Undercover role of wealthy, ex-mercenary boyfriend to Emily

Their jobs are high risk, high reward:

Protect the lives of the powerful and the elite at all cost. Neither expected that one kiss could distract them from their mission. But as the passion mounts between them, their lives and their hearts will both be risked… and the reward this time may well be worth it.

"An action-packed adventure. With a super-stud hero, a strong heroine, and a backdrop of 1600 Pennsylvania Avenue and the world of the Washington elite, it will grab readers from the first page." —*RT Book Reviews*

For more in The Night Stalkers series, visit:

www.sourcebooks.com

I Own the Dawn

The Night Stalkers

by M. L. Buchman

NAME: Archibald Jeffrey Stevenson III

RANK: First Lieutenant, DAP Hawk copilot

MISSION: Strategy and execution of special ops maneuvers

NAME: Kee Smith

RANK: Sergeant, Night Stalker gunner and sharpshooter

MISSION: Whatever it takes to get the job done

You wouldn't think it could get worse, until it does...
When a special mission slowly unravels, it is up to Kee and Archie to get their team out of an impossible situation with international implications. With her weaponry knowledge and his strategic thinking, plus the explosive attraction that puts them into exact synchrony, together they might just have a fighting chance...

"The first novel in Buchman's new military suspense series is an action-packed adventure. With a super-stud hero, a strong heroine, and a backdrop of 1600 Pennsylvania Avenue and the world of the Washington elite, it will grab readers from the first page." — *RT Book Reviews* (4 stars)

For more Night Stalkers, visit:

www.sourcebooks.com

Take Over at Midnight

The Night Stalkers

by M.L. Buchman

NAME: Lola LaRue

RANK: Chief Warrant Officer 3

MISSION: Copilot deadly choppers on the world's most dangerous missions

NAME: Tim Maloney

RANK: Sergeant

MISSION: Man the guns and charm the ladies

The past doesn't matter, when their future is doomed

Nothing sticks to "Crazy" Tim Maloney, until he falls hard for a tall Creole beauty with a haunted past and a penchant for reckless flying. Lola LaRue never thought she'd be susceptible to a man's desire, but even with Tim igniting her deepest passions, it may be too late now…With the nation under an imminent threat of biological warfare, Tim and Lola are the only ones who can stop the madness—and to do that, they're going to have to trust each other way beyond their limits…

"Quite simply a great read. Once again Buchman takes the military romance to a new standard of excellence."—*Booklist*

"Buchman continues to serve up nonstop action that will keep readers on the edge of their seats."—*Library Journal Xpress*

Wait Until Dark

by M.L. Buchman

NAME: Big John Wallace

RANK: Staff Sergeant, chief mechanic and gunner

MISSION: To serve and protect his crew and country

NAME: Connie Davis

RANK: Sergeant, flight engineer, mechanical wizard

MISSION: To be the best… and survive

Two crack mechanics, one impossible mission

Being in the Night Stalkers is Connie Davis's way of facing her demons head-on, but mountain-strong Big John Wallace is a threat on all fronts. Their passion is explosive but their conflicts are insurmountable. When duty calls them to a mission no one else could survive, they'll fly into the night together—ready or not.

Praise for M.L. Buchman:

"Filled with action, adventure, and danger… Buchman's novels will appeal to readers who like romances as well as fans of military fiction." —
Booklist Starred Review of *I Own the Dawn*

Pure Heat

The Firehawks Series

by M.L. Buchman

These daredevil smokejumpers fight more than fires

The elite fire experts of Mount Hood Aviation fly into places even the CIA can't penetrate.

She lives to fight fires

Carly Thomas could read burn patterns before she knew the alphabet. A third-generation forest fire specialist who lost both her father and her fiancé to the flames, she's learned to live life like she fights fires: with emotions shut down.

But he's lit an inferno she can't quench

Former smokejumper Steve "Merks" Mercer can no longer fight fires up close and personal, but he can still use his intimate knowledge of wildland burns as a spotter and drone specialist. Assigned to copilot a Firehawk with Carly, they take to the skies to battle the worst wildfire in decades and discover a terrorist threat hidden deep in the Oregon wilderness—but it's the heat between them that really sizzles.

"A wonderful love story…seamlessly woven in among technical details. Poignant and touching."
—*RT Book Reviews* Top Pick, 4.5 Stars

Light Up the Night

The Night Stalkers

by M.L. Buchman

NAME: Trisha O'Malley
RANK: Second Lieutenant and AH-6M "Little Bird" Pilot
MISSION: Take down Somali pirates, and deny her past
NAME: William Bruce
RANK: Navy SEAL Lieutenant
MISSION: Rescue hostages, and protect his past—against all comers

They both have something to hide

When hotshot SOAR helicopter pilot Trisha O'Malley rescues Navy SEAL Bill Bruce from his undercover mission in Somalia, it ignites his fury. Everything about Trisha triggers his mistrust: her elusive past, her wild energy, and her habit of flying past safety's edge. Even as the heat between them turns into passion's fire, Bill and Trisha must team up to confront their pasts and survive Somalia's pirate lords.

"The perfect blend of riveting, high-octane military action interspersed with tender, heartfelt moments. With a sigh-worthy scarred hero and a strong Irish redhead heroine, Buchman might just be at the top of the game in terms of relationship development." —*RT Book Reviews*

Bad Nights

by Rebecca York

New York Times and *USA Today* Bestselling Author

You only get a second chance...

Private operative and former Navy SEAL Jack Brandt barely escapes a disastrous undercover assignment, thanks to the most intriguing woman he's ever met. When his enemies track him to her doorstep, he'll do anything to protect Morgan from the danger closing in on them both...

If you stay alive...

Since her husband's death, Morgan Rains has only been going through the motions. She didn't think anything could shock her—until she finds a gorgeous man stumbling naked and injured through the woods behind her house. He's mysterious, intimidating—and undeniably compelling.

Thrown together into a pressure cooker of danger and intrigue, Jack and Morgan are finding in each other a reason to live—if they can survive.

"Rebecca York delivers page-turning suspense."—Nora Roberts

"Rebecca York's writing is fast-paced, suspenseful, and loaded with tension."—Jayne Ann Krentz

Betrayed

by Rebecca York

New York Times and *USA Today* Bestselling Author

To trust

Rockfort Security operative Shane Gallagher has been brought into S&D Systems to find a security leak. Confidential information has been stolen, and Shane suspects Elena Reyes, a systems analyst with the access and know-how to pull it off. As he finds excuses to get close to her, their attraction is too strong to ignore, but how can Shane trust the very woman he's investigating?

Or not to trust

Elena has spent her life proving herself, but now she's risking it all: everything she's worked for, and her growing feelings for Shane. Much as she wants to trust the devastatingly sexy, hard-as-nails investigator, she can't let herself fall for him…the stakes are too high.

"Rebecca York delivers page-turning suspense." —Nora Roberts

"Rebecca York's writing is fast paced, suspenseful, and loaded with tension." —Jayne Ann Krentz

Private Affair

by Rebecca York

New York Times and *USA Today* bestselling author

Does everyone have something to hide?

Olivia Winters and Max Lyon knew each other way back when, but she was one of the cool kids, and he was a bad boy from the wrong side of the tracks. Olivia's a successful model now, and Max a PI much in demand. Then Olivia's old high school friend is murdered. And a raft of "accidental" deaths may be murders, too. Max is the only man Olivia can trust to help her investigate.

As they team up, Max is blown away by Olivia's courage under fire, and Olivia finds that the bad boy she remembers from the fringes of her social circle might just be the best man she's ever met...

"*Bad Nights* has everything...drama, suspense, action, and passion." —*Night Owl Reviews*

"Tense and intriguing, the first of York's Rockfort Security books is an action-packed read that promises much for the series to come." —*RT Book Reviews*

For more Rebecca York, visit:

www.sourcebooks.com